An American Sin

"A skillfully crafted, powerful story about the Vietnam War and its legacy, from the viewpoint of an Asian American. Suspenseful and rich with exciting descriptions and characters, this is truly a must-read novel."
—*Margot A. Rowe*, Creative Writing Instructor

"*An American Sin* is a powerful exploration of the personal and cultural cost of the American involvement in the Vietnam War. Guilt-ridden ex-Marine David Wong embodies the bloodstained conscience of a nation as, decades later, he confronts the nightmares of his own war crime. Fighting through horror, anguish, and shame, he emerges to build his own difficult redemption. Su's novel will make you cringe, and weep—and think."
—*Sara Stamey*, author of the Ruth Kurtis series, Ace Books

"Violence and war make me angry! That said, *An American Sin* is very good. The story is very worthwhile, the characters well developed, the philosophy and psychology sound. I just wasn't ready to be brought to tears so many times!"
—*Kate Weisel*, Kate Weisel Creative Resource

An
American
Sin

a novel by
Frederick Su

A bytewrite LLC publication
Bellingham, WA

An American Sin
© 1991 unpublished, © 2001 revised, by Frederick Su

ISBN 0-9711206-0-9

Library of Congress Control Number: 2001130647

First printing August 2001

Printed in the United States of America

Cover Design by Kate Weisel
A bytewrite LLC publication
Bellingham, WA
www.bytewrite.com

Publisher's Cataloging-in-Publication

Su, Frederick, 1947-
    An American sin / Frederick Su.
    p. cm.
    LCCN 2001130647
    ISBN 0-9711206-0-9

    1. Asian Americans—Fiction. 2. Vietnamese Conflict,
1961-1975—Fiction.   I. Title.

PS3569.U14A44 2001   813'.6
                        QBI01-700741

To all the good warriors

And for Gail

This is a novel, or a book of fiction. It comes from the author's imagination and hangs on historical events, which provide the backbone to the story. Some real names are used in the context of history.

History studied in academia can be dry, but the tale of people living through extraordinary events will never be dry.

Because I can hear,
I bow down to Music,
Because I can see,
I bow down to Art.

Because I can feel,
I bow down to Family
and to Peace.

And, especially, do
I bow down to Children—
the torchbearers of Innocence.

The gods don't make worlds; they make music.

Contents

Part I Across Time

Part II Across Space

Preface

February 23, 1991

The Special Forces A Team of eight men was hiding in a large irrigation ditch deep in Iraq. They were there to observe enemy troop movements. The CIA had said there were no villages and civilians nearby. "But we could hear dogs barking that first night," Staff Sergeant Robert DeGroff said.

Around 0900, Staff Sergeant Jim Weatherford, who was standing watch, said, "I hear voices." DeGroff took off his Walkman and listened. He could hear them, too. And the voices were getting louder.

"They're getting closer!" Weatherford said. From his peephole, he could see two girls, about seven or eight years old, approaching. One girl was carrying an eighteen-month-old boy on her back. Curious, drawn by the backlighting of the peephole (there was no roof to the hide site), she drew to within ten feet of Weatherford. The two locked eyes. Then, the girls turned and started moving away.

"She sees me!" Weatherford said.

"She's seen us, Bulldog," DeGroff said to Chief Warrant Officer Richard "Bulldog" Balwanz, rousing him from his rest. "What do we do?" DeGroff exited the hide site and clambered up the side of the drainage ditch, slipping the safety off his sound-suppressed Beretta 9-mm semiautomatic pistol. Sergeant First Class Dan Kostrzebski was right on his heels with a sound-suppressed HK MP5 submachine gun.

DeGroff swung the pistol on the girl carrying the infant. She had turned around, curious, frozen twenty meters away, pure fear on her young face.

"Bulldog, what do we do? Tell me what to do! Should I shoot her?" DeGroff asked.

Balwanz, wide awake now, took only a second. "Don't shoot!" he said. "Don't shoot!"

They're only kids, he thought. In his mind, they weren't there to shoot civilians, especially children. He had kids the same age. He believed in God and had a sense of Right and Wrong. His sense of morality over-ruled his fear, and he was willing to die rather than kill children.

DeGroff exhaled, lowered the pistol, slipped the safety back on, and slid down the side of the ditch. Kostrzebski followed. "Jesus!" DeGroff said. The men looked at each other, relieved but fearful.

They had been compromised. Fear settled over them like a deadly gas filling the ditch. It would only be a matter of time before Iraqi troops moved in on their position. The men looked at Balwanz and thought he had just signed their death warrants. Let me die first, Balwanz thought. I don't wanna see my men die.

Not long afterwards, Iraqi troops piled out of trucks on the nearby highway and moved up the drainage ditch toward them. But the team held them off. It had five sniper-trained members. One shot, one kill. With air support, they were able to escape with their lives.

When Dave Wong heard about it, he said, "I wish I had had such courage."

Part I

Across Time

Is, *was, and shall be are Time's children*

Vyasa, the *Mahabarata* (ca. A.D. 400)

Chapter 1

First Kill

Killing can be a social event.

On the edge of the high Utah desert, the golden windspun aspen leaves had been driven to ground. The nude, outstretched limbs of the trees conjured up images of doomed prisoners. The young man imagined Death blowing through their limbs, leaving as its spoor the faint scent of cordite that settled as a mist in the gullies. He carried his lust for it effortlessly, like a fool.

Suddenly, the sharp cracks of nearby gunfire startled him. Haphazard at first, they became an avalanche fueled by the rhythmic staccato of the semiautomatics. It was a furious fusillade so relentless in its pursuit that he doubted anything could survive it. Then, a buck broke out of the forest on the other side of the ravine. A symphony of guns kicked dust all around the deer as it raced for a thick copse in the draw below. It ran across his line of sight, no more than forty yards away, but the young man didn't raise his rifle. The buck made the thicket, safe for a few heartbeats.

Too many people! He turned east, away from the doomed buck, making his way downslope to flee the noise. He had become separated from his buddies, and now as he broke clear from the trees and walked onto the high desert, he was alone.

As far as the eye could see, the grayish green of the ubiquitous *Artemisia tridentata*, or sagebrush, carpeted the landscape. He inhaled deeply and smelled the sweet, pungent scent of sage, rising slowly on unseen thermals as the land shed its coat of frost. In the distance, softened by the haze, the mountains looked to him like purplish, Brobdignaggian whales breaching a gray sea.

Then, he saw the mule deer. A doe! She was out in the desert about 175 yards away, flushed from the forest by the mob of hunters. It traipsed slowly, then stopped, looking back at him, the large ears at attention. Now! the hunter thought. It would be a long shot, he knew, especially with iron sights. He knelt and pulled the .30-.30 to his right shoulder. He had sighted in the lever action rifle at one hundred yards. He aimed high and squeezed off a round. The bullet hit the ground some five yards short of the doe and left of its haunch. The doe didn't move. Incredulous, the hunter readjusted. He aimed higher and to the right, slightly above the doe's body. He inhaled, then exhaled, letting the exhalation settle easily in his diaphragm, squeezing slowly, steadying the rifle at the last moment with the bottom of his exhalation, which was simultaneous with the last of the trigger squeeze. KABOOM! The doe jumped into the air, snapping at its rear, and then landed bodily on its side. Gotcha! he smiled.

He eyeballed along his line of sight, picking a small downcurve in the profile of the distant mountains as his reference point. He then looked backward, mentally marking the spot where he stood against the nearby hills. He walked through the sandy soil, stepping around the sagebrush. When he thought that he had walked about 175 yards, he lined himself up with the two reference marks. No deer! He pivoted 360 degrees, but could not spot her. He dropped his small pack, and using it as a reference point, started making circles. He expanded the radius of each circle by five yards, and it wasn't until his fourth circle that he found her.

The doe had been hit in the right haunch. She eyed him curiously, head held high. There was no panic in her eyes. But, of course, she had no understanding of what was to come, or that her wound was the effect and he was the cause.

There was a mellowness in her gaze that he found discomfiting, like the trusting innocence of a small child. Almost a bemused smile, he thought. Her beautiful brown eyes held his gaze like a magnet, and he wished with all his heart that he had killed her with the first shot.

This was his first deer hunt. How do you kill her? he asked himself. Should I shoot her in the head or the heart? He raised his rifle, aimed it at her head, but then swiveled it toward her chest. He could not destroy those elegant features. He shot. The doe gasped, breathing harder, head bent over now, coughing little dainty coughs.

"Die! Goddammit! Die!" he shouted at her. "I don't want you to suffer! Please die!" But she wouldn't.

He waited a minute—an eternity to him. She was still alive, suffering. And then the hunter knew what he had to do. She was meat for the dinner table, after all. He could not keep pumping bullets into her. He pulled out his knife, and steeling his heart, grasped her long beautiful snout and cut her throat, spilling her life onto the high desert.

The sandy soil absorbed her blood like a sponge.

Hell, it can even be legal to hunt men!

They went out into the dusk, single file, following the dirt trail through the man-high elephant grass. The moon was a slivered crescent.

"Hey, hey, enough light to kill gooks by," Smitty said, smiling crookedly, fingering his long knife in the last of the waning light.

They walked like ghosts in a two-dimensional world of flat light. There was very little depth perception. And each one's sense of hearing grew to compensate. Their boots felt the path before them; their eyes strained to see the moving mass ahead; they took quick easy breaths, straining to quiet the beating of their hearts and the pounding of the blood rushing by their ears. What they could not see, they had to discern by hearing.

After about half a mile, they stopped. They congregated quietly around Sarge.

"Wolchak," Sarge whispered, "you stay here with Wong. Set up the claymore, five yards away. Then set up your positions on this side." He pointed to the vegetation sloping uphill, away from the trail. The ambush zone would be below them, giving them a fairly free field of fire.

3

"Smitty and Gonzales, you're gonna be ten feet up the trail. Me and Johnson will be up another ten or fifteen feet. Watch your angles. You know this site from the daytime. Don't shoot your own men for Chrissake. From now on, no talking. When you're set, pull the wires. Go!"

With that, they disappeared into the brush, except for Sarge and Wolchak. Sarge set up one claymore mine on the far end of the ambush site. Wolchak, after directing Wong into position, slid out to the side of the trail to set up his claymore at the near end of the kill zone. He was back in a few minutes. "Armed and ready!" he whispered.

Lying down side by side, under the brush, they each laid out two grenades. They checked their M-16s, quietly flipping their safeties off and then back on. Worn smooth, the actions of the safeties made little noise in the night air. They checked the electrical wire, borrowed from the claymore, that served as a silent link between each fire team. Wolchak had it wrapped around his left wrist. He gave a slow tug signaling, Ready! Three fast, heavy tugs on it meant, Enemy! It would work if no one fell asleep.

This was Wong's first night ambush. He had been in-country now for a little over three weeks. He was tired. Always tired. His company had been humping the hills every day. The first week had killed him. Fresh from stateside and Okinawa, he was not used to the incredible heat, the humidity, and the eighty pounds he carried. And at night, stuck in his foxhole, he had alternated with Wolchak, two hours sleeping, two hours awake, then the cycle repeated. The next day, they humped the hills again.

The night air carried with it the scent of danger in Wong's mind. It hung like fruit, redolent with the implied carnage that could come. Whenever he thought he heard something, he would grip his M-16 tighter to him, wrapping his right hand tightly around the stock. But it was always innocent night sounds such as the wind rustling the trees and brush or some animal snorting about. In the distance, every once in a while, he heard the sharp yapping of the village dogs. He strained to see down the path, using only the starlight, for the moon had long since set. But he could see nothing but the vaguest of forms. He thought he could see a large bush on the other side of the trail, a black amorphous shape. Next to it, the ribbon of trail, lighter in contrast. He could not see his comrades, nor could he hear them. It was like an ethereal dream, and he was the only one in it.

The hours passed. Wolchak slept lightly, a barely perceptible snore. He had been on too many ambushes. Complacency had taken over. Wong stifled a yawn. Nothing, he thought. The initial state of excitement had turned into boredom. His grip relaxed on the stock of his M-16. He pushed his shirt cuff back, circling the luminous dial with his hand. Almost 0330. Nothing doing, he thought. It will be dawn soon.

He closed his tired eyes. He let his ears play sentry.

The world awoke with a huge explosion. Sarge's claymore had been tripped. Then the sound and sight of AK-47s and M-16s filled the night air. Then more explosions, grenades thrown by Sarge, then by Smitty and Gonzales. Screams rang out. And yelling, Vietnamese and American. The Viet Cong were firing wildly. Then the sound of pounding footsteps coming their way. And again, the bark of M-16s.

Wolchak, wide awake now, and yelling. "Son of a bitch!" he said, throwing a grenade onto the path. "Fire!" he shouted. "Shoot at the fucking shadows! The silhouettes, man! Shoot!" He let out short bursts of automatic fire. The grenade exploded. Wong followed his example. Screams. Black shadows raced toward them. Wong let loose. Wolchak reloaded, stripping the magazine out, inverting it, pushing its companion back in.

Wong saw bursts of light. Wind blew by his head. The sharp pop of bullets cracked the air and crashed into the bushes behind him. His mind registered those sounds in a split second. But he was focused on aiming toward the flickering lights that were the barrels of the enemies' weapons. Dark shadows were moving away, disappearing. Then Wolchak's claymore blew. Wong quickly reloaded and let out another burst. More screams. Wolchak was firing again. Then, both their magazines spent, reaching for more, they suddenly heard only silence. Their ears rang. Slowly, the moans of the wounded filtered through. The smell of cordite hung heavily in the air. Their hearts raced madly. Their eyes held the bloodlust.

The silence reigned for what seemed like hours. Then Wong heard American voices, yelling. The gray light of dawn filtered through the trees.

"Fucking son of a bitch, that was a good firefight," Wolchak said. "You did all right, Wong. Didn't freeze up."

But Wong, coming down from the adrenalin rush, was shaking now. It finally hit him. This was no longer a game. It was a life where death was a way of living. It was reality more real than he had ever imagined or experienced. He looked at his hands and willed them to stop shaking. But it was like an ague had settled on him.

Wolchak looked at him. "Take deep breaths, man. Don't worry! You'll get used to it." He clapped him on the back. But Wong doubted that he would ever get used to it. He breathed in deeply. After several breaths, the shaking lessened. He continued hyperventilating.

"Wolchak, Wong! You guys okay!" It was Sarge yelling out. "Smitty, Gonzales! Sound off!"

Wolchak yelled, "Okay, Sarge!"

Smitty yelled, "Yo!"

"Secure your area!"

The gray light now gave form to the killing ground. Wong and Wolchak got up and approached the trail. Smitty and Gonzales were already about. Sarge and Johnson were on the trail, Sarge kneeling on both knees, Johnson hovering over him. Four bodies in all, Wong saw at a glance. Two were moving and moaning. Wong's nostrils wrinkled at the smell of war, of blood and fresh death.

Two bodies were on the path, the other two strewn on the slope beyond it. One body was blown into two parts, cut apart at the stomach, flesh stripped clean from part of the skeleton by Wolchak's claymore.

Smitty and Gonzales were sweeping the area from beyond Sarge's up to where Wong and Wolchak stood. Smitty stopped, bent over, working over a wounded, sobbing VC. The sobbing stopped abruptly. Smitty worked at his task, then got up. He laughed with Gonzales as they approached Wolchak and Wong. "Hey, Wong," he yelled. "Look what I found for you!" He held up a severed head, spitting into the face.

First Kill

Wong looked up from the dead VC he was examining. The blood drained from his face. He retched, vomiting until nothing else came out, then dry heaved. "Oh, God! Oh, God!" he gasped, wondering why in the fucking hell he had ever joined the Marines.

"Put the fucking thing down, Smitty," Wolchak said. "We got more important things to do."

Incredibly, one VC was still alive, having gotten beyond Wolchak's claymore. "Yeah, we sure do," Smitty said, tossing the head at Wong's feet. "One gook's still alive."

He was about fifteen, crumpled over in a fetal position, his hands over his abdomen, pushing his intestines back in. He was moaning loudly.

Wong slowly straightened and saw the boy. He yelled out weakly, "Corpsman!" Then inhaling deep breaths, more strongly now, "Corpsman! Corpsman! . . . Johnson, get on over here!" He kicked the head over the edge of the path, viciously, like a man kicking a soccer ball.

"Now wait a minute. What the fuck you want Johnson for?" Smitty asked softly, grinning.

The boy looked at Wong, face contorted in agony, pleading, "Lam on." The fear seeped through, rising above the pain. "Lam on -dung giet toi . . . Anh giong toi."

"What did he say, Wolchak?" Wong asked.

"He said, 'Please. Please don't kill me.'" Wolchak looked at Wong. "He said, 'You're like me.'" The other men's eyes were on Wong, too.

The boy's eyes, Wong thought. Doe eyes. Like in that other world an eternity ago. His first kill. But . . . No! Not this boy! He reeled, suddenly dizzy, knowing what was to come.

"What the fuck you gonna do, Smitty?" Wong cried out, grabbing his arm. "He's wounded! Let him be!"

But Smitty had already unsheathed his knife. In one swift motion, he pulled free from Wong's hand, then came up under his outstretched arms and sliced through the top of Wong's shirt, between the sides of his unzipped flak jacket. He snarled, "Out of the way, you motherfuckin' gook! If you can't finish the job, I will!"

7

Wong stood dumbstruck. And afraid. Wong opened his shirt and looked at his chest. His finger traced the long thin cut, rubbing the blood now seeping out onto his chest. Then fear turned to anger. He gripped his rifle stock harder, swinging the barrel up. But Wolchak stopped him, pushing the barrel back down, glaring at him, shaking his head. "You American, ain't ya?"

Smitty laughed. "Him, American? He ain't proved it in my book yet!" He spat, then leaned over, yanked the boy's head back by his hair and plunged the knife through the side of the throat and ripped out. A whoosh, then a small, gurgling fountain of blood. The boy twitched, then lay still.

"Fuck! Like cutting butter, man!" Smitty said, grinning, wiping the blood from the blade on his pants. "You should try it sometimes, Wong." He bent over again, working speedily. He threw the prizes at Wong's feet.

"Wear 'em," he said.

Wong looked at Wolchak, but Wolchak would not meet his gaze. Then they all turned away, leaving. It was like a dream. Wong heard the garbled static of the PRC-25, messages from company headquarters. Sarge's voice, answering. He heard Johnson, the Corpsman, coming over, saying, "The Sarge was hit. But he'll be all right. Somebody hit over here?" Then Smitty's voice, followed by laughter. They all walked over to Sarge.

Wong looked at the crumpled body. "Son of a bitch!" he cried. Then softly, "That motherfucking son of a bitch!" Two tears trickled down. It was all he would give in front of his comrades.

The dirt beneath the boy was now dark crimson. He saw the boy's eyes. Glazed. And the face, a rictus of pain, frozen in death.

He stood rooted to the earth . . . then, he took a few steps, bent over, picked up the ears, notched holes in them with his knife, and strung the bloody lobes through the chain alongside his dogtags.

Chapter 2

Erlandson

"Why did you pick up the ears?"

"I had to." Silence.

"What do you mean, you had to?"

"I was in a fucking war! Do you know how naked you feel when you don't have someone covering your ass in combat? The way it works is, 'I cover your ass, you cover mine.' If they couldn't trust me to do my job, to be one of them, I doubt if I would be here today."

"I see. I'm just trying to understand . . . I get the feeling you had some affinity for this Viet Cong boy?"

"Yeah!"

"Why?"

"He reminded me of the deer. The eyes. The goddamned eyes. Just like the doe." And here he looks away from Erlandson, saying in a low voice, "He was Asian. I'm Asian."

"You're killing your own people."

Wong squints, then faces him. "Yeah, I guess. He was my first kill. Though I really didn't kill him. But I'm pretty sure I was the one who spilled his guts. I was certainly responsible for his death."

"That's war."

"Yeah, that's war . . . that fucking war!"

"Combat soldiers kill. It's not anything anyone wants to do, but in war—"

"You ever kill anyone?" Wong's voice rises.

"No, but—"

"Then what the fuck do you know?"

"Listen here, goddammit! You came here for help, didn't you?" Not a shout, just a low growl from Erlandson.

Silence. Then softly, Wong speaks, "It is the greatest game, you know, the greatest sport, the greatest gamble, the greatest adrenalin rush, the greatest terror—war is." Wong hesitates. "And it can be the greatest sin."

"Why so?" Erlandson arches his red bushy eyebrows.

But Wong evades the question. "Okay. Maybe that killing got under my skin more than I thought. He was just a kid, a little fucking kid caught up in a stinking little war. That could have been me three, four years earlier. And, yeah, I did feel something for him, because he was like me. We Orientals do look different, you know. Even though I'm American, there was a little tinge of identification there.

"I'm American, was American, will die an American. But in Vietnam, I became too American. After Smitty cut the kid's throat, well . . . I never felt so alone in my life. Jesus, yeah, I felt it. Felt like that boy. Felt like I should have stopped Smitty."

And then Wong burst into a fit of raucous laughter, the sound of a madman. His eyes glare. "But you know, Dr. Erlandson, you ain't heard the half of it yet. I went on killing. I was a green, motherfuckin' killing machine. My American side took over."

"What do you mean, 'My American side took over'?"

Wong looks into Erlandson's face. "I have two souls within one body, you know. I'm as American as apple pie, but I'll always be Chinese, too. The Irish Americans, the Polish Americans, the Italian Americans, the German Americans, the French Americans, well . . . they're all assimilated into the mainstream. They're American Americans. But we Orientals are forever marked."

Wong laughs. "You know I once had someone ask me what country I was from. I said, 'America! Ever hear of it?' What an ignorant, fucking asshole!"

Then, "All I ever wanted was to be accepted as an American," he says, sighing. "How many Americans do you know have strangers ask them if they speak Polish, Italian, German, their grandparents' native tongue? I'm third generation, but I always have people ask me where I'm from or if I speak Chinese. It's because of my slant eyes, you know."

A momentary silence, then Wong speaks again. "You know, they have a saying in the Marine Corps, 'Once a Marine, always a Marine!' Hah! What a bunch of bullshit! I'll never be a fucking Marine again. But, you know what my saying is? How about, 'Once Chinese, always Chinese!'"

"Is being Chinese a burden to you?"

The question brings Wong up short. "You know, I never thought of it that way. But, yes . . . when I was younger, I guess you might have called it a burden. I knew I was different. I was on the outside looking in."

"Did it really bother you?"

"Ha! Ha! What a question! Did it really bother me? Imagine, if you will, a fourteen-year-old boy being called Hop Sing and Ching Chong Chinaman by his peers. Would that bother you?"

Chapter 3

Nevada

The heat rose in waves from the ground. The images beyond bobbed and weaved like kites caught in stiff crosswinds. Out of focus, they seemed like apparitions that balanced on the edge of dreams before the slow cognizance of wakefulness banished them to the unconscious.

The boy was in the back seat of a 1960 Ford Falcon. His eyelids drooped shut. They would remain closed for a while and then, suddenly, he would awake with a start and shake himself, stare outside, and then once more allow his eyelids to slowly close. He was lulled by the motion of the car and the monotony of the landscape. His brother, in the back seat on the driver's side, was in a deep sleep.

"Gahm ngit!" he heard his mother say. So hot!

"Yeah!" his father agreed.

"You all right, On Jai?" his mother turned in the front seat, speaking in Cantonese.

The boy shook his head, fighting off the drowsiness. Then he looked up. "Yeah, Mom, I'm fine." His eyes looked down at the floor behind his father's seat.

"It's not like we going to be forever here," she said in English. "Your father have good job lined up." She smiled.

"I know, Mom," the boy said wearily, once more diverting his attention back outside.

His mother sighed and turned back in her seat. "Nei goh jai youh ngan toe hoc," she said to her husband. Your son has a hard head.

The father laughed, looked in the rear view mirror at his son. "Like father, like son, huh?" he said in Cantonese.

The boy understood, but pretended not to hear. He stuck his hand out the window, feeling the hot blast of air hitting it, squeezing the airflow between his fingers, grasping at the heat as if it were a living animal. He wanted to squeeze the heat out, make the air cool.

He stared at the wide expanse of desert. The plants were drab or dark colored: the brown of the tumbleweed, the gray of the sagebrush, the dark green of the mesquite. The rocks of the drab-colored hills, the gray and brown of the sandy soil, the white veins of the alkali flats all seemed to presage a bitter future for the boy. There were none of the greens of Hawaii, his birthplace, where lush vegetation covered the land from the mountains to the sea. There were none of the colors of the Sierra Nevadas that had captured the boy's wonder and imagination: the life-giving color of the conifers, the blue-green water of the lakes, the splash of colors of the late-blooming wildflowers. Here, everything seemed to have either the whitish gray pallor or the brittle, brown desiccation of death. The boy shivered.

He shielded his eyes to look at a dark narrow strip in the distance. As they closed on it, he could see green and white. Cottonwoods hugged a lonely, forlorn-looking creek. The white turned out to be buildings.

"Should we get gas?" his mother asked.

His father looked at the gauge. It was at a quarter tank. "Yeah, okay. It's probably a good idea. We got another sixty miles to go."

He slowed the car and pulled into a small lot that adjoined the cottonwoods. The white wooden buildings were a grocery store, gas station, garage, and house. His father pulled up to a round-shouldered pump. An attendant sauntered out, a man in his fifties wearing a cowboy hat.

"Howdy, folks. Fill 'er up?"

"Yes, thanks," his father said.

"On Jai, nei jungi oh neu?" his mother asked. You want to go to the bathroom? "Wake Harlan up."

The boy woke his brother. Harlan stretched out, kicking his legs into the back of the driver's seat.

"Let's go to the bathroom, Harlan!" The boys jumped out and ran. Dave turned and yelled to his mother, "Mom, can we go to the store afterwards?"

A few steps behind, she nodded.

Later, the boys wandered through the store, walking on old wooden floorboards that grasped at their feet, tripping them. They settled next to the freezer to scan the ice cream. Dave opted for a cone topped with chocolate and nuts. Harlan chose a Popsicle. Just then, their father pushed the wooden screen door open, stepped inside, holding the door a moment for the gas station attendant, who let it slam with a bang that made Dave jump. Their father headed for the restroom. When he came out, he chose a Dad's root beer.

"Nei jungyi matyeh, ah?" he asked his wife.

She chose orange juice, handing it to him to carry over to the counter.

"Will that be it?" the man asked. "You wanna ring this up together?"

"Yes, please do," his father replied.

"That will be $7.70."

His father gave the man a ten-dollar bill.

"Two-thirty is your change," the man said, handing over the money. "Where you folks from?" A smile on his cherubic face.

"San Francisco."

"Ah! I would have guessed . . ."

How? the boy wondered.

"Don't get too much of your kind out here."

The boy looked at the ruddy-complexioned man. He stood over six feet, towering above his father. His brown hair was turning white at the sides, and when he took off his cowboy hat to wipe his forehead and brow, Dave could see a large bald spot that ran from his forehead past the crown of his head.

His father grimaced, looked at the boy and his brother, and collected them out the door. His wife followed.

"Daddy, what kind are we? Aren't we Americans?" the boy asked.

"Nei umhai baak gwai," his mother said. You are not white. "You're Chinese, On Jai. You are Chinese." She ruffled his mop of black hair.

They had packed their bags and moved what little possessions they had. His father had landed a teaching position with a high school in a small town in Nevada.

As the car rumbled along, the boy suddenly realized his separateness. From what he had seen, this was a land of white. White faces, white bodies, whitish sand. A desolate landscape of small towns with homogenized people. The boy wished he were a tumbleweed, able to be blown away on the slightest breeze back to San Francisco, where at least there was a mix, a spectrum of color.

"Why? Why it come to this?" the boy heard his mother asking his father in Cantonese.

"A little black eye is not going to hurt him," his father replied in English. "We'll review some boxing and judo techniques. He'll do all right." His father looked at him and it seemed to Dave that the weight of the world was on his father's shoulders—that he had put his family in harm's way.

Dave's mother was still shaking with rage. Tears rolled down her cheeks. "None of this would have happened if we had stayed in San Francisco," she said in Cantonese. "No white devils picking on my son."

The father patted his wife's arm, then got up and pulled the boy over. "Okay, Davy, we're gonna practice boxing and judo every night. Okay?" He grabbed his son's shoulders, turned him to set his stance, left foot forward. "We're gonna practice until it's second nature to you." He patted his son's shoulder.

The father got into his fighting stance. "Okay, left lead. Remember. Keep that left foot forward. Jab! Jab!"

"Oh boy!" ten-year-old Harlan said. He jumped off the couch and imitated his father, bouncing around, flailing with his small arms, still thin as sticks.

"Make it snappy, Dave. A jab is fast. Then do your right cross."

Dave imitated his father. Slowly at first, then with the speed of youth. His movements were suffused with anger at his humiliation, still fresh in his mind.

15

"Good, Davy! You haven't forgotten." Years earlier, they had practiced, but had lapsed in training when racial incidents faded into the background, and everyday life reasserted itself. Now, once more, they had a use for it. "Left jab, left jab, right cross, left hook. But don't get into a rhythm. Go!" Dave followed with a swift flurry.

"Good! Continue."

Little Harlan danced around the living room, crying out, "Dah see! Dah see!" Kill! Kill!

"Now remember. Attack! Attack! Counter! Counter his attacks! Don't just sit back and only defend yourself. This ain't algebra, Dave. You gotta change your mindset and really try to hurt the bastard," his father said, trying to explain reality to his scholarly son. "I want you to hit him hard. Understand?"

Dave nodded. He let loose another flurry, with a little more energy. His eyes were narrowed in concentration, lips turned down.

"You're gonna be doing this all your life," his father said.

Dave nodded again. His father didn't have to explain. He looked to his mother, her face still etched with worry. She understood.

They switched to practicing judo, something Dave once trained in. The moves came back to him, rusty at first but smoother with repetition. Ippon Seionage, the defender's right arm shooting under the punch next to the armpit to act as a fulcrum while the left arm pulls the opponent into the hip for the throw. Ogoshi, the around-the-waist-grab throw. The leg sweep. They reviewed the throws, doing them over and over until the old man became tired.

"He's doing real good, Ma." Sweat was beading his forehead, and he was breathing hard.

"And you're too old," she said, smiling slightly. Dave could still see the worry in her eyes. It wouldn't be until years later that he would remember this period of his life and marvel at the seeming radar his mother had for the community sentiment, that she could somehow sense the hate emanating from some of his schoolmates. Once he had wanted to attend a Civil Air Patrol meeting at night. His friend had invited him, and he was to meet him at a local service station. But Dave's mother had refused to allow him to go out alone at night. Dave couldn't call his friend because Dave's family had no phone. How could his mother have gleaned the atmosphere of the place? Was it just the black eye? Maybe it was an unconscious way he hung his head then, though he would never remember himself as hang-dog defeated in these days of his youth.

Dave stopped. "I have a friend I can practice boxing with," he said.

"Nei umh samh kigo?" the mother asked. Can you trust him?

"Yes," Dave replied.

The mother looked from her husband to Dave. "All right, On Jai. Just doan get hurt!"

"Isn't she special," Dave said, looking wistfully at a blonde, lissome figure running the length of the high school basketball court.

"Hmmm, not bad," Mike replied, more interested in the sparring match that was coming up. "Here, tie me up," he said, pushing his boxing gloves in front of Dave.

Dave pulled his eyes away from the girls. He tied Mike's gloves on, then slipped one glove on his own hand, suddenly realizing he couldn't tie his own, nor could Mike help him.

"I need somebody to tie mine," he said.

"Oh, get one of the guys walking by . . . Hey, Tom, give us a hand?"

Tom strolled over. "Yeah, man, what dya want?" A tough, lazy drawl. He was a burly kid, blond hair cut in a flat-top, which most times was covered under a gray cowboy hat.

"How about tying Dave's gloves on for us, man?" Mike asked.

Tom looked at Dave. His lip curled down in condescension. He glanced around. There was nobody nearby. He was one of the guys who hung around with John, the half-breed who had given Dave the black eye weeks ago. His shoulders sagged slightly. With none of his friends present, he was like a boat with sails loosely flapping in the wind, momentarily dead in the water. Mike, who cut no mean figure himself, was watching him intently.

"Come on, man, we ain't got all day!" Mike said. He hit his gloves together in a loud pop. Tom hurriedly tied Dave's gloves, then strolled away to watch the basketball game. Except for a short "Thanks," Dave ignored him.

They were on the mats next to the folded-up bleachers in a corner of the gym. He "felt" her, imagining her eyes staring at him, her gaze boring into his back like a hot iron. Once, he caught her staring. She gave a wry smile. He smiled back. A good basketball player, too! he thought. "Diane," he muttered to himself.

"Come on! Come on! Touch gloves!" Mike pulled him back to earth. Mike was a rancher's son. He had an easy smile that formed from his lower lip and spread to his sideburns and somehow managed to wrinkle his scalp under his closely cropped, light brown hair. Maybe he befriended Dave because he felt sorry for him, wanted to teach him the skills to survive in this rough-and-tumble high school.

Dave and Mike circled each other on the mats. Mike had that build from working as a child in the outdoors. He had a good forty pounds on Dave. He was also taller, stronger, and had the longer reach. Not only that, he had coordination and timing. Nobody picked on him, unlike diminutive Dave.

"Come on, throw a few," Mike urged.

Dave let loose with a flurry: jab, jab, right cross, and a left hook, trying to back Mike into a corner. But Mike let the jabs and right cross bounce off his gloves and danced away from the hook.

"Okay, okay, let's do it again. Put some oomph in it this time."

Dave scrunched down. Left jab, left jab, left jab. Back away, then left jab, left jab, left jab. Suddenly, Dave's head jerked back. Mike had blocked his jab with his right hand and countered with his own left.

"Watch your repetition, man. I'm gonna knock you on your ass if you keep repeating yourself! Mix your attacks!" Mike instructed him.

Dave nodded, then shook his head to get out some of the cobwebs that had suddenly materialized. He circled, threw a left, right, left.

"Come on! Some more!" Mike tapped his gloves together. Dave responded. Left, right, left. Left, right, left. They continued circling each other. Dave now faced the full basketball court while Mike faced the wall and Dave's gaze was inescapably drawn to Diane as she dribbled the ball the length of the court, laying the ball up for two points. She cut a fine figure, he thought.

Mike had both his gloves in front of him, rotating his wrists so that the gloves seemed to take on a periodicity of their own, like the earth rotating about its axis. Dave was mesmerized. Jab, he thought, shaking himself. Jab and cross! Then, out of the corner of his eye, he saw Diane watching them. Was she smiling at him? he wondered.

POW! POW! The mat rushed up to meet his head. Dave smelled the mustiness as he lay there—all the stale odors of hundreds of bodies that had been sweating on the old canvas mat.

"You okay, buddy?" Mike asked, laughing, helping to pull him off the mat. "You're supposed to pay attention!"

Dave straightened up, nodding his head. "Yeah, yeah, I'm okay." He looked across the basketball floor. Diane was laughing, shaking her head, saying something to her girlfriend.

"You wanna go some more?" Mike asked.

"Nah, I think I've had enough today. Thanks a lot, Mike. I gotta run to my algebra class."

"Okay, that's fine." Mike clapped him on the back.

They strolled off the mats toward the cage, stripping their gloves off, untying the first one with their teeth. The girls broke off their game at the same time. Suddenly, Dave found himself face to face with Diane.

"Hi," he said, with a look of chagrin. Showing off, he had instead made a fool of himself.

"Hi!" she said, smiling. "Did you have a good match?" She was almost tomboyish, yet still girlish. Her figure was filling out nicely.

"Not as good as I wanted."

"I saw," she said, laughing. Then, "Gotta go. See you around."

"Yeah, bye!" he said, staring wistfully after her, watching the tight gym shorts disappear down the corridor.

"I know what your mind was on!" Mike laughed, staring with him. "But you better watch out, man. When it comes to fightin', you gotta concentrate on the task at hand. Otherwise . . . you're gonna be on the mat a lot more!"

• • • • •

"Better not fuck with me," John mouthed off. He was a half breed, maybe even some Mexican blood in him. He was taller than Dave, with a marquee body that exuded the wiry strength of a gymnast. He was testosterone personified, controlled by an amoral mind—a dangerous combination. He was showing off in front of a group of boys, his black ten-gallon cowboy hat skewed backwards. His hands were flailing the air in front of him and at the same time he was hopping on his left leg, extending the right in front of him. "I can kick the shit out of anybody." He flung his right leg out in a weak imitation of a karate kick.

Dave, heading to the locker room, saw the hop and the feeble kick as he walked past the group.

"Hey, Chink!" John shouted after him.

Dave's blood froze. He stopped for a second, then ignored him and walked on. Laughter followed in his tracks. But John did not let the matter slide.

Louder this time. "HEY CHINK! HEY CHINAMAN! WHEN I TALK TO YOU, YOU BETTER ANSWER, MOTHERFUCKER!"

"Let it go, let it go," Dave told himself. Ignore him. But it was not so easy. John ran after him, grabbed him, and spun him around. The other boys congregated around them like vultures over the almost dead.

"What . . . what do you want?" Dave asked in a soft voice, the bile slowly rising. John outweighed him by twenty pounds, but Dave's anger suffused his body, winding him tight as a spring. He dropped his gym bag, eyeing John closely. He didn't let him get too close, backing off when John tried to move in.

"I said, 'What dya think 'bout my fighting technique?'"

"It's all right."

"Think it can beat a Chink up?" John laughed. "Did last time, didn't it?" The other boys cackled. Wong grimaced, eyes blinking rapidly.

"You got lucky," Dave whispered, almost too soft to be heard.

"What'd ya say?"

"I said, 'FUCK YOU!'" Dave's voice echoed throughout the gym. Others turned their heads, then started strolling over to watch.

"Why, you little yella fucker!" John came at him, leg extended, try-ing to punch at Dave's face at the same time. This time Dave was ready. Dave grabbed the extended leg, lifted it high into the air, and stepped in with his own right leg to sweep out John's other leg. John fell with a heavy thud onto the hardwood floor, his cowboy hat shooting into the air. Dave was ready to jump on him, but changed his mind at the last second. John's eyes were rolling. He had landed flat on his back, knocking the air out of himself, and had also hit the back of his head quite hard on the maple floor. He was down and dazed.

"Jesus Christ," Tom whispered. He was the one who had tied on Dave's boxing gloves last week. "Did ya see that? Nobody beat up John here, yet! Nobody!"

Dave spun on his heels, lifted his gym bag and left.

"HOP SING! HOP SING!" Tom shouted at his retreating back. He was quite brave now, backed up with four of his friends. "HOP SING!" It was the name of the Chinese cook on the popular TV western, *Bonanza*. This caricature of a Chinese man was the only portrait white America could fathom. It cut to the heart of little David Wong. He turned around to look at them with cold eyes full of hate. At that moment, if he could have killed them, he would have.

"YOU LITTLE CHINAMAN!" they shouted at him. The five boys helped John up. They were still yelling, giving him the finger. John was swaying, unsteady, like a drunkard.

"Okay! What's going on?" Mr. Feldman, the boys' gym teacher shouted, coming out of his office. He was six feet three, broad across the shoulders, like a linebacker.

The troublemakers muttered under their breath, "Nothing, Mr. Feldman. Nothing." They stood around, eyes lowered.

"Well, good, then! If nothing's going on, what are we doing hanging around here?" Feldman asked. He saw Dave's back disappearing through the locker room door. "Time to go to classes?"

"Yes, sir, Mr. Feldman. Yes, sir." They retreated to the entrance of the gym, heading to their classes in the main building. Feldman just shook his head. He could guess what was going on, but he didn't see it happen.

There were too many of them! Dave thought, kicking his gym bag in front of a locker. Too many! How can he fight the world? He slammed his fist into the door of the metal locker. Again and again. "Sons of bitches!" he cried. "Sons of bitches! Can't fight me alone, can you?"

The sun shone lazily and a soft breeze blew, carrying the notes played by the band into the top section of the bleachers. There, Dave and Mike tapped their feet to the strains of "Cathy's Clown," by the Everly Brothers.

It was Sadie Hawkins Day and the festivities were in full swing. The students had been let out early from their classes to celebrate. Most of the students were in the bleachers, but some were still milling about on the lawn. Probably the student body officers, Dave thought, busying themselves with officious duties. One student was talking to Mr. Simpson, the vice principal. After several moments, Dave saw Simpson break away and step up to the microphone.

"Okay, ladies and gentlemen," Simpson liked to refer to the kids as such, as if the label could promote behavior. "Our winner in the egg toss was the team of Tim Snodgrass and Janet Damarski. Everybody give them a big hand. They went forty feet!" The words screamed from the speakers.

Desultory clapping came from the bleachers, punctuated by catcalls. But mostly, kids' voices mingled incoherently into a loud hum, as from a beehive.

"Okay, next up, ladies and gentlemen, is the three-legged sack race. A guy and a girl will be partners." SCREECH! ". . . will stick one leg in a gunny sack and they'll have to run forty yards! Talk about teamwork! The most coordinated will be the winners! Ha! Ha!" Simpson's laughter disappeared in another resounding screech. He continued to work on the microphone.

"Just my dumb luck to draw the ugliest girl in school," Mike said, suddenly worried.

"Oh, give me a break," Dave replied, looking at his handsome white friend, thinking, I'm Chinese! What about me?

"Okay, here are the teams! Gail Benville and Ben Sullivan." The two got up, making their way to the front of the bleachers amidst shouts

22

of encouragement. "Linda Callecon and Henry Allen." Two more got up. "David Wong and Diane Zinner." Screech! Smaller in volume this time. The vice-principal kept reading off more names.

Dave sat in shock. He didn't really want to go, not in front of this crowd.

"Come on!" Mike pushed him forward. "Get down there. I know you can win!"

"You don't understand," Dave replied weakly, still sitting.

"Go! Come on, be a man!" Mike pushed him again.

Dave shrugged, then dragged himself down the bleachers, as if in a dream. It seemed the whole world had stopped and everyone had focused attention on him. He was the only Asian in the whole school; in fact, other than the Indians from the reservation, he was the only minority in the school, the town, perhaps the county, and for all he knew, the whole goddamned state of Nevada. It was the loneliest walk of his young life, for he had an inkling of what was to come.

He stood below, scanning the crowd. Where was she? he thought.

The contestants gathered about Simpson, some chattering nervously, others quietly confident.

"Okay, everybody's here except for Diane . . . Diane! Diane! I know you're out there somewhere!" Simpson called to the crowd, shading his eyes with his left hand, looking for her.

Suddenly, Dave saw her. The blonde hair and the slim athletic body. She stood up hesitantly, looking askance at her friends, then casting a quick glance at the crowd. She hesitated, taking only a few steps.

"Diane! Diane! There you are! Come on down!" Simpson called out. SCREECH!

Dave covered his ears, turning toward Simpson. Damn! Can't he fix that thing? Then, he swung his gaze back toward the bleachers and, suddenly, his world collapsed.

Diane had changed her mind. She had stopped, then shook her blonde head and fled back to the safety of her friends. She scrooched down, trying to make herself invisible. She lacked the courage, as if by associating herself with him in public, she would catch a dread disease.

Dave was left standing alone in front of the crowd. There was laughter and catcalls and, filtering down to his ears, someone had shouted, "Damned Chinaman! Go home!"

Simpson didn't appear to have heard it. Or if he did, he ignored it, like he ignored the circumstances of Dave's discomfiture.

"Okay, it looks like Diane's ill." He fidgeted with the microphone again, craning his head upward, looking at the bleachers.

"Any other young lady out there who wants to be Dave's partner?" Simpson asked. "Come on, now! We need a volunteer! Don't be shy!"

Not a girl stirred.

Dave steeled himself. More jeers. "Chinaman, go home!" he heard. He felt an agony of loneliness. He would never be part of them! he thought bitterly. In this sea of white faces, feeling like an island, he wanted their friendship. If not that, then just to be left alone. No more names. No more fights. Other times, he could feel the hate emanate from some of them, cutting him like a hot knife. His soul raged at the inequity of it all. Because he didn't have the white skin and the round eyes.

He breathed deeply, hiding the hurt with an inscrutable poker face. He felt hollow inside, as if someone had reached into his abdomen and pulled his intestines out, and that all he had was this shell to project to the world. He slowly scanned the crowd, but they ignored him now.

"I'm sorry, Dave," Simpson said, clapping him on the back. He was a pudgy man, his face hidden behind thick glasses. An air of concern always seemed to hover over him. "You know, sometimes I'm damned ashamed of this school."

Dave nodded, said nothing as Simpson got the sack race underway. He looked toward Diane, but she was chatting with friends, not looking at him.

He was on the sidelines again, outside looking in. A social outcast, not by deed, but by his looks. He hung his head—a shame not his own—turned around and walked off the field.

Chapter 4

Jake

Stella stands on tiptoes to pull on the cord. The hinged attic door swings down and she grabs it with both hands, unfolding the ladder. She climbs the wooden steps with a sense of anticipation. When she reaches the top, she steps onto the plywood floor spanning the ceiling joists and pulls the string for the light.

The sixty-watt bulb casts deep shadows, but she can see the row of boxes. Somewhere in there is one labeled, 1967-68. She moves several about, looking at the labels. Then she finds it. She hefts the sturdy white cardboard box, moving it into the open area under the glare of the bulb. She kneels before the box like a monk at prayers, wiping the dust off with her hands, staring at the dates as if she were transfixed in a mantra.

With a sigh, she slips the top cover off. The letters are worn and yellowed with age after almost twenty-two years. But she can still see the big crooked scrawl that spelled out her name and her Annapolis address. Jake's first letter, written in boot camp, is on the bottom; the others as they came, are stacked on top. The last letter—from his buddy—had arrived a week after she had been notified of his death.

It was a tear-stained journey. She rarely chose to relive it. But today she feels compelled to confront that part of her painful past and, per-haps, by recognizing it, to mitigate her bouts of agonizing remembrances.

She leans against the chimney and murmurs, "Oh, Jake," as the past catches up with her, and she is nineteen once again.

"Jake, I'm pregnant," she had told him after dinner. They were newly married, settled into a cheap apartment not far from downtown Annapolis and the Naval Academy. It was June. The small dining room was full of cooking heat from the galley kitchen, and the smell of spaghetti with meat sauce hung heavily in the still air. With no air conditioning, Jake had pushed the windows wide open and had set the front door ajar, hoping for some breeze off the water. He had locked the screen door and then traversed the small apartment to slide the patio door wide open. Still, the mugginess weighed down on them oppressively, like a sea of fog.

The perspiration ran in tiny rivulets down Stella's forehead. She could feel the stickiness on her bottom from sitting too long. Beads of sweat ran between her breasts. She looked at Jake, watching the perspiration roll down his forehead also, along his cheekbones past his strong nose to drip off the lower edge of his jaw. She waited for a response.

But Jake's mind was wandering. "What, honey?"

"I'm pregnant."

"Oh, my God!" he cried out, a look of total surprise on his face. He sprang to his feet and grabbed her hands and whirled her into the cooler confines of the living room, hugging her tightly.

"It's going to be a girl!" he said, laughing.

"Oh, how can you tell?" She slapped at him playfully.

"Oh, I just know it. There's more than enough men on my side of the family." He had two brothers, no sisters. "What we need are females in the family!" He wanted his little girl.

"Well . . . maybe," she equivocated. "Maybe," smiling. Then she screamed, "Jake Abramson, put me down! I'm in no condition for this."

He had grabbed her around the waist, looping her over his hips and hanging her almost upside down above the carpet.

"Jake!" she screamed. But he held her there, admiring her firm thighs and soft curves where her thin dress had fallen away. He let her down gently, dropping beside her on the soft carpet, his lips next to her ear.

"Mmm," he whispered, "dessert time."

She giggled, "No! It's too hot. I'm all sticky."

"Not down here, honey."

She felt the breeze flow across the carpet. "You animal!" They made love, tendrils of air caressing their glistening bodies.

J a k e

. . . . .

"I'm not going to Vietnam," Terry Henderson said, kicking his foot into the sand. "No way I'm gonna go to Vietnam to fight a fucking little war. No way." His jaw, with tendrils of hair sprouting, was set with determination. He was a tall, lanky young man with stringy blond hair that hung down to his shoulders. He and Jake had been friends since second grade. Right now, he looked like a kid throwing a temper tantrum.

Jake heard his best buddy. They were broiling steaks on an outdoor grill on a small beach, one of thousands that seemed to dot the Chesapeake. Jake stuck the grilling fork into the four large T-bones and flipped each one over.

"Shit, Terry! You just don't wanna take the chance of getting killed!" Jake said. He looked at Terry, then down to the girls, who were wandering alongside the water's edge.

Every once in a while they could hear the loud explosions of the M80s go off, amidst the constant harangue of the little firecrackers. The big fireworks show over the harbor would begin in two hours. If they were lucky, they might be able to see some of it.

"Yeah, that's right. I'm too young to die. I admit it. I'm scared of dying." Then, "And I fucking suppose you're not scared?"

"I don't know. Maybe." Jake shrugged his shoulders. "But I still believe in this country."

"Jesus, Jake!" Terry exploded in exasperation. "Johnson got our ass in there in a deep way. And he's digging us in deeper and deeper. It's a bunch of bullshit! You know Jim Ackerbey?"

"Not really. I seen him around some at school before." Ackerbey had graduated a year before and had immediately enlisted in the Army.

"Well, I read in the newspaper the other day. He got kilt. Dumb son of a bitch even got a medal. Trying to take out a machine gun! Jesus Christ! Can you imagine that?"

"Yeah. Yeah, I can imagine that," Jake said, tightlipped, poking the steaks. He was shorter and stockier than Terry, built like a Mack truck, someone once said. In his mind, he imagined himself rushing an enemy machine gun . . . à la John Wayne, pulling the pin of the grenade with his teeth. Of course, he would survive and return as a conquering hero.

"You know what's wrong with you, Jake? You got your head up your ass." Terry knew what Jake was thinking. "You think it's gonna be fun and games like when we were kids playing war games. You think you're gonna be a fuckin' hero." Terry paused, then shook his head, as if he could somehow shake away the future. "This ain't no fucking game, Jake!"

Jake glared at his friend. "Well, at least I'm not running away from my country, am I? Shit-faced and scared! Whatcha gonna do? Run to Canada?" It was a verbal slap in the face to his friend.

Terry's brows furrowed, his eyes grew cold, and his mouth turned down at the corners. "Fuck you, Abramson! Fuck you!" Terry stuffed his hands into his shorts pockets and walked away. After a few steps, he stopped and turned. "What I want, Jake, is love! Make love, not war! I want a wife, children! I wanna fucking die of old age! I don't wanna die young!" He thumped his chest. "Is that too much to ask?" he shouted. He turned and walked toward the distant dock, away from the girls.

The loud roar of an outboard carried over the water. Jake watched the V the boat made as it cut slowly across the smooth, glassy surface of the inlet. The war was like the boat, he thought, upsetting the smooth existence of one's life. And he wondered, Will I live? Will I be around to watch my little girl grow up? Hidden within his bravado was a tinge of fear, and he felt uncomfortable with it.

"How're the steaks?" Stella asked. He broke out of his reverie. The girls were back. He looked at Terry, receding steadily in the distance like some slow locomotive inching through a railyard, being switched toward a destination not yet known.

"They're doing okay. They're fine. Another few minutes for the rare ones," he said, smiling, "and a little bit more for the medium. You girls can start getting the salad ready." He concentrated on the steaks, poking them with the fork.

Silence. Then, "Oh, Jake, what're you and Terry arguing about now?" Stella slipped her arm around his. Jake looked at her and then at Terry's back, wondering how she could pick up the nuances of his moods so easily.

"Same old thing," Jake said, standing up straight, arching his back and extending his hands above him into a stretch. "Vietnam."

The girls sighed. "I'll go find out about Terry," Jenny said.

Stella nodded, then asked, "Why do you always talk about the war?"

Jake dropped his hands. "Okay, Stella," he said, drawing her to him, "no more." He looked at her, then at Jenny running to catch up with Terry in the distance. "And don't worry, if I know Terry, he won't be mad long. His downfall is food. Waft a broiled steak under his nose and all his principles will melt away." Jake laughed.

Stella laughed, too. "You're right!" She nuzzled and kissed him.

He hugged her to him, then patted her abdomen. "How's my little munchkin doing?"

She laughed again. He looked at her, the merriment in her green eyes and the toss of her brown hair. He wanted this baby, his little girl. He felt a chill on this hot Chesapeake summer's day, a shadow that enveloped him, a shadow with arms that dragged him into the still waters in front of the oncoming motorboat. The uneasy feeling was that the vortex of war would cut its swath like a propeller blade across his throat. He smiled and laughed with Stella, but there was a hollowness there, and it frightened him because he so loved this woman and wanted to die of old age with her.

The rest of the summer was hot and humid, as usual. Gradually thoughts of Vietnam receded into the background. She wasn't worried anymore. How could Vietnam touch her? It was so far away. She was too happy to worry. She placed her hand on her abdomen. Is this a girl? she thought. Yes! She would give Jake his little girl!

In late September a chill settled on the land. For days on end the wind blew a cold rain before it, driving the leaves from the trees so that they stood like skeletons against the gray skies. The nights hovered just above freezing, with that damp coldness that soaked to the bones. Summer's benign grasp was ripped from the year, the icy fingers of winter closing in. Even the watermen were complaining, wondering if an Indian Summer would appear at all this year.

The blow fell two weeks after Jake's twentieth birthday. He had finally gotten his draft notice. It was like someone had knocked her onto the ground and then jumped on her abdomen, knocking the wind out of her, trying to kill her and the baby. All she could do was scream. Scream and fight for the breath that could not come. Her sheltered world had suddenly been cracked wide open.

They didn't say much to each other that evening. They went through the motions of supper, washing dishes, and watching television as if they were strangers—newly found roommates tossed together because of economics. Only at night, lying in bed, did they talk.

"Are you going, Jake?" she asked. She knew the answer, intuitively, but she had to hear it from his lips.

"You know I'm going, honey. I love you more than life itself. But I love this country, too. The Communists have to be stopped."

"Bullshit!" she cried out in anger. "What in the hell does a little country halfway around the world have to do with us here? If the Communists want it, let 'em have it! Why should we send men over there to die? Oh, God! Oh, God! Please, please . . . I don't want to lose you, Jake." She had turned toward him, snuggling her head in his shoulder. "We've got something special here. Think of the baby! Don't go. Don't go to war! Please!"

Jake turned away. Already the war was distancing them. "I have to, honey. I have to." It seemed the only way he could speak to her was to bounce his words off the wall. "No matter how much I love you, I have to go. I'm not a man who's gonna run and hide."

The silence echoed throughout the room. It was as if she were viewing herself in a silent movie. She spoke the words, but he could not hear. And she would not hear him in return.

She moved closer again, draping her arm over him. He turned to face her. He grabbed her face in his hands. "Oh, Stella," he whispered, kissing her. "Oh, Stella."

They made love then. Slowly, like in a dream. Quietly, almost dispassionately. In the stillness of the night, she could see the storm clouds rising over the horizon. Growing in height, growing in power.

Chapter 5

Nightmares

He was in the bush again, moving in slow motion down a jungle trail. His buddies were ahead. Then the image of the little girl flitted in. The bush . . . His buddies . . . Then the sight of her, a pretty girl. Suddenly, the Mama-san. He looked at her, bewildered. Like Ahpo, grandmother. Then not. He shook his head, trying to clear it. Was this a dream, or was this real?

Suddenly, the old lady laughed, inches from his face. The ripples of her laughter caused the flesh on her face to rupture along the laugh lines. The eyes turned cold. The flesh decayed, dropping from her face. Then the eyeballs ruptured, spewing maggots . . . maggots everywhere. And the smell!

He backed away in a panic, stumbling into the pretty little girl behind him. He looked at her. A princess she would have been, he thought. The promise of a beautiful woman. Then, before his eyes, her beauty was transformed into death, the young skin festering and putrefying like in a fast-forwarded motion picture, exposing the skull beneath. She, too, laughed at him, girlish giggles that turned into the old lady's obscene cackle.

"Help me!" he screamed to his buddies. But the two ghouls had him trapped. His buddies had disappeared silently down the trail. Somehow, in his panic, he had dropped his M-16. He had only his knife. He pulled it out and nervously flicked his thumb over the blade, testing its sharpness. The Mama-san flew into his face. He almost passed out from the smell. "Die, you old bitch!" he cried out, plunging the knife into her heart. She went down, a look of sadness, it seemed, mirrored in her eye sockets. Then, the little girl came at him. He plunged the knife into her, obliterating her face, closing his eyes and sobbing uncontrollably as he felt the rotting flesh fall away from his fingers.

He stood up. Alive! Relieved that he had won. The two bodies were laid out in front of him, eye sockets pointing toward the sky. Then to his horror they both got up, laughing at the big joke they had played on him.

"No! No!" he screamed. But it did no good. They came closer, caressing him like lovers. He plunged his knife, again and again into both of them. They just laughed, as if the knife were a feather. The smell—so strong—almost made him lose consciousness. It was the charnel house smell of dead bodies after battle, the smell of ripe death, of blood and guts and shit. He could not win. He stood there, head bowed, letting the obscene hands of death caress him.

The Mama-san grabbed his head, forcing it up. Wearily, he looked into the black pits of the Mama-san's skull. Before his incredulous eyes, the cheekbones, chin, and eyesockets realigned, the muscles reappeared, next the skin, then the eyeballs and hair. "Ahpo!" he screamed. "No! Not you!" His grandmother looked at him, pity on her face, changing to disdain. Then her lips curled into a look of hate. And she laughed, pointing her finger at him, exclaiming, "War no good!" Then the flesh fell off, revealing the laughing demon beneath, his great sin mirrored in the black holes of her eye sockets. He felt himself being pulled into that pitiless abyss, screaming all the way.

"God! God!" Wong screams.

He catches himself, stopping the fall, shaking in his bed, beads of sweat staining the pillow. "Oh, Jesus, sweet Jesus. When will it end? When will it ever end?" he cries. His head is splitting. He feels nauseated. He does not remember the ride home from the tavern, or his stumbling into bed. His wife, used to his drunken rages, has locked herself and their daughter, Nancy, in the bedroom. Wong is in the guest bedroom, which was becoming a more common occurrence.

He lies in bed, willing himself to slow the wild palpitations of his heart. He sees a hint of dawn filtering through the sides of the drawn window shades. All is still quiet in the house.

He staggers up, turns on the lights, goes to the bathroom, and returns. He opens the bifold closet doors. Underneath his strewn clothes, he finds his old trunk. He fumbles with the lock, trying to remember the combination; he shakes his head, trying to clear it. On the fourth try, the lock opens. Inside, he finds the knife and a bundle wrapped in black oilcloth. He takes the bundle out and sets it on the desk next to his bed. Unwrapping it, he finds the Colt .45 caliber semiautomatic pistol.

Still in excellent condition, he thinks, through a fogged mind. He caresses its steel blue sides, a lover's caress. He pulls out the magazine. There are no rounds in it. But the box of ammo is also in the bundle, and he finds it easily. Rummaging through the box, he pulls out the .45 caliber rounds one at a time, glancing curiously at the outer jackets. Some still have a certain luster to them; others have dulled with age. It has been a very long time since he had fired the pistol, when it last spewed death.

He sits down at his desk and jams three rounds into the magazine. Why three? he wonders. One would do the job. Just in case I miss with the first two, he thinks, laughing. O-h-h! My head hurts! He grabs his head with his right hand, the one holding the pistol. He waits for the pain to subside, then shoves the magazine into the grip. He draws the slide back, putting a round into the chamber.

He is not really thinking. His mind is numb, in a torpor of sleep and booze. He hears the outside world waking up, signaled by the loud hum of more cars. He stares down at his hands and the pistol. A thing of beauty, he thinks. A tool of destruction, too. But, for myself, it can be a tool for salvation. He flips the safety back and forth, trying to let his mind wander. But his mind will not stray and his hands start to shake. Small shakes at first. But, then, larger motions, as if someone has possessed him, grabbed hold of him, and was physically shaking him, as a parent might shake a disobedient child. With both hands, making sure the safety is in the off position, he brings the pistol to his head, gripping it tightly to release the grip safety.

"Die, motherfucker! Die!" he shouts to himself. The barrel is shoved up against his temple, above his right ear. "You've brought no joy into this world. Die!" He takes a deep breath, pulls the trigger.

Click.

He is frozen. Nothing. A misfire. A reprieve. He starts to shake. He ejects the faulty round, chambers a new one, and brings the pistol once more to his head, but this time he cannot pull the trigger. He can not pull the trigger. He lays the pistol down, ejects the magazine and the round.

He starts to cry. "You sad son of a bitch!" he says. He is convulsed by sobs, a piston of agony fueled by the guilt pumping within him.

After a while, he stands and opens the drapes. The sunlight streams onto his teary face. One more night is over.

Chapter 6

Notification

The lovemaking is slow at first, but the tempo quickens. His lips move over her body in a silken caress, and a glaze seems to have covered her eyes, as if she were dead and looking into a far off distance, a far off time.

"A-h-h!" she screams. She feels herself hurtling over a precipice. "Jake, don't stop now!" she cries. "Keep going . . . don't stop!" And over the edge she plummets . . . a long fall into a sweet abyss until the last of her shudders are spent. She lies there in his arms, suddenly exhausted.

"You did it again, Stella."

"I did what, honey?" She struggles through the torpor of climax.

"You called me Jake. Again."

She twists around in bed, her eyes looking into his for understanding. "I'm sorry, Jim. I'm sorry." She shakes her head, clearing the cobwebs of an old love.

"Christ, even though I've got your body, he's got your spirit. How long has he been dead? Twenty, twenty-five years?"

"Honey, you know I love you." She speaks it, but cannot shake this malaise of remembrance. Her words sound hollow even to herself.

Jim sighs.

After Jake died, Stella had moved to Seattle. Annapolis had held too many sad memories for her. She had lived there for several months in an unthinking fog of grief, a catatonic state of numb denial, expecting Jake to round the corner on Cornhill Street, greeting her with his easy smile, and that they would sit down in some restaurant and feast on crabcakes, clams, or softshelled crabs and laugh at the insanity of her reality—that everything had been a dream. But reality intruded into every breath of her life and, in Annapolis, it choked her like mustard gas.

One day, she woke up, started packing her belongings and, within two weeks, settled her affairs and bade her father goodbye—she was still not speaking to her mother. Then she and the baby headed west in her old VW bug. On the open road across America, she found some salve for her grief. It was as if she didn't have to shoulder it alone, that somehow the landscape of the American West pricked the pus of her pent-up rage and grief and let it run out onto the desert. Not that her grief would be so easily assuaged by landscape, but her suicidal tendencies were alleviated.

Once she reached Seattle, she went back to school and became a receptionist at the Fred Hutchinson Cancer Center. She met Jim Ferguson there, who was then a resident neurosurgeon.

He was attracted to her from the start. She was pretty, svelte, and friendly in a shy sense. He lost himself in her eyes, in the mischievousness of her smile, the arch of her eyebrows. But, it seemed to him, she always had this pensiveness about her, that she lived under a cloud of loneliness and unhappiness. Of course, he didn't find out why until a few months into their dating relationship, which was dominated by his hectic schedule and interspersed by rushed conversations. He looked at her differently then, so sad, so young. But, even then, he knew he loved her and would always love her.

"But you don't love me as much as Jake," Jim says, sitting on the edge of the bed. He sighs again. "I'll always be number two on your list."

A frown forms. He doesn't like being number two, but she is his life and his love. And he has turned the idea over in his mind early in their relationship and came to the conclusion that if he were number thirty-two, well, then dammit, he would wait in the back of the line for her. Still, he would like to move to the front of the line one day.

"I was a basket case, you know." Jim has heard it before. "I had little Sara to raise on my own. You were a godsend. You drew me out of my shell and gave me a reason to go on."

"No, honey, I only drew you half way out of your shell. Your feet are still planted there. I don't think you want to take that last step and leave it all behind."

He turns to her, moving closer. She puts her hand to his face. Jim grabs it and kisses it.

"It seems like it's gotten worse these past few months." He stares at her. "Let it go," he implores.

A heavy silence hangs over the bedroom. The heated passion of a moment ago has cooled. Stella drops her hand and turns away. Suddenly she starts crying . . . small, quiet sobs she stifles with the bedsheet.

"Come on now, honey, don't cry." Jim leans against her. "I know you don't love me as much as Jake. I think I've learned to live with that." He frowns. "Oh, Christ, I am living with it." He stands, throws his hands over his head. "He was your first love and always will be."

"It's not . . . not that I don't love you as much," she says, catching her breath between sobs. "They are two different loves. But . . . but sometimes I can't help myself." She rises to a sitting position now, looking at him, the tears leaving tracks on her bare breasts. "I'm haunted by these visions of him. I can't exorcise his memory."

"Maybe you don't want to, honey. Maybe you don't want to."

"No, no. It's not that. Maybe because it's losing him in that way . . . Some memories have become burned into my mind, you know." She turns toward him, a quizzical look. "He died; I went on living. I suffered the trauma of living without him . . . He was so goddamned young. Just a kid sent off as cannon fodder by the fucking politicians." Her voice is bitter.

His wife is the sweetest person he knows, a caregiver, someone who had a soft spot for every stray cat, dog, and child. She gave to charities and poured out her heart for the homeless, especially the children, but it shocked Jim when he heard her speak of government. Her distrust of the federal government knew no bounds. Her distrust, of course, came from personal experience. And Jim could not fault her for it.

His voice softens. "I only know that I love you just as much as Jake did. Maybe more. Will you accept that?" He lays his hand on her hip.

"Yes." She has turned her back to him. "Can you accept the fact that I'll always remember him?"

"Yeah, I think I can."

She turns again to face him, suddenly shivering. She draws the sheet up to her shoulders. "After almost twenty-two years, it's like a volcano of emotions is building up inside me. There are times when I feel I'm reliving my past. It's so real! Then there are other times when I can't even see Jake's face clearly . . . Am I going crazy?"

Jim laughs at that. "No, you're not going crazy." He gets up to dress. "But you do seem to be under an emotional strain." They look at each other, wondering about the measure of their marriage and this incursion of an old love.

"Honey, I have to go into the office today."

"Oh, no! I thought we were going on a picnic with the kids."

"We are. I'll be back by one, I promise." He sits near her to put on his socks. He then bends over and kisses his wife. "It's that damned Mitchell case. The tumor is back. I've got to talk with Sutherland." Sutherland is the radiologist on the case.

"I promise," he repeats, "I'll be back by one." He eyes her, smiles, then closes the door quietly behind him.

Stella settles back, drawing the sheet to her chin. The house is still quiet. The kids are sleeping in this Sunday morning. "It's like I never really said goodbye to him," she says to herself.

Suddenly the images of him come floating back to her, so young, so proud. But his face is blurred, out of focus. Only the pain is sharp. A shiv stuck into her breast, a focused blow that makes her gasp. Yes! The pain! She almost revels in it. Exquisite! And she is ashamed, because in her soul she wears it like a badge of honor.

When she saw the two Marines at her doorway, her stomach knotted up. She felt faint.

"Mrs. Abramson?" the one had asked, the officer.

"Yes . . . yes," her querulous voice echoed in the empty hallway. "Come . . . come in."

They stepped into the entryway. The officer straightened, looked at the gunnery sergeant next to him.

"Ma'am." She turned to face them. His solemn eyes seemed to bore into her and she felt a chill run through her body. He cleared his throat.

"Ma'am, we regret to inform you that your husband, Corporal Jacob Abramson, was killed in action on 10 February 1968 in the battle for Hue. Posthumously, he was awarded the Bronze Star for Gallantry, the Purple Heart . . . "

She didn't hear the rest. She had fainted. When she came to, the officer was leaning over her. The smell of ammonia was in her nostrils. They had placed her on the couch.

"Mrs. Abramson, are you going to be all right? Is there anyone I should call?" the lieutenant asked. "Your mother?"

"No! I'll be fine." As if anyone could be all right in such a situation, she thought to herself. "I have my . . . father. I have my father. I'll . . . I'll give him a call soon."

"Are you sure, ma'am? We can stay until someone comes to be with you. Or if you like, we can call for you."

Leave! her mind screamed at them. *Just leave!*

"No, please. I want to be alone." She looked at them, her eyes pleading. "Please . . . leave." She hugs herself, gets up, and puts on a sweater.

The two men nodded acknowledgment, looking at each other. "Then we'll be going, ma'am," the lieutenant said. "If there is anything else we can do, please, here's my card."

She palmed the card and ushered them to the door.

"Yes . . . yes, thank you." Her voice was almost a whisper. She closed the door, leaned back against it, and slid to the carpet, sobbing as reality took its impartial hold.

Her grief gradually turned to rage in a cauldron of passionate self-pity stirred by her vehement denial of Jake's death, of God, almost of life itself. She paced the living room floor, shaking in anger, beating her legs with her fists until they were black and blue. "Jake! Jake! You bastard! You promised you would come home to me! Goddamn you! Goddamn you!" she cried. "You fucking bastard!" she railed. "You said you would never leave me!" Back and forth she paced, wearing a path between the kitchen and front door.

"Why?" she screamed, "Why me? Oh, God, we had our lives planned out!" Then, "F-u-c-k y-o-u, God!" A high-pitched wail that reverberated between the walls.

She collapsed on the carpet, against the sofa. The sound of little Sara crying in the next room could not move her. "Oh, Jake . . . Oh, Jake . . . I love you. I love you. Why? Why did you do this to me?" her voice died to a whisper. She sobbed into her arms.

Time passed with no awareness.

When she finally stirred, the slanting rays of the sun through the kitchen window had given way to dusk. She hurried to the bathroom, full of purpose now. She flipped the light switch, opened the medicine cabinet—searching, pushing the pill bottles aside, knocking the cosmetics off the shelves, looking . . . looking. Then, she saw it, the razor blade container. She took out one blade, played with it, her mind fixed on only one purpose. She ran the faucet, tears streaming down her face. Saw the image of herself in the mirror, the woman who was no longer her, who could no longer be her. She looked determinedly at her wrists, grabbed the blade.

Then, as if her mind had been switched to a different frequency, the strident crying of Sara managed to intrude on her grief. She looked in the mirror again and saw a mother. She stared at that reflection, then dropped the blade, wiped the tears from her eyes with the cuff of her sleeve.

She ran to the bedroom, turned the lights on, stood for a moment by the doorway watching her daughter, who was crying, it seemed, with the same rage. She strode to the crib, lifting the little girl to her breast, eighteen-months old and still not weaned. She pulled her blouse up.

"Mommy! Mommy!"

"Oh, honey. Oh, honey," she cooed, rocking the infant in her arms. "Oh, honey, you don't have a f-father anymore!" The words were torn from her mouth. The sobs shook her again, the tears dappling the infant's face at her breast, dripping down to mix with the milk.

Chapter 7

Deacon

"So why didn't you kill yourself?" Erlandson asks, his back turned toward Wong. Then, over his shoulder, "You want some coffee?"

"Okay. Cream, please."

Erlandson sets out another cup. After pouring the coffee, he grabs some half-and-half from the small refrigerator. He strolls back to his desk and hands the cup across the desk to Wong.

"So?" Erlandson's eyebrows arch. He is studying Wong. He sees a defeated man slumped in his chair. He is about five-six and, Erlandson would guess, about 180 pounds, most of it carried in a paunch about his waist. His shoulders are broad yet, hinting of the power the younger man had had. But Wong walks with a slight stoop, shoulders rounded over, the burden of his psychosis weighing him down. The face is long, but the cheeks are somewhat jowly; the hair is streaked with gray, thinning on top. Erlandson looks down at Wong's medical records. Wong was 135 pounds when he was in the Marines.

"I don't know. After the misfire I didn't have the guts anymore. I guess I lost my nerve . . . Do you have a spoon?"

Erlandson sighs, gets up from his desk, and steps to his sink. "Sure, here."

"Thanks." Wong spoons the coffee into his mouth like a kid spooning hot chocolate.

Erlandson gazes at him for several moments, intrigued by this particular mannerism.

"I still don't get the significance of the Mama-san and the little girl."

Wong shifts in his seat. He is more nervous now. He fidgets and looks about the office. His legs are oscillating like metronomes, opening and closing in sync, about two times a second. It seems to work as a pacifier, as rocking a cradle would do for an infant. His hands shake, the cup dips up and down, the liquid inside agitated, as in a wash cycle.

"I don't want to talk about it."

"You don't want to talk about it! Jesus! You almost kill yourself and you don't want to talk about it! How in the hell am I going to help you?"

Wong is really shaking now. "I gotta have my Valium. If I don't take my Valium, I'm gonna fall apart." He reaches in his pockets. He snaps open the pill case and pops four of the little yellow pills into his mouth, flushing it down with coffee.

"And how long have you been taking those pills?"

"About ten years."

"Do you know the long term health effects?"

"No. But, man, I gotta take 'em. Otherwise . . ."

"Otherwise what?"

Silence lingers. The tick, tick of the quartz clock sounds unduly loud to Wong. He hears the low whine of a truck on the street outside, pulling up the long hill.

"I'm scared," Wong whispers.

Erlandson leans closer. "Why?"

"If it were just me, I could handle that."

Silence again. Erlandson sips his coffee. "And?"

"It's . . . it's Cindy. I-I feel like . . . She's not safe with me."

"You mean you want to kill her." The words, when spoken, cut through him like a hot knife.

Wong grimaces, sets the cup on the desk, and slowly gets up. He paces back and forth. "No! I can't kill her. I won't kill her! I love her, goddammit! I love her." But his words don't quite ring true, even to himself. His shoulders sag, his head hangs. "Yes," he admits, "there is this urge within me. Sometimes I just can't control it. Sometimes I feel this great rage . . . especially after we argue. And I carry the grudge. I can't forgive her for it."

"What about Nancy?"

Wong looks directly at Erlandson. "I could never hurt her. She means more to me than my own life."

"But what about when you're drunk and you're all filled with rage. Can't you get back at your wife by hurting your daughter?" Erlandson's face is a frown of concern.

Wong shakes his head. "No, no. No way. Even in my greatest rage, I could never hurt her."

"But you wouldn't be aware of it. You may not see her as your daughter. You may see her as someone else . . . ?"

"Oh, God! I hope not. Late at night, when the demons come, I admit I can't think straight . . . I've put distance between them and me. I've gotten out of bed and walked the streets sometimes . . . two, three, four in the morning. I've even beaten my head against a brick wall."

Erlandson raises his thick eyebrows.

"It's a way of containing my rage." Wong sighs. "Ever feel rage, Doc?" Wong looks up, a challenge in his eyes.

"You're the patient."

"Ah, come on, Doc. You mean to tell me you've never felt like strangling your wife at times." A grin spreads across Wong's face as he leans over the desk, leering into Erlandson's face. A look of almost overpowering dementia shines from his eyes.

Erlandson looks him straight in the eye. "Hell, yes! . . . Hell, yes!" Erlandson is now on his feet, striding in front of his desk, gesticulating with his hands. Loudly, he explains, "But I don't act on it! That is what separates the sane from the insane, the majority of society from the criminals. Can you see that, David? Can you understand that?"

Wong stands still, his dementia deflated like a spent balloon. He thinks back to just last week.

He was drunk as he staggered from the door to the couch, knocking over the small table lamp.

The crash awakened his wife. She came out and switched on the lights.

"Goddammit, Dave," she rasped, "don't wake up Nancy!" Bitterness curled down her lips.

He was bent over the couch. He turned his head to look at her.

"Always drunk! Goddammit, why did I marry a drunk?"

"I dunno why," he muttered. "Beash me."

"Look at this fucking mess you made." She grabbed her broom and dustpan, sweeping up the broken glass.

Dave looked at her. Always so meticulous, he thought. Goddamn her! As if an immaculate house were the highest priority in one's life.

"I didno mean to."

"That's your problem. You never 'mean to' anything, you gobbledygook." He was a turkey to her. And Asian. The term fitted precisely.

"Don't call me . . . don't call me dat." He tried to clear his head.

"I married a fucking gook, a goddamned drunk fucking gook!" Her voice grew more shrill. Her Irish temper was running freely now.

"I said, 'Don't call me that.'" He sat up on the couch now. Then he rolled over and vomited onto the carpet.

"Oh, Jesus!" Cindy yelled. She quickly ran into the kitchen and grabbed a roll of paper towels and a bag. She wiped up most of the spill, wrinkling her nose. She wadded most of the vomit into the towels, dumped them into the small garbage bag at her side, then dabbed at the carpet. "What fucking good are you, anyway?" she ranted. "Always drunk! Can't hold a job for more than three months at a time!"

"What?" Wong asked, more sober, his nausea dissipating.

"You stupid gook asshole!" she yelled. "Always extra work for me!"

The words "gook asshole" cut through his torpor. His eyes grew malignant, a look of madness, his rage bubbling through. She had pushed his button, her words ripping through the thin veneer of his civility. He grabbed her hair with his left hand, wrenching hard. "What didya call me?" he asked, almost stone cold sober. Cindy grabbed his wrist with both hands, struggling to stand. But he managed to stand first.

"Gook asshole!" she screamed out again.

He twisted her head around and smashed his right fist into her cheekbone, knocking her to the carpet. His pent-up rage had found an easy target.

"Son of a bitch!" she cried, crawling away from him.

"You shouldna called me that, Cindy." He followed, bending over her. "Now, doan go calling me that."

She looked at him with contempt and fear, tears falling. "Fuck you!"

He hit her again, the momentum catapulting her head hard against the floor. She screamed in agony.

"Mommy! Mommy! Daddy, why are you doing this?" It was their seven-year-old daughter.

"Nancy! . . . Run! . . . Go! . . . Next door!" The words were weak.

But Wong had already grabbed his daughter's arm. Nancy recoiled, the smell of whiskey and vomit hitting her nostrils. "Don't worry, honey. Daddy ain't gonna hurts you. It's just that Mommy don't like ours Chinese blood. She don't like Chinese."

"Let her go . . . Dave. Let me . . . go," Cindy pleaded. Blood was running from her mouth onto the carpet.

"I'm gonna let her go, dear wife," he said. "Don't worry." Then, "Nancy, go back to your room."

The little girl stood by the doorway, hesitating.

"Go!" Wong shouted.

Nancy had never seen her father like this before. Angry, yes, but not out of control. The little girl retreated, terrified.

"W-h-a-t are . . . you doing?"

Wong straddled his wife, kneeling on the carpet, fingering the knife he had pulled from his pocket.

Cindy's eyes grew wider in fear. "Oh, my . . . God! . . . Oh, my God! Please . . . David. I didn't . . . mean it. Leave me . . . be," she begged.

Wong's eyes looked deranged. A far off look. He fingered the knife slowly. "You know, when I was in Vietnam, I was pretty good with a knife." He smiled.

Cindy screamed and screamed, filling the household with her fear. The nearest neighbor, next door, was two enclosed houses away, doors shut, windows pulled down tight.

No one heard except the little girl. Nancy covered her ears with the pillow. "Mommy, Mommy!" she cried. "Why is Daddy doing this to you?" But her small voice was drowned out by the cries of her mother.

Recalling his rage then, he is deflated now in front of Erlandson.

In the end, he had only nicked his wife's ear. He had been hauled away by police, spent a night in jail. The next morning, he called his lawyer and got out on $1,000 bail, court date pending. Cindy, he heard, was filing for divorce and had gotten a restraining order. He relates this all to Erlandson.

"Am I insane?"

"No. But you're hiding something from me, aren't you? There's something down deep that you don't want to bring out. You don't want it to see the light of day."

Wong slumps in his chair, beaten down and tossed into it like a rag doll. His black hair is matted across his forehead. "There's just . . . just . . . too much . . ." He cries. Soft sobs.

Erlandson lets him cry and finishes his coffee. He shuffles his papers, sifts through them. He comes across Wong's prescreening form.

Erlandson's patients were always asked to write down what they thought was wrong with them, and then to explain why.

Erlandson breaks the silence. "You said on this form that your problem goes all the way back to Deacon. What do you mean by, 'It started with Deacon'?"

Wong sits up. "He was one black fucking son of a bitch."

Erlandson frowns, puzzled.

"Wayne Deacon was his name. But it was just Deacon to us. That's all we knew him by," Wong says, smiling in recollection. "He was my buddy."

"You know the problem wit' you, Wong, is dat you ain't got no confidence. Ya gotta be a good bullshitter, das all. Das how you gets pussy!"

Wong shrugged. He looked over at his friend. It was a handsome face, the color of milk chocolate, intelligent brows over a not-too-broad nose, a firm chin, and an easygoing smile that seemed forever painted on. Wong had never known him to be bellicose. Arrogant, yes.

They were on weekend liberty, walking over the bridge into Tijuana on a sunny June day. Below them, the shantytown sprawled across the landscape like some poor man's subdivision. The houses, sitting on the edge of a huge garbage dump, were made of discarded planks, old plywood, corrugated iron, and cardboard boxes. The rancid smell of garbage assailed their nostrils. The people below walked with a leaden gait, a dead future of unremitting poverty a foregone conclusion.

"That's easy for you to say. Sometimes I think it's easier for a black man than me to get a girl."

Deacon looked Wong over. "Mebbe. But I don't think so. I give my left nut to be Chinese, like you, than black like I's is."

Neither one talked for a while. The only sound was the traffic and the sound of their leather shoes on the pavement.

"So how come you joined the Marine Corps?" Deacon suddenly asked.

"Hell, I don't know. Maybe it was watching too many John Wayne movies." He laughed.

Wong thought back to when he was a desk clerk in a Waikiki hotel and the Marine sergeant on R&R from Vietnam he had met. He was alone. No wife, no girlfriend, trying his luck to pick up women on the Waikiki strip, but to no avail. The man had that thousand- yard stare that looked right through you. He had come by the front desk one night when Wong was on duty. Wong had asked him how he was. Their conversation fell into Vietnam.

"It's a bad motherfucker out there," the sergeant said when Wong volunteered that he was going to join the Marine Corps. The sergeant was leaning on the countertop, blowing smoke rings, looking past Wong. It was a gaze Wong still remembered. "We were setting up positions before nightfall on the side of this one hill, digging foxholes. There was a valley below us. The North Vietnamese was dug in on the other hillside, but we didn't know it. Well, no sooner had we dug in and got into our foxholes, then we got a mortar barrage. Two guys in one foxhole took a direct hit—landed right in their hole. Christ! There wasn't much of 'em to pick up."

His eyes turned sour. He was silent for a moment. Then he shook himself, as if he were just awakening. He looked at Wong, snubbed out the cigarette, said, "If I was you, I'd think twice about it." With that the sergeant left, back to his loneliness and his memories. But he had struck a chord within Wong. There were men dying out there, and he was safe in a dull dead-end summer job with the boredom of another college year approaching.

"Well, you're one dumb sumbitch, Wong." Wong was broken out of his reverie. "What with your college education and all that and you upping for the Marine Corps. Christ, if I was you and had your smarts, I'd be humping all those sweet college girls." Deacon grinned at the idea. He had only gone through ninth grade.

"What about you? What got you into this green motherfucker, Deacon?"

"Hooh! Hooh! Hooh! I didn't have much choice, I guess," Deacon answered. "Like I said, I was a wild one when I was younger. The judge, he said, do the time, boy, or go into the Marine Corps. So I said, 'Yassuh! Ahm a Marine, suh!'"

Wong grinned. "What the hell did you do?"

"I was seventeen and I committed armed robbery."

"Jesus!" Wong whistled. He would never have thought it. "The Marine Corps did straighten out your ass!"

"Hooh! Hooh! Hooh!" Deacon laughed, a wide grin splitting his face, showing his ivory teeth.

"Senor, senor, p-l-e-e-z!" The sounds of children interrupted their conversation. Their hands were outstretched, their bellies swollen, their faces smeared with dirt and filth. They had run out from the adjacent dilapidated houses, up the embankment.

The two Marines looked helplessly at each other, reached into their pockets, and threw a few coins to them. Wong immediately hurried on, but Deacon tarried and was soon surrounded by the kids.

"Senor! Senor! Candeeee! Moneee! Pleeez, senor!" Eight pairs of hands were outstretched.

Deacon reached into his pockets and took out more change and some candies he had. "Ben nose dee ass, mule chacos," he said. Wong strolled back, chuckling at Deacon's accent.

"Jesus Christ, Deacon, you're surrounded."

"Yeah, I know."

"Senor!" one shrill little boy cried out and grabbed Deacon's hands. "My seeester! She young. Feeefteeen! You like?" The boy couldn't have been more than seven.

Wong and Deacon looked at each other. "No, humbray, no. But grazias anyway," Deacon replied.

Then they both noticed the little girl, standing apart. She must have been eight or nine. Already, she had that singular beauty that would mark her in future years. Her jet black hair was tousled, her face smudged, her dress torn and dirty. But her face was angelic, a straight nose beneath beautiful brown eyes. A straight, firm chin. She noticed them looking at her and she smiled sheepishly. Her teeth flashed white against the dark tan of her skin. Wong looked at Deacon above the clamor of the little beggars. Both, sadly, knew her fate.

"Ah, who is dees leetle mule chaco?" Deacon cooed, strolling over to her. The little girl curtsied.

"Well, look at this, Wong! Wouldja believe it? This girl has c-o-o-l-t-u-r-e!"

He reached into his pockets, and fighting off the other kids, he withdrew his right hand and held it high above his head, clenched into a fist. Grabbing her one small hand with his left, he then placed the coin into her palm, closing her hand tightly.

"Gracias, senor." She smiled. Already some of the boys were crowding her. But she turned out to be a fighter after all. She whipped her small body around and bent over, hugging her hands to her small belly, and occasionally kicked out.

Deacon yelled at the boys, "Vomit nose! Leave her alone!" He scurried after them, pushing them from her.

"Andense!" she shouted to their backs. The little boys retreated down the embankment. She spat after them, vicious as a she-cat. Then she looked up at Deacon, holding the silver dollar above her head like a trophy. "Gracias, senor! Gracias!" Then she turned and was gone.

They hurried on. The malaise of poverty had cast its pall over them. They felt beaten down, and they walked in silence. Even the poor pay of a Marine was far more than the sordid poverty they had just seen.

Their hearts lightened when they entered the main street. The sounds and sights of Tijuana tantalized their senses. Here, there were women and more women, dancing half naked, naked, to be felt, to fuck. After months of living with one hundred thousand other men on Camp Pendleton, where a woman was a rare creature indeed, where the sight, sound, smell, and feel of a woman was a forgotten experience, here at last was the incipient pleasure of a woman. They were like lions on the prowl, wishing to leave their seed behind, because death was on the horizon.

"Hey, Marreen, come een!" a hawker shouted to them. Their short hair marked them. Bars, gift shops, groceries, more gift shops, and more bars lined the avenue and side streets. Hawkers stood by every entrance. "Come see, senor! Hey, hey, senor! Girlies! Girls, senor!" The voices became more strident as they came abreast of each shop or tavern. Sex was for sale, in one form or another, and they were window shopping.

They turned off the main drag into a side street. The big neon sign stood unlit as yet so early in the afternoon, but it was hard to miss the large letters that proclaimed The New York Club. The raucous din of rock 'n roll assaulted their ears as they stepped into the dimly lit interior. A girl was on center stage gyrating to the music of Three Dog Night. The bar stools stood almost empty; it was the cubicles instead that were jammed with servicemen and the attendant "ladies." They settled into one, all the while eyeing the gyrating girl. Two other girls, about seventeen or eighteen, slipped in beside them.

"Waas your names, Marreens?" the girl beside Wong asked.

"I'm Wong and this is Deacon," Wong shouted above the roar of the jukebox. The dancing girl was still gyrating, doing a lazy circle, boredom painted on her face.

"I Maria, she Rita," the one beside Wong indicated.

"Senor, you like?" Maria asked, speaking into his ear. She was dressed in a miniskirt and a low-cut blouse. Her ample bosom spilled out in front of his eyes. Her bare legs were rubbing against Wong's. Wong draped his arm over her shoulder and grabbed her left breast, squeezing, then lightly rubbing the nipple.

"I like," he said. "I like."

"Buy drink?" Maria asked.

Wong looked over at Deacon, who was making Rita squirm.

"Whatdya say, Deacon? Should we indulge in some cheap drinks?"

"Hooh! Hooh! Yeah! Ol' Dick's gotta get aroused!" He peeled out a five-dollar bill. Then his hand started squeezing Rita's breast. Wong looked the two girls over, and approved of the fact that he had the prettier one. Deacon wasn't fussy.

When the drinks came, Maria rubbed her hand over Wong's tumescent organ. "Wanna fuckee?" she asked.

"How much?" Wong asked.

"Five dahler," Maria responded. She put Wong's hand between her legs. He felt her smooth thighs. He shoved his hand deeper and she squirmed. "Go upsteears," she whispered into his ear. She held her left hand out. "Five dahler," she repeated. With her right hand she held Wong's hand between her legs. "Fuckee? Suckee?" Wong trembled slightly with anticipation. He pulled his hand out, reached for his wallet, and unloaded the five-dollar bill onto her outstretched hand. She slid out of the booth and Wong followed.

"You gonna go upstairs, Deacon?" he shouted as he passed.

"Yeah, in a minute," Deacon replied.

She led Wong toward the back of the bar, past the other cubicles and the jukebox. The din of rock 'n roll bellowed in his ears as he passed. They entered a back door into a small hallway, at the end of which was a short flight of stairs leading back above the main bar.

Maria climbed before him, wiggling her ass. Wong grabbed it, aroused. She giggled and squirmed away. There was an open doorway at the top of the steps. They went through it. Wong stood shocked; before him lay a sea of writhing, copulating bodies.

"Jesus Christ!" he muttered, standing still, doubtful whether he could fornicate in public.

Maria pulled him. "Come. Come, fuckee!" But Wong held back.

"Come on in!" a sailor, marked by his longer hair, shouted. "Don't be bashful!"

Wong stood a moment. "Oh, Jesus Christ! All right." Maria was already slipping out of her dress. He watched her. Before she took off her panties and bra, she quickly turned and made the sign of the cross.

He quickly stripped, his organ standing at attention, his eyes feasting on Maria's soft curves.

Maria held out a rubber. "Fuckee? Fuckee. Use rubber."

Wong ripped open the packet and slipped the rubber over his penis. He turned Maria around and entered her doggie style. Just then Deacon entered the room with Rita.

"Goddamned orgy!" he shouted, laughing. "Hooh, Hooh, Hooh!" He and Rita quickly stripped and Rita got on top of him, riding him like a cowgirl.

Wong was rocking back and forth, pulling Maria's hips to him, stroking her pendulous breasts. He was riding high on a wave of sexual pleasure, the future and Vietnam far from his mind. The softness of womanhood enveloped him, and his mind found release from the male enclave of Camp Pendleton—that world of warriors and war. He forgot about guard duty, mess duty, fire duty, formation, barracks cleaning, weapons training, first aid, the bland Marine Corps chow, the rules and regulations, the "yes sirs" and "no sirs," the saluting, the standing at attention, the inspections, and the monotony of men—always men, as if there were only one sex in the world and they had all been cloned as Marines.

That other world of civilians was a dim memory, that other world where another gender existed, as common as his personal freedom had once been. For he was no longer his own man now, free to do as he chose. He was Uncle Sam's man, to do as Uncle Sam pleased, sending him to death even.

Here he was making love, not war, and he smiled at that hippie phrase. He was away from the Marine Corps. He was away from Vietnam. He was away from war. And while it wasn't love in the true sense of the word that he was making, it was the next best thing.

They moved in rhythm, gyrating. He felt her smooth buttocks and pulled her to him, pushing himself into the pure pleasure point of her body. He was lost, barely aware of the other bodies near him doing the same thing. He climbed the hill toward climax, gasped, and came to a shuddering standstill, like a mountaineer who has reached the summit. Joyous and spent.

He and Maria dressed quickly. "You like?" she asked.

He smiled at her. "I like."

"Gracias," she said.

"Thank you, Maria."

She smiled back, happy to have a satisfied customer. Then she was gone, to look for new customers.

"Hurry up, Deacon!" he shouted to his friend.

"Yo! In a minute," Deacon replied. "I'm comin'! I'm comin', my man!" His face was a study in concentration. Rita was bouncing up and down like a piston, her forehead steeped in perspiration.

They sauntered aimlessly the rest of the afternoon. Wong ate some food from a street vendor. "Dog!" Deacon claimed. But Wong was so hungry, he didn't care. Only the sauce burned his mouth and even a sixteen-ounce bottle of Coca-Cola didn't help to cool his scorched mouth.

Deacon found another prostitute, borrowing five dollars from Wong. She was chubbier than the first, not really pretty at all. But Deacon wanted her. So Wong waited for him again, some twenty minutes.

"I'm done! I'm satisfied!" Deacon exclaimed, after his second copulation of the day.

They wandered toward the edge of town, heading in the general direction of the border. Suddenly and unexpectedly they stumbled onto a small street fair, rather like a sidewalk bazaar. There were crafts and paintings. The fair stood far enough away from downtown Tijuana that it seemed to cater more to the locals than the tourists, though a few Americans were wandering through.

A young Mexican woman of about twenty stood at one table. Before her, on a white table cloth, she had set small jewelry, mainly ornaments fashioned from silver. There were earrings, bracelets, rings, pendants, money clips, and other items. Her beauty attracted Wong and Deacon to her like iron filings to a magnet. She smiled prettily. "Buenos dias, senores."

"Hi!" Wong said.

"Ben nose deeass, senor rita!" Deacon said, smiling grandly.

Wong rolled his eyes upward. Well, at least, Deacon tried.

The young woman had an air of genteel upbringing. She seemed to generate a subtle electricity that charged the air with sexual excitement, but not in the manner of the early afternoon. She intrigued both of them. But Wong was suddenly stricken with the disease of shyness. Deacon, however, was on the attack.

"My, my, ain't this pretty." Deacon was looking at a delicately carved jade and silver bracelet. Then he picked up a pendant, almost in the same style. He held it up in front of the girl and smiled. "Beautiful!"

Wong had to agree. The smooth turquoise of the jade complemented the smooth sienna tones of her skin. "Gorgeous," he whispered in awe.

"How much?" Deacon asked.

"Ten dollars."

"I'll buy it if you agree to wear it for me," Deacon said.

The girl laughed. "Oh, no, senor! I cannot! I do not know you. How can . . . how can I accept such a gift?"

"Wong, catch me! I think I'm in love!"

The girl blushed.

"Please! You must wear it for me if I buy it," Deacon insisted.

Where in the hell does he have ten dollars? Wong thought, as he wandered off to inspect the other tables. Meanwhile, Deacon was bent on getting to know the girl better. When he got back, Deacon was thumbing through a Spanish cookbook. Wong also picked up a copy.

"Do you know any good restaurants here, senor rita?" Deacon asked.

"Si, senor. And, please, you can call me Carmela," she said, smiling, two rows of perfect white teeth.

"Oh, I'm sorry. My name is Deacon and dis here fellow is Wong . . . Carmela, maybe we could go out to one of those restaurants tonight, huh?"

Wong interrupted. "Spanish cooking? What's the difference between Spanish cooking and Mexican cooking?" he asked.

"Mexico is like America. America to England. Mexico to Spain."

"Oh," Wong muttered, suddenly ashamed of his ignorance.

Carmela turned to Deacon and smiled. "Maybe, Senor Deacon. Maybe."

Deacon winked at Wong. But Wong was unaware that Deacon had just made a date. He was still looking at the cookbook when Deacon grabbed him and steered him a few steps away from the table.

"Wong, can you lend me twenty bucks?"

Wong's shoulders sagged. He was starting to feel like a bank. He knew Deacon would honor his debt, but the weekend wasn't even over yet and twenty dollars would severely strain his remaining cash reserves. He looked at Carmela. She was busying herself, conscious of their scrutiny. She's a beauty! he thought. He quietly slipped Deacon the twenty.

"Thanks, man, I'll pay you back next payday." Then, "You gonna be all right getting back to San Diego?"

"Yeah, hell, I think I know where the bridge is. You take care of yourself."

Deacon turned and went back to chat with Carmela. Wong turned and waved to her. She gave a small wave back and smiled. She looked so much like an angel that his heart ached.

"Lucky bastard," Wong muttered, as he walked away, heading toward the border.

• • • • •

"Sarge says we gotta go search dat fuckin' village," Deacon said. "Moo ain't Then."

"Muy Thanh," Wong corrected him. They were stretched out beneath a few banana trees that marked the edge of the jungle and the village's rice paddies.

"Yeah, moo ain't then. A dumb cow, one that can't moo."

Wong laughed out loud. "You're one dumb motherfucker!"

"And you! Jesus Christ, you becoming more gook everyday here, Wong. You picking up the language."

"It helps with the Vietnamese women, ya know. I kinda like the Ao dais. There's something feminine about those long flowing dresses."

Deacon leered. "I like 'em short myself!"

They laughed. "How's Carmela? Get a 'Dear John' from her yet?"

Deacon slapped Wong across the chest. "Hell no! I'se knows how to keeps a woman satisfied!" Then more seriously, "God knows, I miss her."

Wong looked down at his M-16. He had no one, just family.

"Just 210 more days left in this mother-fucking country!" Wong changed the subject. He had been in-country for almost six months now. Wong would have been surprised if a newcomer had characterized him as having that look combat veterans always have. That thousand-yard stare. A nervous stare that sought to detect the enemy, defining that fine line between life and death. If you were successful, you lived. If you weren't, you died. And luck played an enormous part in it. More than anyone liked to admit.

"Hmmm. I's got 241 days." Deacon had come to Vietnam thirty-one days after Wong. "Shit! I thought you liked this country? I hear you gonna re-up!"

"Fuck no!" Wong smiled, casting his gaze to the village and then back to Deacon. "I kinda like the people. They ain't so bad. But, you're fucking crazy if you think I'm gonna come back for another thirteen months. Christ, I wanna live." Wong's face stiffened. "And I wanna live like a normal man, ya know."

"Yeah, I know. I don't want my pecker or balls shot off."

"There are more important things," Wong said.

"Yeah, like what?"

"How about both legs blown off? How about both arms? Or, worse yet, both legs and both arms, a fuckin' basket case."

"Yeah, yeah. I know." They had been over this before. "But you gotta admit, Wong, a pecker and balls is important! Ho! Ho! Ho!"

Wong laughed. "That's what you got, Deacon. Buku balls, buku pecker." Buku was the Vietnamese pronunciation for the French beaucoup, meaning much, many, a great deal of.

Then they were silent for a minute, listening to the hum of other conversations as the platoon stood down. Wong looked at the landscape, the green jungle and green mountains in the distance. He was amazed at how much this country looked like Hawaii, the home of his youth. Red dirt, banana trees, the green lushness of the plants, the slant eyes of the natives.

"Remember what we agreed on, Wong?" Deacon was rummaging through his pack for cigarettes and candies. He always did this when they went through the villages. The kids almost always crowded around the Marines, especially Deacon. He was a natural.

"What was that?"

"Ya know. If I get my legs blown off, my balls blown off and my guts blown to shit, I don't wanna live like that. Okay?"

They had made a pact. Death wasn't the greatest fear. To live like half a man, or no man at all, for the rest of your life. That was worse. To be a vegetable. To be waited on hand and foot. To be fed like a baby, to have your piss and shit extracted, to not feel sexual pleasure, to not give sexual pleasure anymore. To stare at four walls and a ceiling imagining your previous life before you became a prisoner of your own body. No. There were things worse than death.

"Don't worry, Deacon. I won't let you down. The same goes for me, okay?" They clasped hands, like black brothers. Over the last few months, they had grown closer. In the few firefights, they had tried to look out for each other.

Wong looked over to where Smitty was. Smitty looked up, and Wong felt the cold eyes piercing his very soul. He shivered. "One of these days, I'm gonna take Smitty out."

"Yeah, he is one asshole son of a bitch, ain't he? You better watch your back, man." Deacon looked over at Smitty, too. Smitty was gesturing toward them, and the group with him laughed. "That asshole just as well shoot you in the back."

"All right, listen up!" It was Sarge. "We've been getting some sporadic sniper fire from that village. Muy Thanh, remember? Some eight hundred meters across the paddy there." Sarge nodded toward the village. Everyone looked. "Nothing heavy. There might be one or two snipers there. The lieutenant and captain don't think it's anything serious. 1st and 2nd squad, 1st platoon, have been officially designated the task of clearing the place out."

"Jesus Christ, Sarge," Wolchak said. "Didn't we just do this a couple months ago?"

"Yeah," Smitty said. "Besides there's no good-looking pussy in that village. But, hey, who wants gook pussy, anyway?"

Everybody laughed but Wong. A thin smile settled on his lips.

"Fuck, pussy is pussy. I ain't seen you turn away from that young one we saw the other day, Smitty," Wolchak said.

"Well, she sure was pretty all right. Right pretty mouth. Old Josh was straining."

"Okay, cut the crap," Sarge interjected. "Listen up! 1st squad is going to take the left. We're taking the right side of the paddy. We're going on line." The two squads would be strung across the width of the rice paddy. If there was an ambush from the village, they could concentrate their firepower without hitting each other. "Okay, saddle up!"

The men formed an assault line strung out across the paddy. The mud pulled at their boots as they fought to maintain their line. There was plenty of cursing. The two sergeants yelled encouragement. Wolchak was having a harder time of it because he was carrying the M-60 machine gun.

"Oh, Christ, I just hope there ain't no fuckin' booby traps across here," Deacon mumbled.

"You and me both," Wong said. He was starting to feel nervous. There were another two hundred meters to go. "Why didn't we take the fucking road?"

"Could be mined, man," Wolchak said.

"Yeah, just like here," Deacon said.

Wolchak shrugged his shoulders. If they were hit here, the mud would slow them down tremendously. At least the road would have had surer footing. "Blame it on the fucking captain." They had just lost their old company commander, Algren, to a greenhorn, Jones. Algren had rotated out after his thirteen months.

"Fucking Jones should be here slogging through this fucking mud." Wong was mad. They were getting closer to the edge of the village now, ninety meters. He was straining to see activity in the village. He half expected an AK-47 round to pierce his head. They said you wouldn't hear the round that hit you. The paranoia was very acute at this distance. It was the kill zone. His bowels felt loose.

"Oh, Jesus, Jesus, Jesus. Oh, Buddha, Buddha, Buddha. Help me," he prayed. His boots made sloshing and sucking sounds. He strained to hear above the squad's movement for the chatter of machine guns that could be aimed in their direction. He looked over at Deacon. Deacon was deadly serious, concentrating, eyes fixed on the village. Fifty meters came and went. Still no ambush. Thirty meters, twenty meters, then they were on solid ground, fanning through the village in three prongs, left, middle, right, about the grass hutches. Wong sighed with some measure of relief. At least they were on solid ground.

"Check out each hutch!" Sarge commanded.

The men pushed back the grass curtains, one holding it back and holding a grenade at the ready, the other crouched in a firing position. But most of the hutches were empty. A few had old men, women, and young children. It was over in five minutes. Nothing. The Viet Cong had slipped away again.

"Okay, it looks secure!" Sarge yelled out. "No fucking snipers at least." They congregated near the center of the village. Everyone relaxed.

"Ooh, Ooh, Ooh!" Deacon exclaimed, smiling. "I's gettin' too old for this shit."

"What's the matter, Deacon? Gettin' chicken shit in your old age?" Smitty asked, lighting up a cigarette. Deacon's smile froze.

"Waaal, maybe I'se got more smarts than you's does."

"You callin' me dumb, nigger?" Smitty straightened, unbuckling the snap on his knife.

Deacon moved to meet him, unbuckling his snap, too. Some of the other men started to close around them.

"Hold it, goddammit! Hold it!" Sarge snapped. "I'm gettin' goddamned tired of you, Smitty!" Sarge stepped between them. "I'm tired of you goading Wong and Deacon." He was in Smitty's face now. "You got that, dipshit?"

Smitty scowled, then backed away. "Yeah . . . yeah. I got it."

"Good!" Sarge glowered at him, almost daring him to fight. The men saw that Sarge had loosened his knife buckle, too. He had a reputation as a damned good knife fighter. His men listened when he spoke. "Let's check out the perimeter. Look through the hooches for tunnel entrances." The men turned and left.

Deacon stood alone, relaxed, hanging back from this last chore. He smiled, lit a cigarette. A bunch of kids was approaching him. In front were three little boys and a little girl, ranging in age from five to nine. Deacon reached into his pocket, pulling out candy and more cigarettes. He noticed the little girl had what looked like a lunch pail.

Wong was at the edge of the perimeter, looking into one of the last huts, when he heard the explosion. It almost knocked him to the ground. The shower of dirt and other debris cascaded over him. His ears rang. He could barely hear the shouting and then the shooting. He turned and rushed toward the center of the village. Then he saw the bodies. Little bodies near Deacon. Other little ones that had turned and scattered and then been gunned down by the Marines in a fit of retribution. And Johnson working like a mad man, cutting away at Deacon's trousers and shirt. The lower half of his body was gone, legs like logs a meter away, short stumps where legs had been, guts and blood spilled out into the dirt. Deacon's eyes stared fixedly into space. Johnson was fixing tourniquets on both stumps, pushing a large compress on Deacon's abdomen.

Wong fought his way through the crowd and bent over Deacon, cradling his head in his arms. "You fucking asshole, giving out candy again!" he cried. Tears streaked down his cheeks.

"Fucking . . . kids," the voice was weak. "Wong . . . Wong."

Wong bent over, placing his ear next to Deacon's lips.

"Remember . . . remember." Deacon grabbed his friend's hands, holding tightly.

Wong looked at Johnson, stopping him. "Undo the tourniquets, Johnson."

"He can make it, man!" Johnson stared at him. "He can make it!" His eyes had the look of a fanatic.

"No! Not this way!"

Johnson looked to Sarge.

"You sure, Wong?" Sarge asked.

"It's what he wants."

"Okay. Johnson, let him go." Wong saw the sadness in Sarge's eyes.

Johnson looked at the other men gathered about, shrugged, loosened the tourniquets, and left.

Wong pulled the tourniquets completely off and watched the blood seep into the dirt, felt his friend's hand loosen, saw his eyes gaze into open space.

Oh, Carmela, what can I say? Wong thought, tears flowing. That he loved kids?

Chapter 8

Stella and Sara

"This is for you and me." Stella offers her daughter a small bundle, loosely bound in twine. They are alone in the house, sitting on the large living room sofa. Jim and the kids have left for the Mariners ballgame.

Stella helps unwrap the package. She pulls out a photograph of Jake in his dress blues. "This is your father after he got out of boot camp and infantry training." She hands the photograph to her daughter.

Sara sits crosslegged, placing the pictures on her lap as she receives them from her mother. Some she has seen before. She glances closely at the photos, then lays each one atop the coffee table when she is finished.

The pictures are a time machine, transporting her back into a past she is not aware of. There are other pictures of her father in his dress blues, pictures of her parents in Annapolis, pictures of them with her grandparents—Jake's parents.

"Is this one before the Magic Mountain?" Sara asks, seeing the Disneyland landmark.

"Yes," Stella says, and laughs. "Your father had to drag me on that ride. I was petrified."

Sara laughs, too. "He was handsome, wasn't he?"

"Yes. You two look so much alike." She grabs Sara's hand and squeezes.

"Oh, here are some pictures from the Hawaii trip. You were sixteen months old then. I almost didn't bring you. But your father insisted." There is a wistfulness to her voice.

"I've never seen these Hawaii pictures before." There are pictures of the three of them on Kalakaua Avenue and on Waikiki beach. Sara imagines her father corralling unsuspecting tourists to take their pictures. Others are more candid: her mother changing her diaper on the beach, safety pin in her mouth; her mother lying flat on her stomach, her top undone; her mother sitting atop the tatami mat on the white sand beach, gazing out to the ocean, with a sort of sad pensiveness. Then, she comes upon pictures of her father holding her, kissing her, snuggling her—a beaming, bubbly faced infant staring at her across the years. Then there is the young man— fit, smiling, handsome, so full of life and so short a future.

The sun is higher now. The living room seems bathed in an alabaster white. The sunlight filtering through the clerestories and reflecting off the white walls gives the room a haunting, surrealistic look, like the stark landscape of a Georgia O'Keefe painting. The strains of music from the local radio station add to her sense of physical detachment.

"There is one letter I would like you to read . . . to have. Your father wrote it to you after the Hawaii trip."

"Oh, Mom." Sara already senses the content.

"I was waiting for the right time . . . Maybe I should have given it to you sooner." Her mother shrugs and smiles, tightlipped. "But, I didn't feel . . . the time was right." She hands the letter over.

Sara opens the letter, yellowed around the edges and limp with age. She reads it aloud, the lanky, almost illegible scrawl:

Phu Bai
15 January 1968

Dearest Sara,

I'm hoping that you won't ever have to read this letter. Because when I get back, the first thing I'm gonna do is rip it up. No, the first thing I'm gonna do when I get back is scoop you up in my arms and hug and kiss the bejesus out of you. Then I'm gonna make love to your mother. Afterwards, I'm gonna rip this letter up and be glad that it was all a dumb exercise.

But if I don't . . . Oh, God, if I don't . . . I want you to know that I love you. I love you both, more than my own life. If this war has taught me one thing, it's the value of life. Life is so cheap over here. And so dear. When you can lose it in a blink of an eye, you kind of take a different view of life. Believe me, it's something to be cherished.

There are special moments here, though. Surprising moments. Sometimes, after a night on ambush, when nothing has happened and the sun rises over the mountains and you feel the comforting heat of the sun's rays burn off the nighttime chill, when you see the dawn bring life to a new day—well, those are special times. I think of your mother and the sunrises and sunsets we seen together. And I think of you. Did you know that you came about during one of those sunrise escapades? Your mother doesn't think so. But I do. Oh, how I ache for what I left behind!

Stella gets up from the couch and strolls to the window. She stares out the window to the bay below, her right hand over her mouth, her other hand supporting her right elbow. Her head is bent over.

God, this is a vicious war. Why am I over here? I ask myself that a lot lately. I have to give you an answer. Because, if I don't make it back . . . I at least owe you that much, if I'm not going to be around for your first bicycle ride, your first date, your first boyfriend . . . your . . . h-i-g-h . . . s-c-h-o-o-l . . . and . . .

Sara's voice breaks. A silence envelops the room, except for the woman DJ's sweet melodic intonation:

"For all you lovers out there, a special love song for you by T. Graham Brown. 'Hell and High Water.'" A moment's silence hangs in the air followed by a guitar's plaintive chords. The melody and lyrics float over the room, adding a Kafkaesque feel to the reading of this letter from a long-ago, now-dead love.

She continues to read:

> and your high school . . . and college graduation. You see, in my mind, I already have your future planned. I leave it to your mother to carry it out.
>
> In the beginning, I guess, we thought we could make a difference here, that we could stop communism from spreading. Now, I'm not so sure. The Americans are bearing the brunt of the combat. While there are some good South Vietnamese units, they're kind of few and far between. Most of these guys would much rather be home. Well, so would we! But, Christ, this is their country and they don't give much of a damn about it.
>
> I was thinking about extending my tour, but after seeing so much death . . . too much, really . . . well I'm out of here. I only have 131 days left. Then I'm back to you and your mother. Nowadays, I try mainly to stay alive. My duty is no longer God and country. I can't believe in either these days. My duty is only to my buddies. That's what drives me (maybe more than it should). That and the will to make it back alive and in one piece to you both. I only hope there are no more goddamned wars like this. (Pardon the French. If I get back alive, you won't read this. If I don't, you'll be old enough . . .)
>
> Maybe I was a damned fool for believing in my country. I don't know anymore. And if I should die, I don't wanna condemn you and your mother to sad memories and what-might-have-beens. I don't really wanna do that.

Remember me. Keep me in your hearts. But, please
. . . don't . . . d-e-s-p-a-i-r.

The tears are blurring Sara's eyes. She wipes them off with the cuff of her
sleeve as she fights to regain her composure, to complete her reading.

A-a . . . part of me is in each of you. My spirit will
live . . . forever. And I am so glad to have met and loved
. . . your mother. I only hope you will f-find someone
you can love with as much heart as I do for her.
You are my little munchkin. Forever.

With my undying love,

Your father
Jacob Abramson
Corporal, USMC

Stella turns from the window. "He was killed about three weeks
later." Almost a whisper above the saxophone's melancholy.

"Oh, Mom." Sara wipes her eyes. She rises from the couch, walks to
her mother. "Oh, Mom . . . Hold me, Mom."

Stella brushes her daughter's hair. "I know, honey." She pulls her
daughter to her tightly. "I know," she whispers, looking over her daughter's
shoulders to the glittering waters below.

Sara weeps for a man she has never known.

You are my baby. You are my little baby, Stella thinks. She rocks her,
unconsciously, to the rhythm of the song.

She is caught in the moment, between melancholy and melody. The
daylight reflects off the walls to refract through her daughter's tears into
a rainbow of sorrow. Suddenly, she can feel his presence . . . a slight
exhalation on the nape of her neck.

Chapter 9

Ahpo

"What can I say?" Wong rises from the chair, walks to the window, and stares out. "After Deacon died, I really didn't have a good buddy in the company anymore, at least for a while. Jesus, you know, I started to hate the Vietnamese—the gooks. I didn't feel that they were like me, or that I was like them at all. I mean, what kind of people were they, anyway? How can anybody send kids to kill the enemy like that? Did they hate us that much, to send their own children against us, to sacrifice them at so young an age? Jesus Christ, goddammit! Think about it! Would you send your seven-year-old daughter out with a bunch of C4 to kill the enemy?

"To me it was the most cowardly of acts for adults to do. The VC, in my mind, were cowards. They couldn't stand up and fight. They had no balls. They only committed murder. And yes, it is possible to commit murder in war."

With this last statement, Wong suddenly fidgets nervously, crossing and uncrossing his arms, still looking out the window. He turns, eyes darting all over the room.

"And how do you define murder?" Erlandson asks.

"It's the killing of unarmed civilians."

"But you Marines were armed."

"Yes, we were armed. But the kids—"

"Were also armed. At least that one girl," Erlandson says.

"Yeah, but did she know what she was doing? I don't think so. Some adult was responsible for that. That person was responsible not only for killing Deacon, but for killing all those kids."

"But you said the Marines shot down the rest of the kids. Weren't they culpable?"

"Huh? . . . Yeah, yeah, they were." He hesitates a moment. "Hell no! They had just been attacked by them, for Chrissake!"

"They were still kids."

There was no response for three or four seconds.

"Yeah," he speaks softly, "they were still kids."

"Then why did the other Marines shoot them? Were there anymore lunch pails or grenades the kids had?"

"I don't know. I don't remember . . . Anger? To protect themselves? They couldn't tell. By the time they searched them, they could have had a grenade blow up in their faces."

"Maybe that brings us to the ethics of war."

"There are no ethics in war."

"Surely you don't believe that."

"I don't know."

"You mean, it's all right to kill women and children."

Wong's head jerks up. He looks into Erlandson's eyes, but cannot hold his gaze. "Maybe." His hands are shaking.

"Do you think so?" Erlandson's voice is soft, rising just above the traffic noise from the street outside.

"What do you know?" Wong asks, his agitation gathering steam. He is back on the couch now, fingers splayed against each other, one hand to the other. He stares at his fingers as he presses them in and out like an accordion. He is mesmerized by their motion. "What were you doing during the war years?" he asks. "Were you one of those fucking hippies marching against the war?"

"Yes."

"I thought so. Nice and safe. No bullets, no bombs, no rockets, no booby traps. Just staying home smoking pot and taking part in free sex."

Erlandson smiles at that. "We got the war to end, didn't we?"

No answer.

"What I'm getting at is, how can you sit there in judgement when you weren't there? What is Right and Wrong when Death is the referee?

If you choose Right, we die. If you choose Wrong, they die. What's the difference? Better them than us."

"Give me some specifics. What are you talking about?"

"I mean you can't sit in judgement if you haven't been there."

"Where? Vietnam?"

"No, not necessarily."

"What then?"

"Been face to face with Death. Stared into his eyeballs and know you're not going to get out alive . . . but then you do by the grace of God."

"I thought you didn't believe in God."

"Figuratively speaking."

"Oh, I'm starting to see. It's like that Secretary of Agriculture—what's his name?—Earl Butz during the, uh, I think, Nixon Administration, when they were discussing birth control and the Pope. He said, 'The Pope no playa the game, he no makea the rules.'"

Wong laughs, deep from his diaphragm. "That's good! I like that."

"I thought you might."

"In my case it would be 'No talkee the line if you no walkee the line.' Understand?"

"Yeah, I get your drift." Silence. Erlandson stirs, shifting in his plush swivel chair. "Am I helping? Even though I haven't been where you've walked?"

Wong is silent a few seconds. He sighs. "Yeah. I think it's helping."

"But there is something else eating at you yet, isn't there?"

Wong looks up. "Yeah."

"Wanna tell me about it?"

"It goes back to my grandmother."

My grandmother, or Ahpo as we call her, still lives in Hawaii. And she has always been old to me. When we were really young, she would take care of us sometimes. Even at that early age of four or five, my brother and I knew that we couldn't get some things by her, unlike our mother. If we were out of line we were sworn at and spanked.

She'd yell at us, "Geahm-toh, saht-toh, little sulla bitchee!" Cut your head off, hit your head, you little sons of bitches. Then, she'd whack us. "No good boys! Only good for yahk, mee, oah!" Only good for eat, sleep, excrete.

We had the greatest respect for her. A respect born from fear, really. Only as we grew older did we understand her sense of discipline and how it was needed to keep twelve cousins in line when we little kids worked for her. And worked we did. We became quite a crew. Once every two years or so, we would restain several houses she owned. She would bark out orders.

"Mung Gong, you do roof!" Since Seamus was the oldest, he had the most hazardous job, up on the roof. He would stain the wood shingles. They did that in Hawaii.

"Goch Gong, you paint underside!" By that she meant the eaves.

Then she'd hand out half-filled cans of stain to the rest of us little kids, who would stand and stain alongside the house. Some of the older kids would get up on short ladders to paint higher up and trim the windows.

My grandmother was born in Hawaii. I didn't know that until I was an adult. For some reason, I had always believed she had been born in China and had immigrated here when she was young. Maybe it was because she always had the old ways about her.

She married my grandfather when she was sixteen. He was about forty. I never knew him. He died before I was born. He had immigrated to Hawaii from China to work in the sugar cane fields. His first wife had died. And he had a son, not much younger than my grandmother. When my grandmother married, she was officially the boy's mother. Even at a young age, my grandmother had a lot of common sense. She had warned the young boy not to go barefoot around the lumber yards. They were always looking for scrap wood to add to their huts. But the boy ignored her. What does she know? he must have thought. So the boy stepped on a rusty nail. And in those days, medicine and medical help were almost nonexistent. He died from anthrax, or lockjaw.

Ahpo

My grandmother had eight children, four sons and four daughters in what must have been a marathon session of childbearing. In those days it was a woman's duty and it was taken seriously.

I remember coming back after my junior year at Utah State University. I felt that I wouldn't be going back. Instead, I felt that I should be going to Vietnam. It was a call that beckoned me, a sense of adventure that kindled my imagination. Something exciting instead of the dull, drab student's existence that had heretofore been my lot in life.

I remember it was a couple of weeks of beautiful summery days in Hawaii. By that I'd mean sunny but not too hot. We were laying new wooden shingles on top of one of her rental houses. We'd stack the bundles up above, cut the straps, and spread the shingles about us. We'd line up the shingle by butting them up to a long two-by-four that was referenced to marks on the side of the slope. We'd set the shingle down and pound two nails into it. Then butt another one up alongside it, making sure that the lines between shingles were staggered with respect to the ones below it so no rain would seep in. I remember working alongside Ahpo. It would take me three hammer blows to put the nail into the shingle. She'd consistently only use two. She was seventy-two years old then. Can you believe that? And we also had to replace one of the roof rafters, a two-by-eight. Cutting it to length, well, she could cut it straighter and faster than I could.

One evening I got to talk to her alone. She was in her favorite rocking chair, a maple one my brother had bought for her birthday. Somehow we had gotten around to talking about life in general. I guess it had to do with her buying up the properties she had.

"I nellah cheat. I nellah cheat," she said. "I honest. I pay bills on time. If I late, I pay interest." She was proud of herself. After so many years, she had held on to her code of ethics with a religious fervor.

It was then that I broached the subject that was so heavy on my mind. "Ahpo," I said. "I'm going to Vietnam."

"Heh?"

"I go Vietnam!"

"Veetnam?" She tried to place it. In those days she hardly watched television. And if she did, she needed one of her sons to interpret. "Oh! Ngietnam! . . . Wha' foah?" she asked, suddenly sitting up on the edge of her rocking chair. "Wha' foah go fight Ngietnam?"

"My country needs me," I naively answered.

"Bullshit!" she said. "Why go fight in baak gwai war?" Why fight in a white man's war.

"We gotta stop communism."

"You fulla ohsee, On Jai." Full of shit. "War no good, Davy." Only once in a while she would call me that. "You tink war fun?"

I shrugged, cloaked with the foolishness of youth.

"War no fun. People die. Many die. You tink dying fun?" Then she lay back in her rocking chair and started rocking again. "Hmmph! Only war worth fighteeng is ageens Japanee." Although my grandmother had many Japanese friends, even a Japanese son-in-law, she had never forgiven Japan for the atrocities inflicted on the Chinese during World War II. "You fool, big fool."

We argued a little more. She asked me if I had told my parents. I said, not yet. She kept calling me a fool. But, seeing my insistence and foolishness, she admonished me, "On Jai, don't do foolish teeng. Don't kill Ngietnamese. Don't kill. Don't get killed."

I smiled at what I thought was her foolishness. How could I not kill the enemy?

"Do right, On Jai." Then she looked at me, the eldest son of her eldest son, and frowned. "You goin' regret dis!"

She was right, but how could she have read my future so easily?

"Sulla bitchee baak gwai war!" Son of a bitch's white man's war!

We never did talk about it anymore. I told my parents a couple of weeks later and they couldn't dissuade me. By the early fall I was in the Marine Corps, doing basic training at San Diego.

Chapter 10

The Murders

"So your grandmother is a wonderful person, and wise. What does that have to do with your problem?"

"But, you know, in the twenty-two years since I left Vietnam, I haven't seen her once."

"Why is that?"

Wong sidesteps the question.

"You know why I'm still here?" Wong asks instead. He pauses, and Erlandson allows the silence to linger.

"I still have this urge to kill somebody, then just kill myself. I was shaking so badly I couldn't stop. I had to sit down, grab my hands . . . really concentrate to try to stop the shaking. It was my worse attack yet."

"I thought I was helping."

"You are. I'm still alive." Wong spreads his hands, a thin smile.

"Tell me then. Tell me what's really bugging you."

"I need my Valium."

"I thought I told you to get off those things."

"I need it, or I won't tell the story." A hard set forms on Wong's face as his body starts shaking.

Erlandson is silent for a few seconds. Then he gets up, opens a cabinet door, and pulls a bottle off the shelf. He opens the bottle, takes two pills out, and puts them in front of Wong. "Here."

Wong grabs the two pills, swallows them dry. "More!"

Erlandson tosses two more across the table. "That's it, dammit!"

Wong grabs and swallows the extra two.

"Come on, come on. You've been stringing me along all these weeks. Let's get to the meat of the problem. What's really bothering you?"

"I can't look my grandmother in the eye anymore. For twenty-two years, I have never gone to see her, even when I went to my parents' funerals. Never stopped by to pay my respects to Ahpo. She's ninety-seven years old now. My brother tells me she is feeling her age. He sends me pictures. But, God, when I look at those pictures . . . when I look at her, I see—I want to see her before she dies, maybe before I die. But I only see . . . " Wong chokes, tries to fight back the tears.

The pause lingers and silence sits like a suffocating cloud on the room.

"What? What do you see?" Erlandson asks gently.

It is a while before Wong answers. "You see . . . the main problem . . . the haunting images . . . four months before my tour of duty was up, I killed," Wong looks up to the ceiling, away from Erlandson's face, "my grandmother. And her granddaughter."

The pain is etched onto Wong's face. Sobs shake him. He tries to continue. "I-I . . . we were out . . . on patrol. A long range patrol. For some reason I was put on TDY—temporary duty—with this Force Recon Company. Three of us were there. Wolchak, Smitty, and myself. They needed Wolchak because he spoke Vietnamese passably. They probably liked Smitty because he was one gung-ho killer. And me? Why did they ever choose me? I still don't know to this day. I wish they hadn't.

"We were out on a special assignment. Somewhere near Cambodia. Our lieutenant said it was some top-secret, hush-hush operation. We had radio silence. We were supposed to assassinate a North Vietnamese colonel who was visiting relatives in some small village . . . what was it called? Binh Phong . . . Banh Phong . . . Ving Phong . . . Binh Phuc. Shit. I can't remember. All I know is that we didn't have any support." The words are flowing easier now. "It was enemy country—Indian territory, we used to call it. It was supposed to be two days in, raid the village the dawn of the third day, and then hightail it back out to the designated extraction point ASAP.

"But . . . things never go as they are supposed to go in war. On the afternoon of the second day, we came out of the jungle—that is, the small trails we had been following—and came across this widely used path. The Sarge—Burney was his name—didn't want to use it. But the lieutenant—Manchester—said it would be quicker, and we were behind schedule. The lieutenant won out. Only, less than fifteen minutes later, we stumbled across this old Mama-san and, I guess, her six-year-old granddaughter. Wolchak, the point man, ran into them point blank. They came out of a side trail around a bend. All of a sudden they were there. When they saw us, they screamed, turned, and ran. But, how fast can an old Mama-san and a six-year-old run? Wolchak recovered quickly. He and some other guy corralled them easily enough. Then they tied and gagged them.

"We had to do something. We were still some five klicks, er, five kilometers, from our target village. It was around 1500 hours. We were in enemy territory. We couldn't handle excess baggage. We had to set up positions before dark. Everyone looked to the lieutenant."

I remember how dark it was. Everything was in shadows. It was like dusk. We were painted up black. We were in dark camouflage. The old Mama-san and the little girl were in black. Even the jungle was dark green—black it seemed in the shadows. And our fear spawned a darkness in our hearts.

"We can't let 'em go," Smitty said. "They sound the alarm and we'll have hundreds of gooks out here looking for us."

The lieutenant looked at the two. They were lying on the side of the trail, hands tied behind them. "Get Wolchak up here."

I relayed the message in a soft voice. He was in front, near Jackson. He came quickly and silently.

"Ask them where they're from," the lieutenant said.

"Dung la," Wolchak said. He directed the Mama-san to not scream. She nodded, a frightened look on her face. "Chi o dau?" he asked. I pulled down the gag on the Mama-san.

"Yen Phu," she said, nodding to the east.

"Khoang bao xa?" How far?

She answered.

"She said two klicks, lieutenant."

"What the fuck they doing out here?" The lieutenant's mouth turned down.

Wolchak repeated the question. The Mama-san answered.

"They said they always walked to the neighboring village. It's about four klicks between them. They got relatives there."

"I don't see it on the fucking map."

"Yeah, a lot of times they don't have 'em," Wolchak replied. "They probably live in a small village, six huts or so."

"Tha toi di? Toi khong noi." The Mama-san hoped. Her eyes pleaded. The little girl was crying, tears rolling down her cheek.

"What'd she say?" the lieutenant asked.

"She wants to be let go. Says she won't tell."

"My ass!" the lieutenant said. He looked around. I followed his gaze. The men were nervous, scanning the jungle. We had stayed put way too long. The longer we stayed in one place, the higher the odds we would be discovered.

"Waste 'em," he said. It was like a voice from another world.

Even Wolchak wasn't sure he had heard correctly. "What, sir?"

"Waste 'em," the lieutenant repeated, louder, eyes as bland as the drab dreariness of the jungle, with no spark, no soul.

Smitty, who was nearby, looked up. He had heard the order. Nobody moved. We had some hardcore killers in the bunch, but nobody made a move. Only the silence reigned, broken by the breathing of the men and the weeping of the little girl. The Mama-san smiled weakly, a worried look on her face. She didn't like the silence. She must have known that she had a chance when there was talking. But the talking was all done now.

"Come on, what the fuck's going on?" It was a loud whisper from O'Brien, who was covering the back end. The men looked up to where we were.

Smitty smiled. "Hey, Wong, why don't you waste 'em. Show us you're not a real gook."

His voice seemed to hang in the air. Everybody's eyes were on me. I hesitated, then I pulled my knife out. The whole world seemed compressed. All my existence focused on this moment. Why? I asked myself. Why should I do this? Will I regret it? Will this save the mission? Save our lives? Do I need to prove myself?

"Do it!" Smitty smiled crookedly. "Can't trust the fuckin' gooks. Do it!" he whispered. "Remember Deacon? Can't even trust the fuckin' kids!"

I remembered Deacon, and my knife took on new resolve, glinting in the low light. These were gooks, I thought, where kids were taught to kill. None of them could be trusted. Deacon was my best buddy, and gook kids had killed him. Blown him to shit. I wasn't a gook. No . . . no . . . no . . . not me. I was American, wasn't I? And I could prove it here. In front of all my comrades-in-arms.

The lieutenant looked at me, a look of relief; and there was something else in his eyes. A look of fear? A look of pity?

The old Mama-san, she was scared. She knew what was going down. She begged, she cried. Wolchak had to put the gag back on her. She twisted on the ground, trying to get up, trying to cover the little girl. She scrubbed her cheek raw on a tree and she got the gag off.

She spoke, pleading. She was on her knees now, next to the girl, bending and straightening at the waist, like she was bowing, arms stretched out behind her, wrists straining at the cord. A low moan followed.

I looked to Wolchak. His face was blank. "She said, 'Kill me if you must. But let the little girl go.'"

The Mama-san spoke again, her movement stopped, her back straight. "'She is too young to know anything.'" Wolchak translated.

We looked to the lieutenant. But he shook his head.

I came closer, the knife looming large over her. Her eyes widened. Then she looked me in the eye. It was a look of disdain, total contempt. In those eyes, that face, that race, that culture, I saw my grandmother. But I pushed away the thought. I stabbed, I stabbed. She moaned. I stabbed, I stabbed, until there were no more moans.

My heart had turned as cold and as dark as the jungle. The cold, cruel, silvery blade turned red. Then I looked to the little girl, and I could see the fear in her beautiful brown eyes. Doe eyes.

"It was like a dream. This was someone else doing this. Not me. And, oh God, please help me, the little girl. God! Goddammit! Why? Why?" Wong sniffles, wiping the tears with the cuff of his sleeve.

"After all these years, the nightmares still come back." The words seem to hang in the air. Wong stares solemnly at the carpet. "O-h-h-h," he groans, "if only I could relive that part of my life. But you can't undo an act once it's done, can you?" He is bent over in his chair, head almost touching the carpet, his hands hugging himself.

"No." Erlandson's voice is soft. A sense of pity washes through him. "Was it really necessary?"

"We felt our lives and our mission were in jeopardy," Wong snivels. "It seemed so important then . . . "

"So that makes it all right to kill two civilians?" Erlandson's pity is being washed away by his revulsion of the act.

Wong fidgets. "I killed because I was Asian fighting in an Asian war. How else could I prove I was American?"

"Jesus!" Erlandson's voice is low, but with a bite to it. "Where was your charity of the soul? Tell me, didn't your Asian side know Right from Wrong? Didn't your American side know Right from Wrong? I think that concept extends across cultures, you know."

"Charity of the soul?" Wong laughs bitterly. "In wartime, in the jungle, there is no charity of any sort. Funny thing about life. You crave it and you'll do almost anything to preserve your own life, even killing children. And—"

"Bullshit! Wha—"

"A-N-D as for my Asian or American side, what was I then? What am I now? No, I didn't know Right from Wrong in wartime!" Wong shouts.

"Bullshit! I say. Bullshit! What kind of a world is that?" Erlandson snaps. "And you're American of Asian ancestry."

Wong nods. "What kind of world is war? It's a hellhole," Wong replies. "The hellhole of war. The hellhole of the concentration camps.

Do you think the concentration camp survivors went out of their way to save those women and kids that were being sent to the gas chambers? Hell no! Their rule was to survive! Just stay alive, by God! Even the Kapos, Jewish workers, didn't help the poor fucking kids."

"No, I don't believe in that. I believe that Man can rise above circumstance and privation and make a conscious decision of Right over Wrong, Good over Evil," Erlandson says softly.

"That's easy to say when your life isn't on the line."

"I would stand by that decision even if it were."

Wong looks at Erlandson, sees the look of religious-like fervor on his face, the untested self-righteousness, and shrugs. "Well, you've never been tested, have you?"

Erlandson blinks.

"Don't you think I don't lie around at night and think about it? I think about it a whole hell of a lot."

Wong shifts his weight in the chair. Then, "I've examined my case, and to me," he says, going on a new tack, "it's like a twist on the Oedipus thing, you know. Instead of my father, it's someone like my grandmother. And the girl, like my niece. I sometimes wonder if it was my fate, like Oedipus's. But then I always had the conscious choice, didn't I? To do the act, or not. To kill, or not to kill. If I were a character in a play, it would be obvious, wouldn't it? Just a weakness in the character, a fatal flaw? Well, yes, I guess I could make it one."

"You already tried."

"Yes. Maybe next time."

"We're working on forestalling a next time, right?"

Wong looks up, changing the subject. "To be white! Ah yes, to act like a white man in a white man's war. My grandmother warned me. I ignored her and I killed a part of me, and funny," Wong chortles, as his gaze turns to the far wall, "I can never be truly white—though, as you say, I am American."

He looks at Erlandson, then down at the carpet. Silence for a while. "She was pretty, you know. The little girl. I remember that. A beautiful woman she would have been. But then . . . I guess I took care of that, didn't I?" Wong's voice trails off.

Erlandson tilts his ear, barely hearing the trailing question.

"I never t-told anyone this before. Only you . . . only now."

"So you've been carrying this burden alone for all these years?"

"Yeah."

"You must have repressed it with a vengeance in the earlier days."

"Yeah. I put it out of my mind. When I got back into the real world, after I bummed around for a few months, well, I went back to school. Utah State University. I finished my last year and got my B.S. in physics."

"Most people who go back can't even finish one quarter or semester of school."

"I'm Chinese. All of my life it has been drummed into me the value of education. Oh, sure, it was hard for a few months, getting back into the grind of things. But I guess I reverted back to my old ways. And you know what, for a while there, it was uncanny. It was like I had never left.

"Maybe it was the intense grind of doing physics. I had very little time to think back about Vietnam. It was like a bad dream and if I didn't think about it, it didn't bother me."

"During this period, you weren't bothered at all?"

"Oh, every once in a while, I'd have a crying jag. But then I'd head up into Logan Canyon—which was near the campus—and I'd hike up one of the trails. Then I'd just sit. Just sit and cry."

"Alone?"

"Alone."

"So you never had anybody close to you then."

"My senior year I did. This girl from Hong Kong."

"What happened?"

"God, she was sweet. She was a physics major, would you believe? Her name was Penelope Chen. We studied together. We fell in love. We lived together after college."

"And?"

Wong stares back at Erlandson for a moment, then drops his gaze. "I was in a pressure cooker when I was in college. When I left, it was like the lid came off. I guess it was then that I started to explode. I couldn't keep the nightmares away. I started doing drugs: pot, LSD, downers. My girlfriend, well, what could she do? She couldn't stand a stoned man, one that would occasionally go into a rage for no reason at all . . . " Wong meets Erlandson's gaze. "I'd scare the shit out of her at times. I'd be as high as a kite, demented, caught in my nightmare, and I'd be waving around my .45. Yeah, she was scared . . . And, yeah, I'd hit her . . . Do you think she should have stayed with me?"

Erlandson doesn't answer.

"We separated. I went my way, she went hers. I moved around. California, Oregon, Connecticut, Idaho, Vermont, Illinois. Christ. How do I know how many states? How many towns? I really can't remember. I got real heavy into drugs. And then I got out of it, just like that, except for alcohol. I knew I was dying. While the thought did have its appeal, the coming back was worse than the going in. When I wore off the high," Wong says, laughing nervously, "the nightmares were there, stronger than ever. So, being of sound mind and some deductive ability, I eventually weaned myself off the hard drugs. But," Wong licks his lips, "my weakness is still whiskey."

"But the nightmares still occur?"

"Yeah, but I'm applying my mind nowadays, trying to keep it preoccupied."

"And this is the first time you told anyone about these murders?"

"Yeah." Wong winces at the word.

"Are they getting any worse, then? Like are they as bad as when you were into the hard stuff?"

"Sometimes. It's like they come and go in cycles. Right now I'm into a real heavy dose. Can't sleep at nights." Wong's eyes are red, his lids droopy, his face taut.

"Which bothers you most? The murder of the Mama-san or the little girl?"

The question snaps Wong fully awake. "Jesus! How do I know?"

"Come on, now. Which face creeps up more in your nightmares?"

Wong cringes in his seat. The thoughts of those disembodied faces floating back into his consciousness frighten him. "No, Doc, please. I don't feel like talking about it. Not now."

But Erlandson won't back off. He is on the attack. "The Mama-san was your grandmother. You felt a kinship to her, at least I think you did. Maybe you still do. But what about the girl? Who'd she remind you of?"

"You're grasping at straws. She didn't remind me of anybody. I had never seen her before . . . Only her face keeps reappearing in my nightmare. I see it for a few seconds, before her skin and muscle peel off to reveal the skull." Wong shudders and crosses his arms, massaging himself for warmth.

"What did she look like?"

Wong looks up. "Why are you doing this to me? I want to forget how she looked."

"There's a reason."

"Enlighten me."

"Face her and her image will dim. Run and you will always end up face to face, again and again."

Wong sighs. "As I said, she looked to have been about six. Jet black hair, tied behind her neck. Slanted eyes, of course, but slightly. A curious look to her face. A small pert nose, a firm chin. Nice cheekbones, too, not too wide. I guess you would call it a narrow triangular type face. As I said before, she was pretty . . . And, oh God, she had those eyes . . ." He shakes his head, back and forth, an oscillating pendulum.

"What in heaven's name should cause the death of a child? I was too young, too young . . . I wanted to prove myself . . .

"After I killed the Mama-san, I pulled her body off the child." Wong stops. His face is furrowed in a frown. He stares at a spot on the carpet, some six feet in front of him, off to the side of Erlandson's desk, as if it were stained in blood. The beads of sweat flow. He wipes his forehead.

"The girl is crying, mumbling through her gag. Smitty, that son of a bitch, is yelling in a low voice, 'Hurry up, you fucking asshole, finish it up! Remember Deacon! You can't trust gook kids!'

"Everybody's nervous. I see the girl's eyes, lovely dark brown eyes, crying—and staring at me . . . staring into my very soul. I stand there. I couldn't move. Smitty comes from behind and pushes me. And I snap out of it. I look to Smitty, the lieutenant, at the long, bloodstained knife, and then the little girl. I focus on Deacon, pull the image of him in front of me. I mean, what kind of people would allow kids to kill and die? I have to think of them as subhuman. They sent kids to kill my best buddy, Deacon. I think all these thoughts, pull the anger in front of me. I need that crazy anger. That is the only way I can do this . . . act." He gulps. "Then, I slide away from compassion . . . God! What was it?" Wong wrings his hands in front of him. "That's it! It was an order. I was following orders!"

"Does that make it right?"

"I was caught up in the time and the place. No, it doesn't make it right. That's why I'm suffering and you're sitting on the other side of the desk, supposedly trying to help me.

"Don't you see?" he chokes, his eyes a thin line of pain. "I-I had already cut out my Chinese heart and replaced it with a white American one. But it didn't really fit. T-there was n-no warmth in the latter . . . What was one more life in a shitty, fucking war?"

Silence, then Wong speaks softly. "You've got to realize about time and place and situation." He stops, licks his lips. "Sure, if I could read the future," his voice grows in volume, "I wouldn't have killed either one."

He looks directly at Erlandson. "But we couldn't take the chance!" His strident voice fills the room. Then his voice drops, his eyes staring at the carpet again. "I lifted the little girl up bodily and flipped her over. I couldn't look into her eyes. I stabbed her in the back. Repeatedly . . . How many times? I don't know. It was like I was outside of my body watching someone else do it and I couldn't do anything about it."

A long silence. Erlandson lets it cover the room, like a blanket over a cold soul.

"The music in my soul died that day. A man's sense of self, though I didn't know it then . . . you know, that child part of a person's soul that defines even an adult, that sense of innocence, trust, and wonder—a conscience free of guilt."

Erlandson nods. "That's pretty perceptive." He drums his fingers lightly on the desk, looking curiously at Wong. He is suffering mightily, but he is no fool, Erlandson thinks. He stops drumming. "Was it worth it?" he asks, straightening in his chair. "Was the mission successful?"

For a few seconds Wong does not reply. He bends over in the chair, his elbows on his knees, his head grasped in his hands. Sobs rack his body. Tears flow like rivers down his cheeks. "There w-were no NVA in the village . . . They'd left! A-i-e-e-e!" a scream of agony fills the room.

"I killed them for nothing! For f-fuckin' nothing!"

Chapter 11

First Steps

Erlandson looks at Wong's profile. He flips back to the beginning, perusing the medical records from his active duty Marine Corps days and then his subsequent civilian life. He looks at the personal data. Height: 5'6", Weight: 135 lbs. The rest is uninteresting, blood type, birth marks, etc. He scans through other evaluations done by previous psychologists and psychiatrists. Someone had written: Classic case of Post Traumatic Stress Disorder (PTSD). Exhibits hallucinations, nightmares, poor personal relationships, cannot sleep more than a few hours at a time. Erlandson sees the name, George J. Jackson, Ph.D., San Francisco V.A. Hospital, May 12, 1979. Then, Erlandson sees underlined: Difficult to reach!

Erlandson sighs. More than a decade later, he couldn't say that he had done any better than his predecessor. The symptoms are the same. The Veterans Administration, ergo the taxpayers, are still footing the bill for Vietnam, or rather the aftermath of Vietnam.

The other night, on TV, he saw one veteran refer to Vietnam as "always a war, never a place." For Wong, Erlandson realizes, Vietnam will always be the war. His experiences are forever burned into his psyche, like numbers burned into the skin of Holocaust victims.

But if what Wong had said was true, that this was the first time he had told anyone about the killings of the Mama-san and girl . . . well, maybe he was making progress. He scans through the pages of transcribed tapes from his three months of therapy, glancing at highlighted sections. All roads pointed to last week's startling revelation.

Erlandson sits back in his swivel chair. He puts his feet up on his desk and clasps his hands behind his head. He still cannot get a total grasp on Wong. He feels he understands him to a certain extent. But some questions may never be answered with all the possible permutations within the human brain. How could Wong have lived with this problem for so long? Why was he still alive? A large part of him wanted to die, and a small part of him was struggling like a storm-tossed survivor in a vast cruel sea, desperately fighting the waves to survive.

It was as if there were two personalities within him. But Erlandson feels sure that there is no schizophrenia. There is just this dominant emotion, this excessive guilt, that is wearing Wong's defenses down. It could be likened to a hurricane battering down a seawall to flood any semblance of self-worth Wong has. And by the looks of it, he seems to have damned little self-worth. How to assuage this self-destroying guilt?

But Erlandson is hopeful. In previous sessions, he had felt like a scout, only reconnoitering and probing but never identifying and attacking the enemy position. Now, he has the target identified. The cause that is afflicting his patient's mind has been laid out before him like a cancerous tumor is laid before a surgeon. He has only to excise it, not with lasers or scalpel, nor to kill it with drugs and radiation, but to expose it to the light of day, not once, not twice, but many times. His job is to isolate the instance, examine it with Wong, go into the whys and the wherefors. He feels like a lawyer at times, making an end-run around the facts—he has to pull in the mitigating circumstances that had caused the event, make Wong feel less culpable.

He does not condone Wong's act, and hates war with a passion. But he believes that he understands Wong, understands his predicament, understands his need and drive to be accepted, and understands the ties that still bind him to his culture and his grandmother.

Erlandson sighs. He would enjoy meeting Wong's grandmother, he thinks. Damn! She must be some old lady! He grins.

Erlandson now understands that Wong's killing of other Asians was a stepping outside the norm, outside of the directive given by his grandmother. His guilt is magnified by the fact that he killed not just enemy soldiers, but innocent civilians, as well.

His heart goes out to Wong.

How to help him? How to lead him on the long path back to some semblance of normalcy and forgetfulness?

His intercom buzzes. "Dr. Erlandson," his receptionist calls. "Mr. Wong is here."

"Send him in. Thank you, Sandy."

Erlandson watches Wong come in, crossing the room with a sheepish walk that barely skims above the carpet. He holds his hat in both hands, smiling thinly.

"Good afternoon, Dave. How you doing?"

"Hi, Doc. Not too bad, I guess." Wong sits, a limp, lackluster individual swallowed by the stuffed chair. He looks like a whipped dog.

"Sleeping any better these days?"

"A little bit better." His face is hopeful.

"Good! I think your unburdening has helped and will help."

"God, I hope so."

Erlandson looks at him. "The difference between good and evil is that evildoers make excuses for their actions . . . while the good know they cannot." He pauses, studying Wong's face. "There's good in you, Dave. I want you to know that."

Wong smiles weakly. "Thanks."

Erlandson sits back in his plush swivel chair, shuffles some papers, letting the silence linger. But his mind is at work. Out of the corner of his eye, he studies Wong. He is pudgy. At five-six, he looks almost like a miniature Santa Claus. If he had another twenty pounds, he would fit the part exactly. His hair is thin, with white along the sides. The face is intelligent, settled in behind gold-colored, wire-rim glasses.

Erlandson has treated depression before and prescribed drugs only as a last resort. He is not the type of practitioner who throws Prozac at every manic depressive patient who crosses his threshold. Besides, there is more at work here than with his other patients.

Being a marathoner, he knows the value of physical exertion, of the tie between it and self-esteem. In the 1970s, he had read of studies using running to treat depression. He has kept up his interest, even incorporating it into his treatment of some patients. And, now, researchers are once again using physical exertion to treat depression, because it was found that exertion released not only beta-endorphins but serotonin as well, both naturally occurring feel-good drugs.

From his own experience, he knows physical exertion builds up self-esteem and confidence. It is his belief that building a strong body also builds a strong mind. That from the exertion of the body, the psyche is somehow mysteriously healed. And if not healed, at least the symptoms and conditions greatly alleviated—to manageable proportions. Still, Wong would be a challenge. How to make this man want to live, with such an inordinate guilt pressing him down?

"What's your weight, Dave?"

"Ummh. About 180, 185." As Erlandson writes that down, Wong clears his throat. "Why?"

"Oh, I've got an idea."

Wong sits back in the chair. "Wanna enlighten me, Doc?"

Erlandson pushes his chair backward, away from the desk. "What was your weight when you were in the Corps?"

"Oh, around 130, 135. Why?"

"You ever do any exercise now?"

"Nah. I had enough humping in Vietnam to last a lifetime."

Erlandson looks at Wong's paunch. "Well, I tell you what. I want you to do two things for me. I want you to go to Alcoholics Anonymous. And I want you to go to St. Mary's Hospital. They have a fitness and nutrition program there. I want you to lose about twenty-five pounds."

"Jesus, Doc, I don't want to go to some Catholic hospital. I'm no damned Christian."

"Don't worry about it. They're like a public hospital. Only the name gives them away."

"And why should I exercise and go on a diet? You're a psychiatrist, not a physician."

"Dave, do you want to get well?" A nod. "Then humor me, will you?" Erlandson writes schedules on a slip of paper. "Here, the AA meeting is every day, an hour each day at the local port annex. The fitness program is three to four times a week. Also, as part of the fitness program, you'll be given a physical to check out your heart. I don't want you dying of a heart attack because of me. And we'll get you with a nutritionist. She'll work hand in hand with your exercise physiologist so you can lose that weight." His eyes focus once more on Wong's paunch. Wong's hand unconsciously slips to his belly, massaging it.

"Do you know what I'm giving you, Dave?"

"No."

"I'm giving you the gift of exercise. With it, you will find the fountain of youth. With it, you will find self-esteem. With it, you will find good health. With it, you will find love. Without it, you will fall back into despair."

Erlandson looks at Wong, but sees doubt. He sighs. Only time will teach Wong the truth of his statements. He hands the slip of paper to him. "You need to cut that tie to alcohol. You need positive reinforcement to stay away from it. AA will help do that for you. And the fitness program?" Here he looks intently at Wong. "You have low self esteem, Dave. I want to build that back up. And one way to do that is through losing weight and becoming better physically conditioned." He keeps hammering home this point, trying to mash it into Wong's psyche so that it can creep in by osmosis. "And, Dave, just because you were a Marine once, don't overdo it in the fitness class, will you? Believe me, you'll get better in stages. Now, if you'll excuse me, I'm busy. I can't allot you the full time this week. I'll see you next week after you've started your AA meetings and your fitness class. I'm taking a long weekend."

Wong looks at the paper, stands up, and slips it into his pocket. "Christ, I've got a mental problem, not a weight problem!" he mutters on his way out. "AA? Christ! Every fucking day?"

Erlandson just smiles.

· · · · ·

It is an old bluish gray, Seattle saltbox structure, with yellow trim. Wong tentatively opens the heavy wooden door, steps into a narrow hallway. Several doorways lead from the hallway, signs above them labeling the office space. The third one on the left lists "Alcoholics Anonymous."

He enters the office. Four people are already sitting in a circle, opening their bag lunches. They look up when he enters.

"Hello!" a woman calls out. She is in her fifties, Wong guesses. Silver-haired, corpulent, wearing a black dress that exposed meaty hams.

"Hi," Wong replies.

The others greet him also. Three men, one in his sixties, one in his forties, and one in his twenties.

"My name is Susan. This is Mel, Carl, and Rick." She has unconsciously counted them off according to their ages, Mel being the oldest.

"My name is Dave."

Mel looks at him. "Is this your first time at AA?"

"Yes."

"Well, don't worry," Carl assures him, "everybody has a first time. Rick just joined last month."

Rick, longhaired, wearing blue jeans, nods. "It ain't too bad."

"Well, shall we start?" Susan asks. "Doesn't look like anyone else will be coming." She looks to Wong. "Why don't you start, Dave."

He looks at everyone. "I-I d-don't know where to start." Then he stares at the fir floor.

They all look at him. "Start with why you drink," Susan suggests.

Wong shifts in his chair, squirming. He looks from one to the other, then stares out the window to the American-Pacific mill. A logging truck rolls by, air brakes squealing as it comes to the stop sign. He doesn't reply.

"Maybe one of us should start," Mel volunteers. He is still blondhaired, though streaks of silver are starting to appear. His belly sticks out like a six-month pregnant woman's. He seems amiable enough, smiling widely at Wong. "It's been a month since I last came. In all that time, I only had the urge three or four times. And that was in the evenings when I was alone and somewhat depressed, when none of my family was around. You know, when my wife was at her writing club and my daughter was away at the same time at her woodworking class. When you're alone, you're more vulnerable."

"Mind if I ask why each of you decided to come to AA?" Wong asks.

Carl answers first, stroking his brown beard, his legs extended in front of him. His denim overalls and rubber boots are spotted with excrement, and the smell of manure wafts from him. Wong moves his chair back a foot. Carl takes no notice. "I think it's because we all lost control, and we all wanted a measure of control back in our lives. We couldn't control our lust for liquor."

Everybody nods.

"I was losing my family," Rick adds. He has a nervous tic in his right eye. Dressed in a three-piece suit, he looks like an accountant to Wong. "I was beating up on my wife, and my little boy was having nightmares. I woke up one morning and my whole family was gone."

"It's the same story. Alcohol controls your life. And when that happens, you lose perspective. You become more . . . your cravings become more important than the ones around you," Susan says. "More important than the ones you love." Her voice rises on an evangelical pitch.

"That's true for me as well," Mel adds.

"Any Vietnam veterans here?" Wong asks, focusing on Carl. He seemed the same age as Wong. But Carl shakes his head. The others shake their heads, too. "I don't know. I guess it goes back to my being in Vietnam," Wong says. "I did some pretty bad things over there. And maybe it's my marriage. I guess it's not a good marriage. My wife, Cindy, she drives me to drink, I swear. I can't stand her sometimes. I-I almost feel like strangling her sometimes. And, uh, I got real drunk last week. I-I, uh, sliced her ear with a knife when I was drunk. I, uh, really didn't mean to do it." He smiles sheepishly.

The others look at him, tight smiles sewn on leather-like faces.

"Ummh, we abhor violence, don't we?" Susan says.

"Yes, yes, we abhor violence. Cannot stand for it. No, indeed," Mel adds. Wong looks at the old man more closely. He seems prissy.

"Yeah!" Rick laughs. "No goddamn violence!"

Susan stares contemptuously at Rick, showing displeasure at his profanity. His laughter fades.

"I-I didn't mean to do it." Wong feels like a small child receiving censure from his mother.

"That's just it, Dave," Susan tells him. "You were out of control. The liquor had you in its grasp. It's the devil. It's evil. Once you recognize that, you can fight it with the goodness within you."

"Amen, amen," everybody else chimes in. And suddenly Wong feels like he is at a church revival rather than an AA meeting.

"It's a good analogy, Dave," Mel says. "The liquor is like the devil. It'll always be there to tempt you. What you have to realize is that you're not alone in this battle. We're here for you, dear brother. Between us and Jesus Christ."

Wong sighs. He didn't want religion. He wanted support. Wait till Erlandson hears about this, he thinks.

He sits through the rest of the forty-five minute meeting as silently as possible, talking only when called on for his opinion. He listens to their individual progress reports. And he feels relieved. He does not feel that he is under the control of liquor as much as these people. He only drank when pushed to do so by Cindy. His first AA meeting, and already he feels superior.

They break up. Susan says, "I sincerely hope you'll be back with us again." She smiles, expectant. Others in the group wait, all smiling.

"Sure," Wong replies. "I will most certainly think about it." He smiles in return.

They bow their heads, say in unison, "God, grant us the strength to fight this demon called alcohol."

Wong is already out the door and into the hallway when he hears the "Amens." Jesus, he thinks.

"They're a bunch of losers," Wong says. "They're all religious nuts."

Erlandson looks at him for a moment. "Well, I hate to say this, but it's true. You're a loser, too." Erlandson taps his pencil on the table top.

"No, I'm not."

"I've never heard of any AA meeting being religious convocations."

"Well," Wong snorts, "you should have been at this one. I mean, they were saying, 'Liquor is like the devil,' 'Between us and Jesus Christ,' and bullshit like that."

Erlandson stops tapping the pencil, looks sternly at Wong. "Well, if you're not a loser, you sure in the hell are a quitter. Dave, you couldn't even last a week at AA. You sit through one goddamn meeting and you feel so superior to the others. Why is that?"

"There were no Vietnam veterans there."

"And only veterans can help you?"

"Yeah."

"I'm not a veteran."

"You're different. You're a psychiatrist. You've been trained in handling my type of case. Those people at AA are only amateurs. Think they can help me?"

"AA has helped many people over the years." Then, "You had a chance to go to veterans' groups before. And you didn't."

"There weren't any minorities there. No Asians."

Erlandson shrugs. He thinks it is more than that. A deep shame that Wong probably feels and does not want to share with more than one person. He thinks that Wong would never expose his great sin in front of veterans and then be labeled as a child-killer—no, a child-murderer.

Wong sighs. "Doc, I don't like those AA people. They've got a holier-than-thou attitude. If I want that, I can go to church."

"Jesus," Erlandson throws his hands up in disgust. "I hope you gave more of a chance to your exercise program than you did AA." Erlandson's bushy eyebrows arch.

"Yeah. I think I like it."

He likes it because of Mercury Fanelli. She is blonde, pretty, slim, and graceful, with a wonderful laugh. Erlandson had instructed him to do what Mercury prescribed, and Mercury had prescribed a twice weekly regimen of jogging and/or walking in addition to the twice weekly aerobics session. He has been in the aerobics program two weeks, feeling the sweat flow freely again and reacquainting his body to the pleasant ache of repetitive motion. An ulterior motive, too. He loved the bouncing behinds and breasts, loved seeing the long legs and smooth curves of the women's hips. He always feasted his eyes on Mercury.

Now, he sits in his car at the lake. He has not jogged yet, but has been ordered by Mercury to start this week. He sighs, gets out of the car, squints in the bright sunshine, looking to the Douglas firs and cedars that blanket the far hillside. The water is almost calm, stirred by a slight breeze that blows from the south, causing small ripples. As he walks toward the group, he can see the end of the lake, a gradual tapering of the water into the dark underside of the hill.

The group is on the grass next to the tennis courts. Mercury is there; her lithe figure and blonde ponytail serve as a beacon to him.

They are mostly women, seven of them, and three men. Of the men, they are all heart-attack therapy patients. This he had gleaned from aerobics class. He is the only psychological case, and he is uncomfortable with that. As if he were being singled out with yet another minority trait. He is not sure how much Mercury knows of his case. Surely Erlandson must have mentioned something.

"Hi, Dave!" Mercury calls out.

"Uh, hi, Mercury." He is self-conscious, not having run consistently since his boot camp days. He props his right hand over his pot belly, patting and rubbing it. At least twenty-five pounds overweight and as distended as a pregnant woman. How did he ever let himself go like that? Everyone else seemed fit. Was he the only first-timer?

"Okay, is everyone here? Dave was the last one, I think." She flashes a grin at him. "Okay, good. Let's get into a small circle," she says. They space themselves about eight feet apart on the grass. She directs them through a series of gentle, warm-up exercises: trunk twists, neck rotations, back flexion and extension, hamstring and calf stretches.

"Get into the habit of doing these stretches before jogging," she says, looking at Wong. "Okay, this path, the way we're going, is about 2.6 miles. Don't overdo it if you're out of shape. If you have to walk, walk. In time you'll make it all the way around. As for right now, I don't want anyone to suffer needlessly. And believe me, you don't have to suffer to go jogging." She glances at Wong again. He feels like a novice. Why is she looking at me all the time? he wonders.

"Let's go!" The group starts out. Wong hangs back. He watches Mercury ahead of him, appreciates her long, smooth legs and buttocks as she scampers away like a gazelle.

"Hi, name's Bob." A man in his late fifties or early sixties extends his hand. He is big, perhaps an ex-football player. Wong had seen him in the aerobics class before.

"Dave." Wong shakes his hand, already starting to puff. "How long you, uh . . . mmmph . . . been doing this?"

"Oh, three months, now. Mercury's great. She has a lot of enthusiasm. Gets you going."

"Well, I don't . . . know how far I'm going to-day," Wong puffs.

Bob glances over at him, chuckles. "I was just like you once. Couldn't even make it halfway around the first time I did this. Had to walk."

They jog beside the lake, cross a flat, wide wooden bridge over a sluiceway, then immediately climb a steep hill some fifty yards long. Wong gasps like an asthmatic. Bob takes off with a quick glance behind as Wong quickly falls off the pace. "Stick with it!" were his parting words.

"Come on, Dave, you've only gone an eighth of a mile. You aren't quitting on us now, are you?" It is Mercury. She has backtracked to check up on laggards.

Wong tries plunging up the hill, but he feels like the hill is made of sand. For every step he takes, he seems to slide back two. His breaths come in deep gasps. "Oh, God . . . I didn't think I was . . . this bad."

Mercury laughs. "It's easy to slip into bad habits and put on some extra baggage, isn't it?" She taps him on his distended belly.

Wong frowns, pushing her hand away. "I'll . . . make . . . it."

Mercury turns around, jogging backwards up the hill. "Don't overdo it, Dave. If you're too tired and out of shape, walk. Just walk. There's no time limit to do this loop." With that, she is gone, long strides from graceful legs that fly up the face of the hill.

Wong's legs are burning. His lungs desperately suck in deep drafts of air. His heart thumps madly, jackhammering, the beat resonating from under his ear to his forehead. Sweat breaks out in great beads. His arms feel as if ten-pound weights were tied onto his wrists. Still, he pushes to the top of the hill, then stops, hunching over, gasping big breaths under a stately Douglas fir. His legs are dead and he feels dizzy. Then he sees Mercury running back on the path toward him. He straightens and starts to walk, shaking his arms out, and waves to her to go on. She smiles, nods, and turns back.

The wide path, gravelly with rocks, drops slowly away. Wong, hands on his hips, strides crookedly down the path, breathing raggedly. The path blurs before him; the trees swoon, making circles in his vision. He stumbles on a protruding rock, almost falls, his arms outstretched. He catches himself, stops, then stands on tiptoes and reaches for the sky with outstretched arms, inhaling deeply, and holding his breath for two seconds. Then he exhales slowly while swinging his arms outward and downward, hands meeting in front of his groin. It is a Kung Fu breathing exercise he once learned. He repeats this three, four times, until his breath returns to a sense of normalcy, until his head clears and his vision isn't blurred. He does it two more times, looking above him at old trees that hide the sky.

The others have since left him in the dust. But once again, Mercury is coming toward him, a slight smile on her lips. "How you doing, Dave?"

Wong smiles sheepishly. "Not too well, Mercury. But I'm managing. I think I'd better walk some."

"Mind if I join you?"

"No. I don't mind at all." She falls in step with him. He smells a slight fragrance, almost like rose water.

They walk slowly. "We never did get together to talk about why you're in my class, did we?" she asks.

"How much did Erlandson tell you?"

"Not much. Only that it was a mental thing, also alcohol related. He's a firm believer in physical well-being. Take care of the physical self and the mental things will also be healed, or else lend themselves to better treatment. That's his philosophy."

"Does that mean you've had other cases like me?"

She looks at him quizzically.

"You know, psychological cases like me, not your heart disease cases like you have now?"

"Well, yes, I've had some before."

"Does all this physical fitness stuff help?"

"Yes, I think it does. Though many of those people didn't make a lifetime commitment to it. While they were here, I'm sure it helped their conditions."

"What did Erlandson tell you about my condition?"

Mercury looks at him. "Not much. Only that you were suffering from nightmares. Some Vietnam thing."

"That's all?" He looks at her, a blank look on his face.

"That's all."

They fall silent. In the distance, the loud honks of the resident geese float across the water as the two walk on a six-foot wide path hemmed in by the signature trees of western Washington: Douglas fir, Western hemlock, and Western red cedar. Above them, the hillside rises away, hidden in a forest of two-foot thick conifers, the ground covered by sword ferns, salal, Oregon grape, fungi, broken branches, and duff. The path drops down and they skirt some bogs, the big, broad leaves of skunk cabbage rising above the water. Splashes of salmonberry, head high, line the path.

"It's the first time I've been out here, at least all the way around," he says. Descending a small incline Wong can finally see, through the trees, the water; he also sees the opposite side of the lake, bathed in sunshine.

"It is? How long have you been living here?"

"Five years."

"And you haven't been out here before?"

"Only on the other side. You know, picnicking, that sort of thing."

They are more than halfway through the woods now. The sunlight glistens off the treetops and, once in a while, there is a break in the forest canopy, and bright shafts of light pour through, illuminating the path and casting the blurred shadows of trees before them.

"How did you get into this business?" he asks.

"Oh, I was a kinesiology and physical therapy major at the University of Washington. Then I got caught up in the fitness boom. But I wanted to spread the word, get people interested in fitness as a way of life. Help sick people get better. Now, I didn't want to be a nurse, mind you," she says, laughing. He enjoys the sound. "I do a little physical therapy, but it's mostly related to sports injury kind of things."

She touches his arm at that, and Wong, so unused to physical contact from strangers, feels a strange thrill. He looks at her, her head tilted backward in a soft laugh. Appreciates the fine line of her chin and throat, the twinkle around her blue eyes. He feels an awakening in his loins, a rising from the dead, poking through his shorts. Embarrassed, he says, "I'm feeling better. It's pretty flat here. Wanna jog?"

She looks at him, unaware of his rising interest, and nods. "Okay."

They are out of the heavy woods. Only a few alders hide the view of the lake to their left. The path undulates in minor hillocks with only one small challenge before the path drops down onto the flat terrain of the sunlit, exposed side of the lake near the softball fields.

Wong is puffing hard again.

"How are you doing?" Mercury asks, scarcely breathing hard.

"I've got to . . . stop."

"That's all right."

They walk in silence for a while, heading toward the playground next to the water. He watches her out of the corner of his eye, the blonde ponytail swaying like a pendulum marking each step.

"I don't know if I can keep this up, Mercury," he says, looking at her, a look of defeat on his face.

"Sure you can," she replies, looking at him. "You're an ex-Marine. Never say die, right?"

"I've fought my wars." I don't need this shit again, he thinks.

She looks at him, almost reading his mind. "Do you want to get better, Dave?" They are approaching a log playground of swings and slides. "I really believe, like Erlandson, that this is the way to go."

He stoops over, muscles aching, a small aggravation at the bottom of his lungs. He coughs, his face flushed. "But, God, it's so hard! It's worse than boot camp! I was young then!"

"We just have to do it in stages. Believe me, your body will adjust. You'll breathe easier. Your muscles will ache less. And you'll feel better than ever before," she says, smiling at him. "The whole trick is to not overdo it, okay? Listen to your body. I don't think you listened to your body on that first hill." She taps him on his chest with her index finger, like a coach might a football player. "You looked like death warmed over." She laughs.

Wong laughs, too.

"You want to push your body, but you don't want to kill it. Get what I mean? You want to be able to breathe almost normally, maybe slightly out of breath, but no more," she lectures him. "And keep track of where you start your jogging on this path and where you end your jog—where you have to start walking again. As you get better, you want to decrease your walking distance and increase your jogging distance."

He nods, letting the words sink in. "I used to run, you know."

"A lot of people used to be able to run. I've seen a lot of 'used to bes' in this business. To tell you the truth, I'd much rather have a 'wannabe' in my class than a 'used to be.' At least the wannabes know where they want to go, while a lot of time the 'used to bes' just lie around on their asses. The trick is to keep jogging for the rest of your life. You eat a lot," and here she taps Wong's belly again, "you should exercise a lot."

Wong has never heard a woman spout such philosophy before. She is like an old male sage, someone neophytes climb mountains for in order to seek the meaning of life. He is impressed.

"I have a saying. 'In fitness is the preservation of your self—body and mind.'"

"Aha!" he says. "A play off Thoreau's 'In wildness is the preservation of the world.'"

"That's good!"

"I like Thoreau. He's a damned good writer."

"I'm impressed!" she says, smiling. Then, "You going to be all right? I've got to catch up with the rest of the group and see how they're doing."

"I'm fine, Mercury. And thanks. You'll see me on Thursday." He seems almost convinced.

"Good!" she says, smiling, and with a small wave she is off running again.

Wong walks under the picnic shelter, gazing at the figure fast disappearing down the path. He pats his belly, wanting to lose it, but wondering if he will ever keep up with Mercury. He feels old, not just old with the weight of sin on his spirit, but bodily old. Can I make my body young and fit? he wonders. And will that help my spirit lift the weight of my sin? Will anything lift this sin off my shoulders? he wonders.

But, he must admit, though he feels tired, he feels better.

Chapter 12

Custody

It was a lost cause from the start, and he knows it. But he had to do it, had to fight for his daughter, spend the money—the $75 an hour—for the lawyer.

"It doesn't look good," Nelson whispers. "I don't think you're going to get custody." They are awaiting a decision from the judge, who is in chamber.

Wong nods, wondering why he had hired him then. It was money flushed down a toilet, it seemed. Almost $2,000 so far for his services on the assault and battery charge, which had been plea-bargained down to simple assault—a $3,000 fine and no more jail time. Cindy had refused to testify about her ear, and Wong had sighed with relief. But the relief soon turned back to a tight anger during the custody battle. And now, he wears a weary look of resignation on his face.

"But I think we stand a good chance that they won't make the restraining order permanent. At least, that way, you'll have visitation rights," Nelson says dryly, looking at his client, who is slumped in his chair. "I mean, if they let you have contact with Cindy, they're certainly not going to deny you access to your daughter."

In pleading his case, Wong had gotten up on the stand and had apologized for his assault on Cindy. Then he had recounted his therapy—Erlandson, AA, and exercise. And, yes, he had returned to AA, going at least twice a week during the trial. He would have sat through a board meeting about the various properties of different flames in Hell, if he thought that by doing so he would have a better than equal chance of keeping Nancy.

"All rise!" the bailiff shouts as the judge comes in.

Cindy sits at the other table with her lawyer. Nancy is absent. But, she, too, had taken the stand, at the request of Cindy's lawyer. Her testimony was damaging to Wong, her thin voice, "Yes," going out across the courtroom when Cindy's lawyer had asked her if she had seen her father beating up her mother.

"You may sit," the bailiff announces.

The judge shuffles his papers in front of him. "In Wong versus Smith-Wong," the judge speaks, "I find for the mother. She will have custody." Cindy beams broadly. Wong sits dejectedly. "But the father will have visitation rights, twice a month." Wong sits up straighter. "There has to be an understanding here," the judge looks directly at Wong, "that there is to never be any re-occurrence of what happened before. Is that understood?"

"Yes, your Honor," Nelson quickly answers. "He means that you better not lay a hand on Cindy again," he whispers to Wong.

Wong nods, looking to the judge. "I understand, your Honor."

"Good. Also, the restraining order is lifted. Just behave, Mr. Wong." It makes visitation easier, not having to use a go-between.

Wong nods. "Thank you, your Honor."

They stand. Wong shakes Nelson's hand. "It was the best we could expect," Nelson tells him.

"I appreciate it," Wong replies. "At least I can see my daughter." He smiles. He looks over to Cindy, sees that she is wearing her hair longer, covering her ears. He stares at her, catches her eye. She frowns, then turns away to talk to her lawyer. But Wong is satisfied. It could have been worse.

As he walks out of the courtroom, a beautiful Oriental woman enters, conferring with two men. She is so strikingly beautiful he gasps in wonder. She looks up, sees him, smiles. His heart skips a beat as he smiles back. Then she is past him, setting up at the table he has just left.

Chapter 13

Dinner

"How'd you ever get a name like Mercury?" Wong asks.

He had finally gotten the nerve to ask her out for dinner after a month's worth of jogging around Merritt Lake, but she had invited him over for supper instead. He stands in the narrow, wood-paneled galley, watching her.

He is feeling pretty good about himself. He has lost eight pounds since starting the exercise and nutrition regimen. He can now jog completely around the lake, but slowly. Working with his nutritionist, he has stopped eating junk food, eating more fruits, vegetables, and complex carbohydrates instead. It is as if his pregnant belly is regressing, the fetus of fat slowly disappearing. And his depression is slowly lifting.

"Oh," she says, laughing, "my mother told me I was the result of one hot night of passion when the mercury just shot off the scale." She is preparing a salad, having just checked the chicken casserole in the oven.

"That good, huh?"

She looks up from cutting the carrots and smiles at him—a smile that makes his heart stop. "I guess so."

He smiles in return. "Well, Mercury, in Roman mythology, was the messenger of the gods." He pats his belly unconsciously.

"Well, I'm certainly no messenger of the gods," she replies, noticing his pat with a grin.

"Well, I don't know." He gazes at her figure. "But then again, you'd probably be a goddess." He swallows. Has he gone too far? He is unsure of himself. He doles out flattery as often as Midas doled out gold.

She flushes. "You flatter me." She looks at him. "But, no thanks,

I'm just a woman, no goddess. And no pretensions." She smiles as she says the last sentence.

A cat, a white and orange tabby, rubs and purrs against his leg. He bends down to pet him. "And what is your name?"

"His name is Pickle."

"Huh?"

"Pickle. He got that name because he got his head stuck in a pickle jar when he was a kitten."

He laughs, then turns his attention from the cat to her. She is in her thirties, a few inches taller than he is. He guesses she is 5'-8" or so. She has long blonde hair that she has tied into a ponytail. For some reason the ponytail lends an air of excitement to Wong—a schoolgirlish habit that brings him back to his younger days. He watches her while she finishes cutting vegetables for the salad. She is lissome, not large-breasted, but ample. She is wearing shorts, and her legs are long and tan.

"Would you mind washing out the lettuce?" she asks.

"No. Not at all." He takes the lettuce from her and runs it under the cold tap water, then shakes it out, grabbing a paper towel to damp dry the leaves. She directs him to put the lettuce into the large salad bowl. He does so, then stops to study her again.

"Thank you," she says. She throws in the sliced mushrooms, carrots, tomatoes, bell peppers, the diced pineapple, bean sprouts, and then tosses the whole thing with two large wooden spoons.

She has a pretty face, almost beautiful. Blue eyes above a slightly beaked nose, all set above a sensual mouth—almost sultry—that flashes perfectly formed white teeth whenever she smiles. Wong wonders why he is here. Can he be so lucky? But then he remembers Erlandson's directive. "Go out! Start dating! I don't care if you make a fool out of yourself. I want you to start socializing."

"You have a great place here," he says. "I love the wood paneling."

"That's what made me buy it. I fell in love with the wood, too."

"Yeah, I know what you mean. I get tired of all the white sheetrock they put up in new houses these days."

"I know," she says as she pulls the casserole dish from the oven and forks the chicken. "Almost done," she says, smiling. "Would you mind setting up the table? The dishes and silverware are in the cabinet next to the dining room table."

"No problem!"

He sets out the dishes, suddenly conscious of the music streaming from her stereo. Soft, orchestral sounds, almost like Muzak.

"Would you like coffee or tea?" she asks, almost a shout, from the kitchen.

"Oh, how about tea?" he replies. He wanders back to the kitchen. He sees her back, the fine curve of her buttocks and thighs. He has the beginnings of an erection, but fights to keep it down. Now is not the time.

"Here's the tea bag. Will Lipton do?" He nods. "Good, here, you can pour it yourself."

He stands by the stove, next to Mercury, and smells the clean fragrance of her, like lilacs this time. Small beads of perspiration sit on her forehead. A cool breeze blows in from the nearby window. She feels his stare, looks at him, smiles shyly, looks back down. "I think we're ready," she says. "If you wouldn't mind putting the tea on the table, and the salad, I'll bring the chicken."

Wong does as he is told, making two trips, one for the tea and one for the salad, scooting around her in the narrow corridor linking the kitchen and dining room.

Finally, they are seated. He pours a cream-based dressing onto his salad, then begins eating. "Mmm, excellent salad," he pronounces.

"Why, thank you," she replies, a bold smile and a small dip of her head.

"Here," she says, "let me have your plate." She scoops out the chicken and rice from the casserole dish, then plops in some broccoli from a side dish. "Hope you don't mind broccoli."

Wong makes a face, but smiles. Vegetables are good for him.

"So how come an attractive woman like you isn't married?"

"I was, you know. For almost two years."

"What happened?"

"Oh, it's one of those things. I guess we outgrew each other. Or let's say, I outgrew him. I got tired of his anger. After a while, it was like I was in prison. I mean, I dreaded coming home. There was no warmth in the household or the marriage." She shrugs. "It hurt for a while," and here she looks intently at him, "that I was a failure. But I really couldn't stand the mental abuse. I had to get out. What about you?"

"I'm in the process of being divorced now." His lips are pressed tightly together in a forced smile. He does not volunteer why.

"Any children?" she asks.

"One. A daughter. You?"

"No. No kids. At least Spencer was smart about that, or selfish. He didn't want any, and I wasn't ready then."

"Now, what is it—"

"What do you do—" they both start out at the same time.

"Excuse me, I didn't mean—" she starts out again.

"No, the fault is mine. Please, go ahead." They burst out laughing.

"Now, what is it you do?" she asks.

"I'm a physicist," he says. "Nowadays, I work mainly as a technical writer. I work for a small company in town that designs and builds electronic circuits for radar detectors. I write the user's manuals and the diagnostic manuals." He only works part-time; he cannot hold down a full-time job. But, for the first time, this job has lasted more than six months. And he gets money from the Veterans Administration for his post traumatic stress disorder. But all this he does not tell her.

"Oh, that sounds interesting." There is actually a look of interest on her face, or she feigns it quite well.

"It pays the bills." He hesitates for a moment, then says, "Nah, I guess it's not really that interesting."

She laughs. "No, I guess not. What really interests you?"

Besides you? he thinks, but says, "What I really like doing is writing poetry." This he has not even told Erlandson.

"You do! That's wonderful! I love poetry. I subscribe to a few poetry magazines. Think I can read a few of your poems?" Her smile encompasses the room, casting him under a spell of probable, if not promised, intimacy.

He beams. "Yes. Yes, I think that can be arranged."

"I really like some of these modern poets, like Charles Bukowski, Galway Kinnel, and Carolyn Forché. Kinnel wrote a beautiful ode to his friend Jane Kenyon, who died young. Then there is Bukowski's, 'The days run away like wild horses over the hills.' I saw that when I was in downtown Portland. They have sidewalk poetry there, you know. God, I love that."

He is not sure if she loves the poem or the idea of sidewalk poetry, but he is enjoying himself too much to interrupt her train of thought. He eats the chicken with a bemused smile on his face. Has he struck gold? "Yes, I like that. And, oh, by the way, the chicken is outstanding!"

Mercury smiles. "Thank you." She stops eating and looks at him. "But why do you write poetry?"

He shrugs. "Oh, I don't know. Maybe it's therapy for me." He looks sideways at her. "Why do you read it?"

"It's a mirror into the human soul."

"That it is," he agrees, between mouthfuls.

Then, "Have you read Forché's 'The Colonel'?"

Wong shakes his head.

"Well, it's about her visit to El Salvador. She was invited to a colonel's dinner party. In the middle of it, the colonel gets a box and tosses the contents of it in front of Forché. Do you know what was in it?"

Wong shakes his head again. He forks more chicken breast into his mouth. There is promise to the evening. Who knows?

"Ears! The box was full of ears!"

"Oh?" The blood drains from Wong's face and his appetite suddenly wanes.

She reaches across the table, pats his arm. "I didn't spoil your appetite, did I?" She looks at him closely, suddenly aware once again that he had been in Vietnam and having heard once that the cutting off of ears was done by certain troops. She eyes him curiously.

"I'm okay," he gulps. The color slowly returns. They continue bantering for several minutes about poetry while they eat. But Wong's heart is no longer in the conversation or the meal. He picks at his food, not wishing to be rude.

There is a lull in the conversation and Wong listens to the music. A woman's voice cuts through the air with a haunting melody. He cocks his head, turning his right ear to the music.

Mercury looks at him. "It's Whitney Houston," she says, "singing 'The Greatest Love of All.'"

"I'm s-sorry," he stammers. "I-I don't mean to be rude. But this song. Can we turn it up even louder?" Mercury gets up and obliges him.

The mention of the ears has transported him back in time. His earlier confidence has disappeared. Instead, he is nervous, sweating in his armpits, mouth dry.

Now, the melody and lyrics have tied him to his chair with invisible threads. He cannot move; he feels a pins-and-needles sensation spread throughout his body. He is aware of his predicament, can feel Mercury's eyes on him, but there is nothing he can do. It is like he is outside of his body and the signals he sends to his limbs are short-circuited. Only his ears are fully functioning. He sits, frozen, letting the waves of sound wash over him, hearing Mercury ask, "Dave, is anything wrong?" But he does not answer, can only stare at her with a blank look.

Tears form in his eyes, and he mumbles to himself, "I'm not good enough. I'm not good enough. I've killed the future." He thinks, How can I love myself after what I've done?

The song ends. A silence. Then the next tune.

"Dave, is anything wrong?" she asks again.

He is suddenly back. Tries hard to regain his composure. Fails. He pushes back from the table, tears streaming down his cheeks.

"Please, excuse me. It . . . it was a wonderful dinner. Excuse me, please." He rushes for the door, a man possessed by demons. Mercury stands perplexed and flabbergasted, then follows him to the door.

He stands at the far end of the long porch, leaning one arm on the balcony, sobbing into his other arm. She doesn't know what to do. She doesn't know him that well. She hears him muttering; she is too far away to hear what.

"Children? I've killed a child!" he mutters.

She decides to risk getting closer, having only heard "child."

He hears her footsteps, but does not care anymore. "I'm not good enough. I'm not good enough. I don't deserve this. How can I? I can never love myself." He is referring to the song's lyrics.

She stands there, listening to his monologue. She still does not know what to do. Christ! This guy is weird, she thinks. Finally, she puts an arm around his shoulder. "Dave, can I help?"

He turns and looks at her with cold, dark eyes. She is suddenly afraid. Then a glimmer of warmth, of consciousness, returns to his eyes.

"No," he gasps. "No. Please. I'll be fine. I just need to be alone."

And with that, he is gone. A cold shadow fleeing into the warm, late July evening.

M o m

Stella looks out the window, staring at the gray Seattle drizzle. The rain has dampened her spirits. The city has taken on the gray pallor of death, it seems, broken only by the reflection of light off puddles and the watery sheen covering cars and windows. She shivers, folding her arms.

"Music is the breath of life to her," she says.

Jim arches his eyebrows. "Who are we talking about?"

"Sylvia Scott. You know, the violinist I told you about before. The one who used to play for the Seattle Symphony. Now she teaches. She's such a sweet old lady."

Jim nods.

"Her cancer's back." A grim set to her face.

Jim flinches. "Oh, Jesus. I'm sorry to hear that."

They are eating lunch at a small Mexican café not far from the Fred Hutchinson Cancer Center. With a lull in his case load, Jim had been able to squeeze out some time from his busy schedule as a neurosurgeon.

"Sometimes I hate working in hospitals," she says.

"I know," Jim replies. "It's where life meets death, more often than not." He shrugs. "But we prolong life too, you know." He grabs her hand, squeezes it.

She squeezes back.

"She has such a great sense of humor, a great zest for music and life. You should have heard the story she told about this great violinist who came to play with the Seattle Symphony. They were rehearsing this one piece—a Mozart piece, I believe—and there's a pause. Right in the middle of the pause there's this loud fart in B flat. Guess who let it out?"

"The great violinist!" Jim laughs.

Stella nods, smiling. "She's quite the raconteur. She had the nurses and me rolling in the aisle."

"Who was he anyway?"

"She wouldn't say!" she says, laughing. Turning serious, she looks at her husband. "The tumor came back in her breast, and it's metastasized to the liver."

Jim shakes his head in sympathy. "Who's her primary physician?"

"Endicott."

"He's good. He'll try his best to save her. Chemo?"

Stella nods. "She's losing her hair and her appetite."

"How long has she been on chemo?"

"About a week now. She's suffering a whole hell of a lot, but you know, she doesn't feel sorry for herself. She's also got family to help. Her husband, daughter, and grandchildren." Stella looks away for a moment, then back to Jim. "She's only a little older than Mom."

Jim looks at his wife. "Maybe, just maybe after all these years, you and your mother should sit down and talk things out."

Stella shrugs. She rarely talked about her mother. She had once told Jim that the conflict between her and her mother centered around Jake being Jewish. When Stella's parents came to visit, Jim could see this wall between the two women. It was so evident, it could be likened to a physical barrier. They were always polite to each other, but there was none of the close mother/daughter bond that should normally exist. They never hugged.

"I'm thinking, Jim. I'm thinking I should go east this year. I want to visit the Wall. We can stay at my parents' house, then take the subway into D.C. to the Wall."

"I can't promise anything, honey. It all depends on my case load." He dislikes the east coast, cannot stand the humidity of a Maryland summer. Stella knows this, but the urge to visit the Wall is so strong within her that she will go alone, if need be.

Their food comes—enchiladas, tacos, and burritos. They eat in silence for a while.

Perhaps, after all these years, it might be a good idea to make peace with Mom, she thinks. She and Jake had been married in a civil ceremony with only close friends and family attending. Her father had come, but her mother had not, so adamant was her mother's opposition to the marriage. Stella, stung by her absence, refused to talk to her mother for months. And after Jake died, she had actually hated her mother. With time lessening the pain, her hate was transformed into something akin to indifference. Gradually, over the years, a kind of stilted relationship was established between the two.

She just doesn't *love* her mother anymore, and she understands that her mother knows that. On her parents' last visit out here, she had seen her mother looking at her with pain in her eyes, tears starting to form. A brief moment. Both had turned away. Stella had mumbled something about the kids and left the room, her hands shaking.

She was more comfortable with her father, and she fell into his embrace like the little kid she once was. He was father, friend, and an understanding companion who had an expansive view of the world and the people in it. But her mother did not share her father's world view. Stella wonders at times how the two could have remained married so long, so diametrically opposite they were on certain topics. She once voiced this to her father, and he laughed and replied, "She was once the apple of my eye, and she still is. Whatever differences we have are minor because I love her so much. I think you understand that." She had nodded. Yes, she did understand.

But, how can she reach her mother? How can she love her again? What her mother had done was rip a hole into her soul that perhaps only dying could heal.

Chapter 15

Mercury

The windows of Wong's gray Volvo wagon are rolled down on both sides. He is sweltering in the July sun, but still he sits. He watches the flow of people in and out of the hospital—the infirm, being wheeled in or hobbling, helped by relatives or friends; the firm, visitors or walking patients. He plays idly with the zipper of his gym bag, one part of his mind focused on Mercury, the other dully studying people going by.

He detests hospitals. They are places where the oils of depression, injury, sickness, and death rise to the surface, contaminating the previously pure, uncluttered waters of one's life. He dislikes the contumely so routinely practiced in hospitals. An institutionalized haughtiness beyond the normal pale of everyday life.

Too, the real world had true life, a living that was living and a dying that was dying. In hospitals, dying had become too institutionalized, too antiseptic, too protracted. Dying had, well . . . become white! Pastel even. It was a reflection of the institution with its soft pastel colors on corridor walls, in rooms, behind nurses' stations, in bathrooms. The colors even shaded the dead in the morgue, the white light reflecting the cranberry pink of the walls on the pallid skin of new corpses. Even doctors, nurses, and other health professionals were garbed in white or soft greens or pale blues, an antithetical garb to parry the reality of sickness and death.

Wong's hate of hospitals suddenly wells up in his throat. "A-u-g-h!" he screams. An old man walking by stares at him. Wong scowls and the old man turns away. Wong then turns his hate to Mercury, for putting him in this position. He also blames Erlandson. Goddamn them, he thinks, still twirling the zipper of his gym bag. "I don't need this," he mutters to himself.

It hurts, to have his emotions for someone else drawn out, tight as a guitar string. She is the one doing the plucking. For he wishes to see her; it is almost like a physical ache. He knows she could take him or leave him—more likely leave him.

He wishes to see her, but is filled with a great shame, succumbing to a dislike of himself bordering on loathing. He is full of doubts again, like a high-schooler going out on his first date.

Can I explain myself? he wonders. Will she see me?

In the end, his desire for her makes him bold and resolute. He feels that if he does not take up the pursuit, like a man, he will never see her again. Still, he cannot stand the thought of her looking at him so—that puzzled expression bordering on distaste and condescension—or worse! Pity, even.

"I don't care what she thinks, or what you think she would think," Wong reflects on what Erlandson had said. "I wrote out a prescription for you to take this exercise program and, by God, you'd better complete it. Besides, how many times have I told you to stop running from yourself? Are you going to run the rest of your life? Face it, goddammit! Face the music! You're a man, by God!"

"No! I'm only half a man!" Wong had replied, his bile rising. "Who am I fooling? Do you think a beautiful woman like Mercury would ever be interested in me? I have too many ghosts to carry! And that dinner! Oh, my God!" he cried, his self-pity so myopic.

"Oh, Jesus Christ!" Erlandson had gotten up quickly from his desk, throwing his hands into the air. "What am I doing here? Do I have to beat you over the head? Don't be afraid of failure, of humiliation, of trying. You've got to try! If you don't believe that, then I don't know what else I can do for you!"

It was the only time Wong had seen Erlandson come close to giving up on him. Erlandson had stood silent then. When he spoke again, it was in a low voice. "Try or die!" he had spoken intensely. "Life is a series of trying new things. We're all beginners in some new aspect of life. I believe that firmly. If you're afraid, then all you end up doing is dying, little by little. And before you know it, you really will be dead.

"You've got to find the beauty in life. If you don't, what's the use of living? And love is beauty. Try for happiness, Dave! Try for Mercury's heart. It may be within your grasp. Deserve happiness!"

Wong let the thoughts seep in. "Try or die!" "Love is beauty." "Mercury's heart." "Deserve happiness!" Simple words. But the actions they implied would not be easy for him. At times, he felt he was in a long tunnel, and he could see the proverbial light at the other end. In the beginning, he walked freely. But as he continued walking he discovered he was ankle deep in molasses. As he ventured farther, the molasses grew more viscous and the odor more suffocating. The air reeked, curling his nose, fouling his mouth, not by any innate foulness, but by sheer volume. Halfway through, the end seemed brighter and larger, but the molasses was waist deep now, and he could hardly breathe. The sweat ran in rivulets down his face. His body temperature rose, and he felt as if he were being baked alive.

But, in the end, Wong had promised Erlandson he would try. Now, sitting in his car, he is still overcome by a lethargy inspired by a crazed fear of rejection. He looks at his watch. It is 5:25. The class starts at 5:30. He takes a deep breath, grabs his gym bag from the seat next to him, opens the door, and gets out. He locks the car and heads toward the main entrance, walking like a zombie, his body mechanically shuffling along, his mind preoccupied by the enormity of the rejection he was sure to come.

The exercise class is on the second floor. He takes the elevator up and heads for the small dressing room in the Men's room. He changes with a great weariness, then plods the short distance to the exercise room. He can hear her voice shouting out the cadence of the exercise. The participants are on their collective backs, doing situps, legs in the air, perpendicular to the floor. He enters as unobtrusively as possible. He sees her look up at him, a slight smile curling the edge of her lips. She is pushing her arms, 1-2-3-4, up-back, alternating left hand to right knee, right hand to left knee, curling her body with each touch, letting her shoulders fall back to the floor between touches. He slips into the back of the class and struggles to catch the cadence of the exercise. He thinks, What am I doing here? Do I need her?

But then his other voice pipes in. The voice of loneliness, of depression. And he so wants to hear the music that he has missed all these years—years he had lost with Cindy. The sound of a woman's laughter. The giggles before and after lovemaking. He desires the smell of her, the fresh fragrance without the undue affectation of heavy perfume. He wants a sweet-smelling, subtle odor to stimulate the olfactory senses that connect directly to his brain and from there to his groin.

He wants to feast his eyes. To look into blue eyes, green eyes, or brown eyes. To see the toss of a woman's head, how she can sweep her hair from her face without using her hands. How a woman stands, relaxed on one leg, the other twisted out with her foot in a sort of ballerina's en pointe.

He wants to appreciate the curves in a convoluted, slow-dance time, not the fast, straight-line lovemaking of his youth. The curves of her breast, the flatness of her stomach, the grand arch of a woman's back descending into the sweeping grace of smooth buttocks and thighs and the long sweep of well-proportioned legs. But, most of all—he would be willing to forsake some physical attributes—from experience, he wanted a woman who could also be a friend, a best friend. A friend who could cry with him, love him, like him, laugh with him, live with him. A woman with a sixth sense for his moods, perhaps. A woman, who at a glance, could read his mind. And he hers. At least some of the time.

Was it possible? He didn't know. But there was something about Mercury. She had the physical attributes. That was easily seen at a glance. But Wong had known too many women who had the physical attributes, but were so taken up with themselves that the chemistry was wrong, the catalysis aborted, the reaction stopped.

He does not know if Mercury has that special chemistry for him, or he for her. Wong only knows that he has problems—problems that may be too burdensome for someone of her disposition. He, at least, is learning. He would not be a bargain for her. But, if this relationship is to work, he has to give it a chance, an opportunity to leave the starting gate. Then he would let her make her own judgement. And he would make his own.

He sucks in a huge breath, exhaling loudly. Several women in back turn and look at him, one frowning disapproval, the others merely curious. He smiles. Erlandson was right. He had to try.

He stares at her, and he aches. She is supple grace and power and beauty. A cross between Athena and Aphrodite, the clear intelligence and power of one matched with the natural beauty of the other.

His mind idly wanders through the hallways of his youth as he goes through the motions of the exercises. Certainly, his track record was not one to boast of. From the rejection he felt in high school to his cavorting through whorehouses to the violence running through his previous relationships, his association with women left something to be desired by both parties.

He is sweating profusely now; they have finished the toning exercises and are now stomping and gyrating to fast music. He tries hard to move his hands and feet in choreographed moves to the tempo of the music. 1-2-3-4. He extends his hands in front, left-right-left-right, steps out with the left foot and back, then right foot and back, with a variation of hands alternately shooting above his head.

Caught up in the movement of the exercise, he breathes easily. The beta endorphins reaching his brain have put him into a mild trance. He feels good, as if he could go on forever. From one set of exercises to another, from one song to the next, for twenty minutes, and then the warmdown.

Another thing. Wong has always prided himself as being a man, of doing the manly thing. Yet, here he is, doing exercises primarily geared toward women, in a class mainly made up of women. From the experience of the exercises, he discovers that these women—many of them, in fact—are tougher than he is. They can do more repetitions; they are more flexible. It was his interest in Mercury that killed any prejudice he first had for the aerobics class. Now, the experience and its benefits keep him coming back.

Mercury claps her hand at the end of the warmdown. "That's it! See you next week." She turns the tape player off and picks her towel up from the nearby chair. Three women and one man congregate about her. Wong hangs back, watching. He hears snatches of their conversation. After several minutes, two of the women leave. Wong moves closer, hanging on the fringe of the conversation. Mercury laughs at something the man has said, then she looks to Wong. A noncommittal look. Wong can fathom nothing from it. The man makes another comment, but Wong cannot focus on what he has said. He is fastened on his own thoughts, of what he should say to Mercury. He paces about the group, not too close, not too far, circling like a hawk. Finally, the man and the woman leave, the man looking curiously at him.

They stare at each other, awkward silence like a river between them. "So! I see you made it to class," she finally says, smiling too readily.

"Oh, Mercury, I, uh . . . yes! . . . I-I made it."

She turns from him, packing up her portable tape player, gathering up her gym bag. She is dressed in an aerobics leotard, high cut over her thighs, low cut over her breasts, with signatory rolled-down leg warmers clinging around her ankles.

Wong watches her. He feels a pang. "I w-wanna apologize," he stammers. "There is no excuse for what I did."

She finishes gathering her things. Bag in hand, she looks at him. "I don't know, Dave. Maybe we're too different." She wants to cut him off at the source, before the scene can turn into melodrama. She turns for the door, tightlipped.

Wong stands there, deflated. It is not what he had imagined. He had thought he would get one more chance.

"That's right," he says to her back. "You don't owe me anything."

She is still walking, almost to the door. He is desperate now. What can he say to her? Quickly, he yells out, "Just do me a favor."

She stops, turns to look at him, frowning. He forms his thoughts quickly. What is the one avenue into her good graces?

"Talk to Erlandson about me. He's the one who referred me to your class." If he tells Erlandson that he could go ahead and tell Mercury about his problem, Erlandson would probably do it. But there is still no guarantee that Mercury would ever wish to see him again. She is not a psychotherapist.

"Please, will you at least do that for me?" he asks. He feels his knees weaken for a moment, as if he will come crashing down on them like some knight of old, begging for the grace of her hand. But, suddenly, he straightens. He has done his asking; he will not beg.

She looks at him, seeing him straighten. She likes that. The frown slowly disappears, the crease gone from her forehead. "Can I think it over?"

Wong nods and smiles. She smiles back. Then she is out the door.

He stands there and breathes deeply, a glimmer of hope holding his soul together.

Chapter 16

Jean

The used bookstore is on the ground floor, filled with pine book-cases that rise to a height of nine feet or so. Each shelf looks like the varicolored hues of huge teeth belonging to some benign, smiling mon-ster—part of a gigantic collection gathered by a mad dentist.

A woman stands two stacks away from Wong. At first, he casts sur-reptitious glances at her, but in the end his glances are drawn to her like bees to honey. She is Oriental and a rare beauty. He has a vague feeling he has seen her before, but he cannot remember where. She looks up, smiles. He returns a perfunctory smile, still shy after all these years. She is in her early thirties, slim, with straight black hair that hangs past her shoulders. She wears a pastel cream-colored dress with pale pink floral prints. The dress is cut high, exposing tan shapely legs. Her nose is small and pert, her mouth beautifully swept out into gracious curves exposing beautiful teeth when she flashes her smile at him.

He returns his attention once more to the books, but becomes sud-denly inebriated and woozy in the rarefied atmosphere of romantic possi-bilities—if he plays his cards right. He cannot concentrate on looking for *Macbeth*. His glance is drawn to her once more. She catches him looking, and he blushes. If only he weren't so damnably shy!

He turns back to the shelf, finally locates *Macbeth*, pulls it out and peruses the opening pages. Captured by the imagery of the witches at their brew, he smiles at the genius of Shakespeare. Out of the corner of his eye he can see her coming closer. She is suddenly peering over his shoulder at the book he is holding.

"Oh, *Macbeth*," she says, "a terribly gruesome story." She makes a face, and laughs.

He laughs, too, the ice suddenly broken. "Oh, I don't know. Life is a tragedy at times."

Her smile changes to a look of concern. "Do you really think so?" she asks, reaching out to touch his arm, in that casual feminine gesture he has always found discomfiting. A promise of intimacy before the reality.

"Yes," he says, smiling tightlipped.

"Oh, I didn't mean anything . . . " An inquisitive look. She straddles the line between interest and indifference.

"No. Please . . . don't worry about it."

"It's just to me, well, life is a . . ."

"A comedy?"

She laughs. A beautiful, mellifluous sound. Feminine, not husky like some women, and not too high pitched. "N-o-o . . ." the word is drawn out—monosyllabic but elastic, "not a comedy. Definitely not a comedy." She shakes her head. "But not a tragedy either."

He looks at her, a germ of intellectual interest growing, above and beyond his physical attraction. The Oriental girls he had been out with were reserved. She seems different.

"Then what is it?" he asks, suddenly curious.

She laughs again. "Is this Philosophy 101? Am I supposed to expostulate on metaphysics here, and the meaning of life?"

He likes the sound of her laughter. "No, no. Excuse me. I really didn't mean to quiz you. But you did really get me aroused . . . uh, interested there."

She is bemused, not missing the Freudian slip. "Then how about halfway between tragedy and comedy. A middle-of-the-road approach, neither right nor left, neither all good times nor all bad times." She enjoys the repartee.

"Depends on the person, don't you think?" He lays *Macbeth* down on the lip of the shelf. "Some people are blessed with a bigger amount of those good times. And some unlucky ones have a big dose of bad times. And they keep on coming."

"Maybe so," she says, staring at him curiously.

"I, uh, didn't get your name."

"Jean Chong."

"Chinese!"

"Tohng yahn," she says, nodding. "Nei meng hai matyeh, ah?"

"David Wong."

"Nei jungyi wa tohng yahn ah?" Do you wish to continue speaking in Chinese?

"Uh, sorry. I only know so much Cantonese. I lost it all when I was a kid."

"I know what you mean." She looks at him with a discerning eye. "You want to be American so much it hurts."

He nods.

"And you lose your culture."

He drops his eyes then, shifts them back to the books. The truth hurts. But then he turns back to her and sighs. "Sometimes your identity, too," he says.

"I know."

She is direct almost to the point of rudeness. Wong does not yet know if he likes this in a woman. But he wants to get to know her better.

"So Jean," he says, grabbing *Macbeth* from the shelf with one hand, the other laying hold of her arm and guiding her to the front of the store, "what do you do for a living?"

She lets herself be guided. "I'm a lawyer." He lets go of her, as if his hand had suddenly been scalded. A woman more educated than he.

"What?"

"Public defender, actually. I defend all those people who can't afford lawyers."

"Now I know where I've seen you before." He clicks his fingers. "The courthouse." She smiles. "I didn't know women went in for that kind of thing."

"Why not?" She looks closely at him now. "I believe in the law."

"So you defend all these rapists and murderers?" He frowns.

"Under our system of jurisprudence, everyone is entitled to a fair trial."

"But some of these people don't deserve to live! These . . . these murderers!"

She sighs. "Gee, I hardly know you and already I'm starting to argue with you."

"I'm sorry. I'm sorry." He shakes his head. "Sometimes I get carried away on law and order, on right and wrong."

"It's all black and white to you, is it?"

Wong thinks back to himself. "No. There are times when it is not all black and white. But what do women know about life and death? Most of you are so sheltered."

Jean shakes her head as Wong plops the book down on the front table and pays for it.

"I didn't mean to sound—" he says, as they exit the store.

"So chauvinist?"

"Chauvinist? Didn't that term die out in the '60s?"

"The term may have died out, but the species didn't."

"Hell, you probably weren't even born yet in the '60s!"

"I was, you know." She squints at him. The day is sunny and cool, around seventy-five degrees, with only a slight breeze that stirs her long, straight black hair.

"Oh, how old are you anyway?"

"Over thirty and under forty," she replies. "And how old are you?"

"Forty-five."

"You carry it well."

"Us Orientals, you know."

She laughs at that. They are walking downtown now, past the stores along main street, Puget Avenue. The large department stores have long since abandoned the downtown for the big mall, but little stores and eateries, as well as the banks, keep the downtown vibrant.

"Do you have time for a cup of coffee?" he asks. They are coming up on an outdoor espresso bar.

"Sure."

They pull up short. "Your wish?"

She looks at the menu, thinks for a minute. "Oh, I guess I'll have the mocha."

"Make that one mocha and one latté," Wong tells the girl behind the counter. He pays her, waits for the two coffees.

"So, I'm a lawyer. But you haven't told me about yourself yet," Jean says, as they walk over to one of the outdoor tables with their drinks.

"I'm a physicist. Or shall I say, I was a physicist. Now I'm more a freelance technical writer. I write about software and hardware systems. Mainly training manuals." He sips his latté, grins at the pure pleasure of it—that and the sunlight and the company of a beautiful woman.

"Oh, what kinds of software and hardware?"

"For software, mainly CAD. For hardware, I write about radar, electronics, that kind of thing."

"CAD?"

"Computer-Aided Design. A lot of companies do their design work with computers these days, from screws to houses to aircraft."

"Oh? Sounds exciting." She sips at her mocha.

He looks at her, doubting the veracity of her response. Only physicists and engineers really got excited about such things. He remembers Mercury's response.

He smiles at her. She is a natty dresser, the type who has good taste and the money to afford it. He is captivated by the design of her dress, also by the splendid symmetry of her crossed legs. Her ankles, too, are beautifully, sensually slim; her feet are encased in a pair of carmine pumps and Wong wonders how her feet look, and he suddenly smiles to himself—of how the old mandarins so loved a woman's feet, above all else.

Every once in a while a breeze would stir up and he would catch a fragrance of her perfume. He cannot quite place it; it is a scent akin to plumeria, those fragrant white flowers of his youth in Hawaii.

"How did you ever end up in Marthasville?"

"Oh, I went to law school at Gonzaga. That's in Spokane. When I finished there, I did a stint in Seattle. One day, on my way north to

Vancouver, I passed through town. I liked what I saw, so I started asking
around at the courthouse. Turns out they had a position open for assis-
tant public defender, so I applied." She shrugs. "Seattle is way too crowded
for me these days."

Wong is not deceived by the simplicity of her answer. Many people
came here, only a few with jobs in hand. She must be a damned good
lawyer, good enough to have impressed the establishment to offer her a
position. He drinks more coffee.

"Were you raised here?" he asks. "The Pacific Northwest, I mean."

"No. California, actually. Outside Sacramento."

Another Californian! They had been invading the county, tired of
the urban congestion of Los Angeles and San Francisco, looking for less
sprawl, congestion, and crime, buying up property and driving up property prices.

She smiles. "But what about you? There aren't too many Asians
around here. Where do you hail from originally?"

"Originally? Hawaii, originally. But I've lived in California," he bows
his head to her, "Nevada, Oregon, Utah, Missouri, Connecticut, Vermont, and other states."

"Jeez, you've gotten around, huh?"

"Some, yes."

"And you aren't married?" A sharp thrust into the conversation.

Wong raises his eyebrows at the question. He is picking up
Erlandson's quirks. "I'm in the process of being divorced. And you?"

She smiles. "Yes, I was married for a short while. I'm divorced now.
You know, career . . ." She sighs.

"Yes, well . . . any children?"

"One. A daughter. How about you?" she asks.

"Yeah, no kidding? I have a daughter, too. She's seven! How old is
your daughter?"

"She's ten."

"Would you like to have more children?"

"Perhaps," she muses, eyes bright. "Perhaps."

"Yes, you don't want to have your biological clock run out on you."

It is out before he has had time to think about it, and he immediately regrets it.

She frowns. "If you're implying that I'm in a hurry to get married and pregnant again—"

"No! No! I'm sorry! I didn't mean anything like that at all." He brings his hands out in front of him, placating her. "I just meant that, well, women have to watch how the years sneak up on them more than men, you know." He squirms in his seat. In trying to make amends, he realizes his ankles are already past his mouth.

She looks at her watch. "I'm going to have to go now," she says, a smile returning to her lips. She finishes her cup. "Thanks for the mocha."

He gets up. "I hope I haven't offended you."

"Maybe a little, but I'll get over it." They both stand awkwardly, each waiting for the other.

"Can I see you again?" Wong finally asks.

She smiles. "Yes. I'd like that. I'm in the phone book, under city government, Public Defender's office. Jean Chong." She eyes him. "It was nice meeting you, Dave, and I do hope we'll see each other again." Then, she is off, walking down the street.

Suddenly, Wong is amazed at himself. The possibility of another woman in his life! Chinese, too! He chuckles. Just like his father wanted. And she wants to see him again!

But then he thinks back to Mercury. He doubts that he will ever get into her good graces. But, God, he likes her a whole hell of a lot. Still, he has to let his Chineseness run. This woman is too good-looking for him to deny it. And he is no fool. If one beautiful woman spurns him, he reasons, then he will settle for the other.

Chapter 17

Loneliness

She strides with a quick grace down the sidewalk and glances at her watch—five minutes past noon. She frowns because she is late and is not one to keep people waiting.

Entering the Teriyaki House, she spies him waiting for her—a tall, pale man with an unruly shock of red hair, just like he described himself over the phone. He is eyeing her curiously.

"Mercury?"

"Yes! Dr. Erlandson. How are you? Sorry to be late." She holds out her hand as her words gush out. His hand swallows hers.

"Call me Harry. I only insist on my patients calling me by my title. Have to maintain that small amount of distance and decorum. It's nice to finally meet after talking to you over the phone so many times."

She smiles. "It's nice to meet you, too, Harry."

They order at the counter, then sit in the front corner of the restaurant next to large windows that look out onto the street. A high wall of old red bricks climbs twenty feet to a beamed ceiling, from which suspended fans turn lazily. Ferns, swedish ivy, and wandering jew hang from clay pots. Diffuse sunlight swarms into the establishment.

"So, Dave gave me a call and said that I should talk to you," Erlandson speaks first. "I'm glad you accepted my invitation."

"I was going to call," Mercury says.

Erlandson smiles.

"But the thought of refusing did enter my mind."

"In which case, we wouldn't be here," he says and shrugs. "Look, I'm going out on a limb here. Normally, psychiatrists don't talk to a third party about someone else's, uh, 'affliction.' But, then again, I never was too normal myself. I guess I'm just goddamned unorthodox." He grins, looks at her. "I like Dave. I trust him. He's been through a hell of a lot, and I think you—we—can help him."

She smiles noncommittally.

"Mercury, Dave likes you. At this stage, we don't know if it will ever get beyond a nodding acquaintance." He opens his hands, palms up, over the table. "As you may have noticed, Dave is different—and not just because he's Chinese. It's . . . how—how should I put it delicately? Well, he was mentally ill for a while."

"And now?"

Erlandson shrugs again. He talks to her, while his eyes scan the restaurant. A young couple sits next to them. The young man has long hair tied into a ponytail, like in the '60s. "What can I say? I'm only a psychiatrist. He seems to be getting better. He's improved a lot over the last few months."

"What exactly was his problem?"

Erlandson hesitates. "I know he said to go ahead and tell you everything, but I want you to know that this is confidential, you understand?"

She nods her head.

"He was a Marine, did you know that?"

"Yes. I believe you told me earlier, before he started my class."

"Yes, I did, didn't I? Well, that was part of the problem. In the old days he was what we would today call 'macho.' Too much so," he says, sighing. "You see, him being Chinese was kind of like being on the periphery of American society. He felt that tug of tradition, of all the old values and culture, but he was living the American life. But like all minorities, he was aware of being different," he says, looking sharply at her— she nods—"and how he always will be."

The restaurant slowly fills. Other people crowd around them, and the buzz of conversation fills the establishment, like the low hum of high tension power lines.

"But I know other minorities that have been—"

"You know them on the outside. You don't know their thoughts."

"And you do?"

Erlandson sits back in his chair and shrugs. "I'm a psychiatrist. That's my job, to draw their innermost thoughts out into the open." They are too close to the other table; he can see the young man turn toward them, his ear like a tracking antenna. Nosy bastard! Erlandson thinks.

Their food arrives. "Chicken?" the girl asks. Erlandson points to Mercury. The girl then places the beef in front of him.

"Thank you," Erlandson says. He opens up the Styrofoam container, stabs the meat, and brings it to his mouth. "Dave is car-r-y-ing a g-r-e-a-t weight," he mumbles. He chews quickly. "Excuse me . . ." He swallows. "I'm hungry. Haven't eaten since 6:30, and I only had a muffin and coffee then," he says, smiling. "Dave is under an incredible amount of pressure. You see in Vietnam, he was a killer, you know."

Mercury shakes her head, as she delicately eats the chicken. She mixes the teriyaki sauce on the rice, tastes it, and smiles. Then, "But don't all soldiers kill?"

"Yes. They're supposed to. But, you know, a lot of them really don't. They shoot off a lot of bullets, but confirming a kill is hard to do. A lot of soldiers can't lay claim to actually killing somebody."

"And Dave can?" Mercury pauses in her eating.

"Dave can."

"And that's his problem?" She resumes eating.

"Yes."

"But those that do kill the enemy . . . I mean my father was in World War II. He didn't seem to lose sleep over killing Germans."

"Well, first of all, I doubt that your father would confide in you or even show the effects of battle in front of you. That generation hid a lot of the aftereffects of battle. Besides, that was 'The Good War,' as opposed to Vietnam. There was a great moral purpose to World War II."

He continues to steer the conversation to generalities about men at war, then to generalities about Wong, for most of the meal.

Erlandson finishes eating, puts down his fork, watches Mercury tug at a last piece of chicken, intent on separating it from bone.

He sighs. "And, besides, it wasn't only the enemy Dave killed."

The sentence drops like a bombshell. Mercury stops picking at the chicken. The young man at the other table stops talking to his girlfriend and casts a surreptitious glance at them.

"Wha . . . what? What do you mean by that?" Mercury asks.

Erlandson leans closer and speaks softly. "In Vietnam, Dave committed his great sin. He killed an old Mama-san and a six-year-old girl."

The blood suddenly drains from Mercury's face. "Oh, my God!" She slides away from the table, pushes the remaining food away. "You . . . you mean he's a murderer?"

Erlandson looks at her; he leans back, speaking in a normal tone. "Yeah. Yeah. No doubt about it. But in his defense, there were extenuating circumstances." He glances at the young man. His girlfriend is looking at them, too.

"Are you finished?" he asks Mercury. He nods to the other table. "Too many ears here," he says loudly. The young man turns away, speaking softly to his girlfriend. People at adjacent tables look up.

Mercury turns and glances at the couple. "Sure. Yeah. I'm done. Let's go."

They bus their table and stride through the door onto the street.

"Do you have time for a stroll?" Erlandson asks.

Mercury glances at her watch. "Yes. About ten minutes. I want to hear more." Her face is serious now, like a child's face when she has been set before a difficult task.

They are bombarded by the cacophony of the street. A souped-up 70ish Pontiac, with cut-out muffler, roars by. Erlandson looks disapprovingly, a scowl forming on his face. Some dumb, young kid.

He turns to Mercury, speaking in a loud voice, "In Vietnam, he was an Asian killing Asians, you know. First, being Asian, he had to consider whether his buddies would accept him. Second, like a car run off a road, the danger is in overcorrecting where you steer back onto the road and into a car coming the other way. Dave overdid it; he overcorrected. And he 'done wrong,' as they say." They are standing at a street corner now, waiting for the light to change. Mercury is silent.

"They were on a special mission. They stumbled into the Mama-san and the young girl. Well . . . they had to travel light and fast. They couldn't very well bring them along." Mercury grabs Erlandson's arm. They stand still, ignoring the light and the people sidestepping around them. Erlandson looks at her. "The lieutenant said to waste 'em. Nobody made a move. But Dave . . . well, what can I say? What drives a man to commit murder? He volunteered to kill them, and he did."

"How . . . how could he have done such a thing?" She looks down at the sidewalk, wringing her hands. She blinks repeatedly. Though she doesn't admit it, she was starting to have feelings for him.

"It's hard to get into anybody's mind. Like what motivated him to do that act? I think I've got a grasp on it. He had low self-esteem, still does. But I think the overriding factor was his need to be fully accepted by his comrades-in-arms. There was one guy in the unit who kept egging him about being an American gook. That got under his skin and it kind of grew, like a cancer. After a while, he just couldn't control it. He crossed that thin line of the mind—you know, that line between Right and Wrong. He thought he could become more American by killing the Asian side of him, I guess. And his good buddy had been killed by Vietnamese kids. He extrapolated that as a good enough rationale to kill the girl." Erlandson shrugs, looks down the street and back to her. "It was a shitty war."

Mercury nods. "It sure was."

Standing in sunlight, they are discussing a dark act committed over twenty-two years ago in a dark jungle by someone they both know. A chill creeps over Mercury. She shivers.

"I have to be honest, Harry. I-I just don't think I would like to get involved with somebody like Dave."

Erlandson's eyebrows arch. "I understand. And Dave understands, too. He wanted us to, at least, have this talk. All he wants you to do is to think it over. And if the answer is no, he'll stay away. I'll place him in Kelly Ferguson's class. I don't think she'll mind. And he won't be bothering you again."

"Are you sure?"

"I'm sure." Erlandson smiles. "He's not like that."

"Well . . . okay, I'll at least think it over."

"You know, you would be good for him."

"It's a two-way street. Would he be good for me?"

"He's improving. He's not a hardened criminal. Nor is he insane. He feels remorse, and he feels it deeply. More than you can imagine." He arches his eyebrows, looks intently at her. "There's a core of goodness in there. I think you know that; you've had a glimpse of it. Otherwise you wouldn't be here. The question is if it's worth your while to fight for it."

They cross the street and start walking toward Mercury's car. "I think any relationship is tricky enough, even for normal people. What can I do? If Dave isn't insane, he's still unusual," she says.

"Yes. That's true. But he's curable. I'd almost stake my life on it."

Mercury turns her head. Erlandson meets her gaze. "If I do get involved, I will be staking my life on him," she says, as they reach her car.

Erlandson nods, smiles. "That's true. But I think both of you would be good for each other." They stand awkwardly for a few seconds. "Well, it's been a pleasure meeting you," he says, extending his hand to shake hers once more. "Dave has had a lot of good things to say about you. Now I know why."

"He is too gracious. But I'm glad I came. I learned a lot about him. It explains some things. The way he acted a couple of months ago . . . when I invited him over for dinner." Her voice drops off. She shakes herself.

"Well, it's been nice meeting you, Harry," she says, switching gears. "And tell Dave I'll think things over."

"Will do. Thanks again." Erlandson turns and walks away.

She gets into her car, puts the key into the ignition, then just sits for a moment. She lets out a loud sigh. Why me? she thinks. Is this guy worth the aggravation? Oh, Dave!

The humorless hum of traffic is muted by the closed windows in Erlandson's office. The early October rain, driven by a northwest wind, patters against the panes. Wong can see the tops of some trees, birches he realizes, with branches swaying against the gray sky, shaking loose the small, tenuous, almost heart-shaped leaves. Some are caught in gusts and carried high aloft to float like butterflies before being battered back to earth by the rain.

The dying season reminds him of yesterdays. The good yesterdays he wishes he could relive, over and over. The bad yesterdays he wishes he could undo and forget. He wishes he were God, the great movie director of life, who could run the film backward, reshoot a scene, snip out the old and replace it with the new, and then let the clock run as before with the audience unaware of any editing.

"Are the nightmares still occurring?" The question brings him back to reality.

"I get a flashback once in a while. But mostly I sleep pretty good." He smiles limply. There is an emptiness gnawing at his insides, but he doesn't know how to go about telling Erlandson.

The soft strains of Muzak fill the room. The office is pleasantly heated. Wong can feel himself relaxing. When he first entered, his mood was as dark as the sky outside.

"Then you are getting better!" Erlandson beams.

Wong clasps his hands together under his chin, his eyes downcast. He lifts his gaze. "Better, maybe, in that respect. But, when you think about it, what do I have to live for?"

Erlandson's smile fades into a frown. He sits back, sighs. "Okay, maybe you'd better tell me about it."

Wong sighs, too, a long exhalation. The burden of his sins and the twists and turns of his life sit heavily on him. His soul feels weighted down, as if the heavy clouds outside were pressing on him. "I-I don't have anybody," he says, his eyes downcast. He acts like a child crying for affection, and he knows it, despising himself for it.

Erlandson looks at him. "Dave, look at me." Wong looks up. "Do you . . . are you starting to like yourself?"

Wong shrugs. "Maybe . . . yeah, maybe. Sometimes . . . I actually forget and I do like myself . . . like when the sun is out and it's a beautiful day. B-but when it's raining like this, I-I kinda withdraw into myself, you know. And, I don't particularly like what I see. And, like what we said before, if I don't like myself, how can I get someone else to like me or even love me?"

Erlandson lets the question hang in the air.

"In the old days," Wong continues, "I didn't give a damn. I was too strong to be affected or afflicted by relationships. I mean relationships were for those poor bastards who had this weakness, who needed companionship and solace and love. And me? I didn't need it. As for physical need, I'd just find some whores or else some broad who didn't mind my fucking and leaving her."

"Were you always like that? Even as a kid?"

"Yeah, yeah. Then I guess I wasn't worthy enough. Too much moving around. I went to five high schools, you know. Then, being Chinese . . . well, I just blotted out those longings, that feeling of being one of the crowd with a girlfriend."

"And after Vietnam?"

"It was like you said. I hated myself. How could I find a good relationship when I couldn't even like myself?"

"Well, I think you recognize that wanting to be in love is not a weakness, don't you? It's part of the human condition, a nurturing process, like a child who needs a mother's love. It doesn't stop just because you're an adult."

"I didn't know that when I was young."

"But you know it now, don't you?"

"Yes," Wong says, softly, "I know it now . . . and I want it. I need it."

Erlandson is amazed. At last, Wong has realized that love is not a burden to the human soul, but a blessing. It is the only cure or salve for his morbid guilt.

"I know you do, Dave. I know you do. And we're gonna work on it, okay?" Erlandson smiles. "Did you know that I talked to Mercury?"

Wong sits up straighter. He had been wondering, but did not want to broach the subject and appear overeager like a young pup. "No, I didn't know. How did it go?"

"Well, I told her your problem."

"How did she take it?"

"She was all right about you being in the Marines and killing and all that. But when I told her about the murders . . ."

Wong winces at the word.

". . . of the Mama-san and the girl, that, well, sort of rattled her."

"What did she say?" His face full of anticipation.

"She couldn't believe you could do such a thing."

Wong slides down into his chair, his hope fading. "So she said no."

"No. She said she would think it over. I think she likes you. The question is if she likes you well enough to take a chance on you."

Wong sits up straight, hope on the rise again. He smiles. "Maybe," he says, "maybe. And, oh, did I tell you about this other woman I met? She's Chinese-American, real pretty. Her name is Jean."

Erlandson chortles. "Gee, I was starting to get worried about you all over again. Now you go and find two women who are interested in you!"

Wong smiles sheepishly. "It's only maybe," he says.

"Life is maybes," Erlandson replies, "and you know it. The trick is to turn the good maybes into reality and keep the bad ones at bay."

"That's the Erlandson philosophy, is it?"

"That's right, Dave. And if you think real hard about it, you'll find it's a damned good philosophy, too!"

Wong feels better now. "I will, Doc. I think you may have a good point."

"Oh, and one more piece of advice, Dave. If you can get into Mercury's good graces, well, let me say this, one woman is enough to handle. Two women will stretch you, physically and emotionally."

"I'm not worried. I like Mercury, and I'd like to get to know her better. But I think Jean is really interested in me. And besides," Wong says, smiling, "I've never been stretched by two women before."

"You could've stopped by the class to see me." They are in the hospital cafeteria.

"I just couldn't, Mercury. I-I needed someplace . . . neutral, out of your sphere of influence. Can you understand that?" He had called to set up this meeting, an hour before her exercise class.

Mercury smiles at "sphere of influence," sips her coffee. Facing the windows, she squints, her face as bland as the coffee she is drinking.

Wong picks at a piece of blackberry pie, his heart almost as black as the berries. He swallows his coffee in great gulps, returning once already for a refill. Sunlight, finally breaking through the clouds, streams through the large glass windows, giving the place the feel of a greenhouse. But, still, he feels bleak, under his own clouds.

"Erlandson said that he talked to you." He fidgets with his hands, elbows on the table, clapping his fingertips together.

"Yes, we had a pretty good talk." Then, as an afterthought, "He's a nice man."

"And now you know what kind of man I am."

She looks at him. "Yes." She drops her eyes, sipping her coffee. Then she looks about the cafeteria, unable to meet his eyes. A doctor, in his light blue frock, straggles in. A group of four visitors are engaged in spirited conversation; a few other people, sitting alone, are quietly reading a book or a newspaper. The cafeteria is in a lull between mealtimes.

"Do I look like a criminal . . . a murderer . . . now?"

"But what you did . . ."

"It was war. I'm not excusing myself for what I did. Yes, yes, it was murder. But you don't know the fear we all felt, and my sense of being on the outside, not really being a part of the team. I mean, all my life, I've had that feeling." He speaks softly, eyes flicking between her and the other tables.

"So you had to kill an old lady and a little girl? Murder them in cold blood!" Her lips turn down.

Wong's jaw works nervously back and forth, his frown deepening. "Have you ever been attacked?" he asks. "Have you ever been in fear for your life or limb?"

"No. What does that have to do—"

"It casts a different light on the subject."

"Not in my mind. There is Right and Wrong. I firmly believe—"

"Jesus! You sound just like Erlandson." Wong stares at her. The small, cute beak of her nose. A fine-boned face, surrounded by beautiful

blonde hair. In one fleeting instant, he pictures them together and realizes that she could be his salvation. But the reality of their situation comes
back quickly. He almost breaks, his loneliness sitting on him like an op-
pressive weight, Atlas's globe full of his guilt and pain. He almost begs for
her friendship, her love, as if "happily ever after" could be achieved by
the abject slavering of one for the other. He catches himself in time, what
little self-respect he has left.

The low hum of the cafeteria has suddenly dissipated, many of the
people having left. "I'm not going to beg, Mercury." His words seem to
float in the air, rising to the high ceiling by the windows. "I like you. I'd
like to get to know you better. Maybe there is something I can offer you in
such a relationship. Right now, I-I just don't know what. There are a few
things I have to work out for myself. There must be something, otherwise
you wouldn't be here." He looks at her. "It wouldn't be pity, would it?"

"No, no. God knows, it's not pity." But it is, just a bit. Still, there is
an enigmatic quality about him she finds attractive. She likes his intelligence, his forthrightness, his measured smile, even his ineffable sadness—
something she once found enchanting, before her talk with Erlandson.
When she first met him, she thought that perhaps life only doled out so
many smiles in his lifetime and he had to conserve them. Now she knows
better. He has been so battered down by a tsunami of guilt.

Paradoxically, feeling disgust for what he had done, a modicum of
admiration for the man has still managed to slip through her armor. None-
theless, she is leery about being a nurse to this man's soul. She does not
feel equal to the task, not even the effort. She feels that the plague of his
crime and his remembrance would be too much for her.

"Look, Dave, I'm not going to lie to you. Frankly, I'm nervous around
you now that I know more about you. I-I just don't think it would be a
good idea for us to become involved."

Wong blinks. Involved? He likes the word. But she is slipping away.
He stares at his empty coffee cup, then at the warm sunlight streaming
into the room. But all he feels is the coolness emanating from across the
table. He almost hates her, the cold detachment, the disintegration of
what little relationship they did have. He can remember her warm smile

when he had first met her and how she had helped him learn the aerobics routines. He remembered her help on his first jog around Merritt Lake. In his mind, they were preordained for a life together. He had never felt like that with anyone before. But, obviously, she didn't feel that way.

She gets up to leave. "So you'll be going to Kelly Ferguson's class?" A stone face.

Wong, tightlipped and testy, replies, "Yes, yes. I won't be bothering you again." He remains seated, chair pushed out from the table, legs outstretched.

She stops, looks at him. "I'm sorry, Dave. I'm sorry." Then she leaves.

"I'm sorry, too," he mutters, watching her back. He gets up gloomily, exhales loudly. An elderly woman sitting nearby stares at him. "Too many disappearing backs," he tells her. She smiles sheepishly at him, shrugs, and drops her gaze.

Even with the promise of Jean, he deeply regrets the leaving of this woman in his life. It's as if she were taking all of his future smiles, and that from now on he was condemned to wear the bland, blank stares of the insane or the frowns of the chronically unhappy, forever saddled with dyspeptic eyes and turned-down lips.

He turns and plods wearily over the carpet out the small hallway, past the reception desk, and out into the fall sunshine. He wears his loneliness like leg irons.

Chapter 18

Tet

The rain fell in big droplets, like little mortar rounds that exploded in the puddles. They were back at a forward base camp, behind barbed wire, guard towers, foxholes, and sandbags. Wong was sitting on the covered porch of his hooch watching the rain and the jungle in the evening twilight. Peals of laughter came from the next hooch, music and light streaming out the open doorway. He was alone and, for the time being, comfortable in being alone. Beer in hand, sitting on a wooden chair, he watched the raindrops play across the mud and puddles. He was lost in the pattern of raindrops, the splash, splash of drops hitting water and then the splut of raindrops hitting mud. Splash, splash, splut. A random cantata that hypnotized him, as if he were lost in the flicker of a candle flame and he was far away from Vietnam.

"Mind if I join you?"

Wong shook his head, startled. He looked up. "Naw, Muley, maybe I can use the company."

"Can't stand all those fucking potheads," Abramson said. "Smoke?" he offered.

Wong shook his head. "No. Bad for your health." They both burst out laughing. "But I wouldn't do it out here."

Muley nodded, put his cigarette away. Snipers.

Muley was the new guy. He had joined the unit a month ago, transferred in from some other grunt unit. Wong marveled at his strength and endurance. While everybody complained about the heat, the long hours, about going on point, Muley didn't. In four weeks, he had walked point ten times already—a suicidal desire, Wong thought. They had humped together several times and Wong discovered that he liked the new guy. He filled a vacuum since Deacon died.

"Beer?" Wong offered.

Muley took the beer, sipped. "Hey, not bad!"

"I keep it in the puddles."

The rain fell in a curtain of water that blotted out the jungle. The perimeter lights cast eerie shadows. Every so often, the soft plop, plop of flares lit up the night sky to bare every imagined ghost floating by. They drank in silence, except for some small talk, "Another beer?" "Yeah, thanks," each to his own thoughts, caught in the web of alcohol and rain and jungle and war.

"Do you believe in God?" Muley suddenly asked.

Silence reigned for a few seconds, except for the rain pattering on the roof, splashing on the ground.

"God? How can there be a God? What god would allow this fucking war?" Plop, plop. The flash of light caressed Wong's snickering face.

"Yeah. Funny how this war can make you believe or not. But I can see why some men gotta have something to believe in, you know. Something bigger than themselves. I admit, in a tight situation, I start praying." He looked to Wong. "That's cheating, ain't it, for someone who don't believe in God."

Wong did not answer.

"I mean, I pray that I get out of here alive. If I pray hard enough, I'll get out of here alive. Whatdyathink?" Wong remained silent. "Besides, I got a family to live for . . ." his voice trailed off.

"You can pray all you fucking want, man. If the gods are against you, all you got is shit."

Muley shrugged, then scanned Wong's face in the dim light. He swigged his beer, then in a soft voice, "I heard about you, Wong . . . what you did."

Wong barely heard him, almost let it pass, like a bat flying into the darkness. "Ain't no big thing. I did what I had to do."

"I know, man, but you didn't have to—"

"What are you, huh? A fucking priest? Those other assholes in the squad tell you that they were just waiting for me to kill the gooks—the Mama-san, the girl?"

Muley looked away. "I-I don't know what I would've done."

Wong spat, got up from the chair and walked into the hooch. He came back out after a few moments and threw the knife into the floor, embedding it a good three-quarter inch into the soft wood. "There," he said, "look at it! That's what I did it with."

The knife shone in the reflected light from the perimeter. Long and silver and a thing of beauty and death. The blade was nine inches long, sleek and double-edged, sawtoothed near the handle. The leather thong hung down, swaying in the evening breeze, almost touching the floor.

Muley let it stand, not touching it, watching the light glisten off the blade. "It is Death, ain't it?" Wong did not answer. Then, "Their deaths are gonna fuck you over the rest of your life, if you don't watch out." Wong was standing up, leaning against the side of the hut, staring out into the darkness.

"I can beat it," Wong replied.

Muley shrugged. "I don't think so. Not the way you're going."

"Then what do you suggest?" Almost a snarl.

"You'd fucking better talk about it, buddy. You'd fucking better talk about it . . . I know when I have problems, I always talk about them with Stella, my wife."

"Well, I don't have a wife. No women allowed around here." He laughed. "This is a man's war."

"Hey, I'm here if you need me. In fact, right now, if you want . . . I've been odd man out, too."

Wong smiled, shook his head, looking at the ground. "No. I'm not ready. I don't need it." Then looking at Muley, said, "You've never been as far out as I have, man."

The sound of raucous laughter from the next hooch split the night air. The two men were silent, looking out into the perimeter, letting the sounds wash over them. Muley crossed his arms, suddenly cool and shivering in the night air. A premonition.

"You afraid of death, Wong?"

Silence once more, then, "No!" A guttural exclamation. Followed softly by, "Yeah! Maybe."

All of a sudden, a piercing scream filled the night air. A howl of loneliness and despair split through the curtains of rain and churned past the barren no-man's land into the dense vegetation of the jungle, echoing among the nearby hills. Wong's mouth worked open and closed, a sing-song ululation as he gasped for breath between each scream.

"All right, listen up!" It was Lieutenant Anderson. They were at Phu Bai. The whole company had been moved back to a more secure area. "I'm sure you all heard that there's all kinds of shit going on in Hue. Well, Alpha Company is being sent in. Just our luck, 1st Platoon will ride point."

A groan ran through the twenty-five men, all that was left of the platoon, which at full staff was forty-nine men. The company, ordinarily some three hundred men, was down to about a hundred.

"Shit, I thought this was a fucking religious gook holiday!" Smitty complained.

"Well, it looks like they caught us with our fucking pants down. But some ARVN units holed up in the Citadel are still putting up a good fight. Our job is to go in there and support 'em."

A few moans came from the platoon, but mostly they looked at each other through tired, scared, or indifferent eyes, depending on the man. For a combat infantryman, Death hovered over him in battle closer than any angel ever would. In more secure areas, Death would back away like a vulture on a distant perch, but he was always there, imminent, all-knowing, omnipotent, patient, ready to cut the string of life on a moment's notice. Each man was tethered to him as surely as he was once tethered to his mother by the umbilical.

The company boarded a convoy of ten trucks, which included two dusters. The dusters were Army trucks loaded with four .50 caliber machine guns in front. One duster was in front of the column and one in back. Each truck held about ten to twelve men, with fewer in the dusters.

T e t

As they loaded their gear and clambered into the trucks, Muley said to Wong, "Well, so much for the fucking time off we was gonna get."

Wong nodded, took off his helmet. He studied his calendar. February 2, 1968. He tucked the calendar back into the band inside his helmet and then scanned the column. "Shit, this doesn't look too good," he commented to Muley.

The men lay flat against the sandbags, staring out into the first light of dawn. Within minutes they were rolling along Highway 1, north to Hue. Death's tether was getting shorter.

Wong didn't like the feel of this one. Fifty-two more days and I get killed, he thought. Jesus, he was getting too short for this. He looked across to Muley. Muley looked up. By the look in each other's eyes, they could tell what each was thinking.

"I'm scared about this one," Muley said, above the whine of the truck's engine. He was on the opposite side, leaning over toward Wong.

Wong stared at Muley. "So am I."

"How big a force we going up against?"

"Christ, I don't know. A regiment. Two regiments? Who knows? The captain ain't saying."

Muley reached into his pocket, extended his hand, holding out the photo to Wong. "Me, my wife, and kid," he said.

Wong looked at the photo, then asked, "What in the fuck are you doing here? Your wife is beautiful and so is your kid."

"I ain't one to run to Canada."

"Jesus!" Wong shrugged, handing the photo back.

"If anything happens to me . . . there's an address on back. Can you write my wife for me?"

Wong nodded. "Just don't be stupid out there, okay?"

Muley nodded in return, but Wong knew that his advice had fallen on deaf ears. Wong had already seen Muley in action and thought him to be exceptionally brave, almost to the point of foolishness. It was like the guy had a death wish. It was incomprehensible to Wong, more so after seeing the photo of his wife and baby. How could Muley so tempt and taunt Death when there was life and love for him out in the real world?

All of a sudden the trucks ground to a halt. Everybody looked out. Wong swung out farther to see for himself. All he could see was a concrete bridge, pockmarked with big holes. Beyond, a row of wooden houses formed a gauntlet. The radio crackled. Anderson passed the word. "Be on the alert. Other trucks had been fired on here." All of a sudden the trucks took off, accelerating across the bridge, building up speed beyond it to career through the gauntlet of houses. The .50 calibers of the first duster swept through the buildings when they were about seventy-five meters away. Then there was the return fire of AK-47s. The Marines in Wong's truck stuck their heads down next to the sandbags. As they sped past the houses, they opened up with their M-16s. It was over almost as soon as it began. Their truck was back out in the open on the other side. The men could hear the firing from the subsequent trucks, and then the .50 calibers again, from the second duster. It was their first action of the Tet offensive.

"We're going into some bad shit!" Wolchak said. And they were.

The rest of the way was uneventful, except for a small amount of small-arms fire the convoy drew before pulling into the MACV (Military Assistance Command, Vietnam) compound on the south side of the Perfume River. MACV was the base of operations for the Americans in Hue. Most of the NVA positions were on the opposite side of the river. The ARVN still controlled a part of the Citadel, the old imperial grounds when Hue was the capital of Vietnam, but the NVA controlled the Imperial Palace.

"All right, everybody out!" Anderson yelled. The Marines jumped off the trucks, lugging their equipment. Wong looked around. The walls of the compound were riddled with bullets. Explosions, probably from 120-mm rockets, had blown gaping holes in several of the buildings. Machine gun emplacements had been set up along the wall of the compound. They were sandbagged and manned with a two man crew, mainly M-60s, the 7.62-mm light machine gun.

Most of the Marines plopped down against the walls; a few stood around, smoking. Some were looking through a breach in the wall at the Perfume River and the city beyond. It was quiet. The officers and NCOs were conferring. They would soon be given their marching orders. Nervousness settled in their guts. The dry taste of fear played in their mouths, before the adrenalin of action would pump their hearts bold.

"That's a hell of a lot of buildings to go through," Muley said, looking into the densely packed buildings across the river.

"It's gonna be different from the jungle, all right," Wong replied, following his gaze.

"Don't matter to me where we gonna fight. As long as it's killing gooks. All right!" Smitty scowled, working on taping M-16 magazines together. He carried twelve double magazines and ten grenades.

They were all checking their weapons now. Some doing a quick field strip, cleaning, and reassembly. Others checked ammo and grenades, M-79 grenade launcher, M-60 machine gun.

Wong took out his .45 caliber pistol, pulled the slide partway back to double-check that a round was in the chamber, let the slide spring back, decocked it for safety. Ordinarily, enlisted men did not carry pistols, but Wong had bought it from some REMF (rear echelon motherfucker). Rules were not heavily enforced in combat areas.

"Okay, everybody, listen up." It was Anderson again. "The gooks are holding the far side of the bridge over there." He pointed. "Two platoons from Baker Company have already tried securing it. They were chewed up pretty bad. It's our turn."

There was silence. Anderson continued, "The battalion commander must have confidence in us because he's only sending out 1st Platoon." A groan went up from the men. "1st Squad will be second in line. 2nd Squad will be on point. 3rd and 4th Squads will be right behind. We'll hit the bridge in two columns. Last time there were two machine gun emplacements on the far side, crisscrossing fields of fire. Oh yeah, they got rockets, too. Probably some two-man teams up in the houses on the nearby hillside. We'll be moving out in thirty minutes. We'll have one jeep with a .50 caliber leading. Any questions?"

"Yeah, what if we get across the bridge. Is there another objective? Or do we stand and hold?" Emory, a black from Pittsburgh, asked.

"We stand and hold. Any other questions?"

145

"What casualties did Baker Company take?" Wong asked.

"Eight killed and twelve wounded."

A few of the men whistled. "Son of a bitch!" some mumbled.

"This is where the shit hits the fan," Anderson continued. "Motherfucking payback time," he said, grinning. "We're gonna take that bridge."

A half hour later they were moving out from the compound across Le Loi Street. Wong was on the right side of the road. Muley was opposite him on the left. Ahead were Gonzales, Wolchak, Smitty, the Sarge, and others. Johnson, the corpsman, was behind. The jeep was almost onto the bridge when an NVA machine gun opened up. The .50 caliber on the jeep opened up in reply. Every Marine dove for cover, behind the low walls and behind the steel bridge supports. 2nd Squad was stalled, several Marines sprawled in the middle of the bridge. The fire was withering. Then a B-40 rocket hit the jeep and the .50 caliber was silenced, its gunner hanging over the edge of the jeep upside down, his head slumped on the pavement.

The shouts of the Marines echoed among the gunfire. "M-79s up front!" But the grenades propelled from the M-79 shot beyond the two machine guns. "Get the LAAW!" The Light Antitank Assault Weapon.

Wong watched as one man, a replacement who wanted to be a hero, rushed out from behind cover, kneeling out in the open as machine gun fire raked the area around him. The Marines poured as much covering fire as they could. Wong held his breath. The fucking guy's crazy! he thought. The Marine was just shouldering the weapon when slugs hit him. Wong knew he was dead as soon as he hit the concrete.

Meanwhile, 1st Squad had inched up to support 2nd Squad. There were now bunches of Marines around the supporting structures. Wong ran up, bullets kicking around his feet and pinging off the metal buttresses. He looked up and saw Muley on the opposite side, giving him a thumbs up. Muley pointed to himself and then to the fallen Marine with the LAAW. Wong nodded. They were both about ten meters away from the next structure; the fallen Marine was almost directly at a right angle to it. Go! they both ran to the next buttress, squeezing in among the group of men already huddled about.

"Cover me! Covering fire!" Muley yelled out.

"Cover him!" Wong shouted.

The Marines rose and fired at both of the machine guns. Muley scrambled out into the middle of the bridge. He ripped the LAAW from the dead man's grasp, knelt, shouldered, aimed, and fired. It seemed like minutes to Wong, but it was only seconds. Muley scored a direct hit on the machine gun on the right. He quickly scrambled across to Wong, breathing heavily.

"You stupid shit! You're fucking crazy!" Wong shouted at him.

Muley breathed deeply, laughing, eyes twinkling. The narcotic of battle was in his blood, more intoxicating than love or sex. "Jesus! I didn't think I was gonna make it."

Wong just shook his head.

Their adrenalin was coming down a notch. But there was still one other machine gun. They could see a Marine named Jackson working himself down the left side of the bridge. The covering fire from the right side was heavy. Jackson was about ten meters from the machine gun emplacement. He held two grenades, pulled their pins, and lobbed both of them. As soon as the two grenades exploded, he was over the sandbags, spraying the area down with his M-16 on full automatic. Wong just shook his head again. Such courage!

Once the two machine guns were silenced, it turned into a mopping up exercise. They kept an eye out for the rocket teams hidden somewhere in houses on the near hillside. But they were not ordered to search for them. They got some sporadic sniper fire. But of the enemy on the bridge, five of the NVA were dead. Three wounded were dispatched quickly. The Marines didn't want to fuck with prisoners, unless it was to interrogate them.

2nd squad had taken the heaviest casualties: three dead, six wounded. 1st squad had two wounded. There were three more wounded among the rest of the platoon. The platoon immediately set up defensive positions in case of a counterattack. Anderson radioed back for additional reinforcements and relief. More men filed in from the compound to help secure the bridge.

Half the platoon, with reinforcements from the company, guarded the bridge that night. The other half filed back to the compound. Wong, Muley, and four other Marines were billeted in a small ten-by-twelve foot concrete room. When Wong and Muley entered, they saw three cots with Marines already sprawled on them, sleeping. One Marine was sleeping lightly on the floor, barely lifting his head.

"Goddamn, what a smell!" Muley complained, as they dropped their gear against one of the walls.

Wong sniffed, a scent of death. He followed his nose and pushed aside a curtained doorway. His nose wrinkled. Muley was beside him. "Jesus," he whispered. Body bags were stacked like cordwood—no, like those pods in *Invasion of the Body Snatchers*, Wong thought—almost all the way to the ceiling. They let the curtain drop.

"I can't sleep here," Muley said. "I don't wanna sleep with the dead. I'm not there yet."

"Beats dodging shrapnel from rockets," Wong said, opening the door to look outside. "And it's raining." Wong closed the door and started to pad the floor with some blankets. He arranged his flak jacket and helmet into a pillow.

"Jesus Christ!" Muley relented, making his space ready next to him. "Jesus Christ!"

They were bone weary but alive. They slept fitfully, dreaming of death while inhaling its cruel vapors.

They were on the other side of the bridge now, running from one building to the next. The chatter of AK-47s and a light machine gun greeted each Marine who dashed from cover. NVA troops were set up on the upper floors and roof of a three-story school building. Three streets joined to form a T. The school was at the top of the T, its yard bounded by a five-foot high concrete wall. The Marines moved down the trunk of the T, leapfrogging and zigzagging from one building to the next, heading toward the school. Tall trees obscured any view of the school and yard from nearby buildings, so they couldn't count on any covering fire from Marines there.

T e t

Wong looked out at the street in front of him. One Marine was down in the middle, about seven meters away, screaming "Help me, goddammit! Help me!" The NVA were using him as bait. A Marine named Jonesy, opposite Wong, sprinted four meters to help him. A cacophony of automatic fire erupted, covering fire from the other Marines and the steady staccato of the NVA machine gun. Jonesy was caught and spun around, falling not more than ten feet from the wounded man. Jonesy jerked and was still. The firing ceased, an uncanny stillness reigned, except for the moaning of the wounded Marine in the street.

"Let's do it, man!" Muley was primed to go.

"You're fucking crazy!" Wong responded.

"We can do it! Go!" He was off, the pavement erupting beside him.

Wong and the others provided covering fire. Out of the corner of his eyes, Wong saw Muley grab the wounded Marine by the top of his flak jacket and drag him the four yards to a partial courtyard on the other side of the street. Wong rushed headlong after him, breathing hard, hurdling the dead Jonesy, gasping with relief and fear. The thought flitted through his mind to drag Jonesy to the other side, then he thought better of it. He was dead. Why get killed retrieving the body now? Retrieve it later.

He looked over at Muley. He was laughing. Scared shitless, but laughing. It was like a high to him, Wong thought. "You're fucking crazy," he shouted in his ear, even though the small-arms fire had stopped.

They both heard the noise of the ONTOS on its wheeled track come up the street. It advanced ten meters farther than their position. It had six 106-mm recoilless rifles mounted on it. Wong, covering his ears, watched the Marine fire the rifles. The sound was incredibly loud. But it did the job, pulverizing the upstairs window where the machine gun was and blowing several NVA off the roof directly above it. Cheers erupted from the Marines. They quickly worked their way down the street.

Wong's squad was now bent over in front of the courtyard wall of the school. Several bodies lay near the entranceway, on the opposite side. The NVA had zeroed in on it.

More Marines were sheltered behind trees and in doorways of houses behind them, along the street.

"Okay, who wants to go first?" Sarge asked. There was an eerie silence from the school building.

"I'll go!" Gonzales volunteered.

The other men moved closer to help boost him over the wall. "Now!" Sarge commanded. Gonzales was pushed up onto the one-foot thick wall, legs kicking to propel himself down the other side. A single shot rang out from the building; Gonzales's legs went limp. "Pull him back!" Sarge yelled.

They got him down, plopped him into the dirt. He looked at them, a bullet hole in his head. "Madre!" he cried out, then died.

"Son of a bitch!" Sarge yelled. Then, "We gotta see what's on the other side," Sarge said. The building was screened by a high wall and they were among trees that hid the building from observation by Marines behind them on rooftops. "Any volunteers?"

"Yeah, I'll look," Smitty said. Smitty leaned his M-16 against the wall, moved away from the position where the sniper was zeroed in, pressed the palms of his hands against the wall and inched his head up, the top of his helmet about three inches below the top of the wall. Then he shot his legs up from under his crouch, looked for a split second, and dropped his head back down, his helmet floating above his head it seemed, before cascading down to roll by his feet. AK-47 rounds cracked over his head.

"What you got?" Sarge asked.

"It's about twenty meters to the entrance. The building is upside down U-shaped on this side, the top of the U is in the center." He drew the diagram in the dirt. "That's where the entrance is. I saw some windows above the entrance. I didn't have time to look at the legs of the U to see if there were any windows."

"We gotta know if there are windows in the legs of the U. Wong?"

"Huh?"

"You wanna look?"

"Christ, Sarge, you think I'm crazy?"

Smitty's lip curled down.

"I'll look," Muley volunteered.

"No, no. I'll look," Wong relented. Jesus! What am I doing? he thought to himself. I don't feel like dying today!

"Hold on," Sarge said. "We've got two legs of the U." He pointed to the letter in the dirt with his knife. "I want you, Wong, and you, Muley, to spread out farther along the wall. Wong you go left and look at the right leg. Muley, you go right and look left. You both go up on my signal."

Wong moved about twenty feet away to the left, Muley twenty feet to the right. They cinched their helmets. They crouched next to the wall, palms on the wall, their helmets a few inches below. They watched Sarge raise his fist. When his fist dropped, they both shot up for a split second, then back down. Bullets sprayed over their heads. They scrambled back.

"There are three levels of windows on the right leg," Wong reported.

"Same here," Muley said.

"Okay," Sarge thought out loud. "Okay, I got it. Pass the word. Everybody get their gas masks on." Sarge wet his finger with his tongue and held it up. The wind was blowing toward the building. "Get your CS canisters out." The men dug into their packs for the tear gas and gas masks. "On the count of three, lob those motherfuckers as far as you can. One. Two. Three!"

They hurled the canisters, then fell back to let the gas penetrate the windows and doors. Within minutes, the tear gas did the trick. Several Marines nearby opened fire, cutting down two NVA who had run out into the courtyard. "Okay, now!" Sarge yelled. They ducked through the entranceway.

They entered the building, rolling grenades in first, putting their M-16s on full automatic, spraying the area in front. Each closed doorway was quickly opened or kicked down, a grenade rolled in, then the room sprayed with bullets.

It was hard to see with the gas masks on. Sweat dripped down and water vapor condensed on the lens of the mask, obscuring Wong's vision.

Wong, Muley, and a new guy, Wilson, worked their way upstairs, entering a large corridor, some twelve feet across. A dead end was to the left. They all turned right. Three doors. Two on the left, one on the right. Then the hallway became a T some fifteen meters away. Wong was lead man, hugging the left side of the hallway. Wilson was next, staggered on the right. Muley was close behind. Two more Marines, Wolkowski and Bonaventure, came up the stairs behind them. Wong signaled them to provide covering fire. They worked the first door, Wong pulling it open, Muley throwing the grenade in, Wilson spraying the room after the explosion. Wolkowski and Bonaventure covered the other doors and the hallway. They went through each door of the first hallway that way. At the T, Wong looked out quickly. No report. He looked again. The left side of the T went down a long hallway, at least twenty-five meters. Buku rooms, he thought. The right side of the T branched off left, some ten meters away, into another hallway. The other four Marines crowded around Wong. He explained the situation.

"Fuck, let's go," Wolkowski said, his voice sounding robotlike behind the gas mask.

"Yeah," Wilson agreed, "Bonnie and I will go right and check that other corridor. You three can go left."

"I don't like it," Wong said. They were all sweating profusely behind the masks. Wong pulled his up, took a tentative breath. The smell of tear gas was present, but he could breathe. He yanked off the mask, dropped it to the floor. "Fuck this!" The others followed suit. He looked to Muley, "You, Wolkowski, and me are gonna go down this long hallway?" They nodded.

He looked to Wilson and Bonaventure. "You two gonna cover the short hallway?"

"Yeah," Bonaventure said, "let's go!"

The two groups slid along the walls, tiptoeing down the hallways in opposite directions. Wong was thirty feet down the left side of the T when he heard the shouts and the deafening bursts of AK-47s, the bullets breaking the air past his head, and the resounding answer of the M-16s. Wong dropped low, swung around. Muley and Wolkowski had already taken cover in doorways. Two NVA were in the hallway. Wong let go a burst, cut down one. Muley dropped the other one. Wolkowski shot, too. Life was a matter of split seconds. Wilson and Bonaventure were down. They rushed back to the corner, looked quickly around it. No one else.

"Jesus Christ!" Wong exclaimed, wiping the sweat from his brows.

"Fucking close!" Muley said.

Wolkowski bent over Wilson. "Shit! Wilson's dead. How's Bonnie?"

"He's breathing," Muley answered. He tore out a large gauze pad, pulled Bonaventure's flak jacket and shirt apart. His right chest had two holes in it. He stuffed the pad over the bullet holes, trying to staunch the blood.

Other Marines were now filing into the corridor. "Corpsman!" Muley shouted. Johnson rushed to his side, applying another compress to Bonaventure's back. "Stay with me, man!" Johnson shouted at Bonaventure, who groaned in reply. Johnson injected him with morphine.

Wong looked at the three bodies and the large pools of blood on the linoleum floor. He looked at Muley and Wolkowski.

"Ready?" he asked.

They nodded, rechecking their magazines, breathing heavily, eyes wide. They continued down the corridor, their boots tracking blood, the telltale spoor of battle.

Theirs was an existence of days living in fear, living on the edge, hearts racing, pulses quickening, bowels loosening. An existence where life belonged to the quick, the observant, the lucky.

Each night Wong and Muley went back to the MACV compound to the same room. Every couple of days the bodies were loaded on trucks and shipped out. But every night, it seemed that there was still the same number, sometimes even more. Still, they slept there, when they weren't on guard duty. The smell of death hadn't changed, but they abided it. The room was warm. Outside, a chill wind blew into the compound from the city and rain drummed on the metal rooftop, all night and into the morning. They slept the same fitful sleep.

They were moving behind three M-48 tanks down a narrow street, working their way toward the Imperial Palace. Many of the houses had walls screening small courtyards from the street. Wong, behind the last tank, looked ahead to Muley, who was behind the second tank. Ahead, Wong could see the first tank approach a clearing. The three tanks went on line, the Marines crouched behind them. The tanks started firing at the Imperial Palace. Fucking loud! Wong thought. Just then, they were pounded by a recoilless rifle, then B-40 rockets. All three tanks were hit, though not seriously. They turned in their tracks.

"Let's get the hell out of here!" Sarge yelled. The Marines retreated down the street they had just come up, tanks following. Suddenly Wong saw grenades landing in front of him, coming over the courtyard walls.

"Grenades!" he yelled.

They were coming in bunches, bouncing into the street, exploding their shrapnel. Everybody ran for what cover they could find. Doorways, niches, trees. But it was too late for Sarge. One exploded not two feet away, killing him instantly. "Fuck! Sarge is down!" someone yelled.

Muley ran toward a stone doorway when suddenly a grenade bounced over the wall at his feet. He froze, then turned and ran back into the street. The retreating tank's treads caught him at the waist, running over his body like it was a rag doll. Muley looked down, gasped, wide-eyed in amazement. The grenade exploded harmlessly.

Wong came up. "Oh, Jesus! Oh, Jesus!" he cried. The tank had cut Muley in half, the lower part of his body connected to his upper by thin strands of flesh, his blood staining the road, intestines slipping out.

"Oh, God, it hurts!" Muley's face was twisted in pain. "I'm dead! Shoot me, Wong! It hurts!" The grip of pain and terror on his face. "Shoot me, Wong! Fucking shoot me!" he screamed.

Wong, crying, grabbed the .45 from his holster, cocked the hammer back, stared into those passionate eyes, pointed the pistol at Muley's head.

"S-T-E-L-L-A!" Muley yelled, closing his eyes.

Wong's hand wavered, the pistol dropped.

Eyes now open, Muley appealed to Wong, his face scrunched in agony. "Wong! Shoot me, goddammit! Please! . . . Oh, God! Oh, God! It fucking hurts!" Then in a last passionate burst, "I LOVE YOU, STELLA!"

Wong brought the pistol up again, tears clouding his vision. He steadied his hand. Pulled the trigger.

That night Wong slept fitfully under his poncho in a foxhole, under the teary sky.

Chapter 19

Hope

"Well, what do you think?" Jean asks.

"I thought the performance was choppy in parts," Wong replies, blinking in the bright lights as they shuffle toward the exits.

"Oh, I don't know . . . whoever played Othello was very good." She opens the program and finds the name. "Gene Johannesen."

"A fine Moorish name." They both laugh.

"But I do like *Othello*! I like that undercurrent of racism," she says, holding her hand out, twisting it, like she was dialing the combination on a safe. They are in the lobby now. "How it leads to jealousy and tragedy. Don't you think it's so timely, even today?" Wong helps her into her corduroy coat.

"Yes. Yes, it is." He slips his own jacket on. He holds the door open for her, lingering for the couple behind them.

They step out onto a bricklined patio. A stone wall to their left overlooks the city and bay.

"Did anybody pick on you because you're Chinese?"

He looks at her, caught offguard by the question. "Of course," he says, "probably more than you. It seems to me boys are picked on more than girls in this great land of ours."

The stars are out, a brilliant luminescence above the bay and the islands.

"Yes, I know. I have two brothers. They had to learn how to fight, too. You did learn, didn't you?"

He sighs. "Yes, I did. Judo, boxing, Kung Fu, Tae Kwon Do. I was a jack of all trades and master of none."

She laughs. "But good enough?"

He shrugs. "Would you mind?" he asks, as he leads them to the wall. The lights of the city are to their right, rays skipping across the water like brilliant angel's hair.

A chill wind blows from the bay. Jean pulls the collar of her coat about her, clasping her right hand tight under her chin. "What I'm trying to say is don't you think this play strikes a personal chord?"

"You mean if I marry a blonde beauty and everyone calls me 'my lord.'" He smiles at her.

She laughs.

"Beautiful night!" Wong exclaims, changing the subject.

"Yes," she breathes.

"Look! There's Orion!" He points out the constellation to her. "There's his belt and his sword hanging down." He points out the three bright stars that make out the sword. "His two shoulders, his knees. And over there," he stands behind her, letting her look along his arm and finger, "is Canis Major and Sirius, the Dog Star. The real bright star."

"Oh, this is exciting!" she exclaims. "You didn't tell me you knew astronomy."

"Oh, just a little." He has stepped around to her left, looking at her profile silhouetted against the city lights. Her head is tilted back, looking at the stars. The wind tousles her hair. She is beautiful. A straight nose, fine cheekbones, and a porcelain chin he feels like cupping in his hands.

She drops her head, turns to catch him looking at her, brows slightly arched. "It's getting cool," she says. "Would you mind terribly?"

"I'm sorry. I was just caught up in the beauty of the moment." Did he say that?

She smiles again, takes his arm. "Shall we go, Mr. Wong?"

He is aglow. "Where to?" he asks.

"Oh, I don't know." Her body presses against his as she turns to him, her face inches from his. "Any ideas?"

He is intoxicated by her closeness, almost choking on his reply. "Uh, h-how about the Colophon Cafe?"

Hope

"Sure, Fairhaven. That's a wonderful choice." She grabs for his hand. He holds hers for a few moments, then lets go because his palms are sweating.

They get into his old Volvo. "Hope you don't mind if I roll the window down a little. There's a slight leak from the exhaust manifold."

Jean grimaces, pulling her coat tighter, then laughs. "Almost like a buggy ride, huh?"

Wong nods and laughs, too. They drive to Fairhaven along the Boulevard at the water's edge. Clouds scud by under a slivered moon that hangs above the water; the islands are like huge shadowy ships run aground in the night. Soft music floats from the radio.

"You never did tell me why you came to Marthasville," she says.

Wong hesitates. "It was my former wife. She had relatives out here."

"Oh yes. You mentioned in July that you were divorced. You've got a daughter, right? Six years old?" She looks at him, curious.

Wong thinks for a moment. "She's seven." He concentrates on the road, though the traffic is light as he pulls off the Boulevard into Fairhaven. It is the oldest part of the city, a historical district revamped for upscale tourists. It boasts eateries, coffee shops, bookstores, pottery stores, and galleries. He finds a parking space in front of the bookstore, a rarity.

"What's her name?" she asks, still in the car.

"Nancy." Wong steps out of the car, walks around to the other side, opens the door for her. "My daughter's name is Nancy."

"No, no. I mean your ex-wife's name."

"Cindy. And what did you say your ex-husband's name was?" Her daughter was with him for the weekend in Vancouver, B.C.

"Sahn-Jen Wei."

He looks at her, but she seems more reserved now as they enter the combination bookstore/cafe. At the counter he orders hot chocolate for both of them and a brownie for himself. She begs off on dessert. She sees an open booth and claims it.

He pays and carries the tray over, sits down, and glances at her.

"Thank you," she says.

"You're welcome." He smiles, then looks around. This late in the evening, the crowd is mostly young people—college students—though a few older folks are about. The aroma of food permeates the place: African Peanut Soup, Mexican Corn and Bean Soup, desserts, and coffee. He leans back and notices the high ceiling and, to the left, the ancient, red brick wall behind the counter. It is an elegance of old places.

The motif of the café is cows, especially Holsteins. A mournful cow gazes at customers from a mural on the brick wall. There are Holstein t-shirts, cards, aprons, and hats for sale. A cord of lighted cows hangs alongside the paneled wood next to the booths. Perhaps the owner was once a dairy farmer, he thinks.

His gaze returns and he sees her lips move, but can barely hear her now above the sudden buzz of conversation, laughter, the clatter of dishes, and the hiss of the espresso machine. He cups his hand to his ear.

"Did you enjoy the play?" she asks again, louder.

He nods. "Did you?"

"Yes, indeed! But what a tragedy! For Desdemona and for Othello."

"Life is tragedy." He shrugs, sipping his hot chocolate and nibbling on his brownie. The espresso machine dies down. "Sure you don't want a piece?"

"No thanks." She extends her hand, palm out. "But that's what we talked about before, didn't we? In the used-book store." She is referring to when they first met at Anderson's Books. She leans back and looks fixedly at him. "I'm curious about you!" She sips her drink, waiting for a reply.

He ignores the remark. "Shakespeare has a knack for tragedy, doesn't he? There's your favorite and mine: *Othello* and *Macbeth*. Then there's *Hamlet*, *King Lear*, *Romeo and Juliet*, *Julius Caesar*, and probably a lot more lesser known ones."

"Which one is most like you?" she asks, not letting him sidetrack.

The question takes him aback. "W-what makes you think I'm a tragic figure?" His mouth is slack, eyes disbelieving.

"Woman's intuition. Maybe some of that psychology I took as a student in college. Psychology was almost a minor." She smiles, but it is a tight smile, not relaxed and warm as before.

But she can only be probing. He finishes his brownie. She can't know anything about me! he thinks, as he recalls those murders for "operational expediency" so long ago. He almost blurts out a confession, the urge so strong within him. But he is wise enough to know that now is not the time. He remains tightlipped, chewing, a frown furrowing his brow.

He stares into the night, through the café windows. A couple is standing and talking under the streetlamp's feeble glare, the boy leaning against the long, vertically scalloped ridges of the lamppost. Sometimes he wishes for the guilelessness of youth—to have his life back, before Vietnam, then in some way leapfrogging the war so that he can grow old without nightmares. Maybe even die of old age, which is not a foregone conclusion for him.

"What do you need to know about me?" he asks, shrugging, trying an artful dodge. "That I like you? The answer is yes." He focuses on her face. "We don't have to learn everything about each other in one night, do we?" He smiles.

She smiles back. "But I do believe you are a man who is so full of surprises!" She stares at him for several moments. "You're intriguing— different in some way. There's a certain air about you, a tragic air . . . " she keeps harping.

He chuckles, without smiling, then finishes his hot chocolate. "Is this 'show and tell' on the first date?" She *is* perceptive, uncannily so; and he wonders if his guilt and sin are so easily read by his demeanor, or are they somehow etched on his face, a faint shadow cast from the smoldering fires of his conscience. All of a sudden, he is weary. Bone tired. His body visibly slumps on the soft bench.

"Oh, God! I'm not being too much fun, am I? I'm sorry," she says, noticing, then tapping him on his forearm. "It's a hobby of mine, psychoanalyzing people. I sometimes think I should have been a psychiatrist instead of a lawyer."

Two wonderful professions! Wong thinks. There is an awkward silence. The promise of earlier in the evening gradually dissipates. Suddenly, he straightens and shakes himself, as if awakening, gathers some energy, sighs loudly. "Want to browse?" he asks.

"Sure!"

They rise and make their way from the cafe to the books. Reference and large picture books are straight back in a room by themselves. Biographies and self-help books are shelved in a small enclosure to the right. But Wong's inclination is to novels, and he is drawn to those papered and imagined worlds of words. Jean follows. He moves slowly among the bookshelves, scanning titles, sidestepping around other customers.

"Here's a good book," he says, plucking it from a high shelf. She steps forward, curious. He shows her *Love in the Time of Cholera*, by Gabriel Garcia Marquez. "It's a love story."

"Oh, you're a romantic, are you?" she asks, smiling, as she holds the book in her hands. He feels himself falling under the charm of her smile, as if he were caught in an undertow, and wonders if he shouldn't just succumb. Standing next to her as she reads the cover flap, he inhales the clean fragrance of her. He almost swoons; it's been so long.

"N-no, I only like good books," he manages a reply.

"Whew! A fifty-one-year-old love story!" She looks at him, eyes twinkling. "Can you love someone for fifty-one years?"

A pointed question. "It's fifty-one years of unrequited love." He regards her quizzically. She is anything but coy. He moves to another bookshelf. She veers off, looking on her own.

"Here," she calls to him, "you've suggested a book for me. Here's one for you." She reaches and pulls out *The Joy Luck Club*, by Amy Tan, and hands it to him. "It's about the Chinese. About mothers and daughters, the old country and the new. You do read about the Chinese, don't you?" She smiles, shoulders hunched up, looking at him sideways, as if suddenly shy. And he feels that tug toward her, not only because of her beauty but because she is Chinese, and that is a defining part of his makeup, even though he is *so* American.

"Yes, I was thinking about reading it. I've seen it before, but I never got around to it." He studies the bookcover, and smiles.

"It's a good book."

"You've got a good book, too," he replies, pointing to Marquez's book in her hand.

H o p e

"It's not depressing, not tragic?" she asks.

"Is love depressing? No. It has hope. And mine?"

"It has hope."

The human condition is based on hope. Hope as an escape valve from death. Hope for a longer and better life. Hope for love as an antidote to loneliness. No other animal goes about his life looking to the future the way humans do. Most creatures are caught up in the present; they may prepare for the future, like squirrels caching nuts, but do they ever hope for a better future? Not likely; having hope as salvation from the present is a human trait.

And Wong has hope. He has hope when he enters Jean's home, a small Victorian overlooking the bay, not far from downtown. He has hope when she prepares the tea, and they sit together on the sofa listening to soft music. He has hope when he reaches across to her, cupping her chin in his hands, pulling her close to him, kissing her.

He melts in the moment, dreamlike, when he unbuttons her blouse, frees her breasts for his caresses. He feels the ache in his loins, and half expects to clamber through the clouds of sleep and awaken, grasping air and himself. But he feels her, rubs his hands over skin like smooth silk. They do not speak. The music pulses to the beats of their hearts.

He lies back. Her lips croon and flutter over his nipples; her tongue slides downward, flicks over his penis, continues downward. She puts her mouth over his big toe, sucking on it. He moans in anticipation, the erotic symbolism of it all. She moves back up, now putting her mouth over him, twirling her tongue around him. He moans with pleasure. "It has been so long," he whispers. "So long." She smiles, teasing him, then teeters him on a knife-edge of exquisite agony.

"Yes . . . y-yes," he gasps. He is lost in time, lost in the incurable pleasure of it. Then, he feels a small stirring deep within, like a flute's small, thin note hanging in the air. Slowly, so slowly, the note gathers volume and rises in intensity. Then the other instruments suddenly jump in, drowning him in a deafening crescendo . . . an explosion to silence. Wong shudders, eyes flickering, then lies spent and smiles. And has hope.

· · · · ·

Whenever he reaches for her, it is like he is reaching into his past. To the time when he was a child and all he ever knew were Chinese and all he ever spoke was Cantonese. Back to when his grandmother spewed out invective about bad boys like a dragon breathed out fire. She singed the pants off miscreants, but if you paid heed and did as you were told, she always rewarded you.

Lying in the bed, he smiles at the recollection. He feels a long way from his childhood, from his culture. But this woman beside him, she is his Chinese half, he thinks. Gazing into her eyes, he saw the slant eyes looking back at him, and saw in them a mirror of himself, his background, his culture. Their ancestry flows like different strands of the same rope.

Since that first night, he had gone out with her two more times, once to a restaurant and local tavern for music, the second time to a movie. It wasn't often, since Jean had to arrange times when her ex-husband could take care of her daughter, Mei. She didn't feel right with Wong staying overnight if Mei was in the house.

During those weeks, it was like the magic of Mercury had worn off him; he had fallen out of her spell. Perhaps it was the sex, the comfort of a warm body to chase away the blues. Perhaps it was more. He wasn't sure. Certainly, it seemed that Jean was more interested in him than Mercury was. And a pretty woman's interest, in and of itself, was a magnet to a man's soul.

Last night they had gone to a different restaurant, a Thai cafe in Fairhaven. He had tried the red curry chicken, she the cashew chicken. The meal melted in his mouth, exquisite on his palate, and he had thought he had died and gone to heaven; it was that good.

Back at her house, in a confessional mood somehow—perhaps the Thai restaurant, his Chineseness and hers, the tying together of the Asian strings that wove their existence together at that point in time—he told her about Vietnam. About the Mama-san and the girl. Much to his disbelief, she did not berate him, did not vilify him, did not hate him.

He looks at her now. Her breathing is shallow and slow. A look of peace is on her face as she sleeps, not much different from the acceptance and trust of the evening before when he had bared his soul and told all.

He had expected the worst last night, but she had just sat in silence looking at him for a while.

"Oh, Dave," she said, rubbing her arms in the cool house. She got up to turn the thermostat setting higher. "All those years you must have suffered. I knew there was a tragic air about you!"

"You mean, I don't sicken you?"

"No, I can understand. When I was in high school, I was not part of the clique, you know, those little groups of popular students."

"You? I would think you would have no problem with your beauty."

She made a wry face. "I'm Chinese." A statement like his mother once told him. A forever mark no matter how American you are. "A lot of girls like to have girlfriends, too, you know. To do all that girl talk and all those sort of things. I never did that, never had close girlfriends. And, yeah, maybe I did go out with some of the popular Caucasian boys in the school. Maybe that kind of perturbed the white girls." She shrugged.

"But I killed a Mama-san and a girl! My own kind! Our kind! A girl younger than Mei!"

At that, she turned away. "But I understand."

He sat in shocked silence. How could she understand? "You're too liberal." He was angry. In his self-flagellation, he hated what he was, hated the ready acceptance of some people who said they understood, hated those who patronized him. By so doing he felt they condoned his acts which, in his own mind, were unpardonable.

He got up from the sofa, stalked back and forth on the old fir floors. "You don't really understand!" he shouted.

"I understand that you were different and that caused you to kill."

He stopped pacing. "Yes. I was different."

"And I'm different, Dave."

He looked at her, the upturned face, the dark brown eyes, and sighed. Her difference was minor compared to his. No act of hers could have instilled the kind of guilt and agony he still felt for that act so long ago, which seemed like yesterday to him. Her beauty would never have isolated her from American society, and her gender would never have put her in the kind of position he was put into.

"We are different, aren't we? And you trust me? Around your daughter? Knowing what I have done."

She hesitated. "What you have done is in the past. The man I know now is not like the man you were. Those were extenuating circumstances in a wartime situation."

It was the most immediate acceptance of his actions he had ever known, and something he would have expected out of the mouth of a lawyer. "Is that from a defense attorney defending an accused murderer?"

She sat up then. "Damn you, Dave! I'm trying to help and all you're doing is flogging yourself."

"Maybe that's all I know."

"If that's all you know, then this relationship will go nowhere," she sniffed.

"I find it surprising, though, how you as a woman can accept so readily what I have done." He was back on the sofa, eyes focused on her.

She screwed up her face, pausing, and drew her legs up onto the chaise lounge while mulling over his statement. "I don't know if that is the right wording, 'readily accept.' I understand why you did it, as I said before." The light from the floorlamp spilled across her face.

"You accept the fact that it was wrong? You don't condone my actions, do you?"

"No, no. I don't condone them. Don't get me wrong there. They were morally wrong and totally reprehensible acts." And here she looked at him intently. "But I don't think the person who did them is totally reprehensible."

He did not know whether he should sit in the glow of her affirmation or to take her statement with a grain of salt. He smiled. "Ah, but did you know that for some twenty-odd years, I refused to put the blame on myself. Only after months with Dr. Erlandson, my psychiatrist, did I finally realize that I had to live up to what I had done. And that what I had done was commit murder. Murder. Pure and simple. Even though it was in a wartime situation. *That*, my dear, is hard for me to live with."

Her eyes seemed to blaze with a passion, a missionary zeal. "But you've accepted it?"

"Yes."

"Maybe God and Jesus Christ are watching over you." That was the crack that first appeared between them.

"Oh, Jesus, don't, please. I don't need any sermonizing. God left me a long time ago."

It was a crack that would widen when the religion that poured out of her congealed, freezing his passion into indifference.

"God doesn't leave anyone. Jesus is with all of us every—"

"Stop it!" He was up on his feet again. "If I want a sermon, I'll go to church."

"—day of our . . ." Her voice trailed off. She was taken aback by his vehemence. "I-I'm sorry. I didn't mean to offend you."

He stood before her, his face suffused with anger. "I don't need you spouting your Christian philosophy." His eyes glinted, reflecting the light like hard, cold metal. "You're Chinese. Why aren't you a Buddhist or Confucianist?"

"I-I was raised a Christian."

"Well, so was I. But I am not one now and will never be one again!" He was still pacing. Then, more quietly, "But I guess I am not a Buddhist either, at least a good one. I enjoy too many material things. Maybe a Confucianist?" He shrugged.

"Yes, maybe," she murmured. "But, I'm curious. Why do you hate Christians so much?"

"I don't. Some of my best friends are Christians." He laughed. "What I hate is the pomposity, the bombast, the intractability of righteousness. As if God, if he exists, wears only a vested garment. And sin? Original sin? To be born and live is to sin? What a crock of shit!"

"It's just that there is a lot of opportunity to sin."

"And, yes, those are conscious decisions. Like mine was. But how can innocence, like a child, sin by its very existence? Sure, temptation is there. But if he doesn't succumb? Is he still full of sin?" He let the question hang in the air.

"I-I don't know. I'm afraid I don't know the answers to the esoteric questions about religion."

"Well, I can't say that I do either."

They sat in silence for a while. Wong looked about—eyeing the old, gray, speckled wallpaper, the high ceiling, the old floor—wondering what to do. He did not yet know this side of her. It was new to him. Did he really want to become involved with a Christian?

"But I do remember the moon festival," Jean said, hoping to cover common ground. "It was a Buddhist holiday celebrating a princess's crossing of a bridge from the earth to the moon to meet her lover. Right?"

He smiled at the memories. "Yes. Baht ngit, sup uhm. Eighth month, fifteenth day of the lunar calendar. The bridge would only form on that day. I remember Ahpo coming out and lighting the joss and punk sticks, shoving them into the sand. Then having almond cookies, haam bow, rock candy after we prayed, bye sun, huh?"

She smiled. "Yes, sounds just like ours."

"You know my grandmother never believed that we landed on the moon. My aunt told me Ahpo said, 'Bullshit! No can do! The moon goddess live up there. They'—and here she means the astronauts—'go hide someplace for ten days and then they come back and tell they go moon.' To this day she claims all those pictures on TV were shot on a special stage." They both laughed. He was feeling better now, more mellow. He looked to her, softly asked, "Why don't you sit here?" He patted the couch next to him.

She smiled, got up and crossed the floor to sit next to him. He draped his right arm about her shoulders. "I've missed you," he said.

"I'm sorry it's taken so long for us to be alone again." Her ex-husband had to skip his last visitation with Mei because of a business trip.

He sighed. "It has been a while, hasn't it?" He tilted her chin up to him and bent down to kiss her.

· · · · ·

She was like a narcotic to him, when the rush was all he lived for. He found her body fascinating and enticing, almost a new experience, as if he had never had a woman before. They explored the nooks and crannies of each other's bodies, giving pleasure, melting like old lovers into each other's arms. In those early weeks, she seemed to fit him like an easily gripped tennis racket or like an old ball glove that slipped comfortably over his hand.

But, gradually, in spite of the physical side that fit like hand and glove, the psychic side was not quite so compatible. The driving wedge was her wholehearted and blind, in his mind, acceptance of religion. They argued over it almost incessantly, since the night of his confession.

On weekends when Mei was away with her father, they would sit around early Sunday morning at the breakfast table discussing their views. Jean would then dress for church, but Wong would adamantly refuse to go with her. In his mind, she was the liberated liberal, the church-going do-gooder, who cried for the sociopath, the psychopath, though he had brutally murdered some poor innocent victim. It wasn't all his fault because of his extenuating social upbringing, his underprivileged socioeconomic background. Or, in a lot of cases, they cried for the criminal because the priest or pastor said they should. They poured forgiveness over the perpetrator like holy water; never mind the poor victim or the victim's family.

Morality, then, was a pier with sandy underpinnings to be washed away by the tide of society's indifference, as if family had no say in it, as if a sense of discipline was eroded away by the outgoing tide of loss of the nuclear family.

He had heard her say too many times that such-and-such a person should not be tried so harshly for such a crime because it wasn't his fault. A knocking down of the sentence from first-degree murder to second-degree or even manslaughter. And it ate at him. He would rail at her, at the inequity of her system of values, and she would just look at him and say, "It's in my nature. It's in my Christian nature." That would aggravate him to no end and he would think, She has never been tested, never been victimized to a mortal extent. Through the fire of their arguments, he would feel her accusations about his great sins, though she never said a word about them specifically.

He would rail at her, "What do you know about death! It has never happened to anyone you loved! You have never even killed an animal! What do you know? And yet you defend people who commit murder!"

Her accusations would shoot like laser beams from her eyes. She was accusing and forgiving at the same time. He hated her for it. Hated that aspect of their relationship. He did not want forgiveness from her, did not want it as a foundation for any love that could surface between them. Because he felt that his crimes were against the Mama-san and girl, against his race, against himself, and not against her, though she was the same race.

He thought he perceived in her a Christ figure, a Christ mentality, as if she were ordained to carry the load of the world's sins on her shoulders. Maybe that was one reason she was a public defender. To save the world, you must save the most pitiful, outcast members of society.

"I don't want to save the world," he once told her, "only myself."

She had replied, "You do that by saving the world first." He had looked at her then and just shook his head.

But he always succumbed to the lure of her body, and wondered about himself.

The wedge was there.

Chapter 20

Older

A sense of unease creeping into her existence—not foreboding, not tragedy, just unease—is how she characterizes it to herself. Ever since her mother's call last weekend.

"Mercury, you're not getting any younger, you know. Another November has rolled around and you're thirty-six! And still unmarried!"

"I was once, you know." Though her mother never seems to mention her short marriage to Spencer.

"Oh, he was a jackass! I don't count him."

And he was, she thinks. One of the rare occasions when her mother was right and she, oh, so terribly wrong.

"He's not bothering you anymore, is he?"

"No, Mom. Uh . . ."

"You're hesitating. Is he still bothering you?"

"We're divorced, Mom. He's not bothering me anymore." Which was mostly true, since Spence lived in Seattle. Every six to eight months he would come up to Marthasville to visit friends, get drunk, and appear at her doorstep professing his love. While not physically violent—though the subtle threat was there—he violated her sense of ease, her equanimity, her tranquility.

After the first six months of marriage, she saw the first spark of his irascibility when he went after a woman driver who had cut him off. When she said, "Stop it!", he had rained curses on her, calling her a stupid bitch, a cunt, a fucking whore, just like all the other women he had known.

In the beginning, he begged for forgiveness and she gave it. But weeks later, the incidents repeated themselves and the mental abuse would start all over again. Anything could trigger it: dirty dishes, dirty laundry, not cooking on time, forgetting to pick up his dry cleaning. His temper would flare, they would argue, he would get drunk and more abusive.

He once drop-kicked Pickle into the wall because he thought the cat litter smelled. She hadn't cleaned it out frequently enough to suit him. The cat shrieked and ran for cover, not seriously hurt. It had scared the hell out of Mercury. She screamed at him, calling him a goddamned bastard. He looked at her, cold eyes in a tight smile. She settled down, suddenly scared, breathing heavily, went to the bedroom and slammed the door and locked it. She would retreat into a shell, a mental den that only she could inhabit, and he would leave the apartment. They wouldn't speak to each other for days, living like strangers.

Finally, when she couldn't take it anymore, she moved out and filed for divorce. It was just short of two years, but it had felt like a lifetime.

"If he keeps bothering you, you'd better get a restraining order."

Mercury felt her skin crawl. She had heard about all those poor, helpless women who had gotten restraining orders and then been gunned down by their ex-lovers. She had wondered then how far away she was from that with Spencer. Once, appearing on her doorstep, drunk as usual, he had pushed past her into the house and pulled his knife out and played with it in front of her, flicking the six-inch half-serrated blade open and closed, talking to her in a normal tone about their old relationship.

She couldn't take her eyes off the blade, fascinated and repulsed by it at the same time, thinking, That could be the instrument of my death, and I can't do a damned thing about it. She got him out the door by putting on a strong front, telling him she was late for a patient appointment.

Out of a feeling of desperation and self-preservation, she had gone out and bought a handgun, had even taken the women's handgun course offered by the county parks and recreation. She had told no one about the gun. She felt safer with it in the house. Finally, she could sleep better at night.

Older

Since the divorce, there were a few men, but nothing lasting. They had come and gone in her life like the leaves of autumn, hanging around for a while before being blown away by the wind.

"It would be nice if I could be a grandmother," her mother said, sounding like a broken record every time she called.

Once more Mercury reminded her, "Mom, you're already a grandmother. Richard has two kids, remember?"

"But he's a son. I want my one and only daughter to be happy, to have a family of her own."

Mercury withdrew into herself, felt the fiber of her being turn hollow because she knew her mother was right, that life alone is not much of a life at all. For all of her activities, the sports, the friends—male friends, too—she still had no claim on a single man's heart. Nor had she given, since Spencer, her heart. She had love to give and no one to give it to. Her mother made her wonder why.

Was she setting her sights too high? Were all the good men gone, dead, disappeared, or married away for the duration?

For a while, there was Wong. She liked his sensitivity, even his shyness. She saw him start to lose the pudginess of the middle-aged man he was and turn into the fit young man of long ago, as if he were molting like a snake—not into a larger skin—but into the smaller skin of a fit man. She found him handsome, though she was sure he would not consider himself so. He was not the vainglorious and abusive man that Spence was—at least to her, and that was both a relief and an attractive trait to her. So far, he had never lied, deceived, or betrayed a trust as Spencer had done on so many occasions.

Earlier in their relationship, if you could call it that, there was that mutual liking, that sense of intrigue about the other person that could blossom into the flower of romance. It was there, and she knew it. She liked the feeling of being sought after, that her very presence could bring a smile to a man's face. It had been so long.

"Maybe there aren't too many good men left, Mom."

"Maybe you're too picky, honey. Maybe you're too picky. Sometimes you don't have to be head-over-heels in love. Love grows, you know."

What could she have said to that? She gently changed the subject, asked how her father was doing. He sent his love. They rang off. She promised to call her mother soon.

The gloom of November hangs heavy with the curtains of rain. The Nooksack is threatening to flood. Water is threatening the dikes near Fir Island in Skagit County.

"Flood warnings for the Skykomish, Snohomish, Skokomish, Duwamish, Green, and Cedar Rivers," the TV weatherman warns. All those -ish rivers, she thinks, so lovely on the tongue, so powerful a threat to lowland dwellers.

She pulls the coverlet over her as she lies on the couch, watching as the helicopter camera pans the flooded plain below. She pulls Pickle next to her. He purrs with affection, then lies down next to her face. She can feel his heart beat against her cheek, a steady rhythm of love for her. A rhythm of happiness and contentment.

Can I find happiness? she wonders. The upcoming holidays hold for her the specter of great loneliness. Suddenly, she thinks of Wong, of his sins, of his loneliness, and wonders. It would have been nice to read his writing, some of his poems. But she knows she will never be the one to initiate anything now. It is too late. Her interest has died on the altar of truth. She cannot hide her disdain for what he has done, his great sins.

She turns her gaze from the television toward the picture window and watches the rain speckle the road underneath the street lamp. It is going to be a long winter, she thinks. She nuzzles and pets the cat, sighs, and pulls the coverlet tighter about her.

Wong sits at his desk on this rainy evening, thinking, penning his thoughts. He listens to music. Country & Western. "Music with life experience," the station brags. He agrees. It is so true. He listens to songs about heartaches, broken hearts, love gone astray, and true love.

This technical writer cum poet cuts, slices, and dices his lines, deletes and inserts words, searching for a rhythm to his poem. He titles it "Rain." He has told no one but Mercury about his hobby, and regrets even that, believing that she now thinks of him as a fool.

He has had a couple of poems published in local newspapers. Funny, no one has confronted him about them. Either his friends and colleagues never read those papers or they just wouldn't acknowledge him as a poet. He never used a pseudonym.

When he is finished, he steps back and reads the poem aloud to himself, listening for rhythm, listening for the smooth transitions that a good poem must have, like the shading of darkness into dawn. This act of writing is his pouring of light into the dark abyss of his soul.

Rain

> Sometimes
> I sit and watch
> the tiny rivulets of rain
> stream down the windows.
> Listen to the raindrops
> drum their cadence
> on the near sidewalk.
> Seek the sounds of
> soulfully smooth music
> and gaze at the people walking by,
> mere silhouettes in the
> cold shroud of autumn's rain.
>
> On this gray, lazy day
> I wonder
> how time has slipped away,
> like evening rain
> into the dark chasm of the night,
> across the middle years
> of my life.
>
> And I think of you.

He likes the ring of it on this rainy night. He reads it once more, claps his hands together, satisfied. He leans back in his chair and he thinks, not of Jean, but of Mercury.

Chapter 21

Nancy

"So, how old are you now?"

"Oh, Daddy! You know how old I am! I'm eight years old!"

Wong laughs, as he glances at his daughter. It was his weekend and he had driven down to Seattle to pick her up. He was in the process of making dim sum—Chinese dumplings—and barbecue pork. But he had forgotten the five spice seasoning, so they are driving to the grocery store.

"You have your seatbelt on?"

She pulls on the belt, glowing with the anticipation of the good Chinese food she will be eating. "Yes, Daddy."

"Good. I don't want you hurt, not with all the good food and fun we're going to have this weekend. You like shue mai, char siu, fried rice, tempura, huh?"

The snow flurries are thicker now, but there is no buildup on the road. He looks across at his daughter once again. She is hapa-haole, half white. She has brown hair and a pretty face, eyes slightly slanted.

"Daddy, tempura is Japanese."

"You're too smart for an eight-year-old, you know?"

She giggles. "Mommy makes me study."

"Oh? And how is Mommy these days?"

She frowns for a moment. She has to give an adult opinion. "Don is good for her . . . I think."

Wong smiles. At least she hasn't gotten around to calling her stepfather "Daddy" yet.

"That's good, honey. That's good."

The traffic is backed up at the stoplight. Wong tests his brakes;

the car slips sideways a bit. He corrects the small skid, a frown on his face. It is getting worse, he thinks.

The flakes are getting bigger, falling in slant parallel lines driven by a northwest wind. The traffic moves, but too fast, Wong thinks. They can hear the wind: a murmur rising to a howl, then cascading back down to a murmur—as if a giant had to take deep breaths before each howl. This is unusual for February, he believes.

"Daddy, it's getting worse." She is looking out her side window.

"I know, honey. We're almost there. We won't stay long and then we'll hurry back and start cooking. Okay?"

"Okay." She looks at him and smiles.

He is being tailgated by an American car, a large steel relic with faded paint. An Oldsmobile or Cadillac. Wong speeds up a little. Get off my ass! The car drops off a little. They are almost at the grocery store, which is just past the light and then a right turn down a small hill. The car ahead of him goes straight. The light changes to yellow. Suddenly a large red car in the oncoming lane shoots in front of him, making a left turn.

"Shit!" Wong exclaims, stomping on the brake. He regrets the expletive but is too busy to apologize. The bald tires of the Volvo slide on the newly formed ice. It is like slow motion. Wong, panic-stricken, turns the wheel hard right, stares at his daughter with wide eyes. Then the sickening crunch of metal on metal, glass shattering. And another sound, more sickening than he had ever imagined. The thud of his daughter's head against the hard steering wheel. Somehow her seatbelt has worked loose. He looks in astonishment and fright as his car careens to a halt against another car.

He sits stupefied. Then he unbuckles himself, fights to get his arms around his daughter, seeing the conscious light of her eyes fade, the blood dripping from her mouth. He struggles to get his door open, exits, runs to the passenger side, opens her door, then grabs and carries his daughter outside, cradling her head, yelling, "My daughter! My daughter! My God! My God!"

Cars stop. A man in a business suit rushes out from a white Mercedes, asks, "Can I help?"

"Yes, please! It's my daughter."

"I've got a cell phone," he says. "I'll call 911." He rushes to his car.

Wong lays his daughter on the sidewalk, takes his coat off and covers her. The snow is still falling, flakes covering the girl's face.

"Let's get her under some blankets," a woman suggests. "I've got some in my trunk."

Wong kneels, cradling his daughter's head in his lap. Other cars stop. People congregate. The woman returns and lays one blanket on the snowy pavement. Wong lifts Nancy onto it, cradling her head. They drape the other blanket over her.

"There," she says.

"T-thanks." Wong turns his head, looking for the man with the cell phone, who is rushing back from his car.

"I got 'em. They're sending an ambulance right now. They're not more than a few minutes away, they claim. Hang on, buddy!"

He feels so helpless, kneeling beside her. A pool of blood collects under Nancy's mouth, dyeing the shallow snow crimson, staining the side of her mouth. He brushes her mouth with the cuff of his shirtsleeve. The woman with the blankets kneels beside him. She turns Nancy's head so that she does not choke on the blood. She gently pries Nancy's mouth open, making sure her tongue is free, that she does not choke on it. She produces a bandanna and tries to staunch the blood, then realizing her futility, uses it as a blotter under the girl's chin. The blood keeps streaming, a slow, frightening flow. The woman looks at Wong, worry etched on her face.

He is crying, sniffling, "Oh, God! Oh, God! Don't let her die!"

"Anything I can do to help?" the man with the cell phone asks. No reply. The man then turns to the woman, and they both look to Wong. But Wong is suddenly gone, a man out of time.

The blood. The blood of his daughter has catapulted him back into Vietnam. He looks at his hands, crying, "No! No! Get the fucking blood off me, you bastard!" He stares wild-eyed. "No! No! I won't do it. I won't kill! I won't!" He suddenly jumps up.

The man tries to calm Wong, putting his arm on Wong's shoulder. "No!" Wong screams, pulling away from the human contact. "Never again! Haven't I paid enough for my sins?"

What Wong sees is the girl smiling up at him, dripping blood from fangs like a vampire's, an obscene grin as flesh decomposes before his eyes. He hides his face in his arms, but cannot hide from the vision. Then the girl's face changes into Nancy's, the grin fading, eyes glazing. Nancy dies before his very eyes, blood gushing from her mouth.

"No!" he sobs. "My God! Not Nancy! Please!" Then he hears a loud cackle as the demon once more changes back into the Vietnamese girl. She leers at him, licking up the blood alongside her face with a long tongue, then cackles shrill laughter. Wong squeezes his eyes shut and covers his ears with his hands, trying to shut out the high-pitched laughter. And her utterances, "Now-oou-now!"

In the distance sirens wail, growing louder as the seconds pass. "Thank God!" the woman cries. "Oh, God, I hope they're in time!"

Two police cars and an ambulance arrive, red lights flashing. The ambulance slows and threads its way through the accident scene while the police secure the area. Two emergency medical technicians jump out of the ambulance, black bags at the ready.

"She's lost a lot of blood," the woman tells them.

"Okay, got ya. We'll take over from here."

The woman gets up, relieved. "What's her chances?"

"Don't know yet, ma'am. What we gotta do is assess and stabilize her. If you'll excuse me." He bends close to Nancy. "She's breathing," he says to the second technician.

"How did this happen?" the first technician asks the woman. "Has she been unconscious the whole time? Has she moved? Has her breathing changed?"

She answers the questions.

The other technician kneels alongside Nancy. "Is she shocky?"

"No, I don't think so, Bill. But once we get her vitals, we'll get a better handle on it. Test for shock, will you, while I do the primary survey?" Tom's hands move with a measured hurriedness as he reaches behind Nancy to first feel her cervical vertebrae, then her spine. Next, he feels her shoulders and around her waist, then down her legs, searching for anything out of the ordinary. Then he examines her head.

"No obvious deformity," he concludes, "except for that nasty bump on her head."

"100/70," Bill says. "Heart rate 110. Doesn't look like shock."

More sirens wail in the distance as the first EMT proceeds to hook up an IV.

"I think we got inadequate respiratory drive, Tom. I'm gonna ventilate her." Bill pulls out a mask. He covers her nose and mouth with it. A tube connects the mask to a bag, which he squeezes. "I got her on positive ventilation."

New sirens wail, growing louder.

They watch her for a while. "Good, help me shift her onto the spine board," Tom directs. They lift her gently, then secure her onto the board.

"How's she doing, Tom?" Two paramedics appear on the scene.

Tom looks at the paramedics. "You might have to intubate her, Randy," he says.

"We'll take over from here," Randy says. "And thanks."

Randy looks her over, doing another quick primary survey. Then he checks her ears, nose, and finally her eyes. "Her left pupil is blown." Dilated. "We're gonna have to intubate. Anybody do a neuro check yet?" A neurological test for positive response.

"No," Tom replies.

"I'll do it now," Ken, the second paramedic, says. He pinches her on the arm. The arm pulls away. "Good sign," he adds.

"Great!" Randy replies. He tries to force Nancy's mouth open. "She doesn't want to open up. Let's push some succinyl choline into her, will you, Ken?" It is a muscle relaxant.

"Let's get the gurney here, too," Randy adds. Bill takes off for one. "Where are the parents?"

Tom looks around, then asks the woman.

"Her father is over there," she replies, pointing. "But he seems to have problems of his own."

Randy looks over to Wong. The man in the business suit is still alongside, trying to soothe him. "We're gonna leave for the hospital soon," Randy says, looking at the woman. "Can you do us a favor and find out if he wants to go, or if he's capable of going?"

"Sure," she replies.

"What's your name?" Tom asks.

"Mabel."

"Well, Mabel, you did fine. She did fine," he tells Randy.

Randy nods. "Thank you, ma'am!" He is now able to open Nancy's mouth and inserts a long tube down her throat, into her trachea, then secures it with tape. "Okay, we're ready to move." They get off their knees, lift her and the spine board onto the low gurney, raise the gurney, and push through the small crowd.

Mabel turns and joins Wong and the man. "How is he?"

The man shakes his head. "He's just not communicating. Christ! I can't get through to the guy." He shrugs. "He keeps mumbling about his sins and how he's paid enough for them, like he's hallucinating. Maybe he's on drugs." The man throws his hands up in the air.

Mabel turns to Wong and tries to pull his hands from his ears. "Sir!" she shouts. "Sir! Do you want to travel with your daughter to the hospital?" But Wong only shakes his head and pulls his hands back, trying to block the noise of the demons in his mind.

"Sir!" she tries again, then shrugs helplessly.

"Hey, buddy! Hey!" the man tries shouting into Wong's face, but to no avail.

Tom rushes back. "Any luck?" he asks.

Mabel shakes her head.

"Look, we gotta go. If we can't bundle him in there with his daughter, would one of you mind driving him to the hospital? St. Mary's." He looks at Mabel and the man.

"Sure. Sure. I don't mind," Mabel volunteers.

"Thanks. Come in through the emergency entrance." With that he is gone. Shortly thereafter, the ambulances speed away in a hail of sound.

Mabel watches them go, then turns to the man. "Can you help me get him into my car?"

The man looks at her with doubt. "I'll try."

They both move up alongside Wong. Mabel tries to break through the wall he has erected. "Sir!" she speaks gently. "Let's go be with your daughter."

Mercury is in her car when she sees the ambulance pull up to the emergency entrance, lights flashing. The rear doors swing open. She can only see a small body, lying bundled on the gurney, before the whole crowd rushes through the double sliding glass doors. God! I hope the child is going to make it, she thinks.

She is early for her aerobics class and is dallying, lost in the rapture of one of her favorite songs playing on the radio. A Frankie Valle tune. She looks at her watch. 4:45. She decides to linger for this one song. But then she hears a car screech to a halt. She looks up and sees a white Ford stopping beside the ambulance. A woman gets out and helps a man out of the passenger side, supporting him, as if he too were injured. Mercury looks again. Is that Dave? she wonders. It is! Is something wrong with him? They disappear through the double doors.

Mercury looks again at her watch. Ten till. She turns the key to off, killing the song in midtune. She gets out. She is caught between the pull of her class and the pull of curiosity. God! I don't know if I want anything to do with the man! she thinks. But her steps are directed to the emergency room entrance.

Once inside, she sees the receptionist at the desk, and to the right, swinging double-wide doors. She peers through the two head-high windows into the room. She sees Wong sitting, head in his hands at the far end, a woman in light blue with a clipboard sitting next to him, talking. A man with a white stand-up collar sits on the other side of him. The woman who came in with him is pacing. No one else is in the room.

Nancy

When the pacing woman walks toward where Mercury is standing, Mercury pushes the double-wide doors apart and waves to her, knocking on the wooden door at the same time to attract her attention. The woman looks up and comes, curious.

"Yes?" she says.

"What's going on?" Mercury asks.

The woman frowns.

"I know him," Mercury points to Wong.

For a moment, the woman doesn't answer, her face saying, if you know him, why aren't you there for him? "His daughter. Terrible accident. Head injury. He's beside himself."

Mercury sucks in her breath. Oh, God! she thinks. For a moment, she teeters on the brink. She could just close the door and the book on him, forever—and just walk away. He would never know. She lets the door close; the woman turns and walks back across the room. Mercury stands a few feet from the doors, vacillating.

"Goddammit!" she mutters. "Goddammit!" She walks to the receptionist's desk, points to the phone. "May I? It's in-house."

"Sure, help yourself," the receptionist replies.

Mercury calls the workout room and asks one of her students to lead the class. She hangs up the phone, nods thanks to the receptionist, then strides back to the doors, pushing through. Wong is still seated, bent over, numbed, rocking back and forth.

The woman in blue is still talking. "Sir," her voice is showing some strain. "We need your signature to operate. Your daughter is in very serious condition. We need your permission."

"Sir, your daughter is in grave condition," the man says. "If you'd like to hold hands and pray for her, sir, I'd be glad to lead us." Mercury can now see the cross on his necklace.

The woman sighs, tries again. "SIR!"

Mercury taps her on the shoulder. "Here, let me try."

The woman is dubious. Mabel watches, curious.

"I really do know him," Mercury says, then asks, as an afterthought, "Do you really need his signature? It's life and death, isn't it? Why bother?"

The nurse sighs. "We'd like to have it, but will resuscitation efforts stop? No. The trauma team will work on the little girl, irrespective." She snaps the clipboard shut, stands, ready to give up.

"Let me try," Mercury says, nodding to the nurse.

"Dave," she calls out softly. "Dave." She stoops over, grabs his shoulders, shakes him gently. He looks at her, eyes as vacant as those of a dead man, then looks downward once more. Mercury tries again, then a third time. Then she gets up, sighs.

"He's like in a trance, you know," Mabel says. She introduces herself and explains what happened. "God, it was a ghastly sight. Seeing all that blood coming from her mouth." They both look to Wong again.

Mercury sits down beside him. "Dave, it's me! Mercury!" Slowly, he turns to her, eyes red in a drawn face.

"Why?" he asks, wondering why she is there.

"Dave, never mind why. We'll talk about why later. We need you to sign this form. Nancy needs emergency surgery."

The nurse holds the clipboard in front of him. "Sign here, please." He looks at the clipboard, signs mechanically, then falls back in his seat, staring at the opposite wall.

"Hallelujah!" the nurse says as she hurries through the double doors.

Mabel checks her watch. "Look, do you mind? I'm late. I was on my way to do some shopping. I've got some important errands to run." She looks at Wong, then Mercury. "Since you know him, I thought you'd . . ."

"Absolutely. I'll stay here with him a while. And, Mabel, thank you. Thank you very much. He's been through some hard times in his life. Maybe . . . maybe, this last incident is just too much."

Mabel nods, full of sympathy. "Take care, and best wishes. Oh, and what is the girl's name? I'd like to call back and see how things went."

"Nancy Wong."

"Good luck. I'll pray for her." She leaves, muted footsteps on the carpet.

Wong once again turns toward Mercury. "Why?" he asks.

She looks at him with pity. "Dave, I don't know. Sometimes God works in strange ways."

The chaplain, hearing this, nods. "Sir, it can indeed be hard to fathom God's designs in life. Why put a little girl in jeopardy? Only God knows. We are only mere mortals. We cannot begin to understand—"

"Don't give me that crap!" He stands up now, turning to face them. "What kind of God takes out his wrath on a child?"

"I mean to say that we are only—"

"Shut up!" Wong almost screams, covering his ears with his hands. The chaplain stands, shocked and humiliated, then excuses himself.

To Mercury, "Why are you here? How'd you get here?"

"I saw the ambulance come in, then that woman helping you."

"Well, you can go now. Don't waste any more of your time."

Mercury stands, tightlipped, anger starting to surge. "Are you sure?" Her eyes probe deep within his.

He stares into those clear blue eyes, caught in their spell. "No." He drops his gaze. "Please stay. At least a little while." He is a defeated man.

"Sure." She sits back down, the anger now dissipated.

He stands still for a moment, then starts pacing, a few steps across the carpeted room and then back. "It was the blood. God, it was the blood. I was useless. I-I couldn't even help my own daughter once I saw that blood. It was like I was back in the jungles and it was that little girl again. Her face came back to me—so clear. Then it started to decompose right in front of me. And she was laughing at me. A skull-faced grin." He shudders, suddenly cold.

Mercury stands, draws him near. He smells the sweet scent of her hair, her skin. "Thank you," he whispers. "Thank you."

She steps back and looks at him. "You going to be okay?"

"I'm gonna be okay. You don't have to stay."

She peers at him. "I'll stay until the doctor comes out."

He grabs her hand and squeezes. "Thanks."

They sit. Time trickles like grains of sand through an hourglass, but even slower, because they are counting every grain.

• • • • •

Wong is sitting by Nancy's side. They have wheeled her out of emergency surgery into a critical care room. An IV bottle hangs from a stand beside her bed, dripping glucose into a vein in her neck. Another needle is inserted into her arm.

He had been scared, more scared than he had ever been for his own life. They had waited and waited, hours on end it seemed, the minutes moving like a mountain climber clawing himself up a steep slope. Finally, the neurosurgeon had come out, introducing himself.

"We ran a CAT scan. Her brain is swollen," Dr. Stone had said, looking at the two of them. "She has what we call a generalized cerebral edema from a concussion. We had to go in and relieve the pressure. We drilled a little hole in her head and put a transducer in there to keep track of the pressure in the brain. We also gave here something called Manitol. That's a drug to control her fluids to help relieve the pressure in her skull."

Wong's eyebrows arch.

"She'll be peeing a lot," Stone says. "We want that. Her vital signs are good, but she's unconscious." He had looked at Mercury, then back to him. "And we don't know how long she'll be unconscious."

"What do you mean?" Wong asked.

"She's in a coma," Stone gently replied.

Wong felt Mercury's arm about him. He had almost swooned. "But, is t-that bad or good?" he managed to stammer.

"It's nature's way to heal a damaged brain. She's resting. All she needs now is rest."

"H-how will she be if . . . I-I mean when she comes out of it?"

Stone looked at him again. "You mean whether she will have any long-lasting brain damage? I'm sorry, Mr. Wong, I just can't tell right now. All we can do is hope."

So, once more, his life is centered around hope. He takes Nancy's hand, caressing it with his own.

He thinks of Mercury for a moment. She had left soon after Stone had talked to them. "Call me," she had said, "if you need help, call me." She had looked him straight in the eye. He said he would.

Talk, he thinks. Wasn't it a fact that if you talked to coma patients, they could hear you?

"Nancy . . . Nancy!" he gently massages the little hand in his, struggling for words. "Don't leave me. Don't die! Y-you are a part of me. Though . . . though . . ." he licks his lips; he feels as nervous as a kid put into a stage play against his will. "Your mother and I are no longer close, but you will always be close to me." He looks at her face. No recognition, no movement except for her slow breathing. "You are my life." He holds her hand with both of his, squeezing. "Come on, kiddo!" he begs, searching her face. "Don't die on me."

He continues talking, droning in a monotone, lost in the mantra of his own voice and thoughts. Pictures of her flash through his mind: her first bumbling steps, her first words when she had suddenly smiled up at him and said, "Dah-dah," when she was toilet trained and so proud of herself, and her first lugubrious day at kindergarten with her long face. "Don't worry!" he had said, ruffling her hair. "You'll like school." At the end of the day, she had come running into his arms, a big, beaming smile across her face. "Daddy! Daddy! That was fun!"

"I've always loved you, you know. Even though my love died for your mother . . ." He hangs his head, staring at the linoleum floor beneath the bed. "My love is forever for you." He looks up, wonder on his face. Was there a gentle pressure from her fingers? Or was he imagining it? He presses on her hand, but he does not feel a response.

Then he sits silent. A vision of the little girl he had killed in Vietnam comes to him. But this time, it is not a ghoul. It is her real face.

Wong gasps at the magnitude of what he had done. He had forever stolen a daughter from some parent. Some mother cried over the body of the dead girl, pulled her hair in lamentation, spilled unstoppable tears, cursed him to the deepest hell, swore eternal vengeance, endured unendurable grief.

Now, he truly understands. He feels an exquisite agony, his self-image cut away from him in strips like skin peeled from his body with a filleting knife. Peeling away the layers of his indifference, his shallowness, his excuses, his lies. True. He knew he had done wrong. He had felt guilt, suffered from nightmares. But, compared to now, it was only an uneasiness that weighed on him like a little kid's conscience when he has stolen someone's bicycle.

While Wong has lived under the brutal knife edge of the nightmares, they had not cut him as deeply as this. Now, he has been cut to the core. This . . . this would be a loss of his own flesh and blood. If Nancy died, it would be an amputation of a part of his self, a part of his soul severed and then flung to the high winds, shrieking in agony, blown to the four corners of the earth, unreachable, entropic, lost forever in pieces, quite impossible to glue together again.

Suddenly he can decipher the ghoulish girl's message, the nightmare at the accident scene: "Now-oou-now!" Now you know!

He bends over in his chair, resting his forehead against his hands. "Oh, God, what did I do? Is this punishment? Please, God, let her live. If anyone has to die, let me die. Take me! Take me!" His voice drops to a whimper.

He looks at the little girl in the hospital bed, sees the small rise and fall of her chest as she breathes, hears the rhythmic beep of the heart monitoring machine, sees the jagged pulses running across the monitoring screen—the electronic heartbeat of her life laid out before him.

He rubs his hand across her forehead. "God! Don't let her die!" He cries, his chest heaving as he weeps. He cries and cries, until his body can heave no more. Spent, he falls into a fitful sleep, slumped in his chair.

The nurse sees them through the sliding glass doorway. She comes in, checks on the little girl. She studies the monitor for heart rhythm, blood pressure, and respiration, then feels the girl's hand, examines the IV in her neck and the arterial line in her arm, checks the transducer in her skull.

She looks over to Wong and sighs. She goes to an adjacent room, grabs a blanket from the bed and returns, covering him with it.

She glides silently about the room, like a ghost.

Chapter 22

Icon

He is a silent man standing in a strange place, and is a stranger to them. They turn their faces to him, almost en masse, as if he were a Messiah, capturing their attention by his very presence. No one has done such a thing before, just standing there staring at them. Not friendly, not unfriendly.

A soft uneasiness creeps over them, and the tones of their conversations have shifted from lighthearted laughter and fun to almost frightened whispers as they slowly migrate, unbidden, to the wide stone steps of the school. One young boy stands atop the bottom steps and yells out, "He ain't no bogeyman! And I'm not afraid."

"Well, you'd better be, Bobby Baker!" a girl yells. "Mrs. Lawson said to call her if any strange man ever lurked around out here! I'm gonna tell Mrs. Lawson on you. And I'm gonna go get her right now!"

The young girl, along with her friends, stomp up the rest of the steps and through the oak, double-wide doors into the brick school. Wong can hear the girl's high-pitched voice. "Mrs. L-a-w-son! There's a strange m-a-n . . ." The closing doors chop shut the rest.

The boy, about nine, brown curly hair, is looking at him. A couple of other boys are with him. They are about twenty yards away, talking among themselves and laughing. Wong looks at him. Such a brave boy! he thinks. But I mean you no harm. Wong slowly smiles.

A woman comes out, sees him, and gathers up the boys. "You boys come in right now!" They reluctantly turn and ascend the steps. "You, mister, this is off-limits to adults who don't have a pass!" She stands atop the steps, feet apart, hands on her hips, squinting, challenging him like a gunfighter. "Do you want to come in and talk to one of us?"

Wong shakes his head, mutters, "No, sorry," turns, skirts the chainlink fence, and leaves the school playground.

He stands on the street. He has forgotten how to be a kid. What it was like to be a kid. How he has missed Nancy because of all her days away from him. How she would go back to Cindy once she is better. Already, Cindy is back, the look of disdain and blame on her face. Of course, he had to call and tell her about the accident.

He has lost most memories of his childhood. Only faded, dull images remain. Vivid memories of himself as a child died with the other child. Dead innocence. The child victim. The perpetrator. The body in the former, the soul in the latter—or almost dead in the latter. There is a thread of hope for Wong after all these months with Erlandson, though the memory of his sin sits on his mind like a plague on the land. And he is bitter. What he has done for country, for compatriots, he does not wish on anyone.

He was unseen for a brief while at the beginning, in the schoolyard. He watched the smiles light up the children's faces as they played their games. Heard the childish laughter, like music, soothing the savage beast within him, mollifying the anger, and assuaging the guilt. Saw their almost cherubic faces and sparkling eyes.

He wishes he could grab every child, hug each one in his arms, and weep away the bitter tears of his remembrances. Their innocence would run over him, like floodwaters—inundate, surround, and wash him to his very bones and then, perhaps, provide the means to cleanse his tainted soul.

He thinks of himself as a father and of other people as parents. People become parents because they can recapture their childhood through their children, or perhaps because there is about children a guilelessness and a state of grace that adults have lost. It is a cherished gift adults would once more like to have conferred on them.

He leans against a tree and stares out into the bay, where water and land meet in a curved, graceful line of horizon. He thinks of his child.

Then, for several minutes, he tries to remember his own childhood. Memories that hover in the far distance, in a long-ago time.

Oh, to feel the gift of innocence and to shut out evil! He wishes for that. He stands upright. Almightily, he wishes for that, stretching his arms high above him toward the heavens, almost a Christ figure, this one-time perpetrator of evil and death, an icon of lost innocence.

Chapter 23

More Hope

"Are you all right, honey?"

"Yeah, Daddy. I think so. Just a little sore," Nancy says and smiles.

"You had me worried there, kiddo. Your mother, too." He has her hand in his. The IV bottle is still above her bed, dripping the solution into her thin arm. She is in a semiprivate room, out of intensive care. She had broken out of her coma yesterday, having been in it for a week. Wong had been with her almost twenty hours a day.

A teenage girl, her leg in a cast and suspended in traction, shares the room. A young man stands by her bedside, whispering, holding her hand. Obviously a boyfriend. Every once in a while giggles swim across the room.

"Am I going to be all right, Daddy?" Wong lifts his eyebrows. "I mean, my head, I'm not going to be insane or retarded, am I?"

Wong laughs, the first real mirth he has felt in many days. "You're going to be fine, honey! Just fine! Didn't Dr. Stone just tell you that this morning?"

The little girl turns down her lips. "I don't understand what doctors say all the time."

"Well, sweetheart, you don't have to worry because your old daddy will interpret for you, okay?" He leans over and kisses her forehead, smells the mediciney fragrance of her skin and hair, notices the transducer in her skull is gone, and nuzzles her ear with his nose.

She squirms and shrugs her shoulders. "Oh, Daddy, I'm too old for that!"

"Not in my book, girlie! Not for a good number of years yet. Why, did I tell you what my mother used—"

"Oh, uh, excuse me, I-I didn't mean to interrupt . . ."

Wong straightens and turns. It is Mercury. He smiles. "No. No interruption." She has flowers in her hand.

"I was just passing by and I thought I would stop by and see Nancy." She shifts her gaze. "Hi, Nancy!"

"Hi, Mercury!" It is obvious that this was not the first time.

"I, uh, well . . . once in a while I've been coming over and saying hello to her. You don't mind?" Her eyebrows arch above a smile.

Wong steps from the bedside. "No. No, I don't mind. And, I-I haven't thanked you yet, for that other time, you know, that time in the emergency room. You helped hold my sanity together."

Her deep blue eyes gaze into his. He feels helpless before her. "I wanted to help," she says. "You needed someone."

Wong thinks, Is that the only way I can get into a woman's good graces? Through her pity? "Well, thank you."

Mercury leans against the side of the bed. "How are you, Nancy? Is this hospital taking good care of you?"

"I'm fine, Mercury. Yes, yes. The hospital is good." Her face is so serious it brings smiles to both adults.

"Well, this time I brought flowers. So I'll just put them in this vase you have on the table over here. No candy, this time."

"Oh, Daddy, they were good candy, too! Fudge!"

Wong laughs. He had eaten some, too, thinking they had been left by his ex-wife. He looks at Mercury. "They were good."

She smiles. "I have to go," she says, "but I'll be back tomorrow to say hello again. Okay, Nancy?"

"Okay, Mercury," the little girl pipes.

Wong looks at Nancy. "I'll be back in a while, honey. I want to talk to Mercury." He follows her into the hallway.

"I really meant what I said." He takes her arm, guiding her past the nurses' station into the small waiting area. "I'm glad you were there to help me out in the emergency room."

"Think nothing of it."

Wong exhales, looking intently into her eyes. "Mercury, I lost you once. Don't make me lose you again. I don't want to try to get to know you better and then end up hitting a stone wall, like before."

She nods.

"When Nancy is better and returns to her mother, I'd like to see you again. But if you're not willing to, just give me a 'no' answer now and I won't bother you."

She tosses her hair with a shake of her head. "I've got to go now," she says, flashing a smile at him as she disappears down the corridor. "Does Nancy like chocolate mints? I'll bring some tomorrow. And tomorrow is all right, isn't it?"

He nods. It is the best "yes" he is going to get.

He starts to write in late March, when the days are longer and the sun breaks through the clouds. He has hopes of reaching her, touching her heart somehow, all this after meeting her in the hospital.

He never was the one who could speak well, make the witty comment, praise the pretty girl to her face; rather, he was one of those shy individuals who gravitated to equations and the act of writing because to speak out loud in front of people held such an unholy terror for him. He can still recall taking speech in high school and how he had once gone to math class right afterward where a fellow student looked questioningly at his armpits. Great dark stains had saturated his shirt from above the elbow to halfway down his waist. That was what public speaking did to him. Though he didn't stammer, he couldn't really hide his nervousness either. His sweat glands gave him away. And he suffered unbearably when alone with a pretty girl he liked, seeming a silent fool.

So he writes. He writes of the passion he feels for her. He does so guiltily, because in a way he feels he is cheating on Jean, though he has never sworn any oath of monogamous love to her. He writes now because he is foolish with the spoken word and knows he is better with the written word. He wants to explain, because he will never again subject himself to the pain of her obduracy. Better this time to lay it on the line in front of her and have a quick reply.

He writes and edits the roughly scrawled letter, then types it out. He reads and rereads it, making minor changes, then types it out again, finally satisfied.

Dear Mercury,

Thank you for looking after Nancy. And thank you for being with me when she was in the emergency room. I know you could have turned away. It took courage and a sense of humanity, a sense of caring, for you to come by my side.

The world out there is a cold world. I've been out in it. Have seen the worst of it. Have helped to make it a much worse place. Have felt the loneliness of a man without a God, without a country, without a family, without a lover. But you offer me a glimmer of hope.

I have changed. I have lost weight, become fit, become more well-balanced mentally, and have even once more entered into the social fray of dating. But, in the end, I would like to see you again.

What are you to me? Perhaps it is that lost innocence of my childhood. You are trusting. You are loving. You are easy to get along with. You don't harbor grudges. And, hopefully, I can convince you to take a chance on me.

Your smile is like the sun coming out after a spring rain to kiss the petals of the daffodils. Your hair, blowing in the wind, is like the waves undulating through the grain fields of eastern Washington.

Oh, God, if I could get lost in any terrain, it would be within the depths of your eyes. It's as if I'm peering into a pool of water, when the surface is so calm it acts like a mirror and reflects the image of the mountain. Because then the water is more than water, more than the substance of itself; it is a mirror of the world, a mirror of the beauty around it. Only the goodness of nature is revealed.

I am the mountain, cold and temperamental; you are the still pond. My reflection, in your eyes, is only good. Was good. Before the winds of my confession rippled the mirrored surface of your eyes.

I am writing because I want to see you, to still the choppy waters and look into your warm, soft eyes once again. Because, with you, I am more than I have ever been. Because, with you, I am once more Good, not Evil. I hope you understand.

I'll call you next week.

Dave

He reads the letter once more, satisfied that his soul is bared on that singular sheet of paper. It is his last gasp. If she refuses this . . . well, he thinks, I'll survive and exist, but it will be like a bird with clipped wings who once learned how to fly and can only now dream of it.

He seals the letter in an envelope, affixes postage, and addresses it. The next day he mails it, sailing the letter through the slot, afraid that he might change his mind.

He has cast his name into the fateful pot of love, a witch's brew, a cauldron of bliss and heartache.

After Mercury's visits to Nancy at the hospital and after his letter, Wong goes out for coffee with her. They talk and talk.

"Where'd you learn to write like that?" she asks. "Is your poetry that good?"

"It came from the heart," he replies. "And when it comes from the heart, it's easy." He shrugs off the question about his poetry. Maybe some time in the future . . .

She smiles, intrigued. He asks her out, but she claims other engagements. "I'm sorry, Dave."

He frowns.

"But I will be free April 27th." A whole month away, but it is a "yes," and he smiles.

So he waits, worrying away the long weeks, and finally he takes her out to dinner at Il Pagliatorre, the finest Italian restaurant in town.

She wears a black miniskirt and mauve, square-cut blouse that stands in stark contrast to her light skin and blonde hair, and a light wool jacket the same color as her blouse. A lapis lazuli circlet around her neck complements her earrings, the color almost mirroring the blue of her eyes.

Wong stammers, "Y-you look fantastic, Mercury!" His eyes roam over her body, his interest quickening. He feels like a teenage boy out on a first date with the most beautiful girl in school.

After driving into town and parking, they walk arm-in-arm down the sidewalk, their breaths misting in the cool evening air as their conversation and laughter float away on the night breeze.

The restaurant is a cocoon of warmth and noise, the clinking of glassware and the sound of laughter breaking above the low murmur of conversation.

Once seated, the waiter hands out menus and takes their drink orders. Mercury scans the menu, eyes bright. "They have a broiled halibut in lemon, ginger, and tarragon sauce. Sounds positively enticing to me." She shivers with delight, arms stretched out before her.

Wong smiles at her. "Then, it's settled. I'm for the filet mignon," he says. The diffuse ceiling light glints off her hair. Her earrings sway and sparkle in the dim light. Magic is in the air.

"You look beautiful tonight," he murmurs, amazed at himself for being so forward. But it is too late to take the words back. He does not want it to be like the other night.

She looks at him. "Thank you. And you, you look handsome tonight." She smiles, a lazy, drawn-back curling of her lips, her eyelids almost closed.

"I want to apologize for that other—"

"No need," she interrupts, her eyelids raised now. "I was kind of rough on you, too."

"You had every right to be."

"No, no, please. Don't worry—"

"Ahem, excuse me, here's your wine, ma'am. And your coffee, sir."

They place their orders. When the waiter leaves, they are silent for a moment. "I still don't understand why you came to help me at the hospital—that first time." It was a rehash, but he still feels the need to air it out.

She looks at him. "You know, Dave, I really don't understand it myself. Maybe a sense of duty, pity, goodwill. I don't know." She sighs.

"Pity? Is it pity that you're going out with me tonight?" He feels his bubble bursting.

"No. I'm going out with you tonight because . . . maybe when I saw you at your daughter's bed, maybe, I got a sense of the man that I hadn't known before." She looks at him. "And most women don't go out with a man based on pity. Certainly not me."

"You got a sense of my vulnerability?"

"Maybe that's the most appealing part about you."

"I hate to think that is the only reason you find me interesting."

"Oh, I'm sorry, I didn't mean it that way." She reaches over to touch his hand. "What I mean, a lot of men cover up their feelings too much. They're too macho, know what I mean? I've gotten a sense of you, who you are, from what Erlandson told me and from my observations of you with Nancy."

Wong shrugs.

"My ex-husband certainly wasn't like you. He was Mr. Tough Guy. He couldn't say he loved me. Couldn't cry. Not once did I see him cry, not even when our dog died. That dog was like family, but did he spill a tear? No!" Her face is tight now, frowning. "And I felt less loved than that dog. I was only a body to him. And," here she pauses, wondering how much to tell him about her ex-husband, "he was a real bastard toward my cat. He was mentally abusive to me and physically abusive to Pickle. I don't want an abusive bastard, Dave. I want a caring person. I want a feeling person."

"Well, maybe, I'm too much a feeling person." What is he doing, trying to sabotage himself? He certainly does not want to ruin any chances he has with her by revealing his abuse of Cindy in his raging, drunken days. Those days are over, forever.

The waiter brings their salads. They murmur thank-yous. They pick at them and continue talking.

"I feel like I've been through an emotional wringer, Mercury. You can't imagine the things I've felt. About the m-murders . . . " He still cannot get the word out cleanly. "I've only recently come to call the act for what it is. I made excuses to myself for all these years. Only with Erlandson have I faced up to what I've done. And then, by God, when Nancy was injured . . ." His voice trails away. He looks at her. She stops eating, returning his gaze. "I felt I was going to die."

"Oh, Dave." She puts down her fork, reaches across to cover his left hand. He covers her hand with his right, and squeezes.

He pulls his hands from her grasp and presses both hands against his ears, as if blocking out ghostly calls, bowing his head. He has this great urge to cry, but knows he cannot do it. He fights it off with a great force of will, like squeezing back a sneeze. Then he drops his hands from his head, lifts his chin, and looks at Mercury, seeing the concern in her eyes.

"I'm okay," he says. "Really." He resumes eating the salad and looks about the room. Facing the street, he can see the reflections of the lights and people in the glass. He swings his gaze to his side, but does not see a woman in the back staring at him.

"Your filet mignon, sir. And your halibut, ma'am."

"Ummh, looks great." Wong bites into the steak, playing the morsel of meat along his upper palate with his tongue, then chomps down with his molars, letting the juices flow into the nooks and crannies of his mouth to every tastebud. He sighs, smiling. "This is great steak! How's your halibut?"

Mercury smiles back. "Delicious! Want a bite?" She holds out a sliver on her fork for him. He grabs her hand and guides the fork to his mouth.

"Ummh. Almost as good as mine." He cuts a slice of steak for her. He almost drops the meat; she hurriedly slurps it in before it can fall to the table. Some juices drip down the side of her chin, and she wipes it away.

"You make me eat like a real animal!" she says, laughing.

"You are. We are. I am."

"What?"

"Real animals."

"Oh?" she hesitates a moment. "Oh, of course. But I'm thinking of the connotation."

"That, too." He arches his eyebrows, eyes focused on the soft curve of her breasts showing above the square cut of her dress. The sexual urge runs through him like an autumn wind slicing through trees. She giggles, aware of his attention. Maybe too much wine. Her glass is almost empty.

Wong feels as if the air is electrified, as if they are in tune with each other. He is the violin string, she the violinist. And she plucks his soul like a virtuoso. He is under her spell, trapped by the nearness of her, by the meal, the ambience of the place, the music. In the background, Jose Feliciano strums his heartstrings with "And I Love Her." He unconsciously drums his fingers on the tabletop to the rhythm of the music.

He suddenly has this overwhelming desire to nuzzle her neck, to hold her in his arms, to kiss those sensuous lips, to slowly undress her, to discover the hidden recesses of her mind. To take the years and decades, or whatever years he had left, to make lifelong love to her. With his hands, with his penis, with his eyes, with his tongue, with his mind, with his laughter, with the poetry of his words, and with his love.

"Hi, Dave."

Jolted, he turns. Jean stands in front of him. His mouth drops. "Jean! What a surprise! How are you?"

"I'm fine," she replies. "How about yourself?"

"I'm okay, too!" He is flustered. Of all the people to run into! She introduces Gil to them, and Wong gets up to shake his hand. He introduces Mercury.

Gil is stocky in build, about five-ten. His brown hair is swept long at the side in counterpoint to his bald pate, which makes his forehead seem like a long ski jump. His smile is frozen in place.

The two men talk of occupations and Wong discovers that Gil works for the university administration. The two women speak in low voices. Wong tries desperately to tune his one ear to the slight threads of their conversation as he talks to Gil. He hears Jean asking how they had met.

Mercury's reply about him being in her aerobics class. Then further conversation about each other's occupation. The words ebb and flow, in and out of volume, sometimes drowned by loud laughter from nearby tables. He finds it difficult to answer Gil's questions and after a while they fall silent. He notices Jean staring at him. He looks to Mercury. She flashes him a weak smile. Jean moves closer, edging out Gil, who then moves over to talk to Mercury.

"It's been several weeks, Dave." Her eyes are almost accusing.

"Yes, yes. I meant to call you again. But with Nancy's accident . . ." He lets the phrase hang in the air.

"How is she?" She takes hold of his arm.

"She's doing fine." He pulls his arm away. After he'd called her about the accident, she was properly concerned, but had not accompanied him to the hospital at all, and now a small, guilt-ridden flush plays on her face.

"I'm glad," she replies. Gil stands silently with his hands in his pockets. Mercury watches them.

Wong can't think of anything else to say, and they just stare at each other, tightlipped.

Gil comes to the rescue. "Ready, Jean?"

She looks quickly at him, then turns back to Wong.

"Give me a call, Dave."

"Of course." Goodbyes are said. He watches her slender figure disappear through the maze of tables and people. Gil's right hand is draped over her right hip.

"She's beautiful."

It brings him up short. He shifts his gaze to Mercury. "Yes."

"Anyone special?"

"A friend. Just a friend."

She looks at him. That woman's look, a face conveying disbelief, an intuition beyond words.

He is silent for a while. The lazy confidence and libido of a moment ago have disappeared. The food has grown cold. They eat silently.

They finish the rest of the meal, but without the spark of the early evening. Jean has cast a pall over them. Yet, Wong cannot figure out why. It isn't as if he and Mercury were lovers; by God, they are only on their second date. Still, earlier, he could feel the excitement and promise of the evening. Now? They both pass up dessert. He quickly settles the bill and they stride out into the cold night. He puts his arm around her. She leans her head against his shoulder, and he feels the wind pick up the flames of his hope and desires. A mere flicker. But, driving her home, he feels deflated. Their conversation is flat and boring, like talk among strangers without a common interest.

At the door, she turns to face him, a quick smile. "I had a wonderful evening, Dave."

His expectations die. He is on the verge of saying good night and turning away when he hears her say, "Would you like to have a cup of coffee?"

"W-why, yes," he stammers, a smile forming. He floats through the doorway after her, feeling his wings start to fledge.

Chapter 24

The Beach

The May wind chases the clouds over the town, spilling shafts of warm sunlight that play briefly over buildings and streets. Wong walks out of the shadows into the sunshine, down Bay Street toward the post office. He passes Il Pagliatorre and smiles, reminded of that night almost two weeks ago with Mercury.

A businessman walks toward him, bent over against the brisk wind. Wong watches him fight to hold onto his hat. Suddenly, female laughter shifts his attention; he looks to the left . . . and dies.

It is Mercury, coming out of the restaurant with a tall man in his fifties. Her head is thrown back in laughter so that she does not see him immediately. For a split second Wong wishes he could hide, disappear into the pavement, become invisible. But then he gathers himself. "Hi, Mercury." His voice is almost carried away by the wind.

Mercury stops, her laughter dying. "Oh, Dave!" She catches her breath. "This is Dr. Stan . . . this is Stan Merriman. Stan, this is Dave Wong."

The man extends his hand, smiling. "Hi, Dave, glad to meet you."

Wong nods, shaking his hand. "Same here." But there is no smile on his face.

"We were just having lunch together. Stan works at the hospital. He just joined my aerobics class."

"She does work you out, doesn't she?" Wong says, looking at the man, seeing if he has caught the wisp of another connotation.

Merriman smiles. "That she does, all right. She's tough!"

"What are you doing here, Dave?" She looks at him, curious. A look almost of guilt, he imagines.

"Oh, running errands. You know, bank, post office, et cetera." He has put on his poker face.

"Oh, we're walking down to the post office. Why don't we all walk along for a while?"

"Oh, no. No thanks. I've got some business across the street I have to take care of first," he lies.

"You sure?" Mercury asks.

"Sure," he says, managing a smile. "Nice meeting you, Stan." He extends his hand. "Catch you later, Mercury."

"Bye, Dave." She smiles, brows furrowed, looking at him closely.

He turns from them to cross the street. He waits for several cars to go by, then glances at their retreating backs, her golden hair splayed by the wind, glinting in the sunlight. "Shit!" he mutters loudly.

The phone rings. Wong lets it ring three times before he picks it up. "Hello."

"Hi, Dave."

"Hi, Mercury." He sits down.

"I-I wanted to see how things were with you. I haven't heard from you in a couple of weeks."

He chuckles. "I did call, Mercury . . . When are you going to get an answering machine?"

"Oh, I just hate it when technology takes over a person's life."

He laughs. "It's almost the twenty-first century! Phone answering machines have been around at least ten years. Hell, maybe even twenty or more."

"I know, it's just that I'd much rather have someone call me and be there when the call comes in." She hesitates a moment, then, says, "I want to explain about the luncheon today."

"Mercury, there's no need to explain. We never said we wouldn't see anyone else, did we?"

"No. But . . ." she hesitates, then plunges in. "I felt that I somehow stepped on your toes."

"No." He laughs, a guttural sound. "Just my heart."

There is silence on the line. He can hear her breathing. Then, "David, David, he's just a friend. In this modern world, women can have male friends, can't they?"

He can almost see her standing by the phone, a tight smile on her face, twirling the phone cord with one hand.

"Yes, yes, of course. You're allowed to have as many male friends as you like. I certainly don't have a hold on your heart," he states in a voice as flat as the plains of Kansas.

"Damn you, Dave. Damn you." He can see her frown.

"Did you sleep with him?" He thrusts the question in like a lance.

"Huh?"

"Did you fuck him?" His voice is louder.

"That's none of your business, you bastard!"

He catches himself, suffocates the anger that is building within him, forcing it back down to a manageable proportion. He exhales—a loud, slow rush of air into the mouthpiece. "Mercury, it is. Because . . . because I'm hung up on you. You know that."

Silence.

"Oh, goddammit. Maybe I'm in love, okay? Maybe I'm in love with you, Mercury. Damn! Damn! Damn!"

"You shouldn't have said that." Her voice is like a note from a soft, thin reed.

"Said what?"

"Asking if I fucked him."

"I'm sorry. But standing out there in front of the restaurant, watching you laughing with him, it cut me up."

"Dave, I have friends. I'm not giving them up because of you."

"I'm not asking you to."

"Don't suffocate me, David. I need room to breathe."

Or room to fuck? he almost says it out loud. He almost cannot control his jealousy. It is rising like an incoming tide. Still, he has enough intuition to know if he had said what he had just thought, it would have sunk the ship that was bearing them through the rocky shoals of this romance.

Only the sounds of their breathing break the silence of the line. "Can I call you later?" He is afraid of what he might say.

"Sure," she replies. "You will call?"

"Yes, of course," he says, exhaling audibly. "I'm the one who's in love, remember." He hesitates. "Goodbye, Mercury."

"Oh, Dave, I like you a whole hell of a lot. That's why I called."

Wong sucks in his breath, more hopeful now, but still disappointed, still afraid, still angry. "I'd better say goodbye."

"Dave, wait, I-I—"

He hangs up. Then he stands, leaning his forehead against the wall. Without a thought, he starts to bang his forehead against it. BAM! BAM!

"Love is fun, isn't it?" he says. BAM! BAM! BAM!

He lies naked, under the shade of a coconut tree, the branches swaying lazily in a gentle onshore breeze.

He is lethargic in the heat. A thin sheen of perspiration runs down his chest. He has the park to himself for the moment. But then he hears laughter coming from the beachfront and sees a group coming toward him, all naked also. He watches them, unsure of who they could be. As they get closer, he smiles. It is Mercury, Jean, Cindy, Nancy, and two more—the Mama-san and the girl. He greets them lazily, all female . . . but then he sees a little boy of seven, hidden behind the women. Asian. The boy smiles at him. He smiles back.

"Did you have a good nap?" Jean asks, her smooth skin tawny from the sun, her breasts jutting upward to the sky.

Yes, he replies.

"Well, we brought food," Mercury says, holding out a picnic basket, her breasts swaying.

"A lot of food!" the Mama-san says, laughing. She does not look old.

"I have the drinks," Cindy, his ex-wife, adds. Even she is smiling at him. He lies there in wonderment.

The two girls are playing catch, squealing with delight. He is amazed at the smoothness of their skins. The boy stands aside, watching him.

"Okay, we have norimaki sushi and teriyaki steak," Mercury adds. She is close to him, smiling, and says softly, "And there's me for dessert."

He is languid, but feels himself grow at her suggestion.

Jean has overheard Mercury's suggestion. "Me first," she says.

"No way," Mercury replies. "I'm the favorite of my master." She licks her lips.

Wong watches himself grow in front of them. They lean over and laugh, urging him on. "Grow!" "Get bigger for me!" "I'm the one!" Even Cindy and the Mama-san have joined in.

Mercury props her hands under her breasts. "Oh, Davy," she coos, "don't you love these?"

He looks at Mercury. *I'm mad at you*, he tells her.

Jean has turned around, rotating her buttocks in front of him, spreading her legs. "Oh, but Dave loves my ass, don't you, Dave?" she asks, looking over her shoulder.

He gets up weakly on one elbow. *I don't know which is worse*, he says, *I'm hungry for food and sex*. He is rigid in the soft wind. *But I guess sex is more important.*

"Here, I'll help my Davy." Mercury is between his legs now, putting her mouth to work. "I'm not mad. And there is only you, Davy." She smiles.

His anger melts away in her mouth.

"And I'll help you with your tummy, dear." Jean slices the sushi and some teriyaki beef and gingerly feeds him. It is a strange feeling, having both desires being fulfilled simultaneously.

He eats some, then grabs Jean's hand, pulls her above him, working his tongue into her spot. Mercury's hands brush his nipples as he feels her go up and down on him, her tongue slippery and slithering.

He opens his eyes and sees the boy standing close by. The boy stares at him, not focusing on the lovemaking at all. His eyes seem to bore into

Wong's soul. But Wong is lost in the ecstasy of the moment. Jean has gotten off him and is now nibbling on his nipples.

The perspiration builds up on their bodies. Wong closes his eyes, isolating his one sense, reveling in the feel of his nerve endings. The minutes pass, then he opens his eyes and sees the boy playing with a knife.

It is the knife! Wong reaches out wordlessly, grabbing for the knife, but he cannot reach it. Cannot move beyond the sexual embrace of the women. The boy smiles, fingering the long, obscene blade, as long as his forearm. He reaches for the Mama-san.

No! Wong screams. *No!* He wants to fight off Mercury, but he cannot. He feels himself going over the edge. Her strokes are drawing him toward climax. Wong feels that he can save the Mama-san if he can only just push Mercury aside, stop the climax. Wong reaches for the old lady. The boy has the knife above her.

Ah! but it feels so good! He is bound by chains of pleasure as Mercury brings him over the edge. The boy plunges the knife into the old woman. She screams silently, mouth working, no sounds.

Then the girl. It is as if the boy had a godlike power over them. The little girl submits with a smile. He plunges the knife into the small body. Mercury doesn't stop. The boy pulls out the bloody knife and looks to Nancy. Nancy looks up and freezes.

No! Wong shouts. *No!* He fights now, pushing the women off him, fighting through lethargic pleasure to try to save his daughter. He stretches his arms out . . .

He crashes out of the dream, hitting the stone wall of conscious reality. He wakes up, alone. He grabs himself. He is wet from perspiration, and his sheets are wet and sticky. He starts shaking.

"Oh, Jesus," he cries, "not again." He sits on the edge of the bed, cradling himself. "No," he mutters. "No. Not again."

He wonders why Mercury and Jean and Nancy and Cindy are along in this dream, this new nightmare.

And the little boy?

Wong shivers.

Chapter 25

Letter

Wong lay his M-16 against the stone wall, unslung his pack, sat down, and leaned back. Sunlight streamed into the rough courtyard, then faded with the clouds, and then returned—advancing and retreating like the fortunes of war.

"Hey, Sarge, when we heading back to Phu Bai?" Emory asked.

"Anderson said 1400," Wong replied, looking at his watch. 1040. "He said the trucks should be here by 1230." Wong had been given a battlefield promotion for his coolness under fire and for his part in clearing out the school.

"Shit, that's a long time from now," Wolkowski lamented.

"What the fuck you complaining about, dickhead! Ain't had enough fucking off? You want the gooks to start shooting at you again?" Smitty asked. "That's what's wrong with you fucking new guys. Don't know when you got it made."

"Fuck you, Smitty," Wolkowski said. He was a big man, arms like a middle linebacker's. He had seen enough of war the last week that he was no longer a fucking new guy. And he knew it.

Smitty just whistled, rolled his helmet down over his face, and feigned sleep.

The other Marines were stretched out, talking, laughing, reading letters from home. All glad to be alive. The worst was over. Hue was firmly back in the hands of the Allies. Mopping up the last of the resistance was all that was left, and other units had been assigned to do that.

"Well, s-h-e-e-t, this is the life!" Langley said. He was another replacement. "You know what I'm gonna do when I get back," he said. "I'm gonna go look for pussy."

"Damned straight!" Emory said. "But, hey Langley, how you gonna fuck? Wasn't that your pecker I stepped over on the street out there?" Langley's face turned red while the other Marines hooted.

Wong listened to the banter for a while. But his gaze found the small building where he had slept so many nights, slept with the dead. He remembered how he and Muley had never thought that either one of them would be in the back room in a body bag. How many days ago? Ten, fourteen? It seemed a lifetime.

He turned around, fished in his pack, and got out his writing pad. Gazing around him, he saw the sunlight hitting the building, the first sunlight for what seemed like weeks. The light of life hitting the house of death. He was in the sunlight, too, his body breathing in the warmth after days of cold hell. Oh, he was so glad to be alive!

"Sarge, when we gonna haul ass back to Da Nang?" Langley asked.

Wong looked up. "Don't know."

"Jesus, Sarge, you gotta have some idea."

"I'm busy, Langley." Wong ignored him.

"Christ, Sarge, I just wanna hint, that's all."

"Let him be, Langley." It was Wolkowski.

Wong looked at Wolkowski, and nodded.

How to start a letter to a woman he did not know who lived some 13,000 miles away? She seemed to live in another world, another century. He took a deep breath and started scribbling.

27 February 1968
Hue, Vietnam

Dear Stella,

You don't know me, but I knew your husband Jake. He had asked me to write you if anything ever happened to him. By now, you know that he is dead. I know that there is nothing I can say

that will make it easier for you in your grief. I can only give you a
glimpse of your husband from a different perspective. He was a
husband to you and a father to your daughter, but he was a good
buddy of mine.

We didn't know each other long. But war is kinda funny in
some ways. In all that boredom and fear, friendships can be
made almost overnight. Muley, we called him, because he was
as strong as a mule. Whenever we went out on patrol, he'd
carry extra gear and not complain about it. And to top it all
off, he didn't lag behind. He kept up with us, and even sometimes set the pace. He was one of the strongest men I've known
and one of the most dedicated.

Wong pulled out the wrinkled, bloodstained picture of Muley, his wife,
and the baby. He had pulled it from Muley's pocket after his death. How
strange, he thought, how the camera can freeze time. How the image of
the dead can live forever.

I don't like this war. A lot of us came into it blindly. We
thought it was the right thing to do. I've since changed my
mind. I think I even convinced Muley in the end. He had believed in his country so strongly, even after he got here and saw
all the things that were happening. Things like a lot of the
South Vietnamese not fighting well. The corruption and black
market in Saigon. The wealthy young Vietnamese buying themselves out of the draft while the poor Vietnamese and us Americans were doing the fighting and dying. After a while, it all got
him down. But his responsibilities to the platoon, his squad,
his buddies, the Marine Corps, well, those never wavered. And
while I put off being on point out on patrol as much as possible, Muley never begged off. He was good at it and the lieutenant used him a lot. He was that dedicated; he willingly put
his life on the line more times than I can remember.

And he helped me. I'm Chinese-American. I did some things over here that I'm not proud of. Muley listened to me and didn't judge me. He was like that. Willing to listen. Giving good advice.

I'm sure you've heard of the Battle for Hue. Probably in the newspapers, magazines, and on TV by now. Two regiments of North Vietnamese regulars and Viet Cong had overrun the town and had dug in. It took us Marines about four weeks to drive them out. We took a lot of casualties. One of them was Muley. He was killed by a sniper on 10 February while we were attacking the Imperial Palace.

He was one of the best and one of the bravest. And he was a friend.

With my condolences,

David Wong,
Sergeant, USMC

Wong put the pen back into his pocket, ripped out the pages, and closed the notebook. He stuffed the letter in the envelope and addressed it, using the address on the back of the worn photo.

He looked at the photo once again. He decided to keep it as a memento, something to remember Muley by. Another reason not to send it back to Muley's wife was the blood of her husband on it.

He thought back to Muley. Why did this man, so loved at home with a wife and daughter, why did this man court death so haphazardly as he did? Wong could not understand that.

The lieutenant had said that Muley's death would be labeled as due to a sniper. Wong could not tell Muley's wife otherwise. The thought did cross his mind to visit her when and if he got stateside, but then he felt that he could not hide the truth from her if they ever came face to face.

How can you *not* tell a woman, looking her in the eye, that you put a bullet into her husband's head?

Part II

Across Space

This land is your land,
This land is my land.
©

Chapter 26

Crosscountry

"I'm going to the Wall."

"When?" Erlandson asks.

"Next week." Wong fidgets in his chair.

"Say goodbye to Mercury and Jean yet?"

"No. But I will. I'll keep it short, too."

"So, you're not getting along with either too well?"

"I'm in love with Mercury. Jean keeps pestering me. And Mercury? Well, Mercury is still seeing other men." Wong assumes this.

"That dream, then. You're being pestered by too many women in your life."

"Ah, but there is more, don't you think?" Wong asks.

"Yes, there is an underlying tone of violence, your actions from the past." Erlandson pauses for a moment, then reflects, "There's a link."

"Between the violence of my past and the dream?" Wong frowns.

"Yes, yes. That, too. But I mean between the sexual act and the killing act. Between that most fundamental driving force in life, which is to procreate, and the end of life, death."

"I don't get it."

"Weren't you always after women in your younger days? Didn't want to copulate before going to Vietnam, while you were in Vietnam, knowing that you might die?"

"Yes."

"I think it's a biological drive, a need to leave your seed behind, even though you might die. To leave a part of yourself, to continue your genetic line."

"I used rubbers."

"No matter, the drive is no less real."

"S-o-o? I still don't see the tie-in to the dream."

"One act creates life, the other ends it. Two ends to the same string."

Wong mulls this over. "I still don't get it."

"Your sexual acts are jarring loose more memories of the killings. More guilt."

"Are you saying my dick is like a knife blade. Whenever I'm making a thrust into a woman, I'm killing her? Or reliving the act of killing."

Erlandson laughs. "An apt analogy, but not quite true. I'm just pointing out why I think that particular dream came into your subconscious. It was triggered by the growing involvement with the two women in your life, your sense of conflict there. Maybe by your insecurity regarding Mercury." Erlandson frowns, turning more serious. "You're not harboring any uneasy feelings toward these women, are you?"

"Uneasy feelings? What do you mean, uneasy feelings?"

"Oh," and here Erlandson looks away from Wong, "like you might want to hurt them? Or kill them?"

Wong sits in shocked silence. "What makes you ask that?"

Erlandson turns back to face Wong. "The more I think about it, the dream disturbs me."

"Do you think I could go back to killing women and children?"

Erlandson scrutinizes Wong's face. "No. I don't think so . . . but killing . . . killing someone in an argument or under some extenuating circumstances, I'm not so sure."

Wong sits up straight in his chair. "I think I'll be fine, Doc. I'm getting better. And, no, I don't plan on killing . . . murdering anybody." There, he used the word. "And I only murdered the first time under the most extenuating of circumstances." He smiles, tightlipped. "But I'll tell you what bothers me about the dream," Wong goes on. "I want to know why the boy looked at Nancy."

Erlandson doesn't answer right away. "I don't know. Maybe Nancy's life is or was in danger. Her accident?"

Wong nods. "I don't know. Maybe he knows something we don't. The future."

"None of us can read the future."

"No, none of us can. That's true." Here Wong pauses and reflects. There is still something about the dream, a foreboding he feels. Then the thought slips his mind. "But the past . . . I want to get rid of my past. Like you said before, I should go the Wall. I want to exorcise these demons of my past. My future can only be better for it."

"You realize that even if you go to the Wall, the demons may still be there. We don't know if this will act as a cure—a catharsis."

"I know, but I have to try. And I need a change of scenery. I need to think more about Mercury and Jean. Or," he ponders, "less about them."

"Might be a good idea," Erlandson says, unwinding his big frame from the chair to get up. "You do, of course, know who the boy is."

Wong nods.

July 1990

The sky is the color of gray ash. He threads the car along the wet two-lane road like a silent ghost. He peers out the windshield, past the rhythmic beating of the wiper blades and the misting raindrops, into the cold, wild, lonely landscape that abuts the North Cascades Highway.

He feels a sense of foreboding, an agoraphobia. The huge, hulking mountains and the weather intimidate him. He feels isolated and small against the great massifs of rock. In the warm womb of his car, he feels a cold dread of the outside. He has this sense of mountains as beautiful to gaze at, but he has no intimacy of them.

He loves his car, but at the present time, doubts are seeping in. It is a wonderful mode of transportation around town. The 1970 gray Volvo station wagon has been a fixture in his life since he had bought it used eighteen years ago with 101,000 weary miles clicked on its odometer.

"But it's an old car!" Mercury said when he told her about his trip. Jean had been more pointed. "It's gonna break down, and you're going to be stuck in the middle of nowhere," she said. "Nonsense," he replied. But, now, he is not so sure, and his fear rides as a passenger.

Raindrops form into sleet, then into heavy, damp snowflakes that slicken the road. There is little traffic. He slows down to twenty-five miles an hour and skids as a gust of wind buffets the car. He pulls out of the skid. Jesus! he thinks. Better not break down, car!

He squints at the road, urging the car forward at a snail's pace. Finally, he sees the sign, Rainy Pass. Just five more miles to Washington Pass and eastern Washington.

"KPAR Country," the radio says. "Far out KPAR, where we have the best of Country and Western. Right now we've got the Judds and 'Grandpa, Tell Me About the Good Old Days.'"

The music of the mother-daughter duo floats through the station wagon. Wong sings along, slowly relaxing in the warmth of the sweet music, momentarily forgetting about his car. His throat catches, and tears well up. He thinks, Ahpo! Yes, tell me about the good old days!

Outside, the dark evergreens flee in and out of the mists. The tops of the mountains are completely hidden. On the lower granite faces, Wong sees water cascade as hundreds of little waterfalls to form streams that are channeled into culverts beneath the road, flowing over pebbles and rocks, erasing the mountain little by little over eons.

Wong shivers, a sympathetic reaction to the wet and cold outside. Below Rainy Pass, the sun suddenly peers out of the clouds, timidly, like a child from behind her mother's skirt. Ahead of him, sunlight glints off the rocky spires of Liberty Bells. The sky becomes less dark. He climbs to Washington Pass, 5,477', and switchbacks just once below Liberty Bells in a long downhill grade of six miles.

The flora changes. Gone are the wet westside plants of Douglas fir, cedar, hemlock, and alder. Instead, Ponderosa pine and sagebrush reign. He breathes easier now. The terrain is less steep, more rounded into hillocks. The aggression of the clouds has been dissipated by the mountains.

He passes Early Winters, a small bevy of houses set among trees far from the road, and bypasses the small town of Mazama. Not far beyond, he pulls into the town of Winthrop where, finally, patches of blue splay open the gray sky.

He stops at a convenience store for gas, food, beverages, and the restroom. He hopes to make Spokane by evening. He drives through Twisp, Carlton, Methow, and hits Route 97 to parallel the mighty Columbia River to Chelan, and from there to Wenatchee.

He is driving through orchard country now, the trees set in ordered rows like troops in formation. Sometimes he can see them on hillsides and imagines them as soldiers of old marching down to battle. The arid land has been made arable, fecund even. Apples, peaches, apricots, pears, cherries. All possible because of irrigation from the Columbia River.

"You aren't running away from something, are you?" Jean had asked.

"No," he said. Though, in truth, part of him was. "I've got to go to the memorial. Can you understand that?"

"Yes. But you will call and send postcards?"

"Of course."

It was different with Mercury. He had gone to see her after that episode outside Il Pagliatorre and the ensuing phone conversation. "Oh, Dave, that sounds like so much fun. I wish I could go along."

"I wish it, too. Why don't you consider it?"

"If only I could get away. But I've got all these patient appointments and my commitments to teach all these classes." A pause. "And," here she looked demurely at him, "you've cooled a bit toward me, haven't you?"

"No, I haven't," he replied. They were on her porch. "No!" he yelled out into the streets, like a teenager, his shout echoing off the nearby houses. Wong had learned the futility of jealousy, at least the showing of it before her. He realized that he was maturing in the machinations of love, knowing that if she loved him, he would have no cause for jealousy.

She smiled, pulled him to her, and kissed him. "Call me when you get back. Write postcards to me. I'll still be here for you."

He left off with her then, high on promised ground.

He joins I-90 at Moses Lake, with the sun slowly edging toward the horizon. Wheat fields stretch for miles, as far as he can see. Some fields hold ripening wheat. On others, lonely tractors turn the soil, stirring up dust swirls that run before the wind.

He can see horizon to horizon. Behind him, in the west, some clouds still hover. Ahead, he is driving into clear skies. Small settlements, marked by oases of green trees, pepper the landscape. Sparsely set among the wheat fields he sees dilapidated plank barns, sere structures withered by aridity. He wonders about their history and the people who built them.

The road glides up small grades, a ribbon of highway that disappears into a mirage of land and sky. Just before Sprague, a long lake appears on the right side of the freeway. He sees cattails growing along the near side, then crowding the water on the far side, the desert. A bevy of ducks flies over the water. Two mallards turn to fly over the highway, bodies stretched in flight, their wings flapping at high frequency.

Music is his sole companion. The Seattle station he had been listening to fades in and out, like a ghost caught between two worlds, unsure of which one to dwell in. He switches to a Spokane station, hears the strong signal come in. "Rita MacNeil, 'Why Do I Think of You Today?'" the DJ says, and he is at once caught by the beauty of the singer's voice and the haunting melody.

It is music that grabs him by his soul. He feels himself being passed through a wringer, having the extraneous water squeezed out of the fabric of his life.

Only love remains. Love with all its myriad heartbeats, from a steady rhythm to palpitations to wild drum rolls. Romantic love, sibling love, parental love, filial love. Old love and new love. And he remembers Erlandson's simple statement: "Love is beauty." He did not know this as a young man, wrapped in his own arrogance.

The music has wielded its magic, putting him on another plane of experience, floating him out of body, like death, but for a few minutes. All at once he feels peace, regrets, tears—the nostalgia and pain of old, lost loves and the insecurity of new love. It bathes him in the pathos of his own existence.

He suddenly realizes that he is the maker of his own destiny, his own happiness, his own sorrow. Neither government nor God can mandate happiness and forgiveness for him. Only he is responsible for that. Still, the knowing and the doing are two different things. But, at least, all those months with Erlandson have helped him reach this point of know-ing—an epiphany of sorts.

Suddenly, he has a passion for life. He wants to live. He wants to have more children, and goddammit! grandchildren for his old age. He sighs, and of all the women in his life, he thinks of Mercury as he drives, wrapped in his cloak of loneliness and music, down the long highway to Spokane before a dying sun.

He had decided to drive through Spokane and continue into Idaho the night before. Most of the motels in Spokane were either filled or the rates were too high. Many had an old air about them, like an overused street walker still plying her trade for high prices. He finally found a room for thirty-five dollars in Post Falls, the AAA rate. It was a new motel, too.

Sitting on the edge of the bed this morning, he studies the map, follows the red thread of I-90 through the Idaho Panhandle into Mon-tana. His gaze is drawn to the solid green shading that defines Glacier National Park. He has never been there before and has heard so much about it. He makes a spur of the moment decision, tracing his pen along the thin red line of 93 North.

After settling his bill and gassing up, he continues on I-90. The day is cool and overcast. The evening before, soft, rolling hills covered by dark pines had led his way into Spokane. Now, between Spokane and Coeur d'Alene, the terrain opens up, with small hills retreating in the distance.

Before Coeur d'Alene, I-90 construction forces the traffic onto a local road that hugs the shore of the eponymous lake. Wong sees the breeze create a small chop on the dark green waters. The hills have re-turned to crowd the road. Rounding a downhill curve, he looks up and notices a huge bridge spanning a draw. Large trucks sit atop the bridge like toy trucks on a child's shelf, the repair crew like small stick figures set in motion.

Construction plagues him all through Idaho. Traffic is forced through one small town, where a banner proclaims, "Welcome to Kellogg, Stop and Visit a While." The cars skirt under huge supports of I-90 before making their way back on the freeway proper.

The road meanders like a river now, crowded by small mountains on both sides. The economies of the small towns he passes are driven by logging and mining. He sees the mills and smelters as dominant eyesores in a bucolic sea.

Past the Idaho Panhandle into Montana, the mountains have fallen back and the terrain opens out into wide valleys and plains. The dry green mountains and wide open spaces caress his eyes, fulfilling his vision of the beauty of the American West. The settlements are sparse. A few tourist spots beckon, "Good food, great coffee. See Moose, Elk, Wolves, Bears." But Wong doesn't stop. His singleminded objective is Glacier. He checks the map. He has to take Highway 93, north, before Missoula.

He is not far from the turnoff, listening to country music again when he hears a small clunk. He presses on the accelerator. Nothing. Oh, no! he thinks. His momentum is enough so that he can pull onto the shoulder. When the car stops, the engine is dead. He turns the ignition, hears the whir of the starter motor, but the engine does not catch. He gets out and checks under the hood. Nothing seems amiss, but he needs someone to turn the starter motor before he can make a diagnosis. Cars and tractor trailers whiz by him.

He stands in dumb amazement, mad at his car. How can you do this to me? he berates his car. "I guess Jean was right, after all. Here I am, stuck in the middle of nowhere," he mutters to himself.

For fifteen minutes he fusses with the car. With the ignition set to on, he uses a voltmeter to measure the voltage coming out of the primary wire on the coil. He looks over the distributor. He checks the connections on the battery post, measures the voltage of the battery. He is only guessing. Without anyone to help him turn the ignition to start, he can't do much of anything.

Suddenly a Ford pickup pulls up behind him. A cowboy gets out. "Ya got some trouble here, pardner?" The cowboy is about fifty, almost six feet tall, with lanky strength, brown hair, a weather-worn, wrinkled face, and clear blue eyes. Wong has never seen such clear blue eyes in a man before, and it catches his attention.

"Yeah, sure do. My car just died."

"Well, any way I can help?"

Wong smiles. "How about turning the engine over for me?"

"Sure. By the way, name's Bob Jensen." He extends his hand.

"Hi! I'm Dave Wong." He shakes his hand. "Sure appreciate your stopping."

"No problem." He slides into the seat under the large steering wheel. "Let me know when."

Wong pulls out the high tension wire from the coil to the distributor, holding it in a bamboo salad tong about three-eighths of an inch from the engine block. "Okay, hit it!" The starter and engine turn; a large spark arcs across the gap. "Okay, hold it!" He replaces the wire into the distributor. Now, he has a suspicion. He opens the oil filler cap, sees the rocker arms and valves. "Okay, once again." The engine and starter turn, but there is no motion of the rocker arms. "Okay. Good!" He walks back to the driver's side. "Well, I think I know what the problem is," he says.

"What?" the cowboy asks.

"I think it's the timing gear." He wipes his hand on a rag.

"Well, hey, do you need a ride into town or how about the nearest phone?" Bob asks.

Wong looks at him, smiles. "I'd appreciate it. Yeah, I can call AAA."

Bob gets out of the car. "You'd better get some of your stuff then. There's a gas station and restaurant up ahead. They got phones there."

Wong closes the hood, grabs a light jacket, locks up the car, and jumps into the truck cab.

"Can't tell you how much I appreciate your stopping."

"Hell, no problem. I've been in your position before. Ain't no damned fun, I tell you," Bob says, grinning, as he starts the engine. "So you're from Washington, huh?"

"Yep, north of Seattle, a town called Marthasville, near the Canadian border."

"Oh, I've been there. Nice country. Whatcha doing way out here in Montana?" He checks his mirrors before merging onto the freeway.

"Driving across country."

"That's a mighty old car you're using to go across country, don't you think?" Bob pulls out and accelerates, his pickup bouncing over some bumps.

"Yeah, but I know it and I know how to fix it." Wong looks over his shoulder. "Well, at least most of the time."

Bob laughs. "So where you going across country?"

Wong looks at Bob, his black cowboy hat pushed back off his forehead. Wong still has a distrust of cowboys, a carryover from his Nevada days. He decides he likes this cowboy, but he doesn't immediately answer.

Bob looks over at him. "That is, if you don't mind my asking?"

Wong hesitates some more, then sighs. "I'm going to the Vietnam Memorial."

Another silence, broken only by the loud thrum of a tractor trailer passing them. Bob's face turns serious. He holds his right hand toward Wong. "I was in 'Nam in '67-'68, 123rd Aviation Battalion. Flew fucking helicopters."

Wong relaxes, shakes his hand. "It was a helicopter war, wasn't it?"

"Yeah, damned right," Bob says. "Just mount those M-60s on the chopper and cut loose."

"I was with the First Marine Division, Da Nang and then Phu Bai." Wong looks outside at the rangeland passing by. "Fought in the Tet offensive at Hue."

Bob whistles, pushes his cowboy hat back. "Yeah, I heard about you Marines in the Battle of Hue. That was some heavy shit, huh?"

Wong smiles, tightlipped. "Yeah." He does not want the emotions flooding back. He looks away, out the passenger window. Bob sees his action, claps him on the shoulder with his big hand. They have pulled off the freeway, going up the exit ramp toward the gas station and restaurant.

"Look, Dave, I was out there at the Vietnam Memorial a couple of years ago. It's a hell of an experience." He reflects a moment. "I don't meet too many vets anymore. Maybe I'm too damned busy with the ranch. But let's get your car hauled into a garage and fixed. And, if you've got the time and don't mind, I'd like to invite you to spend the night at our ranch. Vicki, my wife, wouldn't mind at all, and she's a damned mean cook."

Wong thinks for a moment, smiles, and nods. "Sure, why not? Two old vets talking about bad old times. I'd enjoy that."

"Outstanding! Look, I've got some errands to finish up. Let's find out where they'll tow the car to and I'll meet you there in an hour-and-a-half or so."

They go into the restaurant together. Wong calls the AAA emergency road number and is told that a tow truck will pick him up at the restaurant within the half hour. "It's coming from Westsun Garage," he tells Bob.

"Okay, I'll find it. I'll be there in an hour to an hour-and-a-half." He looks at his watch and then Wong. "Do wait, okay?"

Wong looks into the weather-beaten cowboy face. "Not to worry, Bob. I'm not going anyplace."

Bob laughs. "Good!" He claps Wong on the shoulder again before turning to get back into his truck.

The tow is a straightforward business. The driver hooks up his car, Wong rides as passenger to the garage, signs his name to the AAA form.

"Yep, I think you're right," the mechanic tells him. "It's the timing gear. These things give out every 60,000 miles or so." He is a pudgy man with a pockmarked face, stomach straining against his grease-stained blue coveralls. The garage looks like the black hole of Calcutta, formed from grease, oil, and a few windows that grudgingly let in the weak light of the gray afternoon. Old parts are cast about helter skelter. The smell of grease and oil assails Wong's nostrils. "They're made out of some kind of pressed fiberboard, so the teeth kinda wear down," the mechanic continues.

"How much?"

"Two hundred dollars."

Wong's heart sinks. "Two hundred dollars! Jesus Christ!"

The mechanic shrugs. "It's a Volvo."

Wong sighs. He has little choice, even though he knows he is being scalped. He doesn't have the tools, the grungy clothes, the part, or the inclination. "Okay," he mutters.

"We'll have it ready for you, noon tomorrow." The mechanic

wipes his hands on a rag, then picks his nose. His crooked, gray-white teeth beam in his grease-stained face.

Wong nods, then sees Bob's pickup truck pull in. "Okay, I'll be back tomorrow, then." As a grudging aside, he mutters, "Thanks." The mechanic nods.

"How's it going?" Bob asks.

"Two hundred dollars." Wong is deflated. He looks at the mechanic as they depart. "Son of a bitch!" he mutters.

Bob laughs. "Well, hey, at least they'll get it fixed and you'll be back on the road soon. Besides, I called Vicki and she said you're welcome. She said she's going to put some steaks on for us tonight."

"Damned kind of you, sir!" Wong replies, his heart already lifting.

"No problem for a fellow vet!"

They drive out of town into the broad Bitterroot Valley. Stands of Ponderosas run over gently rolling hills, and the overcast sky has broken into flecks of high streamer clouds. Its cobalt blue dome sits like an upside-down bowl on the land.

"Prettiest damned place on earth," Bob says.

Wong whistles as he gazes at the panorama. "It is more than pretty," he says. "It's goddamned pretty. So much so it takes your breath away."

Bob looks at Wong with newfound respect. "Dave, are you a poet?"

Wong shrugs. "Some." The truck bounces along. "Maybe."

"Well, that was damned good!" Bob laughs again. Suddenly, Wong feels as if he has ridden this truck for ages and that this driver was one of those kind white men he has known since childhood—the color-blind type who befriends you based on your character. He relaxes.

They turn off into one of the small side canyons. After a short distance, the road becomes graveled. As they climb in elevation, Wong can see aspens on the hillside, their leaves fluttering in the breeze. The Ponderosas have given way to lodgepole and Douglas fir.

"So, how big is your ranch, Bob?"

"Five hundred acres. Small by Montana standards. We have to lease National Forest land for grazing."

"How many head of cattle?"

"About three hundred. Mostly cows."

"I would have thought it would be steers."

"No," Bob says, chuckling. "We use the cows to produce offspring. Then we sell the calves when they're between six and twelve months old to larger ranches or feedlots."

"Jeez! I wouldn't have guessed."

"It's a living."

"Hell of an office!"

They make small talk as the truck bounces along the potholed road, stirring up great clouds of dust. Wong's gaze continuously scans the landscape, which runs from clearcuts on distant hillsides to meadows and dense forest nearby.

"Is this your ranch?" He notices a marker post, then a mailbox.

"This part is. We just crossed the National Forest boundary."

Wong whistles. "Wish I had land like this!"

Bob nods. "Let me tell you. It's a salve to the soul, especially after Vietnam." He slows the pickup, then turns into a long driveway that circles in front of a log ranchhouse. A large barn sits to their left with a corral next to it and, beyond, the land runs away to the nearby foothills. Most of the cattle dot distant pastures. Some cows are nearby. Wong can hear their lowing, can smell the ranchland redolence.

Two dogs, a black labrador and golden retriever, sprint out from the back of the house when they hear the pickup, barking madly, tails wagging.

"Whoa, Brewster! Sadie!" The dogs jump on Bob, tongues hanging out, tails thumping his thigh. They circle both of them, sniffing curiously at Wong.

"Please excuse the dogs!" yells a petite, attractive woman standing in the doorway of the log house. She is wearing jeans and a white frilly blouse with a leather vest.

"Dave, I want you to meet my wife, Vicki. Vicki, this is Dave . . . ?"

"Dave Wong." He strides to her and shakes her hand.

"Hi, Dave. I heard you were having car problems," she says, smiling.

"Well, nothing that can't be fixed easily, I guess."

A young man steps out from behind Vicki. "Dave, this is Mike, our son." He is about sixteen, a muscular young man in cowboy hat, western shirt, and jeans.

He extends his hand. "Hi!" he says, smiling.

"Howdy!" Wong shakes his hand and smiles.

He is made welcome in the magnificent log home. The evening sunlight streams through a large stained-glass window set above the entrance foyer. A trusswork of beams makes a vaulted ceiling for the living room and kitchen. Everything is wood or stone: oak or tile floors, the huge stone fireplace, the wood furniture shaped into functional—almost artistic—tables, chairs, and hutches, fashioned from maple, ash, or oak.

He and Bob sit and talk in the living room while Vicki cooks. Mike helps her in the kitchen, a pleasant surprise, she says. But Wong surmises the young man is shy. The two men talk in generalities, avoiding the heartache and old wounds. They don't have the true measure of each other just yet. Neither wants to be the first to unburden his baggage. Wong listens to Bob talk about the land, cattle, Montana winters, and environmentalists. He is launched on a tirade against the "goddamned eco-terrorists," who want to raise the U.S. Forest Service grazing rates.

Vicki interrupts. "Not that topic again, Bob! Please, spare our guest!" She smiles at Wong. "Gentlemen, dinner is ready. Please sit." She is the picture of grace, hospitality, and beauty to him on this day.

"Nah, Vicki, I was just getting started when you interrupted us." He winks at Wong. "Probably a good thing," he says as the two men move to the dining table, "because I'm starving!"

Passing the salad around, Bob asks, "Looking back on your experiences, do you think we had a right to be there?"

Wong thinks for a moment. "No. But we speak from hindsight, don't we? After all, we lost the war." Wong dishes some salad onto his plate. "We didn't have the perseverance for it and we didn't want to make more sacrifices. The North Vietnamese were ready and willing to die in great numbers."

Wong pours the salad dressing and starts eating. "Great salad, Vicki." He smiles.

"Thank you."

"We had great hopes in the beginning. To stop communism," Bob says, pausing in mid-bite to reply. "If we didn't stop it in Vietnam, all of Indochina would fall like dominoes." Bob looks at his son, who nods in understanding.

"That was the argument, wasn't it? From Kennedy through Johnson, and finally Nixon saw the light. Only because of massive anti-war demonstrations, though."

"There's steak and potatoes and broccoli on the table. Help yourselves," Vicki pipes in.

The men obey with relish. Wong takes a thick steak, the size of a pancake, cuts into it, and guides the piece into his mouth. "Mmm, wonderful!" He beams at Vicki.

She smiles back.

"Ya know, I used to hate communists with a passion," Bob confesses. "Maybe so much, I couldn't see straight."

"A lot of us couldn't see straight in those days," Wong agrees. "We were led by people who couldn't see straight. We didn't learn from the French experience." Here Wong looks to Vicki. "What did you think in those days, Vicki?"

"I was a Warrant Officer's wife. I wasn't allowed to think, or maybe I didn't want to think. I was like everybody else in the majority those days. I thought it was the right thing to do . . . But, I'll tell you one thing. It was the loneliest, most worrisome time of my life. When I got word that he had been severely wounded in action, I couldn't sleep for days on end." She looks to Bob and closes her hand over his. He returns the squeeze.

"I still remember the time we flew support for this one company sweeping through this village. I had put the chopper down after the sweep was done and was talking to the captain about future logistics. I was a cherry warrant officer, been there less than two weeks. They had found three Viet Cong suspects. Young, thin guys in black pajamas. The South Vietnamese were interrogating them. I was standing alongside, observing all this stuff. The interpreter was relaying all their answers to the captain. We were looking for an arms cache. Nobody would talk."

He stops to down a piece of steak, chewing hurriedly, swallowing.

"Then all of a sudden the ARVN interpreter pulls out his .45 and asks a question. The one suspected VC shook his head. The interpreter shot past the guy's head, barely missing him by an inch. Blew out his eardrum and scared him shitless, but he didn't say a thing. Then the interpreter got a better idea."

Wong continues to eat, slowly, so he can focus on the story.

"Told the captain that we should take all three of them up in the chopper, interrogate them upstairs. I didn't know what the hell was going on. I was just the pilot."

Vicki's face is tight.

"When we got about five hundred feet up, the guy lined 'em up right in front of the chopper door. The captain was just laughing. The interpreter asked the first suspect again where the arms cache was. The poor bastard was shaking so badly he could hardly stand up. Shaking in the goddamned wind. Didn't even look up, kept his eyes down. The interpreter asked his question one more time. The guy shook his head. WHOOSH. Pushed him out the door. I looked back in total surprise. I didn't expect it. I thought the ARVN guy was just bluffing. Same question, next guy. Same result, another dead VC. The third one cooperated." A pause, and then, "I lost my cherry that afternoon."

Mike looks curiously at his father. "Dad, how come I never heard any of this before? Why now?"

Bob looks to Wong. "Because I have a former comrade-in-arms here. Maybe it's good that I talk about it now." He looks at his son, the teenager who is fast becoming a man. "There is no glory in war, son."

They pick at their food now, the war brought back home. Hunger somewhat assuaged, grief and regret become companions at the table.

Wong relates the loss of his two friends, Deacon and Muley. There is not a dry eye at the table when he finishes.

"Why? Why must there be war?" Vicki asks.

Neither of the two grown men can answer.

"It's a male thing," she answers. "The male ego. War is macho."

She stands and gathers up her plate, some food uneaten. "It's the goddamned testosterone!" she mutters, loud enough so everyone can hear.

The two men look at each other, knowing the truth of her statements. Bob looks at his son—a young man anxious to leave the ranch. The men, still hungry, finish eating, though more slowly.

Over dessert, Bob asks, "Dave, are you in a hurry to get to the Vietnam Memorial?"

Wong gives him a quizzical look. "No, not really."

"Why don't you stay a week? We've got a lot of land around here. You could work some for your keep and relax some. I want to show you how this land can help you relax."

"Does that mean I'll have to get up on a horse?"

They all laugh. "It's not that difficult. Besides we have a really laidback mare that is as tame as any horse in the world. Her name is Brandy. You'll love her."

Wong thinks for a moment. "Why sure. I'd love to stay! But I would like to pick up my car tomorrow. Is that all right?"

"Fine. We can pick it up after we do some roundup in the back hundred acres and get your rear end broken in."

Except for Vietnam, he has not lived so close to the land before in his life: rising at dawn, riding during the day when dust caked every pore and the sun baked his skin into leather, when he rode with Bob and the hired hands into the foothills and meadows, heard the birds singing, and saw the wildflowers spread before him like a carpet.

He could hardly walk after the first day. He didn't know he had such muscles in his thighs and buttocks. But by the end of the second day, he felt better, though still sore.

Because he wanted to lose his paunch, he steeled his resolution to continue jogging while on this crosscountry trip. That second afternoon, he suited up, put on his jogging shoes, and headed off the ranch to run three miles on the Forest Service roads. He was slow, but his body has become accustomed to physical exertion. When he didn't run, it was like an ague had settled over him, a dispiriting numbness that would spread through his body to affect his mental well-being, his sense of self. Wong grudgingly acknowledged that Erlandson was right. He had given him the gift of exercise, and Wong craved it as badly as he had once craved booze. Other afternoons, as his body adjusted, he jogged farther and a bit faster. When he finished, he would warm down, doing stretches. He felt alive, energized, relaxed, at peace, a man in love—could he dare say it?—with himself. There was none of the chronic self-loathing.

Then, there was eating. Though he succumbed to Vicki's desserts, he tried to keep portions small. No small feat, because her cooking was superb. He felt he was being rude saying, "No, thanks," to her entreaties to eat more. All he could do was pat his paunch, and say, "I'm trying to lose weight." They understood.

The moon hanging in the evening sky found a smile on his face. Even the two dogs began following him like he was an old friend, indulging his rough petting, lolling their tongues out, and plopping down at his feet when all three of them—and sometimes Mike—sat out on the verandah in the evening to listen to the crickets, owls, and coyotes.

The landscape was a salve to him, gentling his soul, and even easing his torment over Mercury. The couple was also a salve to him. Bob had been to Vietnam and knew what it was like. Vicki had suffered the separation. And that last night of his stay, with the four of them on the porch, he talked about Mercury, the passion of his heart.

"Maybe . . . I don't know. Maybe it's just pity on her part for me." They were watching the light fade over the distant mountains.

"Why pity?" Vicki asks.

"Well . . . " Wong looks to them both. Bob and Vicki are sitting together in a swing, swaying slightly, looking out to their land. Wong sits close by in a wicker chair. Mike is sitting on the porch steps. "I did something over there. What's the phrase? 'A crime against humanity.'" Wong can see Bob looking at him curiously, his blue eyes searching.

There is a silence, except for the loud creaking of the swing and the sound of Mike's knife blade thudding into railroad ties embedded before the first porchstep.

Wong continues, but does not confess his sin in detail. "I committed what I guess you could call murder. My psychiatrist calls it murder.
Mercury calls it murder. And I guess I'm starting to call it murder."

Bob snorts. "Don't you mean 'operational expediency'?"

Wong nods. "Why, yes."

"That happened more times than I like to remember."

The silence hangs once again. Then, "I was at My Lai, flying operational support," Bob says.

"Jesus!" Wong looks at him with renewed interest.

Mike turns his face to his father, wondering.

"The sons of bitches were shooting women and kids," Bob says,
looking to Mike, letting his words sink in so his son can understand. "I
couldn't believe my eyes. Putting them in bunches and mowing them
down with M-16s and even M-60s. I saw three villagers running from
American troops, who weren't far behind. The villagers hid in a bunker.
I put my chopper down between them and the troops. I said, 'What the
fuck's going on? What are you doing, shooting civilians?' I had given orders to Colburn—who was manning the M-60 in the chopper—to cover
me. The fucking lieutenant said, 'Orders, man. We got orders to waste
the whole village, not let anything live.'

"I said, 'Well, you're not gonna shoot those civilians!' I pointed to
the villagers in the bunker, then I pointed to Colburn. That kinda cooled
'em. They just sat down and took a smoke break. We couldn't fit all nine
civilians into the chopper." Here he pauses, reflecting, then looks at Wong.
Wong drops his gaze. "We asked one of the gunships down to help us out.

"There was a boy, about seven or so. He was protecting his three-
year-old brother, hugging him. He was on the ground, just looking at me.
Trembling. Sad eyes." Bob shakes his head. "I couldn't let him stay there.
We had to refuel. What if we couldn't get back in time? I mean, there
were still those murdering sons of bitches roaming about. I lifted him and
his brother into the chopper, pushed them in among the others. One
small tear rolled down the kid's cheek. I still remember that tear.

"I loaded some of the civilians on the one gunship that landed and
the rest on ours. Another gunship flew cover until we could ferry them all

to some safe place. But we were running low on fuel." His weather-beaten face is set with disgust, even after all these years.

"I saw a ditch earlier, filled with bodies—old men, women, children, babies. Some motherfucker was going through the ditch finishing off anyone who moved or moaned. I couldn't believe it. Could not fucking believe it! Couldn't believe that these were American troops!

"Before we took off for refueling, we did one more pass. Colburn saw movement in one of the ditches. We landed and Larry stepped into the dead bodies and retrieved a little girl. She was catatonic. Then we flew back for refueling. By the time we got back from refueling, we couldn't find any more villagers, at least any that were alive.

"I reported it to my C.O., and nobody believed me or the gunners at first. They thought I was someone who got unduly excited in combat. Jesus!" The rancor still sits hard on him. "But I did get them to stop the massacre through the chain of command." He looks at Wong. "Even in war, there is still Right and Wrong."

Wong gets up from his chair, walks to Bob, stands in front of him, and salutes. "I want to shake your hand, too, sir!" Bob remains seated, flabbergasted at first, then stands. The two shake hands, then hug. "What you did, very few did in war. And that was to right a wrong, to stop an evil thing from happening. That took guts, more guts than I ever had or will have. To run against the grain of your peers, fellow soldiers, officers even."

"I didn't save many," he says, staring at the floor of the porch. "Over five hundred civilians were killed." A coyote calls in the distance, the short yip, yip, and then the long drawn-out howl. A plaintive song of life.

"Dad, how come you never told me about this?"

"It's not a proud history for America or for me, son. I also wanted you to be old enough to understand. And, well, I guess this is as good a time as any."

"Mike," Wong says, "your father is a hero with a capital H. Don't you ever forget it!"

Mike looks in amazement at his father, a newfound respect.

"And you know, this whole thing would have been swept away if it weren't for one man, a guy named Ridenhour. Ronald Ridenhour.

His letter to Westmoreland triggered the whole investigation. Ridenhour kept hearing these stories about these widespread killings in 'Pinkville.' The My Lai massacre took place in March 1968. The investigation didn't start until November 1969, about a year and a half later. Then, remember that Life magazine article in December 1969 about the My Lai massacre?"

"Yeah, I remember some pictures from it. All those bodies lying in the road and ditch."

"Americans did this?" Mike asks, disbelief showing on his face.

"Yeah, Mike."

"But why?"

Bob takes a deep breath, the memories coming back to haunt him. "The troops had orders to 'kill everything.' They had been harassed by mines, booby traps, and snipers. So, it was kind of down the whole chain of command. But, only Calley—he was one of the platoon leaders—was ever charged with anything."

"Yeah, I remember him," Wong says.

"Other officers were culpable, too. There was even a cover-up, I seem to remember."

"So many civilians," Wong mutters, shaking his head. Mike continues throwing his knife. "Why so many women and kids?"

"Calley got a life sentence, then it was reduced to twenty years, then ten years. He got paroled early."

"He should have been punished more severely," Wong states.

"I don't understand, Dad. He got off with less than ten years after participating in the murder of over five hundred civilians?"

"That's right, Mike."

"But how?"

"I think because the murders were committed in a wartime situation. Life is cheaper then. There were political forces, too. Some people thought he was a scapegoat."

A silence once more. Mike has even stopped throwing his knife. A look of disbelief and anger suffuses the boy's face. Bob has raised his son well, Wong thinks.

Bob turns and casts a weary look at Wong. "Were you punished enough?" Vicki and Mike turn to look at him also.

Wong sits up. A burden of guilt and shame overwhelms him as a blush spreads across his tan face. He stares at the knife in Mike's hand, suddenly suspended in mid-air. Wong thinks, Here is a round-eye who went out of his way to save the lives of slant-eyes. And he . . . he had gone out of his way to kill slant-eyes. For what? To gain the approbation of round-eyes, because he wanted to be a round-eye. A physical impossibility. A demented delusion of his youth.

Finally, he tells them the story of his sin.

"I've suffered enough," he concludes his confession, almost choking on the words. "Oh, God, believe me when I say I've suffered enough." He looks up, stares at Bob, tears forming. "I'm not amoral."

Bob returns his stare, reflecting a moment. "I believe you, Dave. Otherwise you wouldn't be here. I don't like assholes."

Wong smiles. "I don't either." Then, "Can we switch to something more fun, like women?" They laugh. "I mean it's hard for a woman to love someone she considers to have once been a murderer."

"Dave?" Vicki says, squeezing her husband's hand, "and I think Bob agrees. We don't think you're a murderer."

Wong weeps with relief, the pent-up shame exploding.

"Certainly not in the category of My Lai."

Silence. Wong hangs his head and tries to control his weeping.

Vicki gently changes subjects. "But this woman does like you, doesn't she?" she asks.

"I believe so." He raises his head and wipes his eyes.

"Well, when a woman likes someone, it's usually pretty obvious."

"Ah, but there are other men." He still believes this.

"Oh."

Wong is silent. Bob and Vicki talk about details of the ranch. Which fence to mend, which cattle need medical care.

Though Wong has been haunted all these years by the images of the Mama-san and the little girl, he cannot imagine walking through the field of death that was My Lai. Or being responsible for it. The old men, the women, the little children, the babies.

If Wong's murders were a personal sin, then here—and he remembers it splashed in full color of the major magazines—was a great American Sin. A sin that defined the war, a perversion, a sin as insidious and contagious as any spreading plague. How soldiers, with no conscionable thought, followed orders to mow down people as if they were cattle bound for slaughter. There were some soldiers who refused to do their "duty," Bob said, disobeying direct orders to shoot unarmed civilians. Such soldiers should be commended, Wong thinks. But they were the exception.

Wong wonders how many murderous soldiers suffered as he has. Did they finally find forgiveness for themselves? Did they commit suicide as he almost did, or did they step back from the abyss? Or did they sleep well, believing they had committed no war crime, no crime against humanity, no crime as defined by their stilted, minuscule consciences?

He wonders about himself. Is he any different? The village had been a base for suspected VC operation for weeks—snipers and booby traps. The massacre was an explosion of suppressed rage against an unseen enemy, an explosion of war without boundaries, without rules; it was war in its most evil form. And it was racism in the midst of war, where Vietnamese were gooks—subhumans—thus killable with no remorse.

Wong's circumstances? It was war where the mission was everything, taking precedence over even morality. Isolated, vulnerable, and compromised, he murdered because he thought they were in mortal danger. The troops at My Lai knew there was no more danger. So, the question hangs before him, splashed in neon lights. *Would I have murdered at My Lai?* Was his innate sense of Right and Wrong strong enough to provide the courage to disobey such a direct order? He shudders, feeling chilled.

He looks over to Bob and Vicki. Vicki is leaning her head on Bob's shoulder; he has his arm draped over her. Wong feels like getting up, kneeling and groveling before this man who chose Good over Evil, Right over Wrong. But he knows such an act would embarrass the couple.

The saving grace for Wong is that he has a conscience. It is fertile ground for his nightmares.

H o w a r d   a n d   S a m

He is driving north among the round hills, on U.S. 93 toward Glacier National Park. He had left Bob and Vicki's about eight after a pancake breakfast with eggs, sausages, and coffee. "To set you right for the long trip," Vicki said.

They stood around afterwards like shy youngsters at a dance when it came time to say goodbye. Mike had left earlier, wishing him a good trip to "The Wall." Bob had his left hand in his jeans pocket, a cup of coffee in his right. Wong stood there, both hands in his pockets. Vicki had her arms crossed.

"Oh, Jesus," Vicki finally said, "I hate good-byes." They hugged then. Bob came over, shook his hand. "Take care, Dave. We enjoyed having you over. And if you're ever in this neck of the woods, don't even hesitate to call us." Wong said he wouldn't. He left with an ache in his gut. He had known them one week, but they had the feel of old friends.

Even the dogs seemed forlorn, whining about as he headed to his car. He gently gave Brewster a kick to his haunch. It was a game he had taught the black lab. The dog pivoted away, growled softly, and lunged in at Wong. "You better watch out, Dave. He's gonna take your leg off one of these days," Bob yelled, laughing.

Wong laughed, too. He feinted left, then lunged right, pivoting around on top of the big black lab, lifting the dog up on its two hind legs, hugging him and burying his face into the back of his neck. "You're too slow, Brewster!" Then he pushed the dog off and held his hand out. Brewster came back, sniffing it. Wong rubbed his ears. Then he reached out and scratched Sadie's ears. She kept going back and forth in front of him, bumping her head under his hand like a cat begging for strokes.

He stopped once more to look out over the broad valley and at the mountains in the distance, then waved goodbye to the couple and whispered goodbye to the dogs. The road called to him like an angel of life beckoning the newborn.

The old car runs smoothly. The mechanic had done a good job. Wong pushes the gas pedal down and feels the spurt of acceleration. He is off I-90 now, on two-laned U.S. 93 North, undulating through the hills. On the eastern edge of Flathead Lake, he runs into construction again. He sighs, chews on some cashews he had bought earlier. At last, he is waved on. The road climbs so slowly he is unconscious of it. Only the gradual change in the landscape seeps into his mind. The monopoly of deciduous trees loosens and the conifers now hold sway, all the trees shaped like arrowheads pointing to the sky. He is among the lesser mountains. In the near distance, he sees higher ones, snowcapped, with long ridgelines that outrun the contours of his imagination. The air is fresh, the land a beacon to his soul, pregnant with the possibilities of life and adventure. "The West! Goddammit! The West! I love it!" he yells as he drives along, Country & Western playing on the radio.

He makes the town of Hungry Horse in the early afternoon, stopping at a small gas and grocery store. He checks the map. It is not far from the park entrance.

He looks across the street and sees a huge sign over a building pronouncing, "Huckleberry Store." The store turns out to be a Taj Mahal of huckleberries, serving up huckleberry pancakes and muffins; huckleberry pies; huckleberry ice cream; huckleberry preserves, jams, jellies, syrups, toppings, and even huckleberry fudge. He picks up one jar each of huckleberry jam, jelly, and preserves—for himself and as a gift for Mercury.

"Bears love them," the cashier says.

Great! he thinks. He is planning a short hike in the park and already someone is mentioning bears.

He drives the short distance from the store to the park entrance, pays the entrance fee, and is directed toward the Apgar Visitors Center.

At Apgar, he has trouble finding a parking place. He sighs. It is high summer. The tourists carpet the grounds like army ants cutting a swath through jungle.

Inside the visitors center, he stands in line for information. A small bookshop lies to the left. A three-dimensional topographical map of the park takes up a good part of the floor space to the right. A few stuffed animals sit on pedestals, including a golden eagle, the light somehow caught in the eyes, almost as if it were still alive.

After some minutes, he steps up to the counter, speaks to a young woman ranger, "Hi. I'd like to do a little day hike. Do you have any suggestions?"

"How many days do you have to spend here?" she asks. She is one of those rugged outdoorswomen, tanned, attractive.

"Just today, I'm afraid." He has an appointment to keep in Missouri in a few days.

"Are you going out on the Going-to-the-Sun Road toward St. Mary or Many Glacier?"

Wong studies the map. "Yes. That's right."

She recommends Avalanche Lake, Hidden Lake Overlook on the Going-to-the-Sun Road, and Ptarmigan Falls and Redrock Falls in the Many Glacier area.

"And," she looks at her watch—it is 3:00 P.M.—"you should be cautious of bears on all trails here. I wouldn't recommend walking in the evening twilight or early dawn. And make lots of noise when you hike. Talk loudly, or yell out once in a while." She hands over the map with the hikes she has marked. "Have fun."

"Thanks," Wong replies. Suddenly, he is in a hurry. He wants to get away from the crowds, do the hike and stretch his car-cramped legs, and then find a campsite, perhaps at Rising Sun.

He drives alongside Lake McDonald. Shortly beyond he sees the sign for Avalanche Creek. He turns into a small parking lot, parks, puts on his hiking boots, and dons a small pack. He is among old growth western red cedars, the same as in the Pacific Northwest. They range far and wide, he thinks.

The path is wide and flat in the beginning, then veers right, paralleling a stream. He climbs gradually, happy to be out of the car and glad to feel his muscles at work. He can feel the stretch in his Achilles and calf, the tightening of his quadriceps, the thumping of his heart.

There are several small waterfalls to his left, cascading over large boulders. The forest is small trees here, not the old growth of below, but skinny trees of fir and pine. He looks at the hillsides, looking for movement, looking for bears. He hears noises, but it is human conversation floating down from above. Within minutes he sees two women in their thirties or forties. "Hi," they say. "Howdy," he replies. As he climbs higher, he sees more parties on their way down, young families, couples, older folks. "It's beautiful up there," they tell him.

He has been hiking for forty minutes. He knows he is close to the lake. Suddenly he tops a rise. The trail drops below him into head-high bulrushes. Above them he sees a spire of rock rise from a solid ridgeline. The bulrushes run for seventy yards. He walks through them and is reminded of the head-high elephant grass of Vietnam. He feels an eerie sensation, almost as if somebody were watching him. He sees a large area where the tall plant stalks have been trampled. A bear has been rolling there! He hurries through, breathing hard.

Finally he is at the lake. Slowly, he relaxes, breathing deeply. The lake, near the shore, is full of snags and deadwood. Some hundred feet beyond is clear water. The mountains rise steeply on three sides, at least two thousand feet above the lake. Waterfalls, runoff from glaciers, cascade off steep faces on the opposite side.

A path continues alongside the lake, hemmed in by thick vegetation. Wong is leery of walking a path that looks like an ambush site. It's peacetime, dammit! he tells himself. Still, he cannot make himself walk that path. There are bears around, after all. Instead, he walks the sandy beach, at times stepping into the water and at other times fighting the branches of small trees that overhang the shore. He finally hits a wide beach and sits down to view the vast panorama of water and mountains. He takes off his pack and removes some cookies and eats them. He drinks from his water bottle. He sits for minutes in the silence. A couple walks by from his left. He says hello, they nod and say hello also. The sun hits the tops of the ridges, glinting off the white of the glaciers, the grays of the rockfaces. Wong wishes he has more time to spend in this park. And he wishes Mercury were there with him.

He retraces his path, once again scurrying through the bulrushes. He descends the trail and walks by the stream with its large, flat boulders, and then finds himself in the cedar grove near the parking lot. He hurries; he wants to make the campsite before dark. Luckily, it is not a weekend night, so he is hopeful that he can find a space.

He drives over Logan Pass, awed at the high mountains that look as if they were piled up high, one layer on top of another, the horizontal lines running the length of the mountains. The green of the meadows and the wildflowers remind him of the Pacific Northwest. And while he enjoys the scenery of Glacier, he is at once proud and arrogant about the qualities of his own state.

Driving by St. Mary Lake he sees mountains colored like dark watermelon meat. Even the nearby roadside stones have that pigment. He has never seen such a color in stone before. What could have caused it?

He arrives at Rising Sun Campground around 7:00. He drives through the camping area, relieved that there are at least a few campsites free. He parks and walks to the fee station, registers, and pays. Back at the campsite, he pulls out his tent, an old Moss Eave, and erects it. Then he pulls out his pack and digs in it for the cookstove, an old Svea 123. It is equipment from that hunting trip of so long ago, his first kill.

He thinks of Mercury, the time just before that disastrous dinner, when she had taken the whole exercise group hiking up to Skyline Ridge near Mt. Baker. She had told him during a rest break, "God resides in mountains." In the spring sunshine, sitting next to her, gazing at the beauty of the subalpine meadows and the nearby mountains, he felt it was true.

She had reawakened his love for nature, cajoling some of the bitterness of the jungle out of his soul, so that he could once more love this land, America's land. And how he loved it so: the evergreens and the hardwoods of his youth, the alpine landscape of the continent, not the steamy jungle, overgrown vegetation, and red dirt of Vietnam, or even

Hawaii. He hated red dirt. He hated the jungle, felt hemmed in by it. In the jungle, his fear grew from the claustrophobia he felt when in dense vegetation. He imagined death clinging to him like liana vines, wrapping around him, choking him. It was a place of imminent death, occurring in an eyeblink, where the enemy hid only feet away in the dense brush. And the red dirt was to him a manifestation of solid red blood. In Vietnam, he had walked through the blood of his comrades, the blood of the enemy, the blood of the earth.

After supper, he builds a fire and watches the play of the flames. He hears sounds from other campsites, the cry of children, the laughter ringing out among the trees in the night, the low murmur of adult conversation, the cracking and popping of firewood.

He sees, in the flames, better times. Rather than a crystal ball, his past and future are read in fire. The flames flicker, shaking at the night, and he is lost in fire, the fire of his guilt, the fire of his remaining compassion, the fire of his love for his daughter and Mercury. In the fire's flames, a jittery image forms—the Wall!—a bright shining flame of black granite beckoning him across the width of the United States, across time, across space. He believes that the fire of the black granite will sear away the pain, cleansing and strengthening him, like the searing flame of the blast furnace will burn carbon and iron to form steel.

He departs early the next morning, skirting the rest of the way around St. Mary Lake, past aspens with leaves shaking in the breeze. The visitors center at St. Mary sits in a broad expanse of a meadowed valley surrounded by high mountains. Wong stops on the side of the road for a moment, gazes at real beauty and fixes the image, then continues. He exits the park and drives south on U.S. 89. It is a smooth two-laned road with wide shoulders. The road narrows and winds as it drops in elevation.

The land rolls away in hills covered with meadows and aspens. As he drops in elevation, the land becomes less green and less rolling, and more stark. He has dropped away from beauty to the arid high plains of the American West, both of his imagination and his present reality, where horizons once more stretch to the sky and beyond.

He drives through Browning, on the Blackfeet Indian Reservation, past houses that reflect the drabness of the surrounding landscape. Brown houses, black houses, gray houses, umber, sienna, earth tones, and a white trailer here and there. An auto repair garage, originally yellow, has been smeared black from grease and oil, almost as if the grease and oil had hung in the atmosphere of the place. Old cars sit like derelicts, broken in spirit, giving up their body parts to save their brethren, the Indian nation.

As he continues east, the land once again becomes more rolling and he can see cattle grazing in some of the pastures. Every once in a while he sees a ranchhouse, next to cottonwoods that dot some gully. The road stretches in front of him; only a few cars ply it.

Suddenly, in the distance, he sees . . . motorcycles? The mirage-like images shimmer in the distance. No, they are not moving fast enough. Touring bicyclists? As he closes the gap on this lonely stretch, he sees that they are backpackers! A girl is turned toward him, a beseeching smile on her face, her thumb out. The man is still facing forward, heavy pack on his back, a baseball cap drawn down over his head, shielding his face from the hot sun. He is still walking forward, the girl backpedaling.

Wong steps on the brake; the car squeals to a stop. The couple lumbers hurriedly to the car. He makes room in the front seat, throwing junk from the passenger seat into the back. He unlocks the doors.

"Hi!" the girl says. "Boy are we glad you stopped!"

Wong smiles. "No problem. You two look tired and hot. I've got some Cokes in the cooler there. Help yourselves."

The man smiles at him. "Tank you, sir." He is Chinese, in his sixties, maybe even early seventies, a short white beard, and black and white long hair tied into a ponytail. He couldn't be more than five-four and one hundred and forty pounds. The old man wipes the sweat from his brows.

Wong is surprised to see a Chinese man in the heart of the West, especially in the boondocks. He is curious, but hides it. He gets out and opens the tailgate for them. They shrug off their packs and put them in the back. The old man sits in front with Wong, the girl sits behind the old man. She is about twenty-five, around five-four and ten pounds lighter than her companion, Wong guesses. She has short wavy brown hair and brown eyes, an attractive face—angular, he thinks.

"My name is Dave Wong." He holds his hand out to the old man.

"Name is Hoh Siang Chen. Everybody call me Howard."

"Hi, my name is Samantha Blume. Glad to meet you."

Wong starts the car up, crawling away from the shoulder, like an elephant lumbering slowly off. The car groans under the new load and slowly gathers momentum. The girl opens a Coke and passes another one to Howard. Howard accepts it graciously.

"Thank you, Dave," Samantha says.

He looks at her in the mirror. "No problem . . . What are you two doing out here on a day like this?"

"Well, we went backpacking in Glacier. Since we don't have a car, we decided to start walking out."

"Wow. I wish I had time to go backpacking. I would have liked to go. See any grizzlies?"

Howard laughs. "We saw one. Big one, eh, Sam?"

"Yeah, sifu. We saw a really big one. Must have been a male. It was on the trail about seventy yards off. We just stood in our tracks and waited, holding our breaths. After a minute or so, he wandered off. But that whole day we kinda kept looking all over the place, especially behind us."

"Why do you call him sifu?"

"Oh! That means teacher."

"I know what it means."

"So he's my teacher."

Wong looks to the old man. "So, Howie, what do you teach?"

"The name Howard, not Howie," he says, frowning. The old man then whips his hands out, two smooth moves in a semicircle—knifehand blocks. "Kung Fu and Arnis."

"Arnis? What is arnis, Howard?"

"Filipino martial art. I born and raised in Philippines."

"But you Chinese . . . but you're Chinese, aren't you?" He has to fight from slipping into pidgin.

"Yeah, Chinese. Chinese live in Philippines, you know."

"Oh."

"His family owned an import/export business there. They imported a lot of goods and luxury items from China to the Philippines and exported stuff from the Philippines to China. At least before World War II, before the Japanese invaded," Sam explains.

"So have you learned a lot of martial arts from Howard?" Wong asks Sam.

"I know enough."

"She good." Howard laughs. "Don't fruck with her."

Wong and Sam laugh, too.

"Where you folks headed?"

"St. Louis," Howard replies. "It where we live."

"You came all the way to Glacier from St. Louis?"

"Yeah," Sam answers.

"How?"

Sam holds up her thumb between the two front seats.

"Whew!" Wong whistles. "That's a hard way to travel."

"Not when have her legs," Howard says and laughs. Sam slaps his shoulder from behind.

Wong laughs, too, seeing her turn red.

"Dirty old man," she says.

"Well, you're in luck. I'm going by St. Louis. If you like, I'll drive you there." Then, "But I need you to split the gas?" He turns slightly to watch them.

The girl looks to the old man. He nods. "Sure."

"Good!" Wong says, as they speed down the highway, over the hills. And he is suddenly glad for the company.

Wong drives the back roads most of that afternoon. They hit I-94 at Billings and continue east for a short while before veering off onto I-90 again. The freeway is like an old friend to Wong now. He pushes for Gillette, Wyoming. Both the old man and the girl are dozing, lulled to sleep by the narcotic motion of the car on a seemingly endless highway.

They both awaken as the car slows and turns into a gas station in the town of Crow Agency. "Pit stop!" Wong yells out.

Everyone gets out and stretches. Wong pumps the gasoline while the two go to the restrooms. Wong is checking the oil when the old man comes out.

"How much?" he asks.

"Sixteen-twenty."

"I pay this time. Next time you pay. Okay?"

Wong nods. "Okay, Howard." The old man smiles and retraces his steps back into the gas-and-serve. The oil is fine. Wong slams the hood down. Sam comes out with Howard, candy bars in her hands. She hands Wong a Snickers bar. He thanks her. He chews on the bar as he cleans the front windshield. Sam cleans the back one. Then he goes to the restroom.

"Okay, gotta figure out the miles per gallon." Wong, back in the driver's seat, pulls out his pen and pad and does a quick calculation. "Twenty-five miles a gallon on the highway. Not bad for an old Volvo."

"Should buy Japanese car," Howard says. "Thirty to forty miles gallon."

"I like Volvos," Wong replies.

"Me, too!" Sam says. She looks about the station wagon. "They are usually very nice cars."

The innuendo is not lost on Wong. He looks at her. She winks. He smiles.

"Cost more money," the old man mutters, thinking about having to pay for a fill-up every other time.

"I get to crack." Sam bends over the pool table, lining up her shot. It is their third game; Sam and Howard have won one game each. The cue ball flies from the end of her stick and the pile of balls explode outward, two balls going into adjacent corner pockets. Sam beams.

"Lucky shot," Wong says.

They had arrived in Gillette, Wyoming, around five-thirty. There was a moment of awkwardness at the motel. They looked at each other, then Sam said, "Oh, what the hell. It's cheaper if we all stay together." Once settled, Wong went for a run. After his shower, they opted for a steak dinner at one of the local restaurants. "Can't beat beef in west and midwest!" Howard said. When they finished eating, Wong was tired and wanted to go back to the motel and sleep, but the other two wanted to go to a tavern for drinks and pool. Wong relented and tagged along.

"Good shot, Sam!" Howard says.

Sam lines up on ball 5 for the side pocket. It is a touch shot. She shoots and the ball falls in. Wong frowns. Maybe she is a pool shark! She looks at him and smiles. "Ball 3 in the corner there." The ball plops into the hole. Sam studies the layout. Wong doesn't see any easy shots. "Ball 7 in the side pocket," she says. But she misses.

"About time," Wong says, chalking his cue tip.

It is a small tavern, mostly cowboys lined up at the bar. A few couples are sitting in booths. Neon signs advertising Miller and Budweiser are in the window. A clock with a neon "Michelob" hangs behind the bar. Antlered deer heads gaze down on them from the walls. Two cowboys are playing on the next table and have been there for some time. They laugh loudly, immersed in their own little jokes.

Wong aims for ball 12 in the corner pocket, almost dead on. He puts power behind it, the momentum kicking the ball in to leave the cue ball spinning at the spot where ball 12 had been. "Ha!" he laughs.

"Once in lifetime!" Howard shouts.

"Never again," Sam agrees.

Wong looks at them and beyond. The one cowboy is digging his friend's ribs and whispering, all the while looking at them. He is big and muscular, with a square-jawed face defined by arrogant, cold eyes. His black cowboy hat is pushed back, showing blond hair cropped short. The other one is tall and slender, with a pockmarked face, long crooked nose, and greasy long brown hair. His tan hat has been tossed on a chair.

Oh-oh, Wong thinks. Asshole cowboys again.

Wong steps between the tables to line up his next shot. He eyes ball 10 into the side pocket. The blond cowboy steps into the aisle also. He blows smoke toward Wong. Wong stands up, flicking his hand back and forth, fanning the smoke from in front of his face.

"Hey, Billy, looks like the Chinaman don't much like your smoking!" greasy hair says.

"Waal, if that ain't too much? Maybe we shoulda made this a non-smoking bar, eh?" Billy replies. "Or else kept Chinamen out of this joint, huh?" Billy's face is so close that Wong can smell the beer on his breath.

Sam's smile has vanished. Howard moves over to Wong's side, an insincere smile painted on his face.

"Fuck you!" Wong whispers.

"Whatdya say?"

"Ah, my friend not mean anyting, sir!" Howard steps in. "Excuse him, please, sir!" He bows, playing the obsequious Chinaman, pushing Wong out of the way.

"W-a-a-l, lookee here, Josh! What we got here is a fucking runt China-man! With a pigtail!" The big man laughs, flicking Howard's ponytail.

Sam has stepped around to where Wong is, whispering into his ear, "Don't worry! Sifu is good." Wong turns to look at her, seeing a smile play on her face.

"Yuk! Yuk!" greasy hair laughs. "You're right there, Billy. He's one small runt! And old, too!"

By now, everyone in the bar is watching the confrontation. The bar-tender barks out, "Oh, leave 'em alone, Billy. They ain't harmin' no one."

Billy looks intently at Howard. "Shut the fuck up, Earl. If I want your opinion, I'll ask for it."

"Oh, I thought . . . shit, you bas . . ." the bartender's voice fades into a mutter.

"Kind sir, we only enjoying ourself, playing harmless game of puel." Howard has laid his cue stick across the table. He stands less than three feet from Billy, letting the big man crowd him. "And that ponytail. Not pigtail. There difference."

"Waal, I don't care what it is. Me and Josh here, we don't like Chinamen, do we, Josh?" Josh nods his head. "Especially when they come with a right purty white woman. Now, Josh, what kind of white woman would fuck gooks, eh?"

The word "gooks" splashes over Wong's consciousness like a bucket of cold water. He starts to step forward, spitting out, "You fucking bastard!"

But Sam catches him by the arm, holding him with all her might.

"It's gonna be all right, Dave! Believe me!" she says, getting a firmer hold around his shoulder.

"Sir, my friend here is right! Your line-age—"

"Huh?"

"Lineage, asshole," Sam translates.

" . . . is most questionable," Howard continues. "I think you planted on this world like dung, huh?"

"Dung?" greasy hair asks.

"Like shit," Sam says. Wong laughs.

"Yeah, yeah. I know what dung is," Billy spits out the words. "And you, Chink lover," he points to Sam, "watch your mouth. I got a good use for it."

Sam reddens. Wong starts to step forward, but Howard waves him off and continues, "Yes, like shit. You one big asshole. Everybody has asshole, but you, you have two, huh? Your words come out like shit. What that, huh, make your mouth?"

Wong and Sam laugh out loud now. Even some of the other customers are chuckling.

With that, Billy rears back, his right fist shoots out, faster than Wong would have thought for a big man. But Howard is much faster, stepping away from the punch, blocking it with his left hand and stepping into the cowboy, snapping Billy's head back with a short right to his face. Howard then pulls Billy forward by the lapel with his right hand, driving his right knee into the big man's outer thigh, hard. Done in milliseconds. Fist like a ballpeen hammer, knee like a sledge hammer. Billy screams in pain as he crumples to the floor. Blood flows from his mouth as he grasps his leg with one hand and his jaw with the other, whimpering, "You son of a bitch! You son of a bitch! You broke my jaw and my leg!" He spits out teeth and blood.

Josh meanwhile has picked up his cue stick. Howard, facing him, picks up his own and breaks it in half on the table's edge. It is now about thirty inches long. He meets Josh's wide swing with his stick, moving into him, then sweeps the stick across Josh's right temple, the sound making a sharp thud in the silent room, then flips the stick up hard between Josh's legs. A scream. The tall man collapses, grasping his crotch, whimpering.

"Jesus Christ, mister. I don't want any more trouble." The bartender has rushed to Howard's side. "Maybe you'd better leave. And you owe me money for that cue stick."

Some of the other customers are helping the two men to lean against the wall. Josh still has his hands between his legs and is leaning sideways, dry barfing. Billy, his face a grimace of pain, is massaging his leg. "You broke it, asshole!"

Howard steps over to him. "What you say?"

"I said, 'You coulda broken it.'" His eyes turn away from Howard's piercing gaze. He mutters under his breath, but Howard cannot understand him.

"Maybe we'd better call an ambulance," one of the customers says.

"No ambulance! No cops!" Billy mutters. The bartender shrugs acquiescence. A few acquaintances attend to the two men.

Howard turns to the bartender. "After finish game, sir. We leave after finish game. How much for cue stick?"

"Twenty bucks."

Howard folds a twenty into his outstretched palm.

Wong looks to Sam, then Howard. "Are you that good?" he asks her.

She shakes her head. "No. Not too many people are, you know. But, he *has* slowed down a little in the last five years."

Wong doesn't believe the last statement. He seemed pretty damned fast to him. Sam goes over to Howard and hugs him.

Wong steps over and grabs him by the shoulder. "You old bastard, where'd you learn all that stuff?"

Howard smiles. "I tell you later, Davy. Let finish game, huh?" Then, as an aside, "That how you handle assholes!" and smiles at Wong.

They go back to the hotel close to midnight. Sam sleeps in the same bed as Howard. Wong listens to their gentle murmuring, but does not hear the sounds of lovemaking. What is the relationship between these two? he asks himself. He falls asleep quickly, the hum of the road in his dreams.

· · · · ·

249

After gassing up the next morning, they continue on I-90 toward South Dakota. The land rolls gently. On hillsides the horses and cattle stand like playthings in a child's toyset.

Wong is still mightily impressed by the old man's fighting skills. He looks at him and suddenly sees the tightly corded muscles in the small frame and the litheness with which the old man walks, like a dancer. He sees the polished, scarred knuckles—smooth and hard like steel. Probably breaks concrete, he thinks.

"Will you show me some moves?" Wong asks.

"Certainly. Next rest stop. I show you some inside moves and I show you some stick fighting, huh?"

"Great!" Wong beams, anxious now to stop at rest areas rather than to push the miles.

The land is wide open, arid, punctuated by a few small hills. Billboards and signs are few and far between. The ones that capture their attention come every thirty miles or so, sometimes more distant, sometimes less. "Food," "Ice Cream," "Soda Pop," "Wall Drug." Then, there would be others: "Jewelry," "Old West," "Gift shop," "Restaurant," "Wall Drug." Or, "Tourists stop here!" "Your friends stopped!" "Don't miss" "Wall Drug." The signs run like a series of flip-through picture cards.

"I saw those signs in Idaho," Wong says.

"Mmm, sounds interesting, don't you think?" Sam asks.

"Yes," Howard answers, "we go, huh, Davy?" He looks to Wong.

Wong looks sideways. "Okay, we go." They are coming up to the turnoff. A large billboard, possibly thirty feet long and twelve feet high, sits on the side of a hill proclaiming, "Last chance, next exit, WALL DRUG!" They exit, drive into town, follow the signs, "Buses park here," "Car parking," and follow the arrows. The marked road funnels them into a small downtown area, western in appearance, and bursting with tourists. They have to circle, and Wong finally finds a parking place. They get out of the car, stiffjointed, and stretch.

"Wow, look at all these shops!" Sam smiles in anticipation.

They climb onto the wooden sidewalk and enter the drugstore. Signs and pictures line the wooden walls. The theme of the Old West runs

rampantly through the place, a motif of cowboys and Indians. Southwest-
ern rugs adorn the wooden floor. A woman stands behind a jewelry counter
showing a customer some earrings fashioned from Black Hills gold. To
the right, families wait in line for refreshments at a restaurant.

A sign on a post between the drugstore and restaurant points to the
restrooms, saying, "Make your bladder flatter." Howard and Sam head in
that direction. Wong looks through the postcards. He buys two, one for
Mercury, one for Nancy. He decides he will write Jean some other time.

Sam and Howard browse through the giftstore when they return.
Wong heads to the restroom. When he comes back, they stand in line at
the cafeteria-style restaurant.

"Free donuts and coffee for Vietnam veterans," a sign proclaims.

"Hey, I'm a Vietnam vet," he tells the countergirl.

"Okay, sir, just help yourself," she says, smiling, "and tell the gal at
the cash register that you're a Vietnam vet."

Wong beams, looks to his two companions. "Aha, some small recognition!" They nod, look at him curiously. He helps himself to the dough-
nut and coffee, ordering a hamburger and fries, as well, sliding off his
diet. Sam has ordered the famous buffalo burger while Howard has opted
for a hot plate lunch of meatloaf and potatoes with corn.

"Looks like good Chinese food," Wong says, grimacing as he looks
at Howard's plate.

The old man laughs, shaking his head and swirling his ponytail.
They pay and find a table near the wall and the back entrance.

"You never said you were a Vietnam vet," Sam says, when seated.

"You never asked."

"Howard is a World War II veteran."

Wong looks over to the old man. "True," he says, "I fight Japanese."
Then, he laughs. "Now I like their cars."

They talk about both wars then, in between mouthfuls of food. "I
sixteen, caught in Philippines. After Americans surrender at Bataan, we,
Filipino resistance, fight as guerillas." Howard shoves a piece of meatloaf
into his mouth. "Damn-m-phned bad time! Three-and-a-half years damned
bad time."

"Three-and-a-half years! Jesus, I only had thirteen months in Vietnam." Wong puts down his hamburger, the bad memories seeping back.

"I kill first man at sixteen."

The statement brings Wong back to the present. "Jesus. Too young! Too young!"

"The war. You not own man in war. No fun. No joy."

"You're right. War is no fun, no joy." Wong starts eating again, looking about the wide dining room, filled with people. "How's the buffalo burger?" he asks Sam.

"It's delicious! Wanna try?"

"No, no thanks." But he is too late. She has already broken off a piece and put it on his plate. He picks it up, chews it. A pleasant flavor, lean, very little fat. "Not bad."

"Jap soldier young, too."

Wong is pulled once again into the old man's remembrances.

"But we hate Japs so much. I killed with hate in my heart. No mercy." The old man is lost in that far-off time and place. "Too many my friends die of torture at Jap hands, huh? Good friends, balls cut off. Fingers broken, cut off. Head cut off."

"Oh, God!" Sam says, her head bent over, resting on her hands, elbows atop the table. "Howard, why now? I was eating." She has heard it before. The din of tourists fills the room.

But the old man ignores her. "It where I learn to fight. From my Filipino brethren."

The term "brethren" smacks of communist terminology. What the hell, Wong thinks. I'm no longer fighting communists.

"Tell me of Vietnam," Howard asks.

Wong tells him, about the jungle, about the leeches, about the heat, the monsoons, the fear. "Ah, yes," the old man replies, "same in Philippines." But Wong does not tell him about his sin. He cannot. He watches the old man's face, wrinkled over time, sees even there the war weariness after all these years.

They get up and wander through the other stores, Sam in front, the two men still talking of war. They go through the cowboy store with its western wear and saddles, wander through a gem store where Sam buys some polished stone letter openers, walk aimlessly through a shoe store stocked with boots and moccasins, check out the bookstore and then the jewelry store.

The old man is tired. He sits on a bench alongside a wooden cowboy while Wong and Sam continue wandering. When Wong comes back, he thinks that Howard and the wooden cowboy both look old. The cowboy has skin the color of umber, and Howard is tanned only a few shades lighter. If he were to sit still, he could be mistaken for a wooden dummy.

The old man looks at his watch. "Time to go. Where Sam?"

"She's in the jewelry store, looking for earrings."

"Women."

Just then, Sam comes out of the jewelry store, a smile on her face and a small bag in her hands. She waves the bag. "The most beautiful earrings," she says.

"Women," Wong says, laughing in agreement.

Sam laughs and looks at both of them. "Men," she replies.

"Let's continue through America," Wong says.

Howard is teaching Wong martial arts on a grassy area of a rest stop, oblivious to the people staring at them. Sam practices by herself.

"Here the move I use in bar. You throw right punch, eh?" Howard positions Wong, left foot forward. "Go, throw right."

Wong throws the punch. Howard, with his right foot forward, shows him slowly: block with left, snap punch with the right lead as you slide into opponent, grab the lapel with right, pull opponent into you as you drive your knee into his thigh. Howard repeats it twice, then calls Sam over. She plays the perpetrator. Howard walks Wong through the sequence again. He catches on quickly.

"Good, you coordinated! Practice again!"

Wong goes through it again, until it becomes smoother.

"Good! Good!

"Now," Howard pulls out a stick about two feet long and an inch and a quarter in diameter, "this rattan. Good wood from vine in

Philippines. Light and strong. Hit your head, you feel it. But no kill you, like oak. But it faster than oak. No break either." With that he twirls the stick about Wong's head, changing directions with lightning speed. Wong stands still, flabbergasted at the blur of motion. Then Howard taps Wong across his forearm bone.

"Ouch!" Wong yells, grabbing his arm. Sam laughs.

"Here, you take this one," Howard says. Wong takes it. "Now, stand like me and follow me, huh?" Howard goes through the swinging motions, with his right leg out in front. "This is one," a swing, like a forehand in tennis, to the opponent's left temple; "this is two," a backhand to the opponent's right temple; "this is three," a forehand swing to the opponent's left side at the elbow or ribs; "this is four," a backhand on the opposite side; "this is five," a straight thrust to the opponent's solar plexus. "That enough for now. Practice so you don't forget." Then he watches.

Wong goes through the motions, one, two, three, four, five. His motions are jerky.

"No, no! Don't jerk. This not karate. You take karate before?" Wong nods. "Not karate, huh? Not Tae Kwon Do. Smooth. We follow through." Howard demonstrates, one move flowing smoothly into the other, like ballet. "Try again."

Wong tries. He relaxes his muscles, not tensing at the focus of each blow. He is smoother.

"Good. Keep working, huh?"

They spend another ten minutes on it. Some people have stopped to watch. One young man even asks Sam about what they are doing. "Arnis," she says. "Filipino martial art."

Wong looks at his watch. "We'd better go," he says.

"Before go, we salute each other, huh? End session, Kung Fu style." The old man shows a long ritual Kung Fu form, too long for Wong to follow, though he tries. Wong looks at his watch. Howard, exasperated, shows him the short salute, right hand in a fist clasped by the left, under the chin, and with feet together, a bow of the head. Wong does the short salute.

"We gotta do more. Maybe at night in the motels," Wong says, as they pack up and leave.

Howard and Sam

• • • • •

They are in a small motel on the outskirts of Sioux City, Iowa, off I-29 going south. They had turned off I-90 about two hours ago. The weather had turned from hot to cold as they raced a thunderstorm. The big droplets fell like cannonballs on the windshield of the car, then almost as quickly, the rain turned to drizzle. But the gray of the afternoon stayed for the evening.

Sam has taken the car into town to find a grocery store. "Be careful driving on the wet roads," Wong warned her. "You're in a strange town; don't get lost."

"Yes, mother," she teased.

The old man and Wong are alone. War. Their recollections of it hang in the air of the small room like vapors above a tuberculosis patient.

"I . . . we captured young Jap soldier one time," the old man starts. "We need information about one outpost. How much soldiers? Time they shift guard. How much machine guns? The boy scared. But we need information." The old man gulps. "I selected to get information. I use knife. Cut off one finger. Ask, 'Sahnbolong, do no kurai . . . no heitai . . . ga orinda?'" he rolls the words out slowly, still remembering after all these years. He looks at Wong. "That Japanese for 'How many soldiers?' Sahnbolong is outpost. The boy cry, shake head. I cut off second finger."

They do not speak. The drone of the TV fills the room. Wong rises, turns it off. Silence floats through the room, settling on the cheap shag carpet.

"What makes you better than the Japanese, then? You did the same thing to them that they did to you."

The old man nods, not angry at Wong's impertinence. "Yes. Yes. But we fight for freedom, huh?" He thinks back again. "Still, the soldier no talk. I lift up my machete. Machete good weapon those days. Real sharp. Nobody like doing this kind of things, you know. I look to my friend, Amelio. Even he look kinda sick. But he nod. I chop off his whole left hand. Funny. His remaining fingers jerk, hand lying in the dirt there. Boy scream, but we gag him, eh. He scream again, sound real loud, but it muffled. Only we and jungle hear him. Good looking Jap, too. Has picture of girlfriend or wife on him. She pretty."

255

Wong is silent, caught in the web of his own memories and what he once did. "We tie tourniquet around arm, to keep him alive, so no bleed to death. Tough bastard, that Jap. So young, so tough. But we young, too, and tough."

Silence. There is a glaze of passion in the old man's eyes, and shining through the pupils as if through a peephole, his chronic pain. "Still no talk. So I cut off other hand. He scream again. A great 'Aaaaargh!' from behind gag. Then he cry like baby. We hear crying and sound of jungle. Birds, monkeys. Then, we tie another tourniquet on right arm. Lots of blood! Lots of blood!

"'Do no kurai heitai ga orinda?' I ask again. Still he shake head no. By now, I getting sick. But I no show it. We need information for our survival. I think about Balavia, Ignacio, Saturay, their balls stuck in mouths and their heads stuck on sticks on jungle paths. I think about relatives. I get madder thinking that. I have comrades make him kneel after pull down pants, show his dick and balls. I put wood block under dick. He shake, pull away from block. Take three men to hold him against block. I shake my machete at dick and hold up picture of girlfriend. What good you gonna be to girlfriend now? I ask. What good? Even though he know he gonna die, he don't wanna die like that. I hold machete above dick and ask, how many soldiers? I ready to drop blade when he hold stumps of arms out to me and starts babbling. Amelio pull gag down. He tell everything. How many soldiers, time guards change shift, how many machine guns. He cry and cry. I wrap pistol in old shirt and shoot him in head, him looking at me, smiling. POOMF! the sound gun make. Absorbed by jungle. I then go puke. Never again do I play interrogateur."

The old man sits silent for awhile. "In war, no glory, only killing. Only killing." The old man shakes his head sadly. "Then, fear and memories. Glory only for assholes marching on parade grounds, huh?" He looks at Wong. "It never go away, Davy. I know you like me; you suffer, too."

Wong nods.

"Some part always stay with you. The gods and our ancestors punish us, you know."

"Why did we go in the first place?"

"Because we think we immortal. Because we afraid of dying . . . and not afraid. Because we intent on killing . . . and not intent. Because . . ." he pauses, formulating his thoughts. "Because we young once. And, now, memories haunt us. Old man memories. Forever."

A sick hollowness fills Wong's stomach at those words. How can he carry his own guilt for so many more years like this old man? He hopes fervently that the old man is wrong. Otherwise, what is the purpose of this trip across America? Can the Wall assuage his guilt? Bring him some semblance of relief, some measure of peace?

Just then, Sam returns. Happy Sam, innocent Sam, young Sam, untouched by time and war. She shows them the groceries she has bought for that evening and for the next day's journey. The two men pull themselves together, stepping back into the charade of their present reality. They eat sandwiches and make coffee with the hot pot. They eat packaged pies for dessert.

After supper, they lie on their beds, watching TV, Minneapolis stations. They fall asleep to the TV. Suddenly Wong awakens and gets up to turn off the lights and the TV. He goes to the bathroom. The others awaken and each goes to the bathroom in turn. Afterwards, in the darkness, Wong hears soft sobs, an old man's sobs. And the soft cooing voice of Sam saying, "Sifu, don't cry. Let go of the past. It is done, sifu."

Tears come to Wong's eyes. The past. What is the past? Only the present that has turned into yesterday. But, for some of us, he realizes, those yesterdays reach into the present—long tentacles of time that have never been severed.

The old man is back to normal the next morning, smiling and chipper. The day is sunny with a few high clouds. But now Wong is somber. Where is this trip leading him to? Of what purpose is it, if he has to carry his sins like the old man for the rest of his life? "It never go away, Davy. The gods and our ancestors punish us," the old man had said last night. My God! What if that was true? he thinks.

Even Sam is somber. Wong looks at her in the rearview mirror. Her face is serious, wistful. She stares out the window at the Iowa cornfields.

Wong glances quickly at the rows, too, seeing the lines of corn opening and closing formation in rapid succession, a sea of green waving in the breeze. A Chuck Mangione tune, "Feels So Good," fills the car. Sam looks at him and smiles. Howard taps away with his hand on his leg.

Howard has given up on conversation, getting only "Umms" and "Ahs" from Wong and "Yes, sifu," and "No, sifu," from Sam. The silence rides along with them in comfort. Only good music, the sound of rushing air outside, the hum of the tires, and the occasional creak of the car as it hits a bump are heard.

Wong suddenly feels like they are angels traveling, sent on a mission. He has never believed in angels in the literal sense. But he feels like one of them now, invincible, like he will never die, that he will spend the rest of his days traveling on such long highways in a lonely, far-reaching countryside. He will meet other angels—no, make that the spirits of his ancestors, his parents' spirits, too, in the Chinese belief of life after death—and an old bond will be renewed or a new bond will form among them, as it has between him and Howard and Sam, as it had with Bob and Vicki.

He feels unrooted and he likes it. Not the unrootedness of a man without a home, but that of a traveler who revels in the traveling. As he feels now. At home within the vehicle, rolling the miles beneath his wheels, flowing on a slow river of time to a distant place. The unstructured life on the road that by its very nature becomes a sort of structure of days gone by doing the same old thing. It is a dichotomy of new land discovered and, at the same time, a land that seemingly has not changed much from his remembrance of it as a child. He feels he has driven this road before, traversed this landscape, and believes he will drive these highways in the future. He has immersed himself in the heartland of America, and it is a salve to him, like a mother's heartbeat to an infant. The vastness, the rugged mountains, the endless plains, the rolling hills, the fecund farmlands, the orange sun setting over a majestic land. Gradually, the great land works its magic and dissipates his somberness and melancholy.

"How you doing, Sam?" he asks loudly above the rush of air past the open windows. Howard is slumped in his seat, sleeping fitfully in the heat.

"I'm fine," she answers.

"I guess tonight is the last night we'll be together. We'll be in St. Louis tomorrow." He watches her in the rearview mirror. Small beads of perspiration dot her forehead.

"Yes." Then, "We really appreciate everything you've done, Dave." She has moved closer to him.

He chuckles. "I enjoyed having you two along. Especially in that bar. Old sifu can really fight," he yells.

She grins. "Yes, he can."

He waits a moment, then asks, "Mind if I ask you a question?"

She smiles knowingly. "No."

"Are you in love with him?"

"He's like a grandfather."

"But there's more, isn't there?"

He can see her face in the mirror, her dark eyes probing him, a hint of a flash. "Yes."

"He's a great man."

"Yes. I think so."

"But he is so much older than you are . . . and how old are you?"

"That's what my mother said. But his soul, he has the soul of a thirty-five-year-old adventurer . . . and I'm thirty." She changes gears. "You were talking about the war last night, weren't you?"

Wong nods.

"It still bothers him, you know."

"Yes, I know."

"What did he tell you about?"

"About the Japanese soldier he interrogated."

Sam sighs. A blast of air from a tractor trailer they pass sways the car. "Did he tell you anything else?"

"Like what?"

"Like his parents were killed by the Japanese. That his sister was raped and killed, by bayonet. They carved her up."

Wong frowns. "Oh, God." Wong looks to the sleeping old man. "He's carrying a heavy load."

"And if I can help lighten his load, I will."

"You love him that much, then."

"Yes. He's my Zen Buddhist priest."

"Really?"

"Well, he's not literally a Zen priest, but he has aspirations." She laughs softly. "He believes in the wind, the rain, and the sun. Believes in the natural order of things and how to fit mankind in there somewhere. To him, the wind blows man's soul about until it settles on fertile ground. It's planted. It gets rain and sun. It grows. But what a person does with it determines his or her life, for better or worse."

"I like it," Wong replies. He lets the image float within his mind. He, himself, has grown a crooked stalk. Straightening out is damned hard work. Then, "How did you two meet? I'm curious."

"It was at night. I'd just gotten out of a bar. I got cornered by two jerks—two assholes—" she spits the words out. "Howard came along. No hesitation at all. Well, you saw how he could fight. He saved me from rape, maybe even death. I looked at him. I mean, he isn't any taller than I am and yet he absolutely destroyed my two attackers. I asked him if I could learn to fight like that. He smiled at me and said, yes, if I really wanted to learn, I could. That was seven years ago. So, I'm learning."

Wong nods. About life and death you are learning, too, he thinks.

The miles glide by as the hours pass. They approach Kansas City and catch I-435 to bypass the city. They link up with I-70 east before settling down to find a motel.

Wong goes out for another jog. After a shower and dinner, they retreat back to the motel room. A tinge of sadness hangs in the air. Each knows that separation will come tomorrow. Wong knows that both Sam and Howard like him, and he has grown fond of both of them.

"You have to learn to light up!" Howard advises.

Sam, on the other side of the bed, says, "He means lighten up. He thinks you're too serious all the time."

"I'm too serious?" Wong laughs.

"It true," Howard continues. "You should laugh more, do more, challenge yourself, go out enjoy life. Find woman." He winks at Sam.

"I have some women in my life."

Sam looks up at him.

"They good for you?" the old man asks.

"Not so simple. One I really like, maybe love. The other . . . I don't know yet."

"Ho! Two women!"

"My, a Casanova," Sam adds.

"No, no. Hardly."

"Two women no fun, Davy. Better make decision soon. Find one, and who her."

"He means 'woo' her."

Wong nods. "The old man knows, huh?"

"Damned right! Old man knows." He taps his gray head with his finger.

"Sifu, you didn't tell me you were once involved with two women!" Sam laughs.

"No need tell whole life to such a young one, huh?" he looks to Wong, and winks.

"Try to be happy, huh, Davy. Aim for happiness. Do what you want do. No listen nobody else. Do what right for you, in your heart." He thumps the left side of his chest with his right fist. "That is road to happiness. Listen to it.

"And," he says, "get out of car. Do walking. Backpacking. Bicycle touring. Car, lazy way. Explore America on foot, huh?"

"I didn't hear you complain when I gave you a ride. And I do jog."

"Davy, there is time for car ride. Other times to get away from car and enjoy life, huh? Yes, yes, jogging good. Keep up."

"Yeah," Sam adds, "we're gonna do the Appalachian Trail next spring."

"The whole thing?"

"All 2,240 miles of it. We'll start in May from Springer Mountain, Georgia, and end up at Mt. Katahdin in Maine, probably in October."

Wong tries to visualize such an undertaking and his heart warms to the idea. "That's fantastic! When are we going?"

"Next year!" the old man repeats. "You want come?"

"Hell, yes!" He looks at the old man and then at Sam.

"You welcome come, Davy!"

"I will think hard on it," Wong backpedals a bit. "But, yes, by God, I think I will do it."

The old man beams.

Wong thinks and wonders, though. Even for the old man, there is the scent of sadness about him, hidden behind the smile. He is a man scarred by a youth that will never flee from his memory. The old man looks at him, a crooked-tooth grin. Perhaps these adventures help keep the wolf of bad memories at bay. Nature is like that, a direct throwback to more circadian rhythms, where life is more simplistic.

"Yes, sifu." Wong finally calls him teacher. "Yes, sifu, I will try. I will remember you and try. And I will remember this offer."

"Now, sifu, teach me some more arnis."

The two get up. Wong is drilled in his first five moves. Then the old man teaches him seven more, for a total of twelve. Six, recock the thrust by pulling the stick back to your waist and then thrusting it into the opponent's left eye; seven, then dropping the stick in a wide circle in front of you and past your left knee to continue with a backhand to the top of your opponent's head; eight, pulling back in a continuation of motion seven and settling on your left heel (this is the back leg) to recock the stick with your right elbow in front of your left hip and then thrust into your opponent's right eye; nine and ten, then recocking like strikes one and two but to the knees; eleven, a direct vertical strike like an over-head smash in tennis to the top of the head; twelve, bring the stick in an upward strike to the groin.

"Practice, practice, practice. And make it smooth. Smooth, smooth, smooth."

"Yes, sifu." Wong gets lost in the exercise. A mantra of motion.

The sifu smiles.

The rain falls with a meanness Wong is unused to. Pacific Northwest rain is generally light in texture, but these Missouri raindrops pack a wallop. He has flipped the wiper blades to fast speed and they slide to and fro in a mad frenzy. He turns on his lights so that other vehicles can see him in their rearview mirrors when he passes.

Their mood is a reflection of the wet Missouri woods and farmlands. They are somber, a lazy curling up of each person with his or her thoughts.

Wong pushes seventy and is glad he had bought four brand new radials for this trip. The pavement is shiny wet, but his car holds the road readily. He comes up behind a tractor-trailer rig. He shifts to the left lane and proceeds to pass.

"Watch out!" Sam says.

The spray from the truck's tires whips across the windshield like that from a drive-through car wash. He drives blind for a split second, fighting to keep the car in its lane. He pushes down harder on the accelerator, trying to stare past the hurricane-like blast. Finally, they are past and Wong lets out a small sigh of relief.

"You could slow down," Sam says, arching her eyebrows.

Howard says nothing.

But Wong still pushes the car at seventy. "I've got an appointment today." He is rushing to capture shadows of his past.

Outside Columbia, they fill up on gas, go to the restrooms, and then visit a walnut-wood factory outlet. They wander through the large store eyeing the cornucopia of walnut and other wood products. Howard and Sam buy some walnut bowls; Wong buys a horseshoe puzzle. The puzzle has two iron horseshoes. The end of each shoe is connected by three links of chain to the other so that the whole geometry looks like the perimeter of two horseshoe drives connected by a short road. Around the outside of the chain links is a metal ring, smaller in diameter than the width of the horseshoes. The puzzle? How do you take the ring off?

Back in the car, Howard solves it in three minutes, hiding his movements from Sam. When Sam gets it, she becomes stuck. "Shit! I give up!"

"It's a gift for the two of you," Wong says. "Something to remember me by."

She laughs. "You bastard. Thank you. You just want to make me suffer, don't you." She shakes it and twists it again, once more under the spell.

"Young ones," Howard says. "Must be educational system." He pats his head with his forefinger. "They so slow these days, huh?"

Wong laughs, as he drives back onto the freeway.

"I'm not dumb. I got a lot of A's in college, you know."

"What kind courses?" Howard asks. He already knows.

"Humanities. I was an English major."

"I rest my case," Howard says. He and Wong laugh aloud.

"All right, laugh, you bastards." But she is smiling, her face intent and full of purpose now.

It is still raining, but the mood has lightened. The rain is less wind-driven and even looks like Northwest rain. The music coming over the radio is oldies but goodies from the '50s, '60s, and '70s. They hum along to the songs, a curse escaping from the back seat now and then as Sam becomes increasingly frustrated. "Damn! Damn! I'm not dumb!"

Howard looks to Wong, their gazes meeting.

Sam looks up. "I'm not, you know." She has caught them looking at each other.

"It's a topological problem," Wong says.

"Huh?"

"Think like Kung Fu, Sam. Japanese karate straight. You no solve puzzle using straight lines. Kung Fu circular, huh? Life is circle." He had instructed Wong that if the straight path couldn't get you in to your opponent, then try a circular attack.

"Oh." She is silent. They hear the chains rattling again. Then Dave can see a smile forming on her face in the rearview mirror. "I think I'm getting it. I think I'm getting it." She is like a little girl. "I got it! I got it!" She holds up the ring between the seats for them to see.

"Congratulations." Dave smiles at her from the rearview mirror.

"Yes, yes. Well done," Howard says. He looks at his watch. She took one hour to solve the puzzle. Then he looks at Wong and winks.

"Gee, Dave, I really appreciate this gift. I'm gonna show it around to all my friends at work, too." She works as a receptionist/secretary for a veterinarian.

The rain has stopped and some sunlight filters through the clouds as they approach the outskirts of St. Louis. Sam directs him through the maze of traffic and freeways to their home. They stop in front of a ranch-style house on a circular deadend street.

They unload their packs. Another awkward moment, as he had with Bob and Vicki in Montana. He is making good friends of strangers and hates the parting of the ways.

The rain falls again, a light rain. Sam hugs him, kisses him on the cheek. "You take care of yourself, you hear. Have a safe trip, and do write. Here's our address. We'd love to hear from you. Tell us about the Wall. And we'd love to take you along with us on the Appalachian Trail next year. Give it some serious thought."

He takes the slip of paper from her, says he will write, that he will miss her.

With Howard, he shakes his hand. Then he pulls the old man to him, hugging him. "You're one good old man," he says.

"You good man, too, Davy," the old man says. "Remember, enjoy life, huh? Must have passion for life, huh?" He reaches into his pack and withdraws a pair of rattan sticks. He hands them over to Wong. "Here, Davy. I want you have. Someting remember us by. Also, to fight off ass-holes, huh?" The old man grins. "Plenty assholes around!" Then, words of wisdom. "Can't fight all assholes, huh? Fight only when have to, Davy. Once you fight, no mercy! No mercy for assholes!"

Wong laughs and accepts the sticks. "Dojeh, sifu." Thank you, teacher. He inserts the sticks under his armpit, steps back and clasps his hands in front of his chin, left over right fist, and bows his head.

The old man salutes him back in the same manner.

"Goodbye, sifu," he says. Then he turns to Sam and bows. She bows back.

"Joigin, Wong sinsaang," the old man speaks in Cantonese. Goodbye, Mr. Wong.

Wong looks at them, standing bareheaded in the rain. He captures the image in his mind. Then he gets in his car, waves. They wave back.

And he drives from his uncertain future into his remembered past.

Chapter 28

Augusta

The narrow road curves and undulates through the wet hills, flattens and straightens out on the Missouri River bottomlands, pulling him like a rubber band back to his boyhood.

He has no memory of the landscape, except in vague terms such as green and hilly. The intervening years have erased the specific images of the countryside. He does not remember the large factory on the right, does not remember the small towns, mere bends in the road with not more than grocery stores.

The superfluousness of St. Louis has not yet spread this far west. Still, he imagines that in the years ahead the tract houses and subdivisions will creep slowly forward on the paws of progress. But, for now, he drives with a curiosity and a relief that the land is, for the most part, bucolic.

He sees billboards. And he is curious. Wineries in Augusta? Bed and breakfasts? Restaurants and cafes? Bakeries? Can this be the same town where he spent four years of his childhood? He laughs. Augusta has become a tourist stop!

He gazes at the flatlands, the grassy expanse broken by dark groves of trees. A nearby railroad bed parallels the road for a short time, but there are no tracks on it, only a flat graveled path. Then the road climbs to the right, away from the bottomlands. He climbs and dips and twists through the green hills. Driving atop a long ridgeline he sees, in the distance, a white church sitting on a small knoll. As he gets closer, he sees a road below the church. Then he sees the sign, Augusta, with an arrow pointing left. His heart skips a beat as he makes the turn.

There are certain cherished memories he has of childhood, after the Hawaii of his younger years and before the Nevada of his early adolescence. Memories that now float back to him as he draws nearer to Augusta, Missouri. It was a small town of three hundred fifty where he and his family were totally accepted into a community settled by German immigrants. He had close friends there. He was a Boy Scout. And he played baseball with a passion he has not had since for the sport. He went to Sunday school and church-related activities, even painting a watercolor portrait of Jesus once. It was where he discovered the Missouri woods and hills, learned of osage orange and yew and hickory and black walnut, explored the bottomlands on an old clunker bicycle with pedal brakes, picked wild pecans. He remembers chasing fireflies on balmy summer nights, cupping the insect in his hands with a child's wonderment, watching the fire come alive in his palms. And it was a place where he first became aware of the opposite sex and, for a time, being Chinese didn't matter as it would in later years. It was where he became "American."

The road branches right, down what seems to be a main street. The town seems smaller and drabber than he remembers. Wooden buildings line both sides. To the left, he sees a large grassy area. On the corner is a fire station. There is very little traffic, and Wong surmises that it is the rain keeping people indoors. He makes a left turn by the fire station and unexpectedly comes up to Oak street. "Look for a white house, 4440 Oak street," she had written. He finds 4430, a gray house, but there are two white houses on the same side of the street, no numbers. He stops at one. A man is outside working on the lawn. "Excuse me," he asks the man, "can you tell me where the Kronenbergs live?"

"Next block," he says, pointing at the other white house.

"Thank you." He gets in the car and drives back to the first white house. As he pulls up, an elderly woman steps out on the porch. She has seen him coming.

"Dave!" she shouts.

"Mrs. Kronenberg!" he replies. They hug and laugh.

"It's been thirty-one years!" she holds him at arm's length, looking at him. "Oh, my, it was 1959 when you left!" He was eleven years old then. She looks at him closely. "I would've recognized you." Then, "Come in, come in!"

The house is neat and tidy, covered with plush carpeting. The lights and lamps are on, throwing small circles of light in the room, keeping the outside gloom at bay. A large mirror hangs in one corner, framed pictures of family hang next to it, and a picture of Jesus graces another wall.

"Remember Ralph?"

He is a tall man, handsome, and remarkably unchanged. "Hi, Dave. Been a long time." He smiles widely.

Wong shakes his hand. "Hi, Ralph." He clasps his left hand atop Ralph's. "Yes, too long."

"Sit down, sit down." She makes a fuss over him. He moves to the sofa, sits, and looks at the two of them. Ralph has eased himself into a rocker and Hilda is seated in a plush chair. For a moment, he is lost, does not know what to say.

"You know, when you wrote to tell us you were coming, I pulled out the old yearbook." She picks it off the table and hands it to him.

"Ha!" He laughs. "This is a surprise!" He leans back, cradles it in his lap and flips through the glossy pages. The school had pictures taken of everyone in those days, from grade school through high school. He looks at his youthful self, smiling out of the page. An image of childhood innocence. For a moment, the intervening years seem compressed. He has somehow stepped back into his boyhood shoes.

He sees his brother's picture. Then those of his classmates, John Siegenhaus, Keith Heines, Peggy Sauer, Mary Sandell, Ginny Atwood, Jim Smith, Glen Kratke.

"What happened to Mary Sandell?" he asks.

"She moved away a couple of years after you folks left," Hilda says.

He remembers her. A pretty girl, and intelligent too, with a shy smile that rippled across her face like sunshine slowly breaking through gray clouds. Even now, he remembers his turning away when some bully had made her cry. He sighs. One can still carry the little guilts, even after all these years.

"What about Peggy Sauer?"

"She's still here. She owns the Cookie Jar Restaurant in town. We'll go there later."

Wong mulls this over. It would be interesting to see at least one old face, to see the adult grown out of the child.

"I also have some pictures of your parents," Hilda says. She gathers them from the small table at her side and hands them to him. There are pictures of him with his brother and father in front of the white mansion, of him with his brother and mother in the same setting, and a picture of Hilda and his mother at the smaller house they had moved to from the mansion, a move necessitated by economics. He stares at the pictures. He sees how Hilda is vitality itself, standing straight and tall, not stooped by age as she is now. And how his mother is alive, smiling at him from out of the past. He is thousands of miles from where she is buried, but he has found part of her soul here.

"You can keep the pictures," Hilda says.

He looks at her, a look of gratitude. "Thank you. You are too kind." Then, "May I get a drink of water?"

"Of course . . . Ralph?"

Ralph gets up and Wong follows. "There," Ralph says, pointing through the window, "that's where you used to live. Remember? We were next door neighbors there." It is the old duplex they had once lived in, after vacating the mansion. A lone, wide oak stands by the roadside in front of the house. The grass is forlorn, unkempt. He drinks the water, remembering the power outage he and his family once endured in the dead of winter there. They had had no power for six straight days. Luckily they had a gas stove to cook with and to use for limited heat.

When he gets back to the living room, Hilda says, "We're going to go to the Cookie Jar Restaurant. That's Peggy's place, remember? We're treating."

Wong nods. "Yes, thank you. But I can pay for my own lunch." It is 3:00 P.M.

"We insist," Hilda says, her voice firm. "Now, come on."

Wong laughs. "Okay. Okay."

They put their coats on and step outdoors to his car. "How far is the restaurant?"

"Oh, it's just down the street." Hilda walks slowly. Ralph walks with a limp. Wong ushers them to the car. He makes a U-turn and drives two hundred yards to the end of the street. "Make a left turn here . . . Look, Dave, that's where your family used to live. That mansion, remember."

"Yes, I remember. God, that was a lovely house." He looks at the great white house with its large portico. "What happened to all the peach trees?" Only grass now covered the magnificent, wide, deep front yard.

"Oh, some doctor bought the house and had them all cut down."

"A shame." Nothing stays forever.

"Here, right here."

Wong turns into the restaurant parking lot. It is less than a quarter of a mile from their house. He helps the old people out of the car. "Too bad it's such lousy weather," Hilda says. "I wanted nice weather for you."

"Not much different than Washington state, you know."

She laughs, taps him on the shoulder. "Then you should feel right at home." They step into the small wooden structure.

It is an old-fashioned cafe, checkerboard-cloth tables and a jukebox in the corner, windows front and back.

"Wendy," Hilda says, flagging down a waitress, "this is Dave Wong. He used to live here thirty-one years ago."

She says hi.

"Is Peggy here? I want her to come."

"She's at home. I'll give her a ring," Wendy replies.

Hilda nods approval. "Remember, Peggy went to live in Hawaii. She stayed with your father for a while. That was when your father was building his new home, I think. Peggy and Jeri stayed there for a summer. Peggy met her husband then. Ha! Ha!" Jeri was Peggy's younger sister.

Wong barely remembers that. He must have been away at college or in his booze and drug days then, when he couldn't remember anything that transpired between him and his father.

Hilda calls Wendy over. "Go ahead and order and don't be shy!" He orders a hamburger and fries and a Coke. He has to jog soon, he thinks. The old couple has soup. "Have to watch our digestive systems these days," she says with a smile.

"She has to watch hers," Ralph says.

Hilda laughs. "Yes, Ralph can still eat almost anything."

Wong looks at a poster on the wall near the table, then says, "I still remember you folks liking my mother's chow mein."

Hilda nods. Wong looks to Ralph, who is staring blankly at the front door. Then, Wong remembers that Ralph is deaf. He is misleading. He reads lips so well that most people are unaware that he is deaf. Nor does he garble his speech like some deaf people, exhibiting perhaps a subtle slur, but one had to listen closely for it. Wong repeats himself, looking at Ralph.

"Ah, yes, I loved your mother's cooking," he replies. "All our friends loved it. Remember all those paiute games?" Paiute was a Chinese card game, a cross between hearts and poker. "When your mother cooked, we'd sit down and devour every last bite. Then we would play cards." He grins widely.

They talk some more about old times. And they ask him about his current trip. He relates some aspects, telling them about Howard and Sam.

A dark-haired woman enters. "Harlan?"

"No, it's Dave. Hi, Peggy," he answers.

She is not as he remembers her. She was a pretty tomboy. The woman standing in front of him now is . . . well, grown up. She has rounded, not bony, shoulders. She is not big, but the impression is powerful.

"I heard you're driving across country," she says. "We do that, too, from here to New London, Connecticut. I've got a son in the Coast Guard Academy. In fact, we're gonna go next May. He's gonna graduate." Then, "Where are you going now?"

"The Vietnam Memorial."

"Oh. Did you know that John Siegenhaus was killed in Vietnam?"

"No." Wong frowns. He was a friend, one of the most natural athletes he had known. Even-tempered, easygoing, handsome, athletic John.

"No, I didn't know." He gulps. "I'm . . . sorry to hear that." He looks down. They stare at him, unsure of what to say. He looks up then, smiles wanly. "It was a lousy war."

"Amen to that," Hilda says.

"Amen," Ralph adds.

He and Peggy talk about old times, about her being in Hawaii, about her kids. After a while, the conversation lags. He still has a picture in his mind of the young girl. Peggy looks at the clock on the wall, says, "Well, it's nice seeing you again, Dave, but I've got to get back home to my daughter."

"She's seven?" Hilda asks.

"Six, almost seven."

Wong stands ups, shakes Peggy's hand. "It was nice to see you again."

"Same here. If you're ever in Missouri again, drop by."

"I will."

She turns and exits through the kitchen.

He watches her go, a part of his past, a memory from long ago. He laughs softly. "I still remember the tomboy."

Hilda laughs. "Things change."

He smiles, suddenly hungry again. He wolfs down the remainder of his hamburger. The Kronenbergs have finished their soups long ago. Then a curious thought. "How old are you, Hilda?"

She looks at him. "I'm thirty-eight," she says. "Just reverse the numbers." Then she laughs. "I always tell people that."

"What happens when you turn eighty-eight?" Wong asks. All three laugh.

As he finishes up his fries, Hilda asks, "Want to go see the Mt. Pleasant Winery?"

"Sure."

Hilda pays the waitress; he thanks them profusely, knowing that they are living on a limited income. They clamber back into the car, and she directs him to the end of the short block and up the hill. The winery sits on a bluff overlooking the Missouri River.

The exterior of the shop is red brick. Inside, they walk on knotted, hardwood floors. Hilda's shoes make sharp clacks on the wood. A tasting counter and showroom/gift shop sit on the main floor. A group of tourists is about to go on a tour of the basement.

"This is Dave Wong," Hilda says to the woman in the gift shop. "He used to live here thirty-one years ago! He's an old friend."

"Hi!" she says, smiling warmly. "Would you like to taste some wine?"

For a moment he is tempted, then says, "No, thank you."

"Then how about a tour of our cellars?"

He looks to Hilda and Ralph. "Sure," Hilda replies.

"Okay." He nods.

The saleswoman ushers them to the head of the stairs. "It's just started, sir."

They descend some wide wooden plank stairs. The old couple has difficulty negotiating them. He helps Hilda down.

"Ah, old age," she complains, but she is smiling.

They enter a large, two-pronged cellar, one room to the left and one to the right. The ceilings are about fifteen feet high, the width about twenty-five feet. The rooms are made of concrete and brick. Huge oak casks, eight feet in diameter, line both sides.

"This place was built in 1881," the woman giving the tour says. "The original settlers, who came from Germany, found in these Missouri woods almost the same natural conditions for growing grapes that they had in their old homeland."

"You mean they've been growing grapes and making wine here for over one hundred years?" Wong asks.

"Yes," the woman replies.

Wong is amazed. All those years he lived here—four years of his childhood—and he never knew that it was wine country. They listen for ten more minutes, then Wong gets restless. He nods toward the steps. The old couple nods in agreement.

"There's a nice cheese and gift shop next door," Hilda suggests.

"Sounds good to me," Wong replies. They walk the fifteen yards beneath steadily falling rain to the shop.

The inside of the store is well lighted, counterpoint to the gray skies. Windows face the bottomlands, but the clouds prohibit any viewing of the river from this distance.

Hilda knows the woman behind the desk and immediately explains the situation of old friend again. Then she launches into a discourse about Shelley, the woman's daughter.

He wanders about the store, looking at the various cheeses, snacking, and playing with some of the gift items. He decides to buy some honey, the cherry and blackberry flavors.

"Ready?" Hilda asks, after he pays for the items.

"Yes."

They step out into the rain again. Wong then broaches his plan. "Hilda, do you mind if I drop you and Ralph off at your house. I would like to walk around Augusta for a while. See the old school, the old houses."

"No, I don't mind at all. Come back when you're ready."

So he does that, leaving the car at their place. He walks north from their house.

"That's the direction of the school," Hilda said. "This is too small a town for you to get lost."

He walks past main street, past the church where he once went to Sunday school and church socials. He remembers the old outhouse the church had, a two sexer, male on one side and female on the other side, and how one boy at a time would stick his head down the hole to look when a girl had to use the facilities on the other side. He chuckles. But not me! he declares to himself. His sense of propriety was so strong in those days.

He walks half a block farther to the old two-story brick school. He stands on the bluff above the ballfield where he used to play baseball during P.E., at lunch, and after school. He remembers the 660-yard runs they had to do for their occasional P.E. test in the field below. John Siegenhaus had always run them into the ground, breathing easily at the end. He remembers how he himself would bend over in agony at the end of the run, sucking air in great gulps. John would always smile at him, not arrogant, always encouraging. Poor John! he thinks.

He turns around and looks at the old school. He sees images of himself and his childhood friends running around the playground, ignorant of the specter of Vietnam that lurked in the future. The future that would so define their generation.

He sees the flagpole where his hand had once been badly burned when it had gotten trapped between the ropes during flag raising. He remembers his father as teacher here, how he once had to take a math class from him. He remembers English class, when Mr. Bensol, portly Mr. Bensol, had his weekly spelling bees and how Wong had won the prize, a different box of candy, for five weeks straight. Mr. Bensol finally had to cancel the prizes, because the outcome was always the same.

He remembers Mary Sandell, pretty and intelligent Mary. They had formed a kind of loose-knit team. She was the smartest girl in the class and he was the smartest boy. He was shy and she was shy.

But there were moments, like in biology, when they were learning about snakes. Wong was handling a harmless king snake and Mary had balked in fear. He held it gently in his hand, caressing the cool skin, even rubbing it against his cheek. "It's harmless, Mary." He held it out to her.

She reached out, a tentative touch. Then her smile as she overcame her fear. "Such a pretty snake," she said.

He wanted to say, such a pretty girl. But he was too shy.

He walks back toward the center of town, past the park where he used to also play ball. He still remembers when he was ten or eleven, a sixteen-year-old boy had thrown a baseball at his head as hard as he could from fifteen feet away. He caught the ball. Otherwise he wouldn't be here today, he thinks. He passes the old general store. He remembers walking back from the store with his mother, after she had bought a brand new pair of leather shoes for him for five dollars. He remembers buying bubble gum and trading baseball cards then. Stan Musial. Mickey Mantle.

He turns left, heads up to the white mansion. He stands in front of the big yard. He remembers the living room with the grand old fireplace. He remembers being sick upstairs with pneumonia, almost dying, the worry showing in his mother's eyes, his gruff obliging father agreeing to buy him a dozen comic books at a time while he fought the infection.

How he had to take six to eight large pills at a time, four times a day, for a month or more. To this day he would much rather receive an inoculation than take pills. He remembers his father telling them to go to church, keep up appearances' sake. He remembers sitting Saturday mornings in the annex to watch cartoons. He remembers snow days and sled rides.

Suddenly, he cannot remember any more. Or he doesn't want to remember any more. He wants to leave. He goes back to the Kronenbergs. He sits politely for a while, then gets up. They say goodbyes. He gets into his car, drives past the white mansion once more and continues driving toward the bottomlands, past an old shed on a small farm. He remembers it as the old chicken shed he had once cleaned for twenty-five cents an hour. Ah, the smell! he recalls, smiling.

The road continues, dropping slowly away, then sharply right to the bottomlands. He looks out over the land. It was his playground as a kid. A gigantic nature preserve that he explored on bicycle. One can't do much better for a childhood, he thinks. He turns around, retraces his steps, and then remembers that it was this route he took with his family when they left this town forever thirty-one years ago, when he left behind the innocence of his youth.

He drives north toward I-70, finding a motel for the night. He jogs in the cool evening. Later, he is pleasantly tired but has enough energy to write Mercury about Augusta. He writes of his experiences and memories, telling her of his goodbyes to the past.

> It is difficult to try to recapture one's childhood. Sometimes it's pleasurable to drum up the old memories, sometimes not. For me, visiting Augusta, the memories were pleasant, and not unsad. But time passes. Let's face it, the gift of childhood is only conferred once, Mercury. And, for me, I am so glad I had a place like Augusta.

He writes of the Kronenbergs.

We said sad goodbyes.

Then his storied metaphor of past youth:

"Oh, your mother was a dear, dear friend," Hilda said, when I left, tears starting to form in her eyes. "Come back," she said, "and write." I am a thread to her past, as much as she is to mine.

"I don't know if we'll be here much longer," Ralph added. "Don't make it another thirty-one years."

I laughed. "I don't know," I replied. "I'll try." But my youth has fled. The Augusta of my childhood cannot be recaptured.

The long sled rides on snowy days on the road by the white mansion where we once lived are locked in place now, a man's remembrance of childhood times. The first steep, long downhill rush, the wind blowing in my face, snowflakes catching in my hair. Then, the sharp turn to the right where the grade levels off, and a left curve and gradual downhill followed by a right turn and sharp drop to the bottomlands.

The sled slows and stops on the flat. I roll off the sled onto my back, stretching out on the soft snow, kicking my legs, licking the snowflakes as they fall into my mouth, and I laugh with the sheer exuberance of youth. Then I get up and bend to pick up the sled, grasping metal and wood. Straightening up, the hard wood and cold metal have suddenly turned into empty air. And the snow is gone, too, melted into the memories of my past.

Chapter 29

Annapolis

Stella is caught in a time warp. Something like twenty-two years have passed since she had left Annapolis, returning only now. Occasional visits would have dulled the experience she is now having. Her childhood haunts her, in the hallways, in the guest bedroom that was once hers, in the living room where she lingered on cold evenings in front of the fire-place, outside on the lawn where she once scampered after the falling leaves of autumn. All a prelude for this singular mission of hers.

Mary and Sara had accompanied her on this trip. Jim had stayed in Seattle, too busy to break away from his caseload of patients, as usual. "It's not like I haven't seen them for a long time," he said. "They were just out here last year." Their son, Aaron, his team hot on the chase for a regional Little League championship, had stayed behind, too. Only the girls came. Sara, because she was Jake's daughter, and Mary, because it felt right to bring her.

They drive into downtown Annapolis the next day, crossing the Old Severn River Bridge, next to the Naval Academy. Stella glances at the gray buildings, remembering the occasional walks she and Jake had taken through the grounds.

Her father drives them around for a quick tour: down King George Street, then down Maryland Street, lined with small shops and restau-rants. Stella remembers State Circle, within which stands the brick capi-tol building, the Maryland State House, with its large wooden dome.

"Remember anything yet, Stella?" her father asks.

"Oh, yes, Dad. I remember."

They drive around the circle, exit it on School Street, enter Church

Circle. Her father edges to the right and exits onto Duke of Gloucester Street, pulling into the parking garage.

The day is cooler. High clouds hang in the sky. Stella takes Mary's hand. Sara walks to her left. Her parents, Tim and Maureen, walk ahead.

"Where to, honey?" Her father turns and asks.

"Dad, you don't have to cater to me."

"Nonsense! It's been what? Twenty-two, twenty-three years? And you say we don't have to cater to you. We're so glad you finally decided to come back and visit."

"Okay, then, why don't we start down by the dock and work back up and then over to Maryland Street?"

They cross Main Street and walk down to the dock.

"Remember the old Market House?" her mother asks.

Stella shakes her head. "Vaguely."

"Well, they wanted to tear it down and make a park here. But we citizens organized and fought city hall and won. They renovated the place, instead of tearing it down."

They are in a farmer's-market style store—the Market House. Fresh seafood in open refrigerators beckons them. Crowded shelves with narrow aisles force customers to juggle around each other. Her father buys some scallops. "For dinner tonight," he says.

They wander back up Main Street now, taking their turns exploring the quaint old town. Many stores of her childhood are gone, supplanted by the ubiquitous mall chain stores. Still, the old town has retained that flavor and charm that tourists loved, a mix of the usual and unusual, enough polyglot stores and restaurants to flavor it as unique. Of course, its location next to all that water, the Severn River and the Chesapeake Bay, didn't hurt either.

Sara and Mary are walking with Stella's father. She and her mother are walking together. They wander into a small antique shop, English antiques mostly.

"I still can't understand why it took you so long to come back, dear," Maureen says.

She faces her mother. "There was nothing here to entice me back."

Her mother glowers at her. "How about us? We're your parents!"

Stella, looking at a silver necklace through the glass countertop, raises her head to look at her mother. "Oh, come on now, Mom. It's not like we haven't seen each other all these years. You've been out to Seattle many times."

"Yes. But it's nice to have a daughter come out and visit her parents. We're getting old, you know."

A bemused smile forms on Stella's face as she switches her attention to a vase. "Yes. You're getting old and you're traveling all over the world."

Maureen frowns, hesitates a moment. "You've never forgiven me, have you, even after all these years?"

Stella glances quickly at her father. He is with Sara and Mary, looking at some small items in the corner of the store.

She takes a deep breath. "How am I supposed to feel, Mom? That you were against the marriage from the beginning?" She smiles, tightlipped, opening old wounds, averting her gaze.

"Only because I felt that you were too young."

Stella raises her gaze from knick-knacks to look directly at her mother. "It was more than that."

A flicker in her mother's eyes. "You were too young, honey. Too young!" A silence settles between the two. "Would you want Sara to marry at nineteen?"

"It was more than that," Stella repeats. "You never did like him. You never gave him a chance, just because—"

"I liked him. He was a nice young man." The older woman's face is hard set.

"You hated him from the moment you learned he was Jewish. You didn't want a Jew marrying your precious daughter, as if she couldn't make up her own mind about who she could marry!" The words spill out from the prison of her withheld passion, turned vindictive. She sees her mother cringe, but she does not let up. "You couldn't see past your nose, Mom. Couldn't see the type of man he was. Couldn't trust your daughter's judgement or instinct. Couldn't see that we loved each other . . . so much."

The tears are coming. Her mother is frozen to the floor, stung by her passionate criticism. Stella brushes by her, through the door, into the street, digging into her purse to grab a tissue and wipe the tears from her eyes. She stands outside in the weak sunlight, breathing deeply, trying her utmost to collect herself. A few passersby glance in her direction, but she ignores them. She hears the door open behind her.

Her mother places an arm around her, but Stella pushes it away. Her mother comes about, faces her. "I-I can't say that I'm sorry enough to you, dear. I know I hurt you deeply. I d-don't know if I can ever repay you for what I've done." She looks into Stella's eyes.

But Stella, like a young girl, refuses to meet her gaze. "He died for us, Mom. It was a shitty, fucking war! He died for us—Christians, Jews, white, black, yellow, red, brown. He believed in what he was doing. Even though it was unpopular in those days, he believed in the United States. He died for this goddamned country!" Almost a shout. She lifts her head to look at the sky, the tears running down the sides of her cheeks.

Just then, Tim, Sara, and Mary come out of the store. Maureen waves them off. Tim, seeing what is happening, diverts the girls' attention, taking them down the street to look in the window of a woolens store. Sara looks back.

"Don't you think I haven't thought about what I did?" Maureen asks. "I feel rotten. Oh, God, after Jake died, I knew I had lost you. I knew you could never forgive me. And after all these years I didn't have the courage to approach you and ask you for forgiveness. Can you understand how hard it is for a mother to ask her daughter for forgiveness?"

She takes Stella's head in both her hands, lifts Stella's chin with the fingers of her right hand, forcing her daughter to look at her. She clears her throat. "Stella, I'm sorry. Will you forgive me? . . . Can you *ever* in your heart forgive me?"

Stella still cries, tears streaming down her face, wetting her mother's hands. "M-mother!" She pummels her mother's shoulders weakly, the pain flowing out of her with the tears. "Why? Why?"

Maureen lets her daughter hit her, a small child working out her rage. "I don't know, honey. I don't know. I was such a fool." She pulls her daughter to her. "I'm sorry, honey. I really am."

Stella sobs into her mother's shoulder. Gradually, the torrent becomes a trickle. She stands back, looks into her mother's eyes. "I f-forgive you, Mom."

"Oh, my baby!" Maureen cries, pulling Stella toward her again, stroking her daughter's hair. "You don't know how long I've wanted this to happen. I just didn't have the courage. Oh, baby, I love you so much!"

They stand embraced in silence, a world unto themselves, oblivious to the traffic, the pedestrians, the stares, and time.

"Can we continue the tour, now?" It is Tim, bringing them back to the present. He looks at the two of them and smiles knowingly. Sara and Mary, standing beside him, are wearing question marks on their faces.

"Of course, silly." Maureen smiles as she takes out a tissue and blows noisily. She hands one to Stella, who also blows hard, wiping at the sides of her eyes.

"Come on, young ladies." Stella grasps her daughters around the shoulders. "We're gonna explore the history of this place and then we're gonna have some Maryland crabcakes that'll knock your socks off! I'm gonna show you where Jake and I used to hang out!" They stride up Francis Street, heading for Maryland Avenue.

"You okay?" Tim asks his wife.

She slips her arm into his. "Honey, I'm fine. I think I've just found my daughter again."

As time passes, the uneasiness Stella has worn like a cloak has lifted a bit. The second to last night of her stay, she and her father are sitting in the living room. Her mother, Mary, and Sara have retired for the night.

"Do you still feel the hurt, hon?" her father asks.

Stella looks at him and nods. "Yes, Dad, it still hurts. Maybe not as bad as before. The sharpness is gone, but there is this dull ache. It's like a chronic pain that I think I'll carry for the rest of my life.

"Jim is aware of it. God bless him. I know, in a way, it hurts him. But I guess he loves me enough to put up with me. We're happy, overall."

Stella looks at the oak mantelpiece above the brick fireplace. There, the picture of her and Jake still sits. Their wedding picture.

She gets up, strolls to the mantelpiece, picks up the picture, and examines it closely. "I'm surprised that Mom still has this out."

"You do your mother a disservice. She loves you deeply."

"I know, Dad. I found out."

"What you don't know is that she volunteers for a lot of causes these days. B'nai B'rith, Anne Arundel Aids Foundation, Maryland Literacy Council."

Stella raises her eyebrows.

"She wanted to atone in some way for the way she treated her daughter—and her first son-in-law."

"I owe her an apology."

"Oh, honey, I don't think so. Not after Wednesday afternoon. The two of you made up. That's enough."

They are quiet for a while.

Suddenly, she makes a wry face at him. "Funny, every once in a while I'll look at Sara, and she'll catch me staring at her. I see him in her. She has his strength of character." The silence lingers again for awhile. Only the hum of the air conditioner is heard. She sighs, pivoting in front of the fireplace to eye her father. "God, I only wish he could have lived to see the woman she has grown to be. He would be damned proud of her."

Her father rises from the couch, walks to her. "I wish he can see the woman you've grown to be, honey," her father says softly. She drops her gaze. He reaches around her, wraps her in his arms. "You are one hell of a strong woman. The hell you have bounced back from, well . . . let me tell you, not too many people bounce back from something like that. I'm damned proud of you."

They stand in silence, tears in their eyes. Then, Stella pulls back.

"Dad, tomorrow, I'm getting up early. Would you mind if I borrow the van? We'd like to visit the Vietnam Memorial."

"Of course not. If you need flowers, help yourself out back." He looks at her, the girl he has known, now grown into a woman.

She is a woman who, on the morrow, will confront her painful past.

Chapter 30

The Wall

The tree-shaded path ends abruptly. At its terminus is a road—Henry Bacon Drive—and looming just beyond, the Lincoln Memorial. Stella turns, looking to her right—and there it stands, the lowslung, black, polished granite embedded like an arrowhead into the heart of a nation. Some thirty people are milling about on this early weekend morning.

Nervous but determined, she wills her feet to propel her forward, pulling Mary and Sara with her. To her right, she sees the statues of the three combat infantrymen, staring into the distance, staring at their impending deaths.

The monument is huge! The lines of names! They run on and on, more than fifty-eight thousand of them. How can I ever find Jake? she wonders. Her body starts to tremble.

She looks about and sees large volumes set under glass. There are four stations, people standing in line. One station becomes free. She hurries to it, oblivious to those in the other lines.

The names are listed alphabetically. She looks up Abramson, runs her finger down until she finds Jacob, USMC, and catches her breath. Tears form in her eyes, but she forces herself to look across the column. She finds his name, rank, the day he died, 10 February 1968, and where along the wall his name would be displayed: the panel number, east or west arm of the chevron-shaped monument, and the line number.

One arm of the chevron points to the adjacent Lincoln Memorial. The other points to the Washington Monument. At the vertex of the chevron, the first name starts the run east; and the last name ends there from the west arm. The beginning and the end at a point in space.

She jots down the information and grabs Mary's and Sara's hand in each of hers and, together, they walk along the cut paralleling the wall. There are Joneses, Smiths, Cruzs, Wolchaks, and all the names that are woven across the fabric of America—this flowering youth cut down like early summer wheat.

She comes to the panel number, 40E, starts counting down the lines, her heart palpitating wildly. Finally, she comes across Jacob Abramson. She stares at the name, feeling the etched letters with her fingertips. Then she notices someone else nearby. She begrudges the fact that even in her grief, she cannot be alone.

His feet are unsteady and he is shaking as he looks up the two names. Deacon, Wayne, and Abramson, Jacob. He writes down their locations and turns to walk the path before the wall. The early morning sunlight glistens off the shiny black granite. The roar of jets flying into National breaks the quiet reverence.

He looks for Deacon's name, splaying his fingers and caressing the names of the dead as he walks along. He stops in front of Panel 26E, counts down to line 112. He runs his finger along the long line of names and finally finds it. Wayne E. Deacon, preceded by a diamond, death confirmed. He thinks of his old friend, laughing at their escapades in Tijuana, crying at his death, feeling the sorrow return when he wrote to Deacon's girlfriend of his death. What was her name? God, it was so long ago. Carmen? Carmanda? Carmelda? . . . Carmela! That was it. He had gotten a letter back from her. She had thanked him for writing about the circumstances of Deacon's death. Said she missed him terribly. Said he should come down to Tijuana and visit her. But he had never done so.

He looks at the scrap of paper. Muley's name is several panels away, line 45. He steps over, counts down from the top, high above his head, pointing his finger at the top, doing it by 10s. Ten, twenty, thirty, forty, then forty-five. He can feel the rows now. As with Deacon, he runs his finger across the etched surfaces of the names. Toward the end of the row, he finds Jacob C. Abramson, a diamond preceding the name.

He fishes in his pocket, pulls out the old photo of Muley, his wife, and baby. He stares at it, rubbing one edge between his fingers. He remembers that day, the rumble of the tank, the agonizing scream, Muley torn in half, screaming in shock and disbelief, "Shoot me, Wong!" Those three words echoing across the years. And how he pulled the hammer back of his .45, and then shot his good friend in the head, seeing the bone and brains and blood spatter the pavement. And how he had turned around and retched . . . struggled to a tree and leaned against it and retched some more.

He is crying now, falling onto his knees and leaning against the wall, the tears falling in big drops onto the thin strip of grass. By degrees, a numbness begins to creep into his body. A spirit-numbing torpor. Time is suspended. The grief he feels for his old buddies suddenly shades into the grief he feels for himself. It once again starts to possess his very soul. Vietnam is at once real again to him. The images, the soul on edge, the inchoate fear, the power and the bloodlust well up in his mind, catch in his throat as sobs rack his body. The guilt comes pouring out in great sobs, a catharsis for his great sins. Once again, he sees the old Mama-san's face, the contempt in her eyes. Knowing that her dying would be a more powerful act than all the years of his living. How true! he wails. How true!

Unconsciously, without knowing it, he bangs his head against the harsh black granite with greater and greater force. Blood starts to seep from his forehead, mixing with the tears, stinging his eyes. But he is beyond conscious thought now. Only the hellish images of long ago suffuse his tortured soul. The pictures of the bodies of the Mama-san and the young girl. Like cast-out garbage, detritus from the sick ambivalence of a corrupt war. The images of his guilt flicker on top of the images of his dead buddies. All dead, every one of them. The Mama-san, the girl, Deacon, Muley. Ghostly images, like dancers caught in a strobe light, doing a danse macabre.

But if the images have come back with a vengeance, after a while—how long? Wong has no consciousness of it—they gradually recede. And the aftertaste is nowhere as morbidly bitter as some previous times.

The sobs die down and Wong painstakingly crawls out of the dark abyss of his guilt, feeling cleansed and amazed. The depths of his soul were tested here, but he crawled back. And he wanted to crawl back. That is the difference from some of the other times. He feels as if the Wall has a special power for him, as it has for so many other Vietnam veterans. It has the power to soothe, the spirits of more than 58,000 dead Americans working to lift the heavy cloud of guilt hanging over him.

He is Asian-American, she guesses, and he seems lost in the throes of his own grief, stooped and forlornly banging his head against the wall.

Mary stares at him in disbelief. "Mommy, what is that man doing?" she asks.

But Stella is succumbing to her own grief. She cradles Sara to her. "This is your father, Sara. This is your father." She continues to caress Jake's name with her fingertips. Sara starts crying, feeling the loss of a man she has never known. Stella's tears flow as all the remembrances come pouring back. She can see his face, conjured from the depths of her memory. Blurry at first, then slowly, the face becomes focused.

It was Hawaii. He had served seven months of his thirteen-month Vietnam tour as a grunt, or infantryman. She flew out to Honolulu to meet him, with Sara, sixteen months old. As he got off the plane, he looked extremely fit, almost gaunt. They embraced so tightly that he almost squeezed the air out of her. He picked up Sara in his arms and whirled around in joy. This was his daughter! Flesh of his flesh, blood of his blood. Stella laughed and cried at the same time, overjoyed. He kept whispering, "I love you. I love you. Let's go to bed!" She laughed and agreed.

The hours they spent lovemaking were like playing catchup ball, to make up for all those months of separation and worry. The sun shone brightly outside their Waikiki hotel, but those first few days were almost all spent indoors. Only in the late afternoon and evening did they venture out along Kalakaua Avenue into the tourist strip called Waikiki, wheeling little Sara in a baby carriage. Hawaii was a popular Rest and

Recreation (R&R) spot for many Vietnam servicemen, so they were not alone. Couples were about with men in uniform; but the majority of the veterans were in civilian garb, identifiable by their close-cropped hair in the longhaired age of the '60s.

It was the Christmas season. Carols were being played over loudspeakers; Christmas trees and wreaths adorned shop windows. Though Jake was Jewish, he normally celebrated Christmas as a secular holiday, not a religious observance. Both Jake and Stella were struck by the oddity of a Christmas without winter.

It was a Christmas season without joy. Moments of happiness, yes. Moments of great passion and love. But it seemed to her to be a Christmas lived on borrowed time. She remembered the days and the nights, remembered living them in a blur. She remembered the changed man she thought she knew. The sleeping that was not a deep sleep. The man who now looked over his shoulder quite often, the man who was more aware of his surroundings. Once—luckily she was the one pushing Sara— a car had backfired. She turned toward the noise, then back to Jake, who was flat on the sidewalk. He sheepishly got off the sidewalk, shook himself off, and smiled. People laughed at him goodnaturedly, pegging him for a Vietnam infantryman on R&R.

He was a man who stayed up late at nights, making love to her, watching her, staring out the windows into the gaudy neon night, gazing at the peripatetic flow of people beneath. He was a man who hungered for the touch of his daughter, perhaps aware that he would never touch her again. He had changed. He was not as quick to laugh; he was more nervous, more serious. He did not talk more than, as it were, a few pages out of a tome about his Vietnam experiences. But when he did, he told her he had doubts about God. That God perhaps was an abstraction. "But Death is real. I believe in Death, honey. I seen him a hundred times. He comes suddenly with no impartiality, no favors. He breeds paranoia and hatred. And I sow his seeds."

The seven days passed like a locomotive in the night. Inexorable, the stuff of dreams, wailing away in the passage of time to become mere memories.

That last night he held her tightly and, finally, he confessed his fears. "I've got some life insurance," he said. She remonstrated. But he brushed her objections aside. "It's ten thousand dollars of life insurance for servicemen. Not too many companies are willing to carry life insurance for combat troops. If I should die, please set up a college account for Sara. You can use some of the money yourself. I'll trust your judgement on how much to set aside for her." He looked toward the baby.

"Oh, honey, you're not going to die!" The words came out weakly, tearfully. "You're invincible!" She laughed and cried, tears streaming down her cheeks.

"Yes, yes," he said, laughing softly. "I'm invincible!" He moved slowly toward her, kissing her.

For the first time, she felt his real fear, a subtle shivering of his soul. And in their lovemaking, betwixt their heavy breathing and quiet moans, a part of her heard the shrill revelry of the indolent Waikiki night. A loud cackle that echoed among the buildings, ghostlike, to be suspended in her dreams, mixed with the absurd strains of "White Christmas" floating in the tropical air. This—not the memories of lying on the white sand beach in the bright sunshine—would forever be her image of Waikiki.

Spent, lying in each other's arms, his bravado reasserted itself. He laughed. "Hell, yes, I'm invincible!" She laughed with him. He pulled her closer. "I'll always be there with you, baby. I'll never leave you. You are my heart, you are my soul, like I am to you. I will come back!"

"Yes! Yes!" she whispered. She pulled the sheet up over her shoulders as goosebumps formed on her skin.

As she stands before the Wall, her tears flow, unstoppable. She sees him on the steps of the plane on the last day of his R&R, the last time she would ever see him alive. Her forehead rests on the wall, atop names, and parts of a name become imprinted on her skin. How long? She is unaware of time now; even unaware of her daughters nearby.

· · · · ·

Coming out of his great grief, he is suddenly aware of other sobs nearby. He stands, rubs the tears and blood from his face with a bandanna. He looks to his left. At this early hour, he sees two women and a young girl nearby. The older woman is stretching her fingers, caressing a name. The young woman is bent over, crying. The girl stares at Wong with the unbeguiled look of all children, a mixture of curiosity and awe. She had seen him banging his head, sobbing away like a broken child.

For a chilling moment Wong thinks he is watching a ghost. The girl, blonde and blue-eyed and except for her occidental features, has the same overall facial structure of the young girl in his nightmares. The resemblance is uncanny. The young girl continues to stare, not more than five feet away. Then, suddenly, almost without thought, Wong grabs and wraps her in his arms. The tears flow, but they are different tears now. The mother wakes from her mournful reverie, and is about to remonstrate, but then checks herself. She senses something, senses the need for physical touching that Wong desperately seeks, the touching of two human beings, this strange man and her child. And the child, wide-eyed but unafraid. Then, he puts her back down and pats her head, and mumbles, "I-I'm s-sorry. I didn't mean to upset you."

Stella looks at him, dabbing the tears from her eyes. "I understand," she says, smiling weakly. She pulls Mary to her.

From the time he subjugated himself before the wall to the moment the images receded, the great burden of guilt had been lifted. But it was in that one moment, when he had the girl in his arms and had the power to crush her, only then did he know which way his life would forever be directed. The images would always be there. But now their power to haunt him were diminished. Forever, he hoped.

As atonement, his life's work—what years he has left—will be to work with children. They are the clay to be molded and fashioned for a better world. In that instant, when he held the child, the answer flashed through his mind. War, he knows, will never be banned. But, even in war, there should never be total amorality.

Within the mind of a child, even at an early age, the concept of Right and Wrong is easily planted. Some children never learn morality.

Some do, and yet lose their concept of it as adults. The lessons to be learned are as old as history itself, but the play will continue to reenact itself forever. The guilt of the ages, and especially in Vietnam, is that Morality died. The concept of Moral Right and Wrong, the greater good above and beyond military orders, was ignored too often—something we had so ceremoniously castigated the Nazis for at the Nuremberg trials. Moreover, this concept of Right and Wrong, in Wong's mind, did not come from any deepseated Christian belief. Rather, it came from the Confucian ethic. From family, from society. From the concept of an Enlightened Man. It was a return, though belated, of Wong to the precepts held by his ancestors.

Stella looks to Sara, sees her tear-stained face. She hugs both daughters to her. Then, she lays down the flowers she has picked from her father's garden. She searches for paper and pencil in her purse, and then holds the sheet flush against the wall, atop Jake's name, smearing the pencil lead across the paper—capturing the ghost, as if by doing so, she could prolong her image of him. She stares a moment longer, digs a scribbled note from her purse and leaves it before the wall, underneath the flowers.

"Goodbye, Jake," she whispers, kissing her fingers, transferring the kiss to Jake's name. Then she pivots and leaves, with Mary in hand, Sara following.

Wong, looking dumbly at the family, did not notice that the woman had been rubbing Muley's name. Wong waits, and then out of curiosity, picks up the paper and reads:

Lamentation at the Wall

Dearest Jake,

It was Hawaii,
far removed from war,
where we made long, exquisite love.

You were different,
Still tender,
Yet removed.

I tried to soothe the tortures of your soul,
to love away visions of war.
But the clouds hung above us,
dark and menacing,
a reign of fear
raining fear.

I hoped and prayed
That Death would not touch you
With his cold, splayed fingers.

When it came time to say goodbye
In the bright Hawaiian sunshine,
I saw the sad smile.

And I cried.

He stands there, reading the poem over and over again. Jake. Can it be? He remembers Muley's wife and child were at Waikiki when Jake had taken R&R there. He looks up to where Muley's name is, remembers she was rubbing a name near that area. Can it be? Suddenly remembering the photo in his hand, he glances at it again. He looks closely at the woman in the photo. Could it be the young version of the woman he just saw? He cranes his neck, looking for the family, but they have disappeared over the small knoll and through the trees. Nah! It can't be, he thinks.

He leaves the note, then turns and runs in the bright new morning. Gripping the photo in his hand, he runs toward his past, his present, his future.

· · · · ·

In Seattle, Jim waits nervously for his wife and daughter Mary. Sara's boyfriend had flown out to meet her in D.C., and the two are continuing to Europe.

Jim was always nervous waiting at airports, imagining the worst, even when his rational mind told him airline crashes were rare occurrences. This time, there is more to consider. Over the telephone, Stella had said that she had visited the memorial. The only intimation of her experience was that she had said it was a sad one. Also, that, for a moment, she had felt transported back in time.

How is she? he wonders.

The plane lands. "Come on over here, Aaron," he commands his son. "Your mother and sister will be here soon." He positions Aaron in front of him, draping both arms over the boy. He scans the scores of passengers disembarking, searching for his wife.

Finally, he sees her, with Mary at her side. Moving forward, he gathers his wife in his arms. "How are you?" he asks softly.

She stares into his eyes. "I'm okay," she says. "I made up with Mom."

He pulls her close and kisses her.

She pulls back to look at him. "As for Jake, I guess I'm all right. That part of me will never really be fine, but I think you know that."

"I know. And I also know that I love you as much as Jake ever did."

"I love you, too." She looks deeply into his eyes, tears forming. "I said goodbye, Jim. Like you said I should do."

"I know you did, honey. I know you did." He rocks her in his arms.

"Just be here for me, will you?" she asks. "Always?"

"From here unto eternity," he replies, laughing with joy. He swoops his daughter into his arms, nuzzles her face; Mary giggles. Stella hugs Aaron. The boy stands stiff-armed, embarrassed. She ruffles his hair. They walk arm-in-arm down the long corridor, a child on each side.

Stella tells him about a man named Wong.

B a c k   H o m e

Marthasville hasn't changed much in the six weeks of his absence. The weather is warmer. The trees are lusher, the weeds and bushes are overgrown, and the blackberries hang black and ripe from thick, prickly vines. Roses still bloom on thorny stems. Sailboats ply the bay in a lazy breeze. The town pulses with a soft, measured beat under a lukewarm, late August sun. And his heart still yearns for Mercury.

Her presence seems to have permeated the town. While he did push her into the back of his mind on the crosscountry trip, back home now, his pores soak up the very atmosphere of her existence.

He parks the car near the post office, gets out, and checks his box. He sorts through the mail—magazines, bills, brochures, statements. He sees the yellow card indicating more mail being held in back. He has lost track of the days, but the post office is open. He stands in line, turns the yellow card in, shovels the rest of the mail into a large plastic bag he has carried with him. He moves to a counter to do a quick sort of the mail, looking for personal letters. He smiles, seeing letters from Howard and Sam and the Kronenbergs. He opens them and does a quick read—they are a gush of words saying how glad they had been to meet him, to share experiences.

He packs up the mail; he will finish sorting it later. Mercury's face floats in and out of focus for him. He moves in slow motion under a cloud of uncertainty. He tries to imagine what she is doing at this moment. Will he ever win her over?

Entering his driveway, he sees that the grass is once more overgrown, though he had hired the kid next door to mow it. The dandelions have run amok in the lawn, rising high and proud above the grass. The birch leaves twirl in the slight afternoon breeze. The evergreens still stand like sentries, lined up along the edge of the property, to shield the house from the noise of traffic. Inside the house, a musty odor hangs in the air. He leaves the front door wide open, plops the mail on the kitchen table, and goes around the house opening windows. Next, he unpacks the car, dumping bags and baggage in the living room and kitchen.

He fights to maintain control, to not call her right away, to not appear overly eager. So he whiles away his time, unpacking, cleaning, sorting and reading the mail, cooking, and eating. At the table, over a dinner of fried rice and eggs, he feels as if he has not left, that all is the same with the world, that no matter how much he travels, he has not left. Will never leave. Not with her in this town. She is his other half, like a block of LEGO that fits into its complement. A perfect match. If only she could come to see it the way he does.

In the end, he cannot contain himself and calls her that evening.

"Dave! Where are you?"

"I'm back in town."

"How was your trip?"

"It was great, Mercury! I met a lot of people." He went on to tell her about Howard and Sam and about the Kronenbergs.

She laughs about his exploits with Howard and Sam, the fight in Gillette. She wonders about the Kronenbergs, how they must have changed? How Augusta has changed in his mind? Then, "How'd you feel? At the Wall?"

"It was emotional for me. I felt like I was back in Vietnam . . . for a while." He leaves a pause.

"Did it help?"

"Yes. I think it helped, and I'm glad I went. And would you believe, I met my old buddy's wife!" He gives a brief explanation, promising to tell her more in the future. "But, you know, I think the actual trip helped, too. The physical act of driving across country. It was like I was renewing acquaintances with the land again, with America. I'd forgotten what it was like—driving across country. We'd driven it a lot when I was a kid.

Every summer my parents would bundle us into the car and off we would go. You know what I mean?"

"Yes. Yes, I do."

"I don't think my guilt can be bottled up in such terrain. It's like a drop of water, splattered over dry dirt, soaked up by the vast landscape. There's no room for self pity."

She laughs. "That's a wonderful simile. You should tell that to Erlandson. Maybe he can incorporate it in his therapy."

He laughs. "Yes, I will." An awkward silence pops up. Then, "I'd like to see you again."

She chuckles. "How about this Saturday?"

"Mercury, I'd love to see you," he says, a slow smile returning.

"So it helped, this trip?" Erlandson asks.

"Yes," Wong says, "it helped. Like I told Mercury, this land is big enough to contain my rage and guilt, vast enough to dissipate it. And the Wall, it was like all my guilt was focused there, then defocused. All the ghosts were made diffuse." Wong licks his lips. He certainly hopes so. "The land and the Wall working together. And the people I met. They all helped." He tells him about Bob and Vicki, Howard and Sam, and Stella.

"Howard is you. Bob is what you should have been. Stella? Stella is your forgiveness. I have hopes that you can put your past behind you, more than what Howard has done," Erlandson says, smiling. "I hope that one day, you will forgive yourself for what you have done. Maybe," he pauses, "maybe 'forgiveness' is not quite the correct word. How about 'accommodate'? Accommodate yourself with your sins, so that you have the desire to live. Still, you've come a long way in my book. A damned long way."

"Stella forgave me because she understood the circumstances of her husband's death. I don't think I can ever forgive myself for the murders of the Mama-san and the girl. I don't expect forgiveness from the girl's mother and father . . . and I don't deserve any."

Erlandson has no reply; he only nods.

"I cannot undo my actions. I cannot ask forgiveness from the girl's parents because I'll never see them in this lifetime. There may not be a Heaven, but if there is a Hell, I'm ready to accept it. That is the best I can do." He spreads his hands out in front of him, offering his soul.

Erlandson nods again, still silent.

Wong thinks back to Vietnam. "I was too young. I had no confidence in myself those days. No foundation. So it was easy for Smitty to undermine me."

"What ever happened to him anyway? Did you kill him?"

"Who, Smitty? No! No!" Wong laughs. He then turns serious. "Not that I didn't want to. If I could have gotten away with it, if I had been alone with him, yeah, maybe I would have. But in the end we kind of tolerated each other, especially after I picked up my sergeant's stripe. He extended for another tour. The son of a bitch probably became a career Marine if he wasn't killed during his last tour. I returned to the real world, he stayed in his. He loved killing too much."

Erlandson looks at Wong intently. "You think you can listen to your heart in the future?" he asks. "Instead of listening to outside persuasions like Smitty?"

"It does take self-esteem, doesn't it?"

"Yes."

"Do I have it?"

"Yes. Now you do." Erlandson smiles at him.

"Hi, Dave," Mercury says, greeting him at the door, smiling, followed by a sudden frown. The lazy light of an August afternoon spills through the windows and door.

He is puzzled by her frown, until he sees him. "This is Spence, Dave, my ex-husband."

He is about six foot two, stocky and muscular, with the arrogant handsomeness of an athlete, and towering over Wong by a head. He squeezes Wong's hand into submission. "Glad to meet you, Dave."

"Same here," Wong replies, catching a whiff of liquor. He opens and closes his hand to get the blood circulating once again. Spence smiles.

"Here, I've got some huckleberry jam for you," Wong offers.

"Thanks!" She smiles, looks at the label. "Huckleberry, huh? Sounds delicious and decadent."

"Just like you," he says and laughs.

She laughs, too, then turns serious. "Spence is just leaving. He dropped in unannounced."

"Ah, come on, babe." There is a scowl on his face. He does not enjoy their banter. "There was a time when you didn't mind." He winks at Wong, a crooked smile on his face.

Wong looks at his watch. "Yes, perhaps we'd better hurry."

Mercury grabs a light sweater. "Goodbye, Spence. Whatever has been said between us was said a long time ago."

Spence turns lazily to look at her, then back to Wong. "So now you go out with . . . Chinks?" He waves his hand in Wong's direction.

The comment catches Wong off guard. It came without warning— the slur hanging in the air, alongside the dust particles floating through the shafts of sunlight.

"You bastard," Mercury mutters.

Wong does not know what to do. His balloon of expectations for the evening has burst. He glances at Mercury, then at Spence, and shakes his head, as if to clear his ears. "What did you say?"

Spence smiles, a thincurled uplift of his lips. "I was just wondering why my wife . . . ex-wife . . . is going out with Chinks now."

"What I do now is none of your goddamned business! Now I want you to leave!" The blood rises in Mercury's face.

Wong looks at her ex-husband. He outweighs Wong by a good fifty pounds. He is stronger, no doubt about it. Wong does not relish a fight— does not want to lose and be humiliated in front of Mercury.

"W-a-a-l-l, I was just kinda getting comfortable here, ya know. I was reminiscing with my ex-wife and, all of a sudden, this Chink comes through the door and forces his attentions on my wife . . . ex-wife. I'm having fun, ya know. I'm in no hurry to leave."

Mercury has moved beside Wong. "Let me handle this, Dave," she whispers. Then in a loud voice, "Spence, I swear to God, if you don't leave, I'm gonna call the police and press charges."

He laughs at that. "Well, if you're gonna do that, I'm gonna beat the shit out of you. And your fucking Chinaman friend."

Wong has no choice. He can see the fight coming, like a storm he cannot outrun. He wishes he had Howard along. Howard and his stick. Wong sighs. How much easier it is to have someone else fight your fights. Then he remembers his own stick—Howard's gift—in the car. He whispers to Mercury, "I'll be right back."

He rushes outside, hearing Spence's sarcastic laugh. "Chicken shit!"

Wong jogs to his car, retrieves the stick lying on the floor, and returns with the rattan stick in his hand. "You wanna go outside and settle this." The anger runs looser in him now.

"Sure!" Spence laughs. "Ya think that little fucking stick is gonna help you? I'm gonna beat your fucking brains in, man."

"Dave, no! Don't do this! You'll get hurt. He's bigger and stronger than you are!"

But Wong is already out in the yard, Spence right behind. Mercury follows, full of fear. Wong faces Spence, stick held at the ready. Spence throws his head back and laughs. Wong watches him. All of a sudden, Spence attacks, reaching out an arm to try to collar Wong. Wong, seeing the long outstretched arm, quickly brings up the stick, swatting it across Spence's forearm. A loud scream erupts. Spence cradles his forearm. It stings like hell, but the arm is not broken. Wong watches as Spence works and massages his arm, opening and closing his hand.

"Think you're a smart little bastard with that stick, don't you?" Spence reaches into his pocket, unfolds a knife. It is wicked looking, with a six-inch-long blade, half serrated. A bone cutter.

Mercury rushes at him. "Spence, no! No! Please!" He pushes her off, hard, knocking her to the ground.

The two men circle each other, Spence now giving more respect to the length and power of the stick in Wong's hand, Wong respecting the long, sinister blade.

Wong still feels uncertain. He has not fought since Vietnam. After months of therapy, he finds it hard to shift mental gears from civilized behavior to destructive anger. He is dangerously lethargic, not aggressive at all, mesmerized by Spence, who seems to be an unreal image floating through his mind. He watches in fascination as Spence rotates his wrist, making lazy circles with the blade, just like his high-school boxing friend had made lazy circles with his gloves and then had flattened Wong. Spence senses Wong's lethargy and lunges with the knife.

"Dave!" Mercury yells.

Wong wakes up, as if from a dream. Too late! Spence has grabbed the stick, pulling Wong into the knife thrust. Wong tries desperately to parry the thrust, palm up, and just succeeds, but knows that another slash or thrust is coming. Spence pulls back with his knife on the underside of Wong's blocking arm, cutting the muscle. Wong feels the pain, raises his left arm, feels the wet stickiness of blood, swerves away from the next thrust. Blood oozes like a leaky faucet.

"Oh, Dave! Oh, Dave! Be careful!" Mercury yells.

Wong hears her, but he has a very real problem. Spence still has hold of the stick. Wong cannot risk losing it. He understands that Spence is using it to pull him into the knife. Suddenly, Wong pulls backward with his whole body. Spence is pulled off balance. Wong then executes a sweeping crescent kick to Spence's left arm, breaking Spence's grip on the stick.

"Augh!" Spence screams, shaking his arm.

They circle again. Blood drips from Wong's arm; he tries to ignore the sticky fluid, wiping it quickly on his pant leg. It seems a shallow cut at first, but he cannot be sure. Then realizing its steady drip, he reaches in his pocket, pulls out a bandanna and ties it around the arm with his free hand and teeth, all the while dancing away from Spence. Spence, foolishly, did not pursue his advantage.

"I'm gonna call the cops," Mercury screams. "Stop it, right now! Both of you!" The men continue circling. Mercury does not leave. She is mesmerized by the scene unfolding before her. By now her neighbors are out, watching, wondering what is happening. "Martha, call the cops!" Mercury yells to her neighbor. Her neighbor rushes inside. Others come out of their homes to watch.

Wong concentrates on Spence now. The anger wells up within him. He wills himself to aim for the kill. He feels exulted. Here, before him, is a real enemy. Realizing that he can kill—with legality—in self-defense, Wong slips off the bonds of civilization. He has crossed the fine line between civilized behavior and that of survival. In this respect, he is once again as free as he was in Vietnam, free to kill.

"Give it up, Spence. If you come at me with that knife one more time, I'm gonna kill you." His anger rises, but is checked, under control. He needs the emotion to fill his psyche, but not to overflow. "Controlled anger," he remembered Bruce Lee describe the proper mindset for a fight.

"Fuck you, Chink! You're the one . . . who's bleeding." Spence is breathing hard.

"Then fuck you, Spence. I'm gonna kill you." A mad light gleams in Wong's eyes. His breathing measured, he is not afraid of death.

Spence feints, trying to wedge the knife past the stick again. Wong follows the feint with quick movements of the stick, trying to rap Spence's hands or forearms again.

"Remember, watch out legs," Howard had said. "Remember, use yours. Stay loose; don't drag fight out, eh? If bleeding, finish quickly. Otherwise, get light headed." In fact, Wong's arm seems to be bleeding more. The bandanna is bloodsoaked. He does feel lightheaded, and he is tiring. If he weren't in some semblance of shape, he'd be dead now.

Wong switches to the offensive. "Life is circle," he remembers Howard saying. He feints toward Spence's knife hand, then backhands the stick toward Spence's head. Spence ducks and the stick misses. But Wong is not finished. He brings the stick around in a quick circle, this time catching Spence's knife hand. Almost immediately he jams his right leg into Spence's thigh muscle, hard—Howard's technique.

"A-a-a-h-h!" Spence screams, feeling the pain from his leg and arm, almost simultaneously. The knife falls to the ground. Spence slumps, barely standing.

It could have ended there. But Wong, caught in a bloodlust now, raps Spence across the right side of his face, whipping the stick around like a bullwhip, lightning fast. He hears the loud smack. He comes back across the opposite side of the face, a forehand strike, snapping Spence's head back around as Spence falls to his knees. Wong leaps in back of him, brings the stick across his throat, pulling it up tight, choking off the air. Wong's breathing is faster now as he pulls with all the might in his small stocky frame, his blood dripping down the back of Spence's neck. He drags Spence as he chokes him, preventing him from getting on his legs, to find the balance to resist. It is a killing technique learned in the Marine Corps.

"Enough! Enough! Stop it, Dave!" Mercury screams. "You're killing him!" She claws at his arms.

Slowly, fighting through the adrenalin, Wong comes back down to earth. He looks at Mercury, jerks the stick harder, once, then releases his grip on the stick, and pushes Spence onto his face with his foot. Wong picks up the knife, folds it up, and hands it to Mercury.

Spence is prone, "A-a-a-r-g-h" sounds emanating from him. His fingers are massaging his throat, pulling at his Adam's apple. His face is purplish, puffy, starting to swell like a pumpkin.

Mercury is crying now, shoulders shaking, looking at Wong. He goes and hugs her. "I'm sorry, Mercury. I'm sorry. I didn't start it."

She looks at him. "I know. I know." She takes some tissue paper from her purse and stuffs it over the wound, soaking up the blood. She then wraps her own bandanna around it, putting pressure on the wound. Wong is still breathing heavily.

Spence kneels, bent over, gagging, dry heaving, trying to inhale great gulps of air. He looks sideways at Wong, fear on his face. Slowly, he starts to crawl away.

"Hey, Spence," Wong shouts to his retreating back. "I don't ever want you coming back here again. Do you understand?"

Spence looks back at Wong, nods his head, then continues crawling. He has to stop. He turns and plops on his back, massages his throat.

Wong hears police sirens in the distance. He hides his stick under a bush. Two police officers pull up in separate cars, radios squawking.

"What's going on here?" a female cop asks as she approaches. The name tag identifies her as Sergeant Dougherty.

"A fight. My ex-husband was getting all riled up because I was going out with this gentleman," Mercury explains.

Dougherty looks at Wong's arm, asks, "Need an aid car?"

Wong shakes his head.

"Better go to the hospital later, then, and get that stitched up." She looks to her partner, Hansen. "Jerry, you wanna talk to the other guy? See if he needs an aid car."

"Okay." The big cop wanders off to look after Spence.

Meanwhile, one more cop car pulls in. Dougherty directs the third cop, Boyle, to talk to witnesses. The cackle of radio traffic fills the air.

"You wanna tell me what happened here?" Dougherty asks.

Wong and Mercury explain. Boyle interviews Martha and some of the other people who had gathered. "Any weapons?" Dougherty asks. Mercury hands over the knife; she and Wong are silent about the stick, hoping that witnesses will not reveal its location. Satisfied that Wong didn't start the fight, Dougherty asks Mercury, "You wanna file charges?" She has her book out.

Mercury looks to Wong. Wong looks up, shakes his head. "No. No, I don't think we have to. I think it's settled." Mercury smiles at Wong.

Hansen comes back, confers with Dougherty. "The other guy doesn't wanna press charges either. Just a misunderstanding that got out of hand, he says."

The two officers step away. Boyle joins them. "Looks like two schmucks fighting over a woman," Hansen says.

"It was a real fight, all right," Boyle adds. "The Asian guy had some kind of fighting stick."

Dougherty agrees, nods. "Okay." She snaps her book shut. "The D.A. will never prosecute then, unless we have an aggrieved party. I don't care about the stick; it's not like this knife I confiscated," she says, showing them the knife. "Still, you'd better keep a good eye on that guy." She points to Spence. "If he doesn't come around and his breathing is still labored, we'd better get an aid car over here." Hansen nods. He and Boyle saunter over to look at Spence.

Spence has slowly come back to life, color returning to his face. Hansen asks him how he is feeling. "Better," Spence replies.

"No aid car needed then?" the cop asks.

Spence shakes his head. "No."

The cop then warns him to stay away from Mercury. Spence, stooped over, nods and looks at Wong with a newfound respect, fear even. Still massaging his throat, he straightens and walks about for a while. Hansen tells his colleague to shadow Spence when he leaves. Finally, Spence departs under his own steam, slinking away like a cur with its tail drooping. Boyle follows, to make sure he does not come back to renew the fight.

Wong has to fend off curious neighbors. "What a fight!" a boy yells.

"Where'd you learn to fight like that?" Martha asks. She was the one who had called the police.

"From a Zen Buddhist priest," Wong answers.

Mercury guides him through the small crowd. "Gotta go, folks! Gotta go to the hospital and get him stitched up."

She leans her head against his, looks at him, smiles. "Jesus, I didn't know you could fight like that!"

He chuckles and breathes deeply, smelling the fresh fragrance of her, of life.

They are back at her place. It had taken twenty stitches to sew up the back of his forearm. The cut hurt like a double line of bee stings, one on top of the other. It could have been worse, deeper.

"He's an asshole. Was an asshole, and will always be an asshole."

Wong laughs. "Why did you marry him?"

"I was young. When you're young, it's all loins, no broins."

He laughs again.

She looks at the floor, then back to him. "I was scared, Dave. He's been getting worse in the last six months. There were times when I was even scared for my life."

He pulls her close. "Don't be scared of him, Mercury. You've got me here. I can teach you to fight. If you can play tennis, I can teach you the stick fighting Howard taught me. You'd catch on quickly." Then, "I can even teach you how to shoot a pistol."

She smiles. "You know, I don't like violence. But I've got a gun and I know how to use it."

"Then why didn't you—"

"He wasn't shooting at you."

"Thanks. He could've killed me."

Mercury folds her arms, suddenly cold. "I-I guess I wasn't thinking."

"Oh, don't worry about it. There is some satisfaction in hand-to-hand fighting." He smiles. "But only if you win."

She smiles back.

"He's an asshole. Let's hope he never comes back. I swear, next time I'll kill him."

She shivers, sees the image of Spencer coming for her. "You can't be around me twenty-four hours a day, can you?"

He looks to her. "Do you want me to? I'd be willing to try!"

She snuggles up to him. "I think we can work on that," she says.

Now he turns serious. "There was a time when I would have walked away from this confrontation, Mercury."

"As far as I'm concerned, you should have." She pulls back to look at him.

"What I'm trying to say is that I no longer walk away from such situations. Can you live with that? Can you live with the racial epithets and my not walking away from them? If you become involved with me, that's your future." He is an old warrior revitalized.

She looks at him. "That doesn't give much credit to people and society in general, does it?"

"You've never had to suffer through it. You're mainstream, dear heart. As if you didn't know that."

"I think I can handle it."

"There's also something else. I want to ask you something."

"Shoot."

"I'd like you to go to Hawaii with me."

She is taken by surprise. "To see family?"

"Yes. But especially to see my grandmother. I told you about her before. She's getting on in years. I have to see her before she dies. I want you to come along." He glances expectantly at her. She says nothing. "She is one hell of a woman. You'd enjoy meeting her."

She throws back her head. "Yes!" she says, laughing. "Yes! I'd love to go with you."

He plods up the brick steps. He notices that some of the bricks have worked loose from the mortar. Others have small cracks, a fissure for water that, during cold spells, freezes into an icy prybar to work loose the bricks from their moorings. The grass is long, but not tall, hovering above a carpet of moss that always seems to grow in western Washington. The bigleaf maple provides a wide patch of shade. The leaves of the holly bush shine dark green.

The sun warms his back as he hesitates on the last brick step before entering the wooden porch. He turns to look out over the bay. Tugs tow a barge full of wood chips toward the American-Pacific pulp mill. He sighs, straightens his shoulders, turns to enter the porch, and rings the doorbell.

He hears Mei's voice cry out, "I'll get it!" Shortly thereafter the heavy wooden door opens.

"Hi, Mei." He tries to put on a hearty smile.

"Oh hi, Dave." Her face is blank. "Mom's in the kitchen. Come in."

He steps in under the high-beamed ceiling. Mei closes the door behind him. He stands, unsure for a moment, then hears Jean's voice from the kitchen, "Who is it, Mei?"

"It's Dave, Mom!"

They walk to the kitchen. Jean is rolling out dough on a marble slab on the countertop. She stops for a moment, looks up, smiles. "What a pleasant surprise! I've been trying to contact you. How was your trip?"

"Hi, Jean. Uh, great!"

"How long have you been back?"

"Oh . . . two weeks."

Jean turns to the dough, pushing down hard with her rolling pin. "Ummph!" she grunts. "You could have called." She almost slams the pin down, a tight smile on her face. Then, to her daughter, "Mei, why don't you go back to the living room and continue watching TV, okay? And close the door behind you, please?"

Mei looks quizzically at the two of them. "Okay, Mom."

Wong watches her leave, pulling the door shut. "What are you making?" he asks.

"Cherry pie. Maybe if you stick around long enough, I'll offer you some."

The double entendre catches Wong's attention. "I never said it would be permanent."

"No, by God, you didn't. At least you were honest in that respect."

"I've tried to be honest in all respects."

"Then, is it serious with your blonde girlfriend?"

"Uh . . . I don't know . . . Yes, I guess it is." He paces back and forth now, absentmindedly watching his feet land on the black and white tiles. He turns to look at her. She is so beautiful. Did he really come here to break off the relationship?

"What's wrong with your arm?"

He tells her about his fight with Spence.

"So you'd fight for her, but not for me?"

"That's not fair. I don't think your ex-husband is an abusive asshole."

She changes tack. "How is Nancy? Is she back with her mother?"

"She's back to normal, a regular eight-year-old. She'll be coming out for Labor Day."

"You really miss her, don't you?"

"Do you miss Mei when she's away?"

"Yes." The dough is becoming larger and flatter.

"You're a bastard, Dave. A real bastard!" The words fly like shrapnel, exploding from nowhere. He had hoped to avoid a big scene. He sees a few tears spill onto the dough. She wipes her eyes with the cuff of her sleeve, then turns around and glares at him, still holding the rolling pin.

Wong sits down at the kitchen table. He cannot face her. He stares out the window into the yard. A robin pecks at the ground, then stops, angling its head left, right, eyes searching for danger . . . then it pecks again. Wong turns his gaze to the kitchen table, plays with the salt shaker, and feels bile rising within him, a feeling of revulsion for himself. Why does he always have to hurt the ones he loves? He does love Jean, but he loves Mercury more.

"What do you want me to say, Jean? That I love you? That I want to spend the rest of my life with you? You know the problems I have." He stares at her now, a challenge flashing in his eyes. But she slumps her head, eyeing the floor, hugging the rolling pin to her chest with both arms now, like a child with a doll. He continues to watch her. He sees a silent shaking; her hair, from his angle, hides her face. Only the muted sounds of the television in the next room filter through the silence. The minutes are slowed, each second carrying lead weights, an agony for both of them. "I-I . . . you don't know me that well. Did you know that I sliced my ex-wife's ear? Took ten stitches to set it right."

She suddenly looks up, wipes her face, and finally puts down the rolling pin. "I hope she fucking put you in jail!"

"Yes," he says softly. "She did."

"They shouldn't have ever let you out." She turns back to the counter.

"Oh, come on now. I served my time."

"Not enough."

"You're talking!" His ire is rising now. "What about that murderer, Quentin, you defended. What? A lousy fifteen to twenty years for murder? When will he be eligible for parole? Five years?" Quentin had killed a young prostitute, claiming self defense because she had attacked him with a knife she was carrying. But it had been the prosecution's contention that she was the one acting in self defense.

Her back straightens as she once more starts rolling the dough. "It was manslaughter."

"You mean you plea-bargained it down to manslaughter. Where is justice these days?"

"Who the hell are you to talk to me about justice. Y-You killed your own kind! Asians! Civilians!" she spits out the words. "And for what?"

Wong sighs. For once he refuses to rise to the bait. "Yes. I did it. I've lived with that memory all of my life. And it will be there with me till the day I die. And I will surely go to Hell for it."

She stops rolling, looks at him. "I-I'm sorry. I shouldn't have . . ." She wipes the flour from her hands on her apron. "So, you really love her?"

"I don't know. I think I do. There is some chemistry there."

"And there wasn't any between us?"

Wong doesn't answer.

"If there wasn't any, Dave, then I've never been so wrong in all my life. I felt it. I think you felt it, too." She looks closely at him. He drops his eyes to the floor. "What are you afraid of, Dave? Are you afraid of me? Are you afraid of getting involved with an Asian? Is that why you're so all fired up over a white woman? Are you white? Wake up, Dave. Look in a mirror. Do you think it's been easy for me to function in this white, male-dominated world?"

"I'm American."

"Well, goddammit, so am I!" she cries out. "I'm American, too!" she screams.

Wong has no answer. Again the silence surrounds them. Then they both look up at the sound of the door coming ajar.

"Mom, is anything wrong? What's the matter?" Mei stands in the doorway, concerned, a frown on her face.

"It's all right, dear. Dave and I are just having an adult discussion." She smiles tightly. "Why don't you go back to the TV and close the door behind you."

The girl looks at the two of them, shrugs, then does as she is told.

"Do you think I'm proud of the way I've turned out?" he asks. "One act, one stupid act more than twenty-two years ago, has made me into the man I am now. Do you want to live with me? I'm still a possible time bomb."

"And your blondie?"

"Maybe she's less sensitive than you are. Tougher."

Jean laughs sarcastically, throwing up her hands. "Yes, one does need toughness for love these days." She paces across the room. "Dave, we're both Chinese. I can understand parts of your character your blonde girl-friend—what's her name?"

"Mercury."

"Mercury . . . Well, I can understand you better than she ever can. She's not Chinese. No matter how American you are, you'll never completely divorce the Chinese part of you. And you'll only be kidding yourself if you think you can."

"No. You're wrong. She can understand me better than you can. You think that just because you're Chinese you have an inside track? I'm more American than I'm Chinese. You married a Chinese man before. Where did that get you? She knows what I've been through. And she's helping me get through it."

"I know what you're going through, too, Dave. Didn't I help?" Then, "Maybe there is something else here that you're not telling me. Is there?"

Wong turns away from her. "No. There is nothing else."

"Maybe there is, but you're not telling me, are you?" She moves to stand in front of the kitchen table. "I don't think you like Mei, do you?" Silence. "Goddammit, Dave! I deserve an answer on this one!" She pounds her fist on the table in front of him.

"If it were only Mei, it would be so simple. Don't kid yourself, Jean. It's more than that." But that was part of it. Wong had never felt too comfortable with the girl. She was shy and reclusive. He had never gotten close to her. Wong had seen in her the same stony silence he himself used to erect before people. "No, it's not Mei," he repeats.

The friction between them, he feels, is the taut rein Jean seems to want to put on him. Tension sometimes seemed to exude from her and it would be carried over into their relationship. With Mercury, he could do almost anything he wanted, within reason. He didn't feel so confined, so trapped. With Jean, there arose images of Cindy raising her ugly head. Her prying, her aspersions, her nitpicking. With Mercury, he remembers the statement she had made, "You make your own life, I'll make mine, and in the twain we'll meet." And again, Mercury saying, "I'm easy."

Wong could only characterize Jean as saying, "I'm fussy." Perhaps fussiness went hand-in-hand with determination. Jean's career engulfed her, and any marriage with her would have to bend to her schedule, her demands, her flexibility or lack of it. At almost fifty years of age, Wong found that he was stiffer, less flexible in a lot of things. He had his own baggage to carry. If anything, a woman would have to bend to him.

Then there was religion. Organized religion would never be part of his life. With Jean, it was as much a part of her as her race was. She could no more divorce herself from Christianity than she could divest herself of her slant eyes, black hair, upbringing, and culture. But they had been over this road before, and he didn't want to travel it again now.

Jean leans against the counter, arms hugging herself. Her words are soft, almost a whisper. "Is that all?"

"I guess."

"Then maybe you'd better go now." She is sobbing softly.

Wong stands, takes a few steps. He almost feels like hugging her. One last time. But she makes no move. He flops his arms, an awkward gesture, watching the tears roll off her cheeks onto the clean tile floor. He treads lightly to the closed door, opens it, turns to face her one last time.

"I'm sorry, Jean. I really am."

She is still staring at the floor, not even a glance up. He closes the kitchen door behind him, strides to the front door, does not even say goodbye to Mei. He closes the front door and feels a great heartache. His legs are wobbly going down the brick steps.

Suddenly, he remembers the first time he had made love to Jean, after seeing *Othello*. It had been a magical night, a night that had saved his soul.

He is tempted to turn around, to not lose this woman in the forest of his past.

Chapter 32

Hawaii

The house doesn't look any different than when he last saw it. They pass the chain link fence put up by his father twenty years ago to keep burglars out. The house paint seems new, as yet unblistered and uncracked. The yard is well kept. The lychee tree is gone. In its place are small papaya trees, the fruit hanging pendulously, some carrying the yellow color of ripeness.

"It's been a long time," Harlan says.

"How long?" Mercury asks.

"About twenty-three years," Wong replies, since he had last seen Ahpo. He wipes his hands on his shorts. He is sweating profusely in the hot, humid climate. "So who's taking care of her today?"

"Auntie Kate."

They reach the door. Wong knocks. His aunt walks over, unlocks the screen door. "Davy!" she cries out. "Oh, my God! How long has it b-e-e-n?" She clasps him in her arms—an uncharacteristic exhibition of emotion from someone Chinese. He towers above her sheepishly.

"Hi . . . hi, Kate. Uh, since my father died. Eighteen years?" He had seen his aunt then, but he had not called on his grandmother.

"Well, it has been too long! What you been doing all these years? Harlan said something was wrong . . . " She stops, seeing Harlan shaking his head. Then she looks at Mercury. "And this is . . . ?"

"This is Mercury. She's a friend."

"Hi," Mercury says, offering her hand.

"Well, glad to meet you, Mercury!" Kate takes Mercury's hand in both of hers. "Come into the living room . . . Ma! Ma! Look who's here!"

It is the same living room, the walls studded with pictures of her extended family. The same furniture, it seems, occupies the room. The old settee with a futon pillow, the old stuffed chair, the wooden rocking chair, the small table on which the telephone sits. He gazes at the oak floor, pitted and scratched, victim of a bevy of grandchildren and great grandchildren. She is sitting on a soft rocker. Wong hears a soft hum and sees his grandmother rising and falling in the chair. An inflatable cushion of some sort is in back of her. Wong immediately recognizes it as the massage rocker Harlan told him about.

My God! he thinks to himself. She looks so old! All skin and bone. Her right eye is closed. She looks at him closely with her left. "Who dis?" she cries out. "Who?"

"It's Dave, Ma!" Kate shouts into her left ear. "It's On jai!"

"Huh!"

"Kin Sum's son!"

She looks closely at him, then her face cracks into a wide grin. "On jai! Davy!" Then, just as quickly, a frown. "Why you no come visit before?"

He stands above her, grabbing her frail left hand. "Ahpo! Oh, Ahpo!" He cannot speak for a moment. He remembers the old lady of yesteryear, the strong old woman who could work him into the ground, that indomitable woman of boundless energy and spirit. His eyes mist over. He has been gone too long.

"Damned fool! Why stay away? Ahpo no hate you. You no like Ahpo?"

"I no hate you," he replies, slipping automatically into pidgin.

"Huh? What say?"

He leans closer, shouts, "I no hate you. The war . . . the war make me . . . bad. A bad man."

She looks at him, smiles. "No, no, Davy. The war bad. I told you so. The war bad. You not bad. I tell you, 'No go fight baak gwai war.' You remember?"

He smiles down at her. So long ago, and she still remembers. "I remember."

She leans back, a smile of smug satisfaction on her face. "Nei yaak m'yaak, ah?" Did you eat?

"You folks eat yet?" Kate asks. Then to her mother, "Ma, this is Mercury!" She points to her. Mercury stands and smiles at the old lady. Ahpo smiles back at her, a toothless grin.

"Hou leng baahk mui, huh?" Good looking white woman.

Mercury stands, puzzled.

"She says, 'you're good looking,'" Wong translates, laughing.

"She's not bad herself," Mercury says and laughs. Kate translates. Ahpo grins again.

"Her mind is still clear, you know," Kate says. "She's just getting old. She's ninety-eight, you know!" She clasps her hands together, laughs, and gets up. "I forgot. Did you folks eat yet? It's her lunch time." Still the obedient daughter, she goes into the kitchen.

"How about papaya?" Wong asks, following her. "It's been a long time since I've had fresh papaya."

"Sure." Kate pulls a papaya from the refrigerator. She hands it over to Wong. "Do you still know how to eat one?" she asks, laughing.

Wong smiles. "Sure." He washes it, cuts it lengthwise, then scoops out the salmon-egg-like seeds. He places the halves on a plastic plate and rejoins his grandmother in the small living room.

"You long time gone, On jai," Ahpo says. "You better go put flowers on your parents' graves."

"You can come over my place, yeah?" Kate offers, coming back from the kitchen with a plate of char siu bao, that doughy dim sum filled with barbecued pork. She passes the food around. Wong offers some papaya to Mercury. "Plenty of flowers. We got plenty. Bird of Paradise, Haleconia, ginger." She smiles. "Oh, your parents will be so glad you came home!"

"Thank you." Wong looks to his brother. "Tomorrow, Harlan?"

His brother nods. "Yeah. Tomorrow will be a good day."

"Is that all right with you, Mercury?" Wong asks.

"Oh, fine. Yes, that'd be fine."

"When go?" his grandmother asks.

"Tomorrow!"

"Huh?"

"Tomorrow!" Kate gets up from her chair, leans over and yells into her left ear. "Tingyaht!"

"Oh! Good, good!" Ahpo looks at Wong, smiles. Wong smiles back.

"I didn't really realize she was so far along . . ." he says.

"It has been a long time, you know. Big difference, yeah? Since the last time you came. Even five years ago, big difference," Kate says.

"Yes, she's old. And I always thought she would live forever."

"Hah! Nobody lives forever. I'm getting old, too. But her, she has a strong constitution, you know. She's old, but she won't let go. I tell her, 'Ma, when the good Lord calls, you don't have to fight it. Let go. There's lots of relatives on the other side. They'll take care of you.' But she's a fighter. She told me that one night she heard 'Anh yanh!' You know what that means? It means Mother-in-law."

Wong nods. His mother!

Kate nods. "Yes, it was your mother calling her. But she wasn't ready to go. The Chinese have a belief. They say that at night you don't answer the first call. Only ghosts call once. Living people will call more than once. So she didn't answer."

"She's scared, isn't she?"

Kate nods.

"I remember that she didn't want to come to my mother's funeral. Or my father's. She didn't want to see them put into the ground."

"Yeah, she is so strong . . . her mind is. You know, she is so stubborn. She says she wants to die, but a part of her still clings to life. Like her subconscious wills her to live, even though she knows she is a burden to us. She has only known life, and she clings to it with all her might.

"We've been doing this for five years now. Lewis puts up with me. And your Uncle Frank comes on the other days. We alternate. Harlan comes every night.

"But her mind is still first rate. She can still control her bladder and bowel, you know. I told her once she loses that we have no choice but to put her in a nursing home."

Wong looks at his grandmother. She is still rising and falling in the chair, pushed by the automatic air bladder behind her back. She can't last much longer, he thinks. She has wasted away so much!

She smiles, her teeth all gone. "You fine, Davy?" she asks. He nods. "You parents be proud of you," she says. "You good son. Of course, Harlan better. He take care of me."

They all burst out laughing. "If I live here, I take care of you, too, Ahpo!" he yells. "You my favorite grandmother!"

"Huh?"

Kate translates, yelling in her left ear. The old lady smiles, chuckles to herself. "Eat," she says, "eat."

Wong has already eaten, but he is still hungry. He moves over the old floor in his bare feet, asks Mercury and his brother if they want more food. Mercury shakes her head no, Harlan says yes. He clutches two halves of a char siu bao, gives one to his brother, and returns to his chair to eat. He feels he is home again. His grandmother is skin and bones and near death, but she does not remind him of that grandmother from the jungle. The skin on Ahpo's face does not fall off; maggots are not climbing out of sightless eyes. All Wong feels is a great love. When he thinks about it, that has always been what he had found with this old woman. Suddenly he feels he has to say something the old lady has probably never heard in all her days. He looks to his aunt.

"How do you say, 'I love you.'" he asks.

A shy smile forms on his aunt's face. They know that she has never said such a thing to her mother before. It has never been the Chinese way. "Ngo oi nei."

Wong gets up. In that house, so full of Chinese tradition, with a picture of his grandfather—whom he has never known—hanging over them, he bends over his grandmother and kisses her cheek. She sits like a stoic. He yells, "Ngo oi nei, Ahpo! Ngo oi nei!" Five, six times, he yells, free of Chinese reserve, his American soul expressing itself. He feels as if a great weight has been lifted from his shoulders. At least this time he could say it before she died, unlike with his own mother. His grandmother understands, smiles and looks at him, a tiny tear rolling from her left eye down her cheek.

"Are you sure you won't mind?" Harlan had asked. "I'm going out to a movie tonight."

"No, we don't mind at all. I'll be glad to take care of her. Have a good time."

"I'll be back about 11."

They hear a humming sound when they enter her house.

"What is that noise?" Mercury asks.

"I don't know. I'll pop in and look." The hallway light is on. The light in her room is off. Only the stray light from the hallway and that from the street lamps filter their way into her room. She is lying on her back. Wong sees her massaging herself with an electric massager. He steps back out into the hallway. "It's her massager," he says softly.

Mercury chuckles. "Mind if I sit out here and read?"

"No, of course not."

Wong steps back into the bedroom, alongside the bed, which has steel rails so that she does not roll off. Her walker is butted up against the bed so it would be close by when she rises. A step away is a wooden seat made by her son to function as a toilet, an oval hole cut in it, set over a plastic pail filled with water.

"Ahpo! It's me, Dave."

"Where Harlan?"

"He went movie, Ahpo!"

"Oh."

He takes the massager, a long rod with a vibrating end, from her right hand and takes over for her, rolling the vibrator over the left side of her neck and shoulders and then down her left arm and around her left hip. She lies silently. The breeze blows in through the jalousies. A dog barks, a loud puncture of the lazy Hawaiian night, again and again, a sound to wake the dead.

He talks to her. "You were right, Ahpo. It should not have been my war. The things I did . . . made me ashamed . . . of being Chinese, even of being human . . ." He rambles on, pouring out his confessional to the last old person alive from his childhood he has always loved.

He continues to massage and talk. She stares listlessly into the dark night. He knows she does not hear him, does not understand all he says, and she does not bother to reply. She is suspended on this side of sleep, awake, waiting.

Wong checks on Mercury in the living room. She has slipped sideways in her chair, dozing quietly, the magazine opened on her lap.

"Oh niu," Wong hears. "Oh niu."

He rushes back into the bedroom. He takes the massager, places it on the side table. He then grabs her under the armpits and sits her up on the side of the bed. "Let her stand; she can help you," his brother had said. "That way you won't kill your back." He drops the bedrail, pulls her up so that she can stand, supports her as she steps to the wooden toilet, pulling her shift up before sitting her down. She sits and pulls her shift down, her last measure of modesty before her grandson.

"Pau," she says. So quickly? Wong wonders. He stands her up, moves her backward against the dropped rail, lifts and turns her onto the bed.

She sighs loudly, looks at him with a measure of recognition. "Old!" she says. "Old."

"You're still great, though, Ahpo." But the sentence slides right by her; she has drifted into her lethargy again. He starts to massage her once more. They are yin and yang, night and day, male and female, age and youth, life and death, the one the progenitor and the other the product of her genes.

"I killed them, Ahpo. The little girl and the old lady." He finishes the telling of his story. She looks at him then, her mind swooping in from distant thoughts.

"Killing no good," she says. She turns to look at him, then rolls her head back so that she stares fixedly at the ceiling. She drifts away again, her consciousness seemingly caught on the currents of the night wind. A faint fragrance of plumeria wafts in through the jalousies.

Anh Yanh, she hears. This time she answers. "Seu Kung!"

Wong hears his mother's name on her lips.

The hubbub of the crowd and cars is like the distant roar of a great waterfall. The sound rushes in from all four corners and is focused onto the open stage area near the escalators of the Ala Moana Mall.

"You dumb pake." Three teenage boys are standing next to him. The one in the green Hawaiian shirt is the one who spoke. Pake is Hawaiian slang for Chinese.

"Hey, I no dumb. You pupule!" the boy in yellow fluorescent shorts replies. You crazy, like a mental case.

The sound of pidgin splashes across Wong's eardrums.

"Kiss my okole," the first one replies.

"You pau argue?" the third one asks. He wears loud orange shorts and matching tank top. Finished arguing? "Let's go." The three of them walk away, still arguing goodnaturedly.

Wong watches them wander off, a gaudy splash of color and language. Mercury has disappeared into the Honolulu Bookstore. She wanted to look for a book on the history of the islands. He told her that he would be out here, in the open area. He continues to watch the waves of people walk by. They are a primordial soup of cultures congealed in the pot that is Hawaii: Chinese, Japanese, Korean, Hawaiian, Filipino, Samoan, other South Sea islanders, Portuguese, haoles, blacks, and others. A melting pot of Americans—outside the normal image conjured up by mainstream Middle America.

They will be flying to the Big Island tomorrow. They have plans to climb to Red Hill on Mauna Loa. It would be a four-day trip, with a layover in Kona, then the next night at the cabins at Namakani Paio in Volcanoes National Park. The third night would be at the 10,000 foot mark on Mauna Loa, then back down the fourth day to fly out of Hilo back to Honolulu. The following day would be Ahpo's funeral. Then, since Mercury was due back, they'd have to return to Seattle right after the funeral.

Thank God! he thinks. Erlandson was right. He had made it just in time. Any later and he wouldn't have seen his grandmother alive. He smiles, remembering her welcome, her saying, "I told you so," about Vietnam. He loved her for her brashness and affability, her sense of caring that ranged down to the wide, deep roots of her extended family.

He becomes bored sitting and watching the crowd, and starts to pace. His interest captured by a picture, he wanders into a gallery. The framed print, four feet tall and three feet wide, depicts a Japanese woman in a red kimono. He reads the card next to it. "Hanayome: Passion." The painter is a Japanese artist named Otsuka, who relocated from Japan to Hawaii.

He stares at the painting. The face of the woman is painted white, with the slightest tinge of pink in the cheek, below the eyesocket and above the chin. The face is framed by the woman's hair, which is bundled on top, held by red and white ribbons, with a few grayish green flowers tucked in. Her eyes are slanted delicately upward. Her lips are two graceful red curves, slightly darker than the red of the kimono, which takes up almost the whole of the painting. The kimono is brilliant, more brilliant than the red refracted light of a prism. Hundreds of small squares of dark red cover the kimono, perhaps a thousand or more, painstakingly done.

Wong imagines the artist making the brushstrokes with a crimped and cramped hand. He'd have to flex his fingers every few brushstrokes.

The broad flowing collar of the kimono is checkered with white squares in the same pattern as the red of the kimono is. Below the waist, the red is broken by flowing, folded designs that drape off the figure to trail on the floor: smooth cornered squares, drawn shutters, rolled scrolls, wheels like dartboards, sashes, flowers—in blue, red, black, gray green, beige, pink. The designs are complicated, yet pleasing, representing gaily decorated carts. The carts allude to the legend, Wong reads, of a nobleman who courted a beautiful poetess for ninety-nine evenings.

The figure stands out alone against a pearlized white background. A thin red border in the matting highlights the red. Gold trim, adjacent to the red trim, and wide off-white matting, held in a black frame, complete the framing of the print.

The colors seduce his sense of vision. He can imagine the passion the artist must have had to complete this painting. His passion for art, his passion for women, his passion for living, and his pride in being Japanese. Distinctly different from the rest of American society, this man has found his niche in his art. An embrace of the old in a new world, an embrace of a foreign tradition—an old culture—in a new one. He has done it well.

Through his art he has pulled Wong into Japanese culture and tradition, bridged the enmity that once ran like rivers between the two cultures of their ancestors. Shunted the anger of his grandmother against the Japanese, diluted the memory of Howard torturing the young Japanese soldier. Eased his pain. Through the beauty and grace of the painting, a common thread is captured. The adoration of beauty. Of womanhood. Something that transcends all cultures and politics. An adulation of lovers.

"You like that, don't you?" Mercury asks. She has appeared behind him, a package in hand.

He looks at her, shifting his gaze from the print. "Don't you?"

She studies the print. "Yes, I like it. Very much."

He stares at the print again. "It's called 'Hanayome: Passion.' Hanayome represents the eternal flower of the home and is unselfish female devotion." He looks at her. "That's the Japanese man's ideal of femininity."

"It's not mine," she says, smiling at him.

He circles her waist with his arm. "I know."

But he cannot take his eyes off the painting. The faint, subtle suggestiveness of the woman's pose. A Japanese subtlety, an invitation to erotic interludes. In the tilt of her head, in her gesture, in her kimono, in her demureness.

"Can I help you, sir?" A saleswoman approaches.

"Yes, how much is this?"

"Hanayome: Passion. One of our bestselling prints, sir. We have only about ten left out of 450 limited-edition prints." Wong looks at her with impatience. She clears her throat, smiling broadly. "It's $2,500, sir."

$2,500! he thinks. God! How can I afford that?

"This is his third in the Hanayome bride series. The first two were Serenity and Happiness. Purity will be out soon."

"I love this print. What do you think, Mercury? Is it worth it?"

She laughs. "It's your money, Dave. Can you live without it?"

He thinks for a while. He has some money saved up. "I think I'm gonna get it," he says, smiling. "Yes, I'm gonna get it."

They go with the woman to fill out the sales form.

"That's a lot of money," Mercury remarks.

"Yes, it is," he agrees. Then, he takes her hand and he walks her back to stare at the painting again while the woman runs a check on his credit card. "Perhaps, it's my Asian side calling out to me," he tells her. "Can you understand that?"

"Why didn't you pick Jean, then?"

"I'm American, too, you know. I've just learned today, looking at this painting, that I don't have to shut out my culture and ancestry. I'll always be American, but I'll always be Chinese, too. I can get the best of both worlds." He drapes his arm around her shoulder.

She laughs at his Chineseness, his American Chineseness. Because he has found himself these past few months, he has found her, and she is glad. She whispers in a low voice, "Have you found your passion?"

He laughs at her. "Yes," he replies, turning her around to him. "Yes."

Their boots echo on the worn, red pahoehoe lava as they walk through the grove of ohi'a trees. Looking above them, they can see large clouds start to shroud the upper part of the mountain's broad flank. The mountain has impeded the clouds' movement from the sea, backing them up like cars on an overcrowded freeway. Down below, shafts of sunlight brighten the arid lava flats, pushing through gaps in the clouds.

"Looks like rain." Wong looks at his watch. It is only 10 A.M. When Wong had awakened at 6 A.M. in their cabin at Namakani Paio, he had gotten up and stood under the koa trees to see a clear, blue sky. Not one cloud was evident, not even about the mountain. The leaves of the koas rustled in the slow, lazy breeze and the fragrance, like eucalyptus, wafted to his nostrils. A beautiful day, he had thought then.

"Doesn't look too good, does it?" Mercury agrees.

"Hawaii and rain." Wong shifts the pack on his back, pulling on the shoulder straps to cinch the pack closer to his body. "I forgot. That's why everything is so green."

They leave the forest of ohi'a trees quickly behind, walking almost exclusively at these elevations on pahoehoe. The pahoehoe lava is smooth, looking like petrified cowpies in a farmer's fields, or like coils of rope. After about ten minutes, they pass through a gate set in a barbed wire fence used to keep out foraging feral goats and pigs. The vegetation, at 6,600 feet, is mainly small yellowish green shrubs called ohelo. Together with the ohi'a trees, they provide the only splash of green in the vast, forbidding landscape.

"Seven thousand feet," Mercury says, a short time later, spotting a sign rising out of the porous ground.

"Another three thousand feet to Red Hill, then."

"How're you doing?" she asks.

"I'm fine. It's good to be away from crowds." They had not met anyone else on the trail.

They continue up, following lava cairns, or as the Hawaiians call them, ahus. Rounding a small bend in the trail, they come upon a pronounced reddish coil of pahoehoe lava that looks like tentacles from an octopus, draping from more than seven feet high.

"I've got to take a picture of this," Mercury says, unslinging her pack, reaching for her camera.

Wong stands idly by, looks skyward toward the upper slopes of the mountain. The clouds directly above them are silvery gray; light still filters through. But higher up, they are dark and forbidding. Wong grows uneasy. It was Mercury's idea to do this climb, at least to Red Hill Cabin. Wong, who grew up for part of his life in Hawaii, had never thought of the mountains as a place to go. It had always been the beach for him and his cousins. They were flatlanders on islands built by volcanoes.

"It would be a great climb," she said. "Who wants to lie around the beach all day and do nothing?"

He agreed. The beach no longer had the attraction it once did. "Do you think I can make it?" he asked.

"Sure. You're in shape."

He had agreed, he thinks back, because he had learned to love mountains. But this mountain is unlike any other he has seen close up or been on. He looks at its long, desolate flank. Lava, lava everywhere. Ten thousand cubic miles of it! he remembers reading. The mountain rises to a height of 13,679 feet above sea level and more than thirty thousand feet from the ocean floor. Mt. Shasta in California, by comparison, only filled a mere eighty cubic miles.

He feels small, infinitesimal even, swallowed in the vast immensity of the landscape. The thought of the clouds they are heading into sits uneasily on his mind. He turns his gaze from the mountain's naked flanks back to Mercury. She is still angling for snapshots.

"Mercury, can you hurry up!"

She stops, turns to face him, her face questioning.

He looks up at the mountain, points to the dark clouds.

"It's only rain, Dave."

He feels sheepish. She is right, but he cannot shake a sense of dread. They are like ants, the mountain looming over them, intimidating. The clouds trigger memories of Vietnam. Of Tet. Of being out in the open, caught in the falling rain. The wind sneaking up on your back, like whistling death.

She finishes up, slings her pack back on. "Let's go!" she says and smiles. They slog on under threat of rain.

Above 8,500 feet, Wong remarks, "There are no trees!" The last ohi'a tree stands on a little knoll behind them. Silhouetted against the gray sky, it takes on the aspects of a lone bonsai. A tree clinging to life before the mountain's destructive majesty.

To the right, some four hundred meters off, they see a large ridge of black lava. It is a long, wide arm extending down from the mountain, runoff from the last eruption perhaps. They eye it like castaways on a boat might eye a limitless expanse of ocean. It defines their existence.

Only, this ocean is formed of splattered, flowing, broken, porous stone. In the dim light of the overcast day, the ridge seems colorless—a deep, ominous black.

If God resides in mountains, as Mercury once said, then the god on this mountain is a god of destruction, a god of death, a slayer of life, a god indifferent to human concerns and frailty. Akin to the Hindu god, Shiva the Destroyer, he thinks. Microscopic is his ego before this mountain.

In another half hour they enter clouds. "Better get our jackets on," Mercury warns. They stop, doff their packs and reach in for the Gore-Tex jackets. The jackets shield them from water droplets and the wind, which blows cold clouds across their path.

They hit a wide field of a'a lava. They stumble upward on coarse, broken chunks that worry their feet. There is no form or order to a'a, only a jumbled mass spread over a wide area that looks like a field of dead, charred human limbs of various sizes burned down to mere stumps, some aimed in supplication to the sky, others broken into charcoal-size pieces. Green crystals of olivine, within the broken a'a, catch their eye as they stumble upward.

The ahus flit in and out of their vision, veiled by the clouds. Man high, they seem like ghosts. In that black and brown environment, the fog isolates the two in a desolate land that grows fearsome in their imaginations. They hardly speak. Only the wind and their footsteps, a sound almost like walking on broken glass, breaks the silence.

After a while Wong asks, "How you doing?"

They stop for a minute, standing and trying to peer beyond the pale curtain of fog. "I'm fine," Mercury replies. "You?"

"I'm okay. I'm just wondering how much farther it is."

Mercury looks at her watch. "We passed the 9,000 foot mark about twenty-five minutes ago. Can't be much farther."

"Okay." He shifts the pack on his back, then starts off again, heading up a steep, red, gravelly slope. It starts to rain hard. They lean into the hill, left shoulders dropped against the wind, their eyes focused on the path. The rain does a tap dance against his jacket, felt hat, and bare legs.

It is the steepest slope they have yet encountered. But Wong has relaxed, almost feels exhilarated. He is dry, warm, and comfortable, unlike the damp, numbing cold of Vietnam after a wet night in a foxhole with a poncho and cotton clothes. He feels the stretch in his muscles, extending and contracting as he climbs, a steady, rhythmic cantata of exertion.

Wong raises his head. He sees several large ahus and what looks to be a sign silhouetted against the gray sky. "It looks like Red Hill," he turns around to Mercury and shouts. "We made it!" The heavy rain has stopped; only the mist remains.

"Here, here!" he says, directing her to stand next to the sign, "PUU ULAULA REST HOUSE, ELEVATION 10,035 FEET." He pulls out his camera. "Smile!" She smiles seductively, striking a pose like a chorus girl, left hand on hip, her right hand extended high above her head, her right leg stuck out. He snaps several pictures.

They turn and walk into a small circular depression where the cabin sits. The cabin is formed out of rough, vertical wooden planks and has a corrugated metal roof. A small outhouse sits to the side. There is a catchment basin for rainwater that drains from the roof.

The reddish color of the lava suffuses the place. The result of oxidation of iron in the lava, it looks like a tsunami of blood has washed over the broken, jagged lava. The color covers the vast Martian-like landscape.

They step onto the sheltered porch, their boots clomping loudly on the wooden floor, and push through the door. No one else is there. Wong looks at his watch. Five minutes past 2 P.M. Not bad, he thinks. Only four hours to get here.

Bunk beds are set against the back wall. Another bunk lies against the right wall. The cabin has mundane, rectangular windows on three sides. A table and two benches sit on the left side of the cabin. A small galley with a wooden countertop extends from the table to the front of the cabin.

They unsling their packs and lean them against the bunkbeds. "Want some coffee?" she asks.

"Yes. I'd like that."

They doff their jackets. Mercury rummages through her pack for the cookstove. "Good. I'll light the stove and you can get water."

Wong picks up the plastic water jug and steps outside to fill the jug from the spigot of the catchment basin.

She fires up the stove. Wong returns with the water and fills the pot from the jug. She takes the pot and nestles it on the burner.

"It's quiet up here, isn't it?" she asks, her blue eyes sparkling.

"Not anymore with that stove blasting away." He goes to the door and opens it, venting the carbon monoxide.

"Oh, you know what I mean."

He laughs. "Yes, there's not a sound outside. No birds. No plants growing. No other animals. Only the wind and the rain." He unpacks and changes out of his damp shorts into wool pants. Mercury starts to unpack, occasionally checking the pot. She changes into wool pants, too.

She spoons out instant coffee and pours hot water into their cups. "Thanks," he says.

She smiles at him. "Wasn't so bad, was it?" She turns the stove off.

"Just a lot of rain." He sips his coffee, staring across the table at her.

She smiles at him. "It's just rain, Dave."

"Yes." He smiles back. "It's just rain."

He gets up to close the door now that the stove is off. They drink lazily as a warm silence settles over them. He looks at her. She is studying the map. She has done wonderfully well, he thinks, assimilating herself into the Chinese cultural aspects of his family. That part of him was always on hold when he was on the mainland, but as soon as he came back to Hawaii, it reasserted itself. He had to go bye-sun or pray at his parents' graves. He had to make the rounds to all of his uncles and aunts. He relived his history in the islands when he called on them. He socialized with his brother and cousins, visiting Chinatown. Of course, he had to call on Ahpo, which was the main reason for his coming back. He could even understand her Cantonese, but he had difficulty formulating the words to speak. Now, her funeral was the day after tomorrow.

"It's 11 1/2 miles to the summit cabin from here," she says. "Another 3,000 feet in 11 1/2 miles. Certainly not steep."

"But it's long. Long and desolate."

"Ah, but it would be fun, and a challenge."

"We'll come back, Mercury."

She smiles, closes her map. "I know we will, Dave."

Wong gets up and steps into the galley. He picks up a book, returns, and sets it on the table. "It's a log," he says, when she raises her eyebrows.

He flips through, reading entries aloud to her. "'I am furious at my husband. On the way to the summit he left me alone. We got caught in heavy rain and wind about two-thirds of the way up. I at least had a poncho. Pierre didn't believe in a raincoat in Hawaii. Ha! When I got to the summit cabin, there was Pierre in his sleeping bag. He was shaking so bad from hypothermia. And he felt so cold! I jumped naked into the sleeping bag with him. But I didn't have any heat either. Finally, I got up and boiled water, made tea, and poured it down his throat. I also filled a water bottle with hot water and stuck it inside the sleeping bag with him. After three hours, he started to get better. Oh! I am so mad at him. Imagine that! Almost dying on our honeymoon!'

"Interesting story, isn't it?" He laughs, looking across at her.

"Yeah. The husband wasn't too bright. Not bring a raincoat when you're climbing a mountain?" They both shake their heads.

He continues reading. "'I ain't never experienced so much pain as climbing up here to Red Hill. I was tired, the altitude killed me, I puke all over the rocks. No more.' Here's someone who really loves this mountain. 'I've been climbing this mountain every year for ten years now. I love it. It gives you a sense of who you are in this world, doesn't it? One has to get away from Honolulu and the hustle and bustle of Waikiki. Here, fellow hikers, is Mother Nature beneath your feet in all her splendor and power! This is the place for solitude, meditation, for finding out about yourself.'"

He looks at Mercury. "A wise man," she says. He nods.

He reads on. "Oh, oh," he pauses.

"What?"

"'We settled in for the night and then all of a sudden at about 1:30 we felt the cabin shake and heard this long, rumbling type roar. Looks like Pele was turning around in her sleep!'" He looks at Mercury. "Just what I needed to hear."

Mercury laughs. "Oh, don't worry!"

The hours pass as he continues with stories of hikers from California, Montana, Germany, New Zealand, Australia, Italy, even Washington state. In a lull, Wong looks out the window. The rain still falls outside, a gray drizzle. The cabin is warm, almost too warm. He stands, stretches. "I'm going outside," he says. She looks up at him and nods.

He grabs his jacket from the nail, puts it on, and closes the door behind him. He turns to look above the door, sees a wooden sign with the words, The Red Hilton, etched into it. He smiles. Someone has a sense of humor. He sits down on the wooden floor, leaning against the planked wall. He gazes out into the rain, a soft gray cover over a harsh red land. He sits like that for five minutes. The door opens. Mercury, her coat on, asks, "Can I join you?"

He smiles, pats the floor beside him. She scoots up next to him. He drapes an arm about her. They sit in silence, listening to the raindrops patter on the roof above them, seeing the rain form into little puddles in pockets of lava. Once again, he is watching falling rain. There are tears in his eyes, dripping down his cheeks.

Mercury turns, wipes them from his cheeks. Does not ask why.

But he tells her. "It's because I'm happy," he says. "I'm so goddamned happy I'm scared. Scared that it won't last. That such a thing could ever last in my lifetime."

She looks at him. "Nothing lasts forever."

"No. Not even pain. I've been in pain all these years, Mercury. Suddenly, it isn't there, at least in a real hurting amount, and I don't know what to do."

She laughs at his foolishness, his masochism. "But why should you want pain? You should want happiness!"

"Ah, but don't you see, happiness is foreign to me. I'm afraid of the new, the foreign." He has been staring at the red landscape, but now he changes his gaze to her. "And I'm afraid of losing you."

"Don't be afraid," she whispers. "Don't ever be afraid." She looks into the barren landscape, then softly says, "Dave, there's only you."

He turns his head to her and smiles, then kisses her. A warmth suffuses him, and he tells her of that time so long ago when he and Muley had sat out on a porch to watch the rain. About Muley's warning him about the great load he was carrying.

"It was the rain," he tells her, "like it was presaging our future." He tries to relate a sense of time and place, of how the clouds weighed on his mind, smothering him under the great uncertainty of war and his sin.

He tells her of Tet, about the battle for Hue, of his killing Muley. Tells her more of his trip across the country, and specifically about visiting the Vietnam Memorial. Then he tells her about meeting Stella.

When he had run from the Wall, he had looked all around for them. He didn't see them walking down the path by the Reflecting Pools, did not see them on Henry Bacon Drive, did not see them on the steps of the Lincoln Memorial. His heart sank. Next, he thought of going into the Lincoln Memorial. He ran up the steps, stood before the great statue of the man, scanned the crowded interior filled with people. Then he spotted them, standing before the mural of the Gettysburg Address, their heads tilted upward, in adoration it seemed. He hesitated, unsure now of what to do. Could it be? he asked. Could it really be? As he got closer, he compared the young woman of the photograph he held in his hand to the middle-aged woman in front of him. Yes, there was a similarity. He approached the woman on wobbly legs. "Ma'am?"

They all turned around. "Yes?" she asked.

"Ma'am, I-I saw you there at the Vietnam Memorial?"

"Yes. Yes, I remember."

His throat was dry. He coughed. "T-there was a name there. You rubbed a name there, didn't you?"

"Yes. Yes, I did, but why—"

He plunged in. "It wasn't Jacob Abramson, was it?"

The color drained from her face. "My God," she whispered. "My God!"

"I knew him in 'Nam. I was with him when he died."

She was crying now. No sound escaped her lips, though Wong could see her mouth working, trying to form words.

"Can we go outside, where it's quieter?" the young woman with her asked. "And, oh, my name is Sara Abramson. This is my mother, Stella. This is Mary." The little girl peered at him with curious eyes. "I'm Jake's daughter," Sara added, shaking Wong's hand.

The daughter chaperoned her mother out onto the stone steps where the crowd was thinner. He told them then. His name. About Jake, about Tet, about the battle for Hue. And about how much Jake had loved them. Finally, he told them about that last day. Even the final act of his pulling the trigger. The shot that ended her husband's life. She stood there, shock on her face.

"He was suffering tremendously," he explained. "He was dying." He looked to Sara, saw her grimace, looked to the little girl, her face upturned in wonder at him.

"I understand," Stella said. "I understand." Then with eyes brimming full of tears, she hugged him to her. "And yes! I remember now. Your letter after he died. Wong! Oh, thank you! Thank you!" she said.

"We all cried, right there on the steps of the Lincoln Memorial," he tells Mercury. He pauses, looks out to the raw, red landscape. "Then we went to an outdoor cafe near the Washington Monument. Sara and Mary decided to go into the monument, which gave the two of us a chance to talk some more."

He tells Mercury what he told Stella then. Hours before Jake's death, they had been pinned down by sniper fire. They were in a wide boulevard crouched within doorways, behind stone walls and trees, waiting for the tanks. It seemed that the North Vietnamese had zeroed in on anything that moved. Suddenly a little boy had come running out of one of the doorways after a toy he had left in the street, the shouts of his mother echoing after him. The mother started to run after him, but shots rang out and the mother pulled back in fear. But the North Vietnamese did not shoot the kid.

"They were using him as bait," Wong said. "I mean they were deliberately missing him. The kid was just standing there bawling. The mother was screaming and bawling. 'Giup Do! Giup Do! Halp!'" He looked to Stella, then sipped his Coke, continuing. "Jake just looked at me. You see, I was frozen with fear," Wong said, licking his lips, then drinking his Coke. "I wasn't going to risk my life for that kid. Jake? He just shook his head, looked out along the street and said 'Cover me!'"

Stella listened intently, staring at Wong. "We covered him. He sprinted those ten yards, scooped the kid up, and ran like hell. Bullets were ricocheting all over the place, but he made it to the doorway where the mother was. We all cheered! But that was like him." Wong looked at Stella, said, "That's the measure of the man you had married."

Stella was crying now, shoulders shaking. Other patrons in the cafe were staring at them, but neither of them cared. Wong brushed the tears from his eyes.

"What I didn't tell her though, Mercury, was the look Jake gave me. I can still remember it, a look of reproof. That war was not for children, should not be brought to children . . . which was, of course, what I had done. We used to argue about that. I told him about Deacon. He'd say, 'But they're kids, fucking little civilians! They're not all like that, for Christ sake!' He said he'd risk his life for them and he did. He was the bravest man I ever knew. A man of honor and principle among all that madness."

"You have some honor and principle, too," Mercury pipes in, a small smile.

He looks past her, ignoring the remark, surprised and feeling unworthy of it. "When I was with Stella, for a moment, it was like I was suspended in time, almost like Jake was there and I was talking to him. Like I was caught between past and present."

He turns his gaze to her. "Ever get that feeling?" Mercury shakes her head. "Between sin . . . and innocence," his voice drops off. "I killed a child . . . Jake saved a child." His voice is like a soft rustle of leaves stirred by the wind. "Sometimes I wonder why I lived and he didn't." He is not sure if Mercury has heard him. She is looking out over the desolate landscape. But she nods.

Wong wipes his eyes. Mercury turns back to him and he sees tears trickling down her cheeks. Soft rain on smooth skin that is a counterpoint to the rainfall that plunges onto the harsh lava. He wipes a tear off her cheek with his finger, looks at it before it slides off, and then he gazes at the raindrops hitting the puddles in the small depressions of the lava. The lifegiving rain, like tears from the cheeks of the gray clouds.

"And, would you believe it?" he says. "She lives in Seattle!"

Mercury laughs softly. "To think all these years, she's been living so close to you."

"And I gave her the photograph. It was old, bent, faded, and blood-stained, but it was one of those things she was glad to have. She cried when I gave it to her."

They sit silently, gazing out at the red lava, seeing the jumbled, frozen chaos out there. Nothing alive. But there is no Death out there this time for Wong. None of the soil of war where Death grows as a common weed; only lava lies before him, a primordial soil. From its flowing pahoehoe and its catapulting a'a, life begins anew. He is like the seed of an ohi'a plant blown by the wind to find a crevice in the harsh, hard lava, put down roots, break the lava into soil, turn its face to the sun, wind, and rain, and thrive.

Too, for him, the color red no longer connotes the color of blood, the color of death. Here, among the red lava, the color signifies the color of life, the Chinese color for good luck.

He suddenly has this vision of himself rising like some phoenix out of the ashes of his self-pity, out of the devastation of his past, because of Erlandson, and because of this woman sitting next to him.

The light dies slowly, the gray and red converging into darkness. Mercury shivers. "Want to go in?" he asks. She nods. They get up. "It's time for supper anyway," he says.

They cook their freeze-dried dinner, make instant coffee, and finish up with store-bought danish.

After dinner, Wong washes the dishes and tidies the place up, setting aside the rubbish they will carry out tomorrow.

The darkness is broken by a small circle of light thrown by a candle lantern hung above the table. Occasionally, they use a flashlight to find items in another part of the cabin.

They make ready for bed by 8 P.M. Mercury climbs onto the top bunk, gazes quizzically at him. "Are you coming?"

"I'll be right there," he replies. He has the log book and is sitting at the table under the candle lantern. In the rarefied air, away from the harried pace of civilization, after all those months with Erlandson, he sees himself, perhaps more clearly than at any other time in his life. No excuses, no self-pity, as if he has come naked onto the mountain. He writes on a piece of scratchpaper, pausing and working the phrases. He looks over to Mercury, sees the quiet rising and falling of her chest in sleep. He shifts his glance back to the paper, studies it, scratching at the words, inserting others. Then, satisfied, he writes in the logbook:

> Higher and wider
> Grows the sin,
> Like a fungus,
> In the dank darkness
> Of a man's soul.
> But shrivels before
> The bright light
> Of day.

He reads and rereads the poem, then smiles. He knows he is an unforgiven man—unforgiven by the girl's parents, unforgiven by himself. He will always carry the guilt, an innate burden like his race, but more bearable now. If he died on the morrow, this would be his epitaph.

He douses the candle lantern, takes the lower bunk beneath Mercury. He sleeps peacefully. Around 2 A.M. he feels a small rumble.

He awakens, and sees starlight diffusing through the window. He does not know if he has dreamed the rumbling roar or if it was real, shaking him awake. He sleeps fitfully for another two hours, then gets up.

"What're you doing?" Mercury asks.

"I'm gonna watch the sun rise. It's clear outside. Wanna come?"

She hesitates, lolling on her bunk. "Okay."

They get up in darkness and put on their clothes and boots and step outside. The air is not too cold. The stars sparkle, beautiful and alluring diamonds cast upon black velvet. They climb the knoll behind the cabin, following the worn path by flashlight. The sun is below the horizon, the stars still brilliant pinpoints of light. The constellations, at so low a latitude, look unfamiliar to Wong. With difficulty, he can make out Orion, Canis Major and Minor, Auriga, and a few others. He searches for the Southern Cross, but cannot find it.

After forty minutes, the first light of dawn eases over the horizon, pushing back the night. The bright stars turn dim, fleeing before the oncoming radiance. Low, horizontal clouds hug the ocean and an orange blaze fills the northeastern sky.

"It's beautiful!" she whispers.

"Like you!" he says, laughing. He pulls her close to him.

Slowly, slowly, the sun creeps above the clouds, and they can no longer watch the white hot orb. The sweet, warm innocence of the light washes over them. Washes away the darkness.

Between love and light, he has become part-child again.

Acknowledgments

Without good teachers, the world would be a lesser place. The author wishes to thank his creative writing instructor, Margot Rowe, who cultivated his love of writing and taught him the nuts and bolts of writing both fiction and nonfiction.

Thanks to all the old timers at her Bellingham Vocational Technical Institute "blue collar" creative writing class who critiqued the original manuscript: Sue Norris, Alta Bode, Bonnie Foster, Sharon Mitchell, Jim Bailey, Earlene Luke, Rhonda Howard, Michael Wilson, Joanne Roosma.

Thanks to later critiquers, too: Amelia Pryor, Jan Christian, Julie Straight, Alaine Borgias, Sara Stamey for line-editing the final manuscript, and Kate Weisel for the final proofreading.

Thanks to the following people:

Dan Cantrell, Lima 3/5, 1st Marine Division; Tracey Barnett, Public Information Officer, St. Joseph's Hospital; Margie Campbell, ICU Nurse Manager, St. Joseph's Hospital; Marc Pierson, Regional Vice-President of Clinical Information and Process Management and former Emergency Room physician, St. Joseph's Hospital; Dave Tveit, Paramedic/Firefighter; Steve Mann for police procedural.

Hiroshi and Meiko Takaki for translations into Japanese. My aunt, Vera Ah Choy*, for translations into Cantonese. A Vietnamese woman, who had wished to remain anonymous, for translations into Vietnamese (leaving off the diacritical marks was the author's decision).

Susan James, editor of the defunct Fishwrapper!, who published excerpts of *An American Sin*. She believed in it when no one else would.

Bob Jensen is the fictional representation of Hugh Thompson, the hero of My Lai, who was responsible for saving the lives of Vietnamese civilians and getting the slaughter to stop. The author salutes him and his crew members, Larry Colburn and Glenn Andreotta*. A salute, as well, to Ronald Ridenhour.

For the Preface, thanks to Daphna Rubin, SEH Productions, Producer of *American Commandos*, for her help in tracking down members of the Special Forces A Team. Thanks to SFC Pamela Smith, US Army Special Operations Command, Public Affairs Office, Ft. Bragg, N.C.

The author also salutes the members of the Special Forces A team (especially R.B.): CW2 Richard Balwanz, SSgt Robert DeGroff, SFC Charlie Hopkins[†], SFC Rob Gardner, SFC James Honermale, SFC Dan Kostrzebski, SSgt Terry Harris, SSgt Jim Weatherford.

[*]deceased

[†]In memory of MSG Charlie B. Hopkins, Team Sergeant of ODA 525 (The Sharkmen). He represented the best of the best. May he rest in peace. —R.B.

Another bytewrite LLC publication:

A Step-by-Step Guide to Changing the Timing Belt on the 240 Volvo non-B230 Engine (i.e., 1976-1984)

$12 U.S./$16 Canadian

Save $150 by doing it yourself!
More detailed than the Haynes or Bentley manuals.

A two-wrench job! Moderate difficulty.

Visit www.bytewrite.com for details.